Loans
not re
at th
3 tim
Plea

1

0

1

S

Ch
to
w\
w\

The Edinburgh Bride

Also by Anne Douglas

Catherine's Land
As The Years Go By
The Butterfly Girls
Ginger Street
Bridge of Hope
A Highland Engagement
The Road to the Sands

The Edinburgh Bride

Anne Douglas

PIATKUS

Visit the Piatkus website!

Piatkus publishes a wide range of best-selling fiction and non-fiction, including books on health, mind, body & spirit, sex, self-help, cookery, biography and the paranormal.

If you want to:
- read descriptions of our popular titles
- buy our books over the Internet
- take advantage of our special offers
- enter our monthly competition
- learn more about your favourite Piatkus authors

VISIT OUR WEBSITE AT: www.piatkus.co.uk

First published in Great Britain in 2007 by
Piatkus Books Ltd of
5 Windmill Street, London W1T 2JA
email: info@piatkus.co.uk

The moral right of the author has been asserted

A catalogue record for this book is available from the British Library

ISBN-10: 0 7499 0838 6
ISBN-13: 978 0 7499 0838 6

Set in Times by
Phoenix Photosetting, Chatham, Kent
www.phoenixphotosetting.co.uk

Printed and bound in Great Britain by
William Clowes Ltd, Beccles, Suffolk

Author's Note

Although the Queen's Theatre, a feature of this novel, was suggested by the history of Edinburgh's old Theatre Royal, and occupies its site next to Saint Mary's Metropolitan Cathedral, it is quite fictional as a building and in its style and aims. All characters connected with it are completely imaginary, as are the inhabitants of Victoria Row and the women's hostel, Adelaide House. There were tenements around the cathedral, but these were demolished many years ago and have no connection with my invented buildings, and although there have always been charitable homes in Edinburgh, Adelaide House never existed.

Acknowledgements

In my background research for this novel, I found the following books on the theatre particularly helpful:

Bond, Daniel, *Stage Management*, Black, 2nd ed., 1997
Fraser, Neil, *Stage Lighting Design*, Crowood Press, 1999
Kidd, Mary T., *Stage Costume*, Black, 1996
Thomson, James U., *Edinburgh Curiosities 2: A Capital Cornucopia*, John Donald, 1997

Part One

Chapter One

The card was in the newsagent's window.

> Lodgings – Suit Young Person. Nice clean room in respectable flat. All meals found. Apply Mrs Beith, Number Eight, Victoria Row.

Maeve Clare O'Donovan, usually known as Mae, stood with her finger to her lip, reading the card again. She was just twenty years old. Tall and slender, with a fine complexion, Irish blue eyes and black hair recently bobbed. Rather late in the day, perhaps, to be modern, for this was 1928 and bobbed hair was nothing new, even in Mae's village in County Cork.

All the same, her employer had sighed and her da had groaned, but here was Mae in Edinburgh, beginning a new life, and glad to look different. Sure, her old life could go with her great knot of hair, as far as she was concerned. Too late now to bring it back.

Yet this new life of hers, she had to admit, had not got off to a good start, for hadn't there been a tragedy before she'd even unpacked her bag? Shivering a little, Mae quickly opened the shop door. She had decided to ask inside, if they knew anything about Victoria Row.

'Victoria Row?' repeated the woman at the counter, straightening magazines with hands black from newsprint. She had a thin, avid face and inquisitive eyes. 'Why, it's just across the road, hen! Is it the lodgings you're after? Wi' Mrs Beith? One o' ma customers, and a nicer woman you couldnae meet, I'm telling you!'

'Just across the road?' Mae repeated.

'That's right. You go out o' here, at the top o' Broughton Street.

You've Victoria Place on your left and the Catholic cathedral and the Queen's Theatre opposite, and straight across from them is Victoria Row.' The woman nodded. 'If I was you, I'd try for the room, lassie. It'd suit you fine.'

'I think I might,' said Mae. 'But there was no rent mentioned on the card.'

'It'll no' be very dear and you can just have a look, eh? No harm done.' The woman's eyes were travelling over Mae with continuing interest. 'You're no' from round here, are you?'

'From Ireland,' Mae answered reluctantly.

'Ireland? Well! I was just thinking, this lassie here could be Irish!'

'Thank you for your help. I must be going now.'

'You from Miss Thorburn's hostel, then? Just along the street? We get a lot o' girls coming in here from her place.' The woman gave a sniff. 'All smokin' and turnin' over ma magazines without buyin'. If you're in there, I'm no' surprised you want out!'

'Thanks again,' said Mae coolly. 'You have been very helpful.'

'Nae bother!' called the woman, as a man, entering, opened the door for Mae to leave. 'Any time!'

If I need a newspaper, I think I shall go elsewhere, thought Mae, for the interest of the woman behind the counter had not appealed. And why should she have been so unkind about the girls from the hostel?

It was true that Mae was staying in Adelaide House, Miss Thorburn's hostel, and also true, as the newsagent had guessed, she was not the same as the rest of the girls. But then they were unfortunates, some of them expecting babies, others the victims of violence, and Miss Thorburn herself had founded the hostel for such poor souls and should be given every credit.

Settling her cloche hat more firmly against the chill April wind, Mae reached the top of Broughton Street and looked about her for a place to cross. Sure, the traffic here was as bad as the City of Cork's, or even Dublin's. You just had to take your chance. Dive in through the motors and taxis, the bicycles and horse-drawn carts, and come up outside the grey stone building of the cathedral and its neighbour, the Queen's Theatre, that was all gables and turrets, and darkened by time. What a strange thing, then, to find a theatre and a place of worship jammed up against each other! But Mae hadn't time to ponder on it. She was looking for Victoria Row.

*　*　*

It was a long line of tenements, directly across a slip of a street from the cathedral and the theatre. Solid stone houses, several storeys high, blackened, like the Queen's, with the soot of years; some with windows sparkling clean and curtained, others not. And of the children playing at the doors, some were wearing boots, and others not. A varied sort of place, then, but not a slum.

I'd be all right here, thought Mae.

The door to Number Eight was open. Perhaps it was never locked? At least it had been painted recently, and gave on to a wide passage that had been swept. There were two closed doors and a flight of stone stairs, on which sat two small girls with rough fair hair and freckled faces that lit up when they saw Mae.

'Who you wantin', Miss?' cried one, running towards her.

'Seekin' the lodgings?' asked the other.

'Susie! Jannie! Leave the lady alone!' cried a fair-haired young woman appearing at one of the doors. Clearly the mother of the girls, she gave Mae an apologetic smile as she pulled them out of her way. 'Sorry, hen. They're that excited, you ken, watching the folk going up to Mrs Beith's.'

'There have been a lot of people round?' asked Mae, with sinking heart.

'Aye. Well, this is a good place to stay, you ken. Nice and central. There's been plenty looking.' The young woman hesitated. 'Mind, up till now, Mrs Beith's only taken young men as lodgers. Thinks they're useful. Likely to do little jobs.'

'Denny was a young man,' one of the children put in. 'He went to Glasgow.'

'I liked Denny,' said her sister. 'He gave us pennies.'

'Maybe I have a penny—' Mae began, but the young woman shrieked and bundled her daughters into her door.

'Och, what a shame you are to me, you lassies!' Mae heard her crying. 'Hinting for money, what next?' Then she put her head round the door, as the girls began to wail, and told Mae to go on up.

'Second door at the top, hen. Mrs Beith'll be all ready and waiting, dying to see who's next. But she's no' seen any young men yet, I can tell you that.'

'I am hopeful, then,' Mae answered, with a smile, and began to climb the stairs.

Chapter Two

The woman who opened the second door on the top landing looked to be in her middle forties. Her face was round and smooth, and her light-brown hair, touched with grey, short and wavy. She wore a hand-knitted cardigan over a print dress, and the pale-blue eyes she fixed on Mae were friendly.

'Mrs Beith?' asked Mae.

'That's me, dear.'

'My name's Mae O'Donovan. I am here about the lodgings.'

'Come away in, then, come away in!'

Ushering Mae into her living-room, Mrs Beith went immediately into her patter.

'You'll like ma room, though I say it maself. No' many folk have got a spare room, you ken. Och, no! Lodgers sleep on the floor, as often as not. Never expect a room like mine. But there's only me, you ken, since ma husband died, and ma Norrie joined the Argylls.' She pointed to photographs on a heavy Victorian sideboard. 'That's ma Frank there, and that's ma Norrie. He's abroad.'

Mae looked at the studio portraits of the serious-looking man in stiff dark suit, and the young fellow in soldier's uniform, his round face like his mother's, and made appreciative noises.

In fact, she was appreciative, not only of the photographs, but of the living-room, which seemed to her so clean and well-cared for, with the blackleaded range gleaming, the shabby old pieces of furniture polished, every dish on the dresser shining. Mrs Beith was obviously house-proud and could make things comfortable.

'You're no' Scottish, are you, dear?' asked Mrs Beith, watching her.

'No, I'm from County Cork.'

'An Irish girl? Fancy! A long way from home, eh? Are you looking for work here, then?'

'I had a job.' Mae hesitated. 'Well, I was thinking I had, but – something happened. The lady died. Before I arrived.'

'Oh, my Lord! What a terrible thing! Whatever did you do?'

Mae was thinking back to the awful moment when she'd arrived at the house in the New Town and been told that her new employer, Miss Ennis, had died of a heart attack the day before. Her niece, a married woman from the south side of Edinburgh, was closing up the house and preparing to organise the funeral. There was no longer any place for the new maid from Ireland.

'You could try for a bed at Adelaide House,' the niece had told Mae distractedly. 'It's a women's hostel off Broughton Street. Aunt Beatrice used to give them donations, I believe. Then maybe you'll go back to Cork?'

But Mae had said she would not be returning to Cork. She had her new life to think of, here in Edinburgh. And why she wanted a new life – well, that was her affair.

'I was given a bed in a hostel near Broughton Street,' she told Mrs Beith. 'Adelaide House. Perhaps you know it? A lady called Miss Thorburn is in charge.'

'Och, yes, I know it, and Miss Thorburn as well. A real lady, eh? Goes to ma kirk. But what she's doing, giving all her life to thae girls, I canna think! What a collection, eh?'

'They are not bad girls,' said Mae. 'I feel sorry for them.'

'But you wanted away, all the same.' Mrs Beith laughed a little. 'Come, now, I'll show you the room.'

It was small and neat, with a single bed, a chest of drawers, and hooks to hang clothes; not unlike the room Mae'd had when in service with Mrs Fitzgerald in the City of Cork. But very different from the room she'd shared with her cousin in her father's cottage in Traynore. Sure, you could hardly call that a room at all. More like a loft, with a stair that was only a ladder, and nowhere for the girls to put their things.

Even so, a little pain made itself felt round Mae's heart when she thought of it, for when her mother had been alive, that had been her room and her da's, and Rosaleen and Mae had slept by the peat fire downstairs. Now Ma was dead and Rosaleen away to America. With Kieran Connor.

'It's lovely,' Mae said, clearing her throat. 'It is a very fine room indeed.'

'I told you you'd like it.' Mrs Beith smiled proudly. 'And the other thing you'll like is ma bathroom.'

'Bathroom?'

'Aye, and I'm the only one to have such a thing in Number Eight, I can tell you! Well, ma Frank was a plumber, you ken. At least, he worked for one. I says to him, I says, you get the landlord to put us in a bath and tell him you'll get it cost. And that's what he did.' Mrs Beith's smile faded. 'Now's he gone, and ma laddie's away, and there's only me to use it. Except for ma lodger.'

'Your husband would have been glad he made it for you,' Mae said softly.

'That's what I tell maself,' Mrs Beith heaved a sigh. 'Would you like to see it? It's just here.'

When she had admired the tiny bathroom, Mae was taken back to the living-room, where Mrs Beith, wiping a tear from her eye, asked her to sit down.

'To tell the truth, Miss O'Donovan, I've only had young men as lodgers since Norrie went away. They're handy, you ken, putting in nails and things like that.'

'I can put in nails,' said Mae.

'Aye, well, no doubt. Thing is, I've had a lot o' folk around, you ken, wanting ma room, and I've told 'em I'd let 'em know.'

'And will you be letting me know?'

Mrs Beith's eyes rested on Mae's face. 'I've never had an Irish girl before,' she said slowly. 'I suppose you'll be one for the cathedral?'

'I am not always at church.'

'We've the Queen's Theatre opposite, as well.'

'Maybe I will go to the theatre.'

'They put on some good plays, and it's only ninepence for the gallery.'

'And how much is the room? Supposing you were to let me have it.'

'Seven shillin' a week. I canna afford to take less, even if you're no' wanting meals.'

Mae looked down at her folded hands. 'I understand. When I get a job, I could pay that.'

8

'But what sort o' job would you be looking for? No' live-in service, eh? Seeing as you're looking for lodgings?'

'I have been thinking I'd like something different from service. Maybe work with my needle. The nuns at school taught me to sew, but Mrs Fitzgerald, the lady I worked for in Cork, taught me to dressmake. She said I was talented.'

'She must've been nice. There's no' many ladies teach their maids anything except work.'

'She is nice.' Mae hesitated. 'I felt bad about leaving her.'

With her gaze still fixed on Mae's face, Mrs Beith said lightly, 'What a shame you had to, eh?'

But Mae did not rise to the bait; she said nothing, and after a moment, the older woman looked away.

'I've no' said I've decided, you ken, who I want to take.'

'No, but you are going to be letting me know.'

'Aye.' For some moments, Mrs Beith sat, seemingly lost in thought. Suddenly, she clapped her hand to the table. 'Och, what's the point in waiting? Miss O'Donovan, I'm letting you know now. I'd like you to have ma room. I think we'd get on. What do you say?'

Mae gave a quiet sigh. 'I say, thank you. I am very pleased that you would like to take me for your lodger. You will not regret it, I promise you.'

'I ken that. Now, when would you like to move in? Everything's ready. Clean sheets on the bed and everything aired.'

'I could come any time. I need not give notice at the hostel. Should I perhaps sign something?'

'Och, no! If things dinna suit, there'll be a week's notice either way. Shall we say, next Monday? Start o' the week? I'll have your rent book ready for you then.' Mrs Beith jumped to her feet. 'Now, what about a cup o' tea? The kettle's on the boil.'

Returning down the stair, Mae met the little girls again.

'Let me find you a penny,' she told them, looking in her purse. 'Well, two ha'pennies. Can you buy some sweeties?'

'Oh, yes, yes!' They danced around her. 'Are you the new lodger, then? Are you, are you?'

'I am. I am moving in very soon.'

'Mammie, Mammie!' they called through their open door. 'The lady's the new lodger. She is, she is! You said she wouldnae be, but she is!'

9

Their mother appeared in the doorway, trying to laugh. 'I never said any such thing!' she cried. 'What are you lassies talking about? How would I know who was going to be Mrs Beith's new lodger?'

'You said the lady was Irish, Mammie, you said she'd never do,' the little girl called Jannie said earnestly. 'Is that no' right, Susie? Is that no' what Mammie said?'

'Heavens, what nonsense bairns say, eh? You canna believe a word of it.' The young woman put out a strong hand to shake Mae's. 'I'm sure I hope you'll be very happy, lodging here. Ma name's Rona Walker, and these are ma wee lassies. Is it true you're Irish? I wasnae even sure.'

'Yes, I'm from County Cork. My name is Mae O'Donovan.' Mae gave Rona her sweetest smile. 'I am very glad to meet you. I hope to see you again soon.'

'Well, if there's anything I can do when you move in, you just let me know, eh?'

'Thank you, that's very kind.'

Outside in the street, Mae's smile vanished. Was this what it meant to be Irish? At least young Mrs Walker had had the grace to feel embarrassed over what she'd said. But how sure she must have been, that Mrs Beith would not take Mae because of who she was. Well, she'd been wrong, hadn't she? Mrs Beith had picked Mae from all her applicants. Quite a feather in Mae's cap, that was.

But she was still a little troubled, as she made her way back to Adelaide House. She felt very much alone.

Chapter Three

Noises and cooking smells. That was Adelaide house. The noises were all different – shrieks, giggles, clatterings, bangings, even babies crying – but the cooking smells were always the same. Beef stew and acrid cabbage. Yet, the residents did have other things to eat. How did everything end up smelling of stew and cabbage, wondered Mae, letting herself into the hostel.

Once, it had been a pair of elegant terraced houses, probably lived in by the quality; later it had become flats. Now, as Miss Thorburn's hostel, it had returned to two houses, with accommodation in the first for girls alone, and in the second for mothers with babies. Naturally, the original woodwork was not what it had been, and partitions now marred the proportions of the fine old rooms, but who was complaining?

The hostel was a place to put your head when you'd nowhere else, and Mae was as grateful as any. As someone from outside Edinburgh, she wouldn't have been allowed a bed at all if it hadn't been for Miss Thorburn's kind heart, especially as she wasn't 'expecting', and hadn't been thrown out by her family, or battered by a husband. All she'd wanted was a place to stay while she found a room somewhere, and Miss Thorburn had given it to her. Mae just wished she could have done something in return, something to help, but Miss Thorburn's only helper, apart from the residents themselves, was voluntary, and Mae couldn't afford to be that.

Both Miss Thorburn and Miss Dow, her assistant, were in their office, when Mae found them to give them her news. It was a tiny room, created from a butler's pantry of long ago, with space only for a desk, a filing cabinet and a couple of chairs.

'Here's Mae!' cried Miss Dow, who was a fairish, placid woman in her forties and an ideal foil to the slim dark looks and fizzing energy of Miss Thorburn. 'Any luck, dear?'

'Ah, Mae, I can see by your face that you're leaving us,' said Miss Thorburn, smiling. 'Did you try the newsagent's as I suggested?'

'I did so, Miss Thorburn, and there was a card there for lodgings in Victoria Row. I went along and the lady said I could have the room. I am to move in next Monday.'

'Well, you're a quick worker and no mistake!' cried Miss Dow. 'But, Victoria Row, that's not bad, eh? Nice and central.'

'And close to your cathedral, as well as the Queen's – you've a bit of everything there,' said Miss Thorburn. 'I think you've done well, Mae.'

'Always provided the theatre doesn't burn down again!' Miss Dow laughed. 'Och, I'm only joking, dear. It's many years since the last time. But there were four fires on that site, so I've been told, and one of 'em melted the lead on the tenements' roofs.'

'Don't frighten the girl, Harriet.' Miss Thorburn stood up. 'As you say, it's a long time since the last theatre fire. Eighteen eighty-four, if I'm quoting correctly.' She put her hand on Mae's shoulder. 'I think you'll be very comfortable in the Row, my dear. They're good, solid houses and the tenants are respectable people. I'm sure you'll settle in well. The only thing is, we'll be sorry to lose you here.'

'I am grateful that you let me stay, Miss Thorburn,' Mae said earnestly. 'Sure, I was at my wits' end, when I found out what had happened to Miss Ennis. I had no idea where to go.'

'Poor Miss Ennis – she was a true friend to us. It was a tragedy she died as she did. But we're glad you stayed, Mae. See how good you've been with the girls! And they like you, you know. I think they'll miss you.'

Mae flushed a little. 'I cannot believe I've helped 'em much.'

'You listened to them, you gave them sympathy. They don't get much of that.' Miss Thorburn turned back to her desk. 'But how about the rent for this place? Will you be able to manage it?'

'Well, I have some savings and then I'll be finding a job as soon as I can.'

'I wish I could have offered you one here, but, as usual, there's not enough cash in the kitty.'

12

'Time the council gave us something,' put in Miss Dow. 'Why should you run this whole place yourself, Anita? I know the council's got the workhouses to see to, and the orphaned bairns to help, but our girls come pretty low on their list, if you ask me.'

'I suppose it was my own idea to open the hostel.' Miss Thorburn turned back to her desk. 'And I do appreciate the council's problems. But, oh Lord – shouldn't we be able to do more?'

There was a silence, as Mae remained quiet, awkwardly aware that she should perhaps have left the two women to their discussions, until Miss Thorburn cried, 'Oh, poor Mae, I'm sorry to be involving you in our difficulties. You go along now and have your tea. Be prepared to tell the girls all about your lodgings, they'll be longing to hear.'

'And envying you,' Miss Dow added dryly.

'I'm afraid so,' sighed Miss Thorburn.

Would she really be missed? As Mae took off her coat and washed her hands in the downstairs cloakroom, she felt happier to think that it might be true. Irish or not, it seemed she had made friends here, and that gave her confidence.

Even so, the future itself was far from certain. All she could cling to was her determination to make her way in Edinburgh, and not run scuttling home to take up the same life as before, while Rosaleen sailed to New York as Mrs Kieran Connor. Ah, now, why go remembering that? Because she never got it out of her mind, that was why.

'Mae!' voices called to her, as she neared the dining room, from where she could already hear an immense clashing of dishes and cutlery, as those girls whose turn it was, set out the meal. 'Mae, hen, how'd you get on?'

Soon she was surrounded by young women of various looks and manner, some in maternity clothes, others still painfully thin, but all marked with an anxiety they could not conceal; an anxiety recognised by Mae because, to a lesser degree, she shared it. Only those uncertain of their future looked like these girls; only those who were in some way afraid.

Chapter Four

In the dormitory, Mae had a corner bed nearest the door, next to a girl called Sandy Corrie. She was eighteen, with thick ginger hair unevenly cut, and a bar of freckles across her turned-up nose. Nervy and at times difficult, she considered herself alone in the world, having parted from her family in the Old Town, while the father of her baby due in a week or two, had parted from her.

'As though I care!' Sandy had cried, tossing her head, when she told Mae. 'I dinna need him.'

Mae had wondered if Sandy might not make it up with her family, but her reply was evasive.

'Surely, when the baby comes, your mother will want to see her grandchild?'

'It's being adopted. Did you no' ken that? Miss Thorburn's arranged everything. Going to a lovely family, she said.' As Mae gave a sympathetic sigh, Sandy shrugged. 'Och, it's for the best, eh? What sort o' life could I give a bairn?'

Lying sleepless in the dormitory, thinking about her new lodgings and wondering how she would get on, Mae became aware of Sandy tossing and sighing close to her. It was not unusual. Many of the young women were too uncomfortable or too anxious to sleep well, and there was always someone moving restlessly and groaning, or, if asleep, crying out in dreams. Still, Sandy was near her time and Mae, worried for her, leaned across to whisper, 'Are you all right, Sandy? Can I get you anything?'

'Thanks, it's just ma heartburn.' Sandy sat up, staring at Mae in the faint light that came from the landing beyond the open door. 'And you ken what – you'll laugh, eh? But I'm scared. I'm scared of having the babby.'

'Sandy, why should I laugh? Sure it's natural to feel afraid. But then the baby comes and everything's all right.'

'What if it's no' all right, though? What if I dinna get through? No' everybody does, you ken.'

'You're young and strong, it will be all right for you,' Mae said firmly, making a great play of confidence and at the same time asking herself how she had the nerve, when she'd had no experience of childbirth. 'Mrs Mennie will look after you.'

'Mrs Mennie? I dinna want Mrs Mennie! Calls herself a midwife, and then she just lets you get on with it, everybody says so. No, I want Dr Rick. He's that kind, eh? And handsome!'

Mae smiled and nodded. All the girls thought the hostel doctor, Dr Rick Hurst, another prince for Cinderella, and he was certainly a pleasant young man.

'Let's hope you will not be needing him, Sandy. Is he not only called out for emergencies?'

'Mebbe I'll be an emergency, then. Och, I wish it was over and I could get ma figure back! You're so slim, Mae, I wish I was you.'

'Better not talk any more, we are going to wake the others.'

'But I've got this terrible heartburn, you ken. Let's go down to the kitchen and make cocoa, eh?'

'I say, let's just try to sleep.'

'No, come on. I'll never sleep, the way I feel. Come on, let's away, then we'll feel better.'

'You are just like my cousin, Rosaleen,' sighed Mae, pushing back her bedclothes. 'She could always get round me.'

The kitchen of the hostel was not an attractive place by night. There were always scuttlings in the shadows cast by the gaslight – mice, or black beetles – and with the stove damped down, it was usually cold. There was, however, a gas cooker where they could boil a kettle, and when they sat at the table, wrapped in their coats and drinking the cocoa Mae had made, it was true, they did feel better.

'Tell us about Rosaleen,' said Sandy, taking out a peppermint tablet. 'Is she as pretty as her name?'

'Yes, she is very pretty.'

'I'm sure no prettier than you, Mae.'

'She has a way with her. She charms people.'

'Men, you mean?'

'Everyone.'

'And she stayed with you and your folks?'

'Yes, she was an orphan. First, her da was drowned. He was my da's brother. They were both fishermen. Then her mother died, so my mother took her in, though she didn't live that much longer herself. Rosaleen and me looked after Da.'

'And you lived in a wee house by the sea?' Sandy sighed. 'Bet it was nice, eh? I've aye loved the sea.'

'The sea can be cruel, Sandy. We are never forgetting that.'

'But gives your folks a living.'

'It's true, we make a living. And Da says things are better than they were. But everyone I know in Traynore is poor, except the quality.' Mae shrugged. 'And things may be changing for them, 'tis said.'

'Aye, well, most folk I know are poor. And you'd have had the fresh air and the sky and all o' that. Never see the sky from a tenement, you ken.' Sandy chewed on her peppermint. 'Mae, why'd you come away?'

After a long moment, Mae answered. 'I was working in Cork and I suppose I felt like a change. Da was managing all right, and Rosaleen was wed—'

'Rosaleen was wed?' Sandy's eyes gleamed. 'Who'd she marry, then?'

'A boy from the village. Kieran Connor. His da kept one o' the pubs.' Mae cleared her throat. 'He was always a wild one, but now he's gone to New York to be a policeman. His uncle's there and done well. Kieran will do the same. With Rosaleen.'

'Is he good-looking, this Kieran?'

'People think so.'

'Do you think so?'

Mae lowered her eyes. 'Rosaleen and himself – they made a handsome pair.'

Sandy was silent for some moments, then she said softly, 'I think I know why you came away, Mae.'

'What are you meaning?'

'Och, you should hear the way you say his name! Take ma advice, hen, never say his name.'

Mae leaped up, her face burning, and put the cocoa mugs into the sink. 'Reading my heart,' she whispered, turning back. 'You're a devil, Sandy, so you are!'

16

'Aye.' Sandy smiled. 'Some folks do say.'

She rose with an effort and put her hand on Mae's arm. 'But dinna be mad at me. I'll no' let on. Who to, anyway? Nobody knows the laddie here. And it's no disgrace to be sweet on some-body, eh?'

'I used to think he was sweet on me,' Mae murmured. 'But when my cousin came back from Dublin, I knew I was mistaken.'

'You'll soon forget him in Scotland. Why, I bet you find a nice Scots fella and get married and all!'

'To find somebody, you have to be looking.' Mae reached up to the mantle to turn out the gas. 'And I'm not looking.'

'Nor me,' said Sandy, walking heavily from the kitchen towards the back stairs. 'Men? They're nae good to anybody.'

'Even Dr Rick?' Mae asked dryly.

'He's the whatever it is that proves the rule.' Sandy gave a breathless laugh. 'Used to say that at school. Listen, I think I might sleep now. Dinna ken why, but I suddenly feel that tired. Seems a long way to ma bed.'

'Here, lean on me, I'll help you,' said Mae, and the two young women made their slow way up the kitchen stairs back to the dor-mitory.

For a long time after Sandy had fallen asleep, Mae still lay awake, thinking of home. Of her da and his Katie, her long dead mother. Of Rosaleen. And Kieran Connor. No, no, hurry away from him. Back to Da, sitting by the peat fire, turning the pages of his books when he was home from the sea, for he was a great reader. Sir Walter Scott and Dickens, stories of the Irish heroes, legends, poems, anything in print. Didn't he spend any money he had, going round the second-hand bookshops in Skibbereen and the City of Cork?

'Sure, I am more than a fisherman,' he would say, and tap a fin-ger to his weatherbeaten brow. 'I have a life up here, like all Irish folk. We are for the literature and the poetry. Remember that, girls, remember that.'

And Rosaleen would sigh and close her violet eyes, and Mae would say, 'Yes, Da.'

Ah, but there was no need to worry about Da. He had Annie Morragh to look out for him – she only lived next door – and would probably be taking him down the aisle one of these fine days. That same aisle in the little Catholic church where Da himself had given Rosaleen away, into the care of bright-haired Kieran Connor.

And I was her bridesmaid, thought Mae. And I made her dress. Oh, but I will not be thinking of all of that now, I will not. I've promised myself, so I have.

But it wasn't till her eyes finally closed and sleep came, that her promise was kept and she need not face the thoughts turning round and round in her mind.

Chapter Five

Even Dr Rick was at the front door to say goodbye to Mae the following Monday, though in fact he'd only called to check on Sandy's swollen ankles. Still, there he was, giving Mae his wide grin and firm handshake, wishing her all the best, along with Sandy and some of the residents who'd remembered Mae was leaving.

'I could give you a lift, if you liked,' Dr Rick told Mae, eyeing her large case. 'I've a visit to make near the cathedral.'

But Mae, looking a little forlorn in her too-large coat that had been her employer's, said it was very kind of him, but Miss Thorburn had ordered a taxi.

'A taxi?' squealed Sandy. 'Och, you'll be grand, eh?'

'I said I could go on the tram, but—'

'But I said that was nonsense,' Miss Thorburn cut in crisply, and pressed a shilling into Mae's hand. 'There is no convenient tram to Victoria Row from here, and I never let my girls strain themselves with luggage. Not when I have my little fund ready for just this sort of thing.'

'But you need all your money for the hostel—'

'Just take it, dear,' called Miss Dow. 'You'll never win a battle with Miss Thorburn – and there's the taxi now!'

With one last tight hug from Sandy and promises to come back soon, Mae took her seat in the back of the taxi, waving like someone grand to those waving back, and was driven away. Her last sight from the rear window was of Sandy turning back to the house and of Dr Rick's tall figure stooping to give her his arm. No doubt he was telling her to rest, get her feet up, and no doubt she was sighing and saying she'd die of boredom. Poor vulnerable Sandy.

If only I could have done more for her, thought Mae. The others, too. But she knew well enough that the problems of the girls at Adelaide House were too great for her to solve. You just had to be like Miss Thorburn, and do what you could.

It was the same with the Irish. No one thought, because they'd got their independence in 1921, that their troubles were over. There was just the hope to cling on to, that one day they would be.

And what about Mae herself? Her gaze was sombre, as the young taxi-driver drove at speed through the city traffic, showing off his driving skills to his pretty young passenger. Another chapter had ended, and what was to follow? A new job and a new life with the Scots folk of Number Eight. How would they be? Not as friendly, perhaps, as the girls of the hostel.

Whatever happened, she decided, setting her chin, as though someone were arguing with her, she was not going to apologise for being Irish. They must take her as she was. For why should they not? She wasn't really different from them. Ah, but they would think so, wouldn't they?

'This is you, then, Miss,' called the young taxi-driver, pulling up at the kerb outside Number Eight, Victoria Row, where the Walker girls and other interested children were already trying to look in at Mae. 'Want a hand wi' that case, then? Second stair? Nae bother!'

'Miss, Miss, are you coming to stay?' cried Susie and Jannie, running up the stair after Mae and the taxi-driver, who was leaping ahead, carrying the case as though it were no weight at all. 'We'll tell Mammie, eh? She's been lookin' out for you, you ken! We've all been lookin' out for you!'

'Come on, you bairns, now, out the way,' said the driver, laughing as he set down Mae's case at Mrs Beith's door and waited as she found the money to pay. He was very thin, quite a featherweight, but not even out of breath. 'Should you no' be at school, anyways, eh?'

'We've BEEN tae school,' Susie said scornfully. 'School's OVER!'

'It's TEATIME,' said Jannie. 'We're going for our tea.'

'Aye, away you go.' The driver, pleased with the tip Mae had given him, grinned and touched his cap, as the girls melted away. 'Best o' luck, then, if you're just movin' in, Miss, and I hope you get something tasty for your tea and all.'

20

'Something tasty?' echoed Mrs Beith, suddenly appearing at her door. 'I should say Miss O'Donovan'll get something tasty! There's nobody makes a better meat and tattie pie than me!'

'Meat and tattie pie? Beats a sheep's heid or a penny fritter, eh?' the driver cried cheekily and ran lightly away down the stair, with Mrs Beith staring crossly after him.

'Impudence!' she cried. 'Och, the way folk talk today doesnae bear thinking about. Whatever would ma Frank have said? But come away in, Miss O'Donovan, come away in!'

'Please, Mrs Beith,' said Mae, carrying her case into the flat, 'call me Mae.'

Chapter Six

When Mae had unpacked and put away her few clothes – it always surprised her that her case should be so heavy, when she seemed to have so little to wear – she washed her face and hands in the bathroom, and combed her thick black hair. Thank heaven, no need now for long brushing and pinning! And the short style suited her, or so she hoped.

For a fleeting moment, she studied her face in the mirror over the hand basin, and thought she looked well; even pretty. Not as pretty as Rosaleen, whatever Sandy said, but there was no need to compare herself with Rosaleen now. All that was in the past. She was on her own, and glad of it.

'Mae!' she heard Mrs Beith's voice at the door. 'Are you ready for your tea? It's on the table.'

'Well, then what d'you think?'

Now Mrs Beith was looking anxious, as she watched Mae take her first mouthful of the famous meat and potato pie.

'It's very good, Mrs Beith.' Mae was genuinely enthusiastic. 'It's really – as you were saying – tasty.'

'I've aye been known for ma pastry.' Mrs Beith, satisfied that Mae had passed her first test, picked up her own knife and fork and began to eat heartily. 'Now, there's some'll tell you they canna afford to make a pie like that, but it's no' true. You just need time, eh? Buy cheap cuts o' meat and give 'em plenty cooking time, that's the thing.'

'Even cheap cuts of meat are too expensive for some, though.'

'Aye, well you'd know about poverty in Ireland, eh? Is it true they live on tatties, then?'

22

'At one time, they did, but things are a little better now. And my father is a fisherman. We always had fish.'

'And Irish stew?' cried Mrs Beith. 'If you could get the mutton, eh?'

'If we could get the mutton,' Mae agreed with a smile.

'Well, one thing's for sure, you'll be better off here than at Miss Thorburn's, eh? She's on a tight budget at that hostel, you ken. What she doesnae get from charity, she's to put in from her own pocket.'

'The food was not bad. But we had to take it in turns to cook, so a lot depended on who was cooking.'

'Just ma point. Some o' those girls'd be better at smokin' their Woodbines than scrapin' a carrot.' Mrs Beith shook her head. 'Poor lassies, though. You canna blame 'em. Dragged up, with no proper guidance. Och, Miss Thorburn's got a job on with them, all right. And talking o' jobs, I've an idea for one for you.'

'For me?' Mae's blue eyes were bright. 'Is it in the newspaper?'

'No, I heard about it. Just let me get us our afters and I'll tell you.'

With maddening slowness, Mrs Beith brought bowls of stewed apple, then a jug of custard, while Mae, having been told to sit still after offering to help, fiddled with her spoon and waited.

'There we are, all set.' Mrs Beith poured the custard. 'Now, this job – it's for a lady who lives in Victoria Place across the road from the theatre. Nice houses. Better class than the Row – at least, the folk there like to think so. Got more money than us, anyway.'

'And this lady wants – what?' asked Mae.

'Och, a maid, o' course! No' to live in, so it'd suit you. Her name's Mrs Cameron. I do a bit o' spring cleaning for her sometimes, when she wants an extra pair o' hands, you ken, but she sent word yesterday to say her girl's gone and would I oblige full time? That's too much for me, but I told her I knew the very one for her.' Mrs Beith smiled confidently. 'She says, will you go and see her tomorrow?'

'Domestic work, again.' Mae was drooping over her apple and custard. 'I was hoping to find something else.'

'Aye, but you need the money, eh? You can look for something else later. I'd go and see Mrs Cameron, Mae, if I was you. You'd have your wages to keep you going, and you have to think o' that.'

'Yes, it's true.' But Mae was leaning her cheek on her hand, and looking down at her empty bowl with such a lack of enthusiasm that Mrs Beith sighed and clicked her tongue.

'Och, you're disappointed. But what did you expect? You were going to work as a maid before, eh? For the lady who died? What's different?'

Mae looked up and made an effort to smile.

'I'm thinking it would have been different. Miss Ennis was an old friend of Mrs Fitzgerald's, the lady I worked for in Cork. When she asked her to recommend an Irish maid, Mrs Fitzgerald was after giving my name. Because she knew I wanted to leave Ireland and see something new.'

'I see,' said Mrs Beith blankly. 'Well, I canna say I do. You were still going as a maid to this Miss Ennis, eh?'

'I was, but Mrs Fitzgerald was saying she'd teach me things and I'd be more like a companion, not just a maid.'

'A companion. Well, dear, I'll have to be honest. You'll no' be a companion to Mrs Cameron. She's got a husband and a daughter – about your age, or a bit younger. She doesnae need a companion.'

'But, it's true, I need the money.' Mae stood up. 'My savings will not last for ever.'

'You'll go and see her, then?'

'I will go and see her. And thank you, Mrs Beith, for thinking of me. You've been very kind.'

'Why, lassie, I want to do ma best to help. And you need a bit o' help, eh? Being on your own, and all. Now, I'll clear away.'

'And I'll help you wash up.'

'No, no, I've never expected ma lodgers to do that.'

'Your lodgers have always been men.' Mae was laughing again. 'Men are never expected to wash up.'

'Ah, now, I'll no' treat you different, Mae. You pay the same, eh?'

'I want to help, though. And afterwards, I could make you a cup of tea.'

Mrs Beith's eyes wavered, and she put her hand on Mae's arm. 'I've no' had anyone to make tea for me for years,' she said softly. 'Thanks, Mae.'

When the washing up was done and Mae had been instructed in how to make tea as Mrs Beith liked it, they sat together to drink it, Mrs Beith in her own armchair, Mae on the sofa.

'I was thinking mebbe I should get a wireless,' said Mrs Beith, setting down her cup, and taking a stocking to mend from her work basket. 'It'd be nice to have, eh? One or two folk here have got sets. On the never-never, you ken, but I'm no' keen on that. I like to pay ma way.'

'Miss Thorburn has one in her own flat, somebody said.'

'Aye, she would have. She'd be one who'd like to keep up wi' the news.'

A silence fell, as Mrs Beith put on her glasses and stitched away at her stocking, while Mae looked up at the mantelpiece clock. The girls at Adelaide House would be having a last giggle together, before going up to bed. Probably, there had been a quarrel over the washing up – there usually was. Somebody not doing their share, or dropping cigarette ends in the water; something of that sort. It didn't take much to get the girls going, and Mae gave a reminiscent smile. Talk of Irish tempers! Those Scots girls could give as good as the Irish any day of the week.

'Missing the hostel?' Mrs Beith asked shrewdly, looking up over her glasses. 'It'll be quieter for you here.'

'I never mind being quiet.' Mae hesitated. 'Mind if I ask you something, Mrs Beith?'

'Ask away, dear.'

'Why did you choose me as your lodger? Was it because I was on my own?'

'And needed help? Mebbe. But I thought you were brave.'

'Brave?' Mae stared. 'I would never be calling myself that.'

'Well, I could tell you'd some sort o' sorrow inside, and you'd come away to try to get over it. I thought I'd like to help. So, I offered you ma room.'

'I'm glad you did, then. But I'm not really sorrowful. Just – disappointed.'

'Over a young man?' Mrs Beith snapped off her thread, studied her mended stocking, and smiled. 'No need to say any more, Mae. Just remember, though, that broken hearts get mended. Why, in no time at all, you'll no' even be remembering what he looks like!'

No time at all? Mae shook her head. She couldn't imagine it. But as she lay for the first time in the spare-room bed that was now hers, she thought how wonderful it would be, not to remember Kieran Connor at all.

And then other things came into her mind. Sandy's swollen

ankles; Dr Rick's cheerful smile; the lady she had to see tomorrow called Mrs Cameron. How would she get on? She'd have to do her best. Mrs Cameron represented money to pay the rent for her lodgings. And maybe something better was round the corner. Maybe.

Chapter Seven

Women were standing on the stair when Mae, wearing her cloche hat and a blue jacket and skirt, reached the floor below Mrs Beith's the following morning. She stopped when she saw them, for their eyes had immediately moved to her and she thought she should perhaps make herself known. But Mrs Beith, from above, called out 'Good Morning', at which they stood aside for Mae to pass. Still she hesitated, glancing up at her landlady to introduce her.

'This your new lodger, Clara?' shouted a stout woman, with a pail of water by her feet and a mop in her hand.

'This is Miss O'Donovan,' Mrs Beith answered sharply.

'Oh, Mae, please,' said Mae, smiling, at which there were cool smiles in return. 'I'm very pleased to meet you.'

After a moment's hesitation, the woman with the mop and pail extended a damp hand. 'I'm Tilda Tamson. That's ma door there.'

'And I'm Emmy Alpin,' put in a thin, fair-haired woman. 'I'm on the top. This is Maggie Sims – she's one down – and Freda Burns – she's ground floor. Lives next door to ma daughter, as a matter of fact.'

'Would that be Mrs Walker?' asked Mae, as Maggie and Freda, both in their thirties, inclined their heads without smiling. 'I met her when I came about the room. She has two little girls?'

'Aye, that'd be ma Rona,' said Emmy. 'Bonnie, eh, the wee lassies?'

'Very.'

'You Irish, then?' asked Maggie. 'We heard Clara'd taken on an Irish girl.'

'She's from County Cork,' Mrs Beith called down. 'She's no' long arrived.'

27

'Come here to work, eh?' asked Freda. 'You found a place yet?'

'I am going now to see about a job with Mrs Cameron,' Mae answered before Mrs Beith could speak for her, and was surprised when Tilda Tamson burst into loud laughter.

'Mrs Cameron? Och, good luck, then, hen!'

'There's no need to put the lassie off,' snapped Mrs Beith. 'I've always got on well with Mrs Cameron.'

'Aye, well, we're no' all as tough as you, Clara,' said Tilda, who looked tough enough, the good Lord knew, thought Mae, now continuing to descend the stairs. She felt uneasy, leaving the women, as though their stares at her back were cold; as cold as the waves of the sea in Traynore Bay. But then Tilda called to her.

'Hold on, lassie! Here's a nice laddie'll see you oot!'

'Och, it's Harry,' said Emmy, smiling, as Mae turned her head. 'Ma son, you ken. He stays with me and his dad.'

A tall, loose-limbed young man dressed in rough jacket and flannel trousers, was running lightly down the stairs, and at her first sight of him, Mae's heart missed a beat. Kieran Connor! Oh, so like, with the blond hair and the height, and the way of holding himself.

But a second look made her breathe again. This young man might have seemed, just for a fleeting moment, to resemble Kieran, but his face was his own. A handsome face, yes, with hazel eyes and high cheek bones, but Scottish, not Irish, the eyes deeply set, the upper lip rather long. When she realised that she had been staring at him, the colour flooded Mae's face, and she looked hastily away.

Had he noticed? He had seen her at once, she felt sure, but he was laughing at his mother, accusing her of gossiping, and the neighbours were joining in.

'Supposed to be going for the messages, eh?' he asked Emmy. 'And this is as far as you get.'

'I'm no' going for ma messages, I've no' even got ma bag! I was just having a bit crack with the lassies.'

'And here's a new lassie for you to meet, Harry,' said Tilda. 'Mrs Beith's lodger, from Ireland.'

'County Cork!' cried Mrs Beith, not wishing Tilda to be taking over the introductions. 'Her name is Mae O'Donovan.'

'Hello, then, Miss O'Donovan,' said Harry Alpin, his eyes now freely searching her face. He put out his hand, which she briefly shook. 'I think ma mother's told you who I am. Welcome to Victoria Row.'

'Thank you.' As her colour receded, Mae smiled. 'I'm sure I'll be happy here.'

'Sure you will.' Harry glanced back at the watching women. 'So long for now, Ma – ladies.' He turned to Mae. 'Maybe I can see you on your way, Miss O'Donovan?'

As the two young people left them, Harry putting on his cap, the neighbours exchanged glances.

'He's taken wi' her, eh?' Maggie murmured. 'You can tell.'

'Better watch out, Emmy,' said Tilda, finally sinking her mop into the pail of water. 'The colleen might be setting her cap at him.'

'And she might not!' cried Mrs Beith.

'You'd better get on washing the stair, Tilda,' Emmy said coldly. 'It's your turn.'

'What does it look like I'm doing?' cried Tilda. 'Dinna take it oot on me!'

'Take what oot?'

'Och, nae bother.' As Tilda began to wash the top landing, Emmy and Mrs Beith went into their flats and closed their doors, while Maggie and Freda drifted away down the stair.

'Which way are you going, Miss O'Donovan?' Harry asked, when they had reached the street. 'I'll walk a bit o' the way with you, if you like.'

'I'm only going across the road. To Victoria Place.'

He grinned. 'And I'm only going to the Queen's Theatre.'

'You're an actor?'

'Sort of. No' exactly got ma name in lights.'

'Oh, but that's exciting! To be an actor! Sure, it's a wonderful thing to be.' Mae sighed. 'But all I'm trying for is a maid's job again. I'd really like sewing. Dressmaking, if possible.'

'Work like that might turn up.'

'Hope so.'

They had reached the dark bulk of the theatre building and halted for a moment, looking at the posters advertising the current play.

'*Hay Fever*,' Mae read aloud. '"A Play by Noel Coward". Are you in that?'

'No' that one.' Harry put his hand under her elbow. 'Come on, I'll take you across to Victoria Place.'

'There's no need.' She laughed. 'I can take myself across the road.'

'Traffic's bad this time o' day. Have to see you get there safely.'

'Aren't you needed for a rehearsal, or something?'

'Plenty o' time.' Allowing no more argument, he walked with her across the road, his hand very firm on her arm, his eyes more on her face than the traffic. 'What's the number o' the house, then?'

'Thirty-five. This is it.' Mae at once removed his hand from her arm and stood looking up at the well-kept façade of Mrs Cameron's terraced house. It was solidly built of stone, with lace-curtained windows and a handsome front door, beside which was a brass bell-push – the only thing in need of a clean, as far as Mae could tell.

'I wonder if I should go down to the area door?' Mae murmured. 'Mrs Cameron will not want me to use this one.'

'Piece o' nonsense, that! You're coming for a job, you should use the front door. Go on, ring the bell.'

'Only if you leave, Mr Alpin.'

'Harry, please.' He touched his cap. 'Aye, I'd better clear off, eh? Might no' look too good, to arrive with a fella for your interview. But you tell me how you get on, eh?'

She nodded, waiting impatiently for him to leave her, and only when she had watched his tall figure cross the road and reach the theatre, did she ring the bell.

'Yes?'

The front door had opened and a woman stood looking out at her. She was quite small, with a narrow face and water-grey eyes. She wore a smart grey two-piece with a white blouse, and her hair was dark brown, coiled in a knot, with waves on either side of a neat parting. Everything about her was, in fact, neat.

'Mrs Cameron? Good morning, ma'am, I'm Mae O'Donovan,' said Mae. 'I've come about the vacancy for a maid.'

'You should have used the area door,' the woman told her in pinched Edinburgh tones. 'But, no matter. Please, come this way.'

Good luck, Tilda Tamson had wished Mae in her dealings with Mrs Cameron, and as she followed the small, erect figure downstais to a basement kitchen, Mae was already beginning to believe she would need it.

Chapter Eight

The kitchen was large, but comfortless. Small windows below street level allowed in little light, and the heavy iron range that needed blackleading was scarcely warm. There were pans on open shelves and a dresser with plates, but at the long wooden table that dominated the room, were only two chairs. Mrs Cameron, having placed her handbag on the table, seated herself on one of the chairs and pointed to Mae to take the other.

'Now, Miss O'Donovan,' she began, 'I understand you are in lodgings with Mrs Beith in Victoria Row?'

'I am, ma'am. I've just moved in.'

'From Ireland, where you were in service with a lady in Cork, Mrs Beith informed me. Do you have a character reference from her?'

'I have.' Mae took papers from her bag. 'And I've another from Sister Teresa at my school.'

'I shall not require the reference from the school.' Mrs Cameron took the papers Mae passed to her and quickly ran her wintry gaze over them. 'This seems very satisfactory, but of course it is rather awkward that the lady in Cork is so far away.'

'Sure, the post is quick, if you want to write, and Mrs Fitzgerald would be glad to write back,' Mae told her.

'Would she?' Mrs Cameron studied Mae's face for some moments. 'I'll be honest, I've never employed an Irish girl before, but Mrs Beith is of the opinion that you would be a very hard worker.'

'I've always given satisfaction, ma'am.'

Mrs Cameron folded Mae's reference but did not return it. 'Mrs Beith also told me that the lady you were to have worked for died suddenly, leaving you without a place. Why did you wish to work for her, anyway? I mean, why leave Ireland?'

This was the question for which Mae had prepared herself.

'I wished to better myself,' she answered, crossing her fingers for the white lie. 'And I thought Scotland would be a grand place to come to for that.'

'You're not alone in that, my dear. This country's full of your countrymen, who have come to work here because they say there's nothing at home. You did have a job, though, didn't you?'

Mae hesitated. 'I thought it would be good for me to see something away from Ireland,' she said at last.

'I see.' Mrs Cameron took a notebook and pencil from her bag and made a note. 'Well, I'll tell you what I'm prepared to do. I've taken Mrs Fitzgerald's address and I will get in touch. In the meantime, I'll take you on with a month's trial. Here is your reference.'

'Mrs Cameron, ma'am, what are the wages?' asked Mae.

'Wages? What you would expect. Fourteen shillings a week. One weekday afternoon and evening free and every Sunday from two'clock. Hours from seven in the morning until dinner has been cleared away, with an hour off for lunch and a half hour for tea.'

Fourteen shillings a week. Mae sat rigidly on her hard wooden chair. She's offering me less because I'm Irish, she thought. Everybody knew that Irish maids were supposed to be cheap. Why, even Miss Ennis had not been going to pay as much as Mrs Fitzgerald, but this one's offer was even less. Mae tightened her lips.

'I was to be paid more than fourteen shillings by Miss Ennis,' she said quietly.

'How much more?'

'Two shillings.'

Mrs Cameron's eyes flashed. 'Ridiculous. And were you to live in?'

'Yes, ma'am.'

'Even more ridiculous. I can't be doing with staff living in. They are far too demanding, and expecting meals and breaks at all hours of the day. And then to be paid sixteen shillings a week! That's over forty pounds year!'

'I have my rent to find. I really need the extra money.'

There was a silent battle of wills, as water-clear eyes met brilliant blue, and it was the water-clear eyes that wavered.

'Very well, I'll offer an extra shilling,' said Mrs Cameron coldly. 'That will bring you up to fifteen shillings a week, and don't forget, you will be getting your dinner here, and your tea.'

'Thank you,' said Mae.

She still had not decided whether to take the job or not, for it was plain that Mrs Cameron was as hard as nails, and had only backed down over the wages because she knew she'd been offering rather less than the standard rate in the first place.

On the other hand, the house was convenient for Mae's lodgings and she could probably begin earning very soon. From the look of things, it seemed likely that Mrs Cameron hadn't had help for a week or two and would want her to start tomorrow.

'In addition to a maid, I employ a daily cook,' Mrs Cameron was saying, watching Mae closely. 'Mrs Ord comes in at four, to prepare the evening meal, but I prepare lunch myself. You would be expected to help.'

'Yes, ma'am.'

'There are only three of us in the family – myself, my husband, who works at the Edinburgh Bank, and my daughter, who stays at home. Not a large household, obviously—'

Mrs Cameron broke off, as the kitchen door opened. 'And here, for some reason, is my daughter,' she snapped, frowning at the young woman who had appeared in the entrance. 'Charlotte, can you not see that I am busy?'

'I'm sorry, Mother, but there's a telephone call for you. I think it's the butcher.'

'You're always so indefinite. Is it the butcher, or is it not?'

'It is the butcher.'

Mrs Cameron heaved a sigh. 'Then I'd better speak to him. He's probably going to argue over the chops he sent, which were certainly not gigot chops, as I ordered. You must excuse me, Miss O'Donovan – Mae, as I shall call you.'

As soon as her mother had swept out, the young woman took a step or two towards Mae. Her eyes were the same as her mother's – water-clear grey – but her hair was mouse-brown and short, and her face waxen pale. She's like moonlight, thought Mae, there's not a scrap of colour to her. Why, you'd hardly know she was there!

33

'Nice to have a telephone,' she remarked, to break the silence that had fallen.

'Oh, yes, it is very useful,' Charlotte Cameron answered quickly. 'Are you going to be the new maid?'

'I cannot be saying.'

'Hasn't my mother offered you the job? She's desperate for some help, since Trina left us.'

'She's offered me the job, but I haven't made up my mind to take it. The hours seem very long.'

Charlotte smiled. 'I wouldn't worry about that. Mummy goes out a lot. She's on a load of committees, and plays bridge three times a week. Trina just put her feet up, as soon as Mummy was out of the door.'

'And why did Trina leave?'

'Oh, there was a row, of course. All our maids have rows with my mother.' Charlotte looked quickly into Mae's face. 'Shouldn't have told you that, should I? When I want you to stay?'

Mae raised her eyebrows. 'Worried about the work not being done?'

'No, it would just be nice to have someone young here again. Someone like you. You're Irish, aren't you?'

'Yes. I'm thinking your mother's not happy about that.'

'My mother's not happy about anything,' said Charlotte. She put a finger to her pale lips. 'Listen, she's coming.'

'Tiresome fellow!' Mrs Cameron cried, as she returned to the kitchen. 'Took me a while to make him understand that he'd sent me the wrong chops, but he's agreed to adjust my account. Remind me to check on that, Charlotte. Now, Mae, I'm sorry I had to leave you, but when can you start?'

Mae hesitated, her eyes going to Charlotte's face, reading the message in the large clear eyes.

'Whenever you wish, ma'am,' she answered, and sensed Charlotte's relief.

'Tomorrow would be excellent.' Mrs Cameron allowed herself a brief smile. 'After Trina MacDonnell let me down so badly – just walked out, can you believe it? – I was beginning to despair of finding someone I could trust. Just look at the way she left the range, for instance! And the front-door brass! I can hardly go out and clean it myself, or ask my daughter to do it. But I have every hope of your being satisfactory, Mae, for Mrs Beith said you'd be

34

a good worker and she knows who will suit me. Have you your uniforms?'

'I have two print dresses for morning, ma'am, and two black for afternoons.'

'Excellent, again. Of course, I'll pay you for them, but as they are second-hand, we shall have to work out a fair price.' Mrs Cameron put a hand to her narrow brow. 'We can talk about that and other formalities tomorrow when you come at seven. I shall have to let you in, but eventually, of course, you will have your own key. Goodbye, for now, and I hope you will be happy with us.'

'Thank you, ma'am. I'll do my best to give satisfaction.'

'Charlotte, will you see Mae out the back way, please? I really feel quite weary now. I think I shall have to make a cup of tea and take one of my tablets.'

'This way,' whispered Charlotte.

At the door to the area, the two young women exchanged cautious smiles.

'I'm glad you decided to take the job,' said Charlotte.

'I hope I can please Mrs Cameron, Miss Charlotte.'

'Oh, please don't call me Miss. And only my parents say Charlotte. My friends call me Lottie.'

'I am not exactly one of your friends,' Mae said gently, thinking that Lottie, who must surely be nineteen or twenty, seemed very young for her age. Old enough to have learned the difference between a maidservant and the daughter of the house.

'You will be,' Lottie said earnestly. 'I just feel that you will be.'

It was Mae's private thought, however, as she ran up the steps to the street, that she would probably not stay long enough at Mrs Cameron's for that.

'I will be here tomorrow,' she called down to Lottie, who waved and closed the area door.

Chapter Nine

As soon as Mae arrived back at Victoria Row, Mrs Beith began her interrogation. How had she got on? Had she liked Mrs Cameron? Had she taken the job?

'I have taken the job,' Mae told her, taking off her hat and jacket, running her hands through her hair. 'I start tomorrow.'

'Tomorrow? Must have thought it all right, then?'

'I would not be saying that.' Mae sank into a chair. 'I think I will not find it easy.'

'Mrs Cameron's no' so bad, though? A wee bit sharp, mebbe, but could be worse.'

'All her maids have had rows with her, her daughter told me.'

'Poor little Miss Charlotte? She's that quiet, eh? Well, Mrs C does expect the best, and I suppose she doesnae always get it.' Mrs Beith took her great brown teapot from the side of the range and poured Mae a cup of tea. 'You have this, now, while I get our dinner.'

As Mae sat, gratefully sipping her tea, Mrs Beith began peeling potatoes. 'It was me said you'd be a good worker, you ken, and I'm sure you'll do fine over there.' She gave Mae a covert glance. 'How did you like Harry Alpin, then?'

'He seems a nice young man.'

'The neighbours were saying he was taken with you.'

'He just walked with me to Victoria Place.'

'Oh, yes? He could've left you at the theatre.'

Mae brightened. 'It's interesting he works there. I've never met an actor before.'

'An actor?' Mrs Beith stared. 'Did he say that? Did he tell you he was an actor?'

36

'He said "sort of" an actor.' Mae set down her cup. 'Is he not, then?'

'He's an assistant to the lighting man. That's what he is.' Mrs Beith shook her head. 'Fancy him saying that, then. An actor!'

'He told me a lie?' Mae had turned pink; her eyes were stormy. 'Why should he do that? Why should he pretend to be an actor?'

'Mebbe he thought to impress you. I mean, being a lighting man's very good, but some folk get excited over actors, you ken. Queue up to see 'em, and that sort o' thing.'

'He thinks me a fool, then. A silly Irish girl who'll believe anything.'

'He's the one who's a fool, Mae. He'd know you'd find out soon enough, that he was having you on. What got into him, then?'

Mae stood up. 'I shall not trouble to find out, anyway. Now, I think I will go and change from my best skirt. Then, if you will show me the iron, I will press my uniforms for tomorrow.'

'Dinna let Harry worry you,' Mrs Beith said quickly. 'He's a good lad, at heart. If he was wanting to impress you, it's just because – like they were saying – he was taken with you.'

Mae put her cup and saucer in the sink. 'These neighbours,' she said, after a pause, 'are they happy about me?'

'Happy about you?'

'Me being an Irish girl.'

Mrs Beith's eyes flickered. 'Why should they no' be happy? What's it to them?'

'I had the feeling – they were not welcoming.'

'Och, it's just their way. And then – well, we've had one or two Irish folk here who were no' like you, you ken. That's all it'd be, Mae. They'd be thinking o' them.'

'What were they like, then, these Irish folk?'

'Well, no' keen on taking their turn at the stair, and that. And then forever arguing, and letting the bairns fight and tease, you ken. They'd plenty bairns, and all.'

'Nobody thought all Irish people were not the same?'

'That's the way it goes, eh? The Irish have got their reputation in Scotland. Canna deny it.'

'The Irish do good work in Scotland, is what I have heard.'

'They do, they do. But then, they're no' kirk goers. That's another thing. Different religions can cause problems.'

'That should not be.'

'I agree, Mae. But we dinna live in a perfect world. All I can say is, I've never let religion bother me. Live and let live, is ma motto.'

'I know that, Mrs Beith. You took me as your lodger.'

'And I wasnae wrong to do that.' Mrs Beith filled a pan with water and set it on the range to boil for the potatoes. 'Away you go, Mae, and I'll get the dinner. Then you can do your ironing, eh?'

As she changed from her best skirt and blouse, Mae's eyes suddenly filled with tears. It was good to know that there were people like Mrs Beith, so kind, so welcoming to people like herself, who were strangers. Even, to some, aliens.

In spite of her kindness, though, and the friendship shown her by everyone at Miss Thorburn's hostel, there were times when homesickness came over Mae like a rush of sea water flooding up the beach at Traynore. All she wanted then was to be with folk like herself. Her da. Rosaleen. Even Annie Morragh next door. And Kieran Connor? Oh, God. She'd better find a handkerchief, then wash her face before Mrs Beith called her for her dinner.

It was evening when the knock came at the door. Tea was over and Mae had pressed her dresses for next day, and also washed her hair, pushing it into place with her fingers, drying it near the warmth of the range.

'I'll see who that is,' said Mrs Beith, putting aside her knitting. 'Likely somebody wanting to borrow milk, or an egg, or something. Folk here, they run out of everything.'

She came back in a moment with an odd look on her face.

'It's Harry Alpin, Mae. Wants to have a word.'

Mae shook her head. 'Say I am busy.'

'Ah, no, just speak to him, eh? Mebbe he wants to say sorry about that actor business.'

'Maybe.' Mae rose reluctantly and went to the door, where Harry Alpin was standing waiting, the gaslight shining on his hair so like Kieran Connor's. When he saw her, his face lit up.

'My evening off, Miss O'Donovan, so I just called to see how you got on today. Did you take the job.'

'I took it.' Her face unsmiling, Mae studied Harry's face. He did not look to her in the least apologetic. 'Are you not required at the theatre, Mr Alpin?'

'No' just now. Like I said, I'm no' in *Hay Fever*.'

'But are you not working on the lights?'

The colour rushed to his face, rising to his brow, as his eyes filled with recognition of what Mae knew. He put out his hand and drew her on to the landing, closing Mrs Beith's door behind her. 'Oh, God,' he said simply.

'You are a lighting man, then? Not an actor?'

He wiped his brow. 'I never really said I was an actor.'

'You let me think it.'

'Aye. I feel bad. Dinna ken what got into me. Did Mrs Beith tell you?'

'She did.'

'She'd think I was a fool, eh? Pretending to be something I'm not. It was just a spur o' the moment thing, you ken.'

'You thought I'd be impressed.'

'No, no, believe me.'

'Mr Alpin, I have to go now.' Mae put her hand on the door knob. 'I'm sorry.'

'But can we no' talk? Please? It's a grand evening, we could walk—'

'I'm sorry, I have things to do.'

'You could spare a few minutes, eh? I wanted to ask you to walk with me, anyway.'

'It is not what I want, Mr Alpin, to walk with you. Goodnight.'

Without looking at him again, Mae went into the flat and closed the door.

Mrs Beith looked up. 'Well, did he apologise?'

Mae shrugged. 'Sort of.'

'Poor laddie! I bet he feels bad, eh? Getting off on the wrong foot wi' you.'

'He wanted me to walk with him, but I told him I was not interested in walking with him.' Mae fixed Mrs Beith with a look that warned her to say no more. 'That is the truth.'

'Oh, well, then.' Mrs Beith began to knit again, clicking her needles and bouncing the ball of wool from her knee. 'You know best what you want, Mae.'

'I do,' said Mae firmly.

Chapter Ten

Polish the front-door brass. Brush the stairs. Wash the hall. Clean out the sitting-room grate and lay the fire. Blacklead the kitchen range. Run down to do the breakfast.

'Mae, we cook the porridge on the gas stove. There's the pan.'

'Mae, the master likes eggs and bacon for breakfast on weekdays and kippers on Sundays. Crisp the bacon please, and be careful to keep the eggs in shape.'

'Mae, the toast goes in the rack. It needs cleaning, but you can do that later, with the rest of the silver.'

'Mae, when you've cleared away, can you make a start on the dusting? Don't forget, when it gets towards lunchtime, you'll need to do the vegetables. Then you can set the table again. You know where everything is, now.'

'Very well, ma'am; all right, ma'am; certainly, ma'am.'

Working for Mrs Fitzgerald was never like this, thought Mae, her head in a whirl at the end of her first morning at Mrs Cameron's. Of course, the work of the Georgian house in Cork was there to be done, but at a nice gentle pace, and sometimes Mrs Fitzgerald would say, 'That's enough for today, Mae, let's put on our hats and go to the galleries.' Or, it might be that she'd want to supervise Mae's sewing, or her reading list, or help her with her spelling when she wrote home to her da.

Why ever did I leave her? Mae groaned to herself, having her own lunch in the kitchen with her eyes half closed in weariness. I must have been crazy! Oh, God, there was the bell from the dining-room! As she got up to answer it, she was half-deciding that if Mrs Cameron didn't go out that afternoon, she might just put on her hat and coat and walk out herself.

But then there was the pale wraith of Lottie drifting around and fixing Mae with her large hopeful eyes. Couldn't do that. At least, not yet.

In fact, at two o'clock, Mrs Cameron did go out.

'I have decided after all to go to my bridge group this afternoon,' she told Mae, who was putting the last plate on the dresser after finishing the washing up. 'You've managed so well – I'm really pleased with your work – I think I might leave you.'

'Is there anything special you'd like me to do, ma'am?'

'Well, there's all the silver to clean, but maybe there isn't time for that today. Just answer the door, if anyone calls.'

'No one will call,' Lottie murmured, from the kitchen door.

'It's true, everyone knows Wednesday's one of my bridge days.' Mrs Cameron adjusted her old-fashioned, brimmed hat and pulled on her gloves. 'But be ready, in your black, Mae, just in case. Charlotte, you'd better go and change our books at the subscription library. I don't want you talking to Mae and getting in her way.'

As Lottie sighed agreement, her mother hurried out, then hurried back again, to remind Mae that Mrs Ord would be arriving at four and would she please help her if required and set the table for dinner?

'Very good, ma'am,' said Mae, asking herself – would this woman ever go? And then – oh, joy! she did.

'There, she's away,' said Lottie, listening to the front door bang. 'And won't be back till well after five. Let's have some coffee.'

'Coffee?'

'I'll make it. I make good coffee. I learned at Atholl Crescent.'

'What's Atholl Crescent?'

'It's a sort of college where you can learn how to cook and run a home. Mother thought it'd be useful for me to do a course, for when I get married.'

'You are getting married?' Mae asked with interest.

'No, that's just what she wants me to do.' Lottie was busying herself measuring out coffee beans for the grinder and setting a pan of water on the gas cooker. 'But let's not talk about me. Tell me about Ireland. Tell me about your home, Mae.'

'Sure, it'll not take much telling,' Mae answered, unwilling to reveal as much of her life to Lottie as to Sandy. But Lottie was pressing and Mae eventually told her a little about Traynore and her father, pretending again that she had come away only to try for a better living. Lottie seemed interested, but when they were sitting together at the kitchen table, drinking her strong, delicious coffee, she began to droop in her chair like a flower out of water.

'I do envy you, Mae,' she whispered. 'You're so free. If you want to leave home – there you are, you do it. It must be wonderful, just to go!'

Mae's blue gaze on her was astonished. 'I'm free?' she asked. 'To work for other people?'

'Oh, I'm sorry!' Lottie flushed, very slightly. 'I didn't mean to say your life was easy. I know it's not. Honestly, I do.' When Mae said nothing, Lottie's flush deepened. 'I suppose you think I'm lucky?' she asked huskily. 'Got nothing to complain about?'

'You have three good meals a day,' Mae said shortly.

'Yes, I'm very comfortable. I just have no life of my own, that's all.'

'It's not for me to say so, but you could leave home yourself, if you wanted to.'

'I'm not trained for any job.'

'You could do cooking.'

'Cooking? I was hopeless on that course! All I can do is make coffee.' Lottie laughed a little, then she leaned forward. 'You know what I want to do, Mae? More than anything in the world? I want to act.'

'Act?' If Lottie had said she wanted to fly, Mae could not have been more surprised. Her face darkened as she remembered Harry Alpin. She wasn't sure she trusted people who talked about acting. 'Have you tried it?' she asked cautiously.

'Yes. At school and then with an amateur group. I was never so happy in my life. I never wanted the plays to end.'

'What's wrong with being an actress, then?'

'Nothing, except in my mother's eyes.' Lottie's tone was bitter. 'She won't hear of me going to drama school. She won't even let me go to the theatre. Says it's not "suitable". Amateur theatricals – yes, they're fine, and I might "meet people". Young men, she means. But going into the commercial theatre – oh, no, that's out of the question.'

'What's your father say?'

'Daddy? He says what Mummy says. You saw him at breakfast, didn't you? Can you imagine him arguing with her?'

Mae, remembering the small grey man hidden behind his newspaper, shook her head. Probably Mr Cameron let his voice be heard at the bank, but at home only one voice counted and that was not his.

'I can't see what you can do, Miss Lottie,' she said, rising to clear away the coffee cups.

'I bet if you were me, you'd think of something.'

Mae gave a wry smile. 'We've only just met. Why are you thinking you know me?'

'I don't really know you, but I'll tell you this, Mae. You're different from our other maids. You're strong, and I think you're clever. Maybe you won't always be a maid.'

'And maybe you will not always be at home, Miss Lottie.'

'I did ask you not to call me "Miss". We're just two young women together, aren't we?'

'Except when your ma's around.'

'I'm talking about when she's not.'

They exchanged conspiratorial smiles before Lottie left to change her mother's library books, and Mae put on her black dress to be ready for callers. As Lottie had predicted none came, but Mrs Ord, a short, stout woman wearing a beret over her greying hair, bounced in at four o'clock, made herself tea, and began slicing and chopping meat and vegetables, while keeping up a conversation with Mae.

'Och, you're a bonnie girl, then, eh? And straight from Ireland? Aye, I can tell. Look at your complexion! That's the rainwater, they say. Lovely and soft. Well, ours is, too, but we dinna end up looking like you. How d'you like it here, then?'

Mae was still considering what to say, when Mrs Ord said it for her.

'Bit of a tartar, eh, the Missus? But could be worse, I'm tellin' you. And Mr Cameron, now, all he wants is to be left in peace wi' his glass o' port and his cigar, and that's him. No' like some men, eh? Tryin' to kiss the maid when the wife's away!'

Mrs Ord laughed cheerfully. 'Dinna worry about folk, I say. If they dinna like you, that's their look-out. You can always find another job, you ken.'

'I am not worrying,' said Mae, which was not strictly true, for she was worrying about Lottie. Poor little Miss Charlotte, as Mrs Beith had called her. Would she ever be free? At least, she had her dreams, however impossible they might be. But thinking of Lottie's dreams brought the theatre to Mae's mind, and the theatre brought Harry Alpin. Would he be waiting for her, when she walked home after this interminable day? She thought it unlikely.

The day's work ended at last, with the dinner dishes washed and the kitchen tidied. While Lottie hovered, smiling, Mrs Cameron told Mae again that she was pleased with her.

'Mrs Beith was right, you are a good worker, Mae, and the house is looking better already. Well done!'

'Told you she's no' so bad,' said Mrs Ord, as she and Mae went up the area steps together. 'Fair, anyway, and you canna ask for more. Goodnight, then, I'm away for ma tram. Are you no' lucky? You've just to cross the road hame!'

Thank the Lord for that, thought Mae, as she dodged the traffic, feeling fit to drop. People were just arriving at the theatre and she stood for a moment, looking up at the façade blazing with lights, wondering in spite of herself how Harry Alpin was faring, as he waited for curtain-up. Not so nervous, perhaps, as if he'd been the actor he'd pretended to be, but then his job, even as assistant lighting man, must be complicated enough. At least, she needn't worry about seeing him. Except for his evening off, he would never be free at this time. What a relief!

But when she arrived back at Number Eight, Mrs Beith met her in a flurry of excitement. Harry Alpin had called earlier, on his way to work.

'He says he'd like to see you on Sunday afteroon, if you've got that off? He'll just come down and explain. Poor laddie, you'll have to see him, Mae. He's that upset.'

'I'll think about it,' said Mae, sliding into a chair. 'Mrs Beith, is that tea you're offering? Ah, you're a wonderful woman, so you are.'

Chapter Eleven

While Mae was dressing in her best blue on Sunday afternoon, Harry Alpin was up the stair, looking at himself in his mother's kitchen mirror. It was so spotted with age and gave so shadowy a reflection, he called over his shoulder that it made him look like the Demon King in a Christmas pantomime. 'What d'you think, folks?'

'You look fine,' snapped his mother.

'Put some water on your hair,' Ben Alpin, his father, handsome still, though more grey now than fair, lowered his Sunday paper. 'It's standin' on end.'

'Och, no.' Harry ran his hands over his blond hair. 'I'll get ma stuff.'

'Why all this fuss?' asked Emmy. 'You said you weren't going out with that Irish girl. You said you were just going to speak to her, though why you have to speak to her, I canna imagine.'

'Just want to tell her something about the theatre,' Harry muttered, desperately rubbing oil on to the rebellious tufts of his hair. 'Stop going on, Ma.'

'Aye, stop going on,' said Ben. 'If you could just hear yourself, Emmy. Ever since you heard Harry was meeting that Irish lassie, you've never been off his bones. He's no' getting married to her, as far as I know.'

'I should think he's not!' cried Emmy, breathing fast. 'You'd sing a different tune if he was, Ben Alpin!'

'Och, he's got more sense than you give him credit for, I'm telling you. He just wants to speak to the girl, that's what he said.'

'It's a nice afternoon,' Harry murmured, finishing with his hair. 'We might go for a bit of a walk.'

'So, now it's a walk—' his mother was beginning, when the door opened and Susie and Jannie Walker came hurtling through, to fling themselves on their grandparents, followed at a quieter pace by Rona and her thin, quiet husband, Jake.

'Hello, hello, anybody home?' cried Rona. 'Just popped in to see if anybody wants to walk up Calton Hill with us? Come on, it's a grand day, it'll do you good!'

'Your dad and me can come,' Emmy said stiffly. 'Your brother's got other plans.'

'See you later,' said Harry, quickly, and slid away to the door, before any more could be said to him. 'I'll no' be late back.'

Mae was standing outside Mrs Beith's closed door, looking up and down the stair, as though interested. When she saw Harry thundering down towards her, she gave an uncertain smile.

'Hello, then.'

'Hello.' He took off the cap he had just put on over his newly flattened hair. 'You're wearing your blue hat.'

'Why not?' she asked with a smile.

'I mean, you're ready to go out.'

'Were you going to talk to me on the stair?'

'Lord, no!' He grasped her hand, then let it go. 'I was hoping we could walk somewhere. It's a grand day.'

'It is.'

They walked down the stair as stiffly as a pair of soldiers on parade, and even in the street, where they met warm spring sunshine, did not relax.

'Where to?' asked Mae. 'Someone told me I should climb Calton Hill, so see the views.'

'No, no! I mean, no' today,' Harry said hastily. 'Let's just make for Princes Street Gardens, eh? I expect you'd like to see the flowers.'

Mae felt like telling him she would rather hear what he had to say, but held her peace as she walked by his side. As they made their way up Leith Street and into the east end of Princes Street, she could sense his strain and felt a certain guilt. He was so clearly upset, as Mrs Beith had said, but what did it matter, after all? It was scarcely a crime, what he had done, and it was only because she'd made a fuss about it, that it had seemed so.

'Mr Alpin—' she began, and paused, trying to decide what to say.

'I wish you'd call me Harry.'

'Well, you should call me Mae.'

He looked down at her, his troubled face lightening a little. 'I'd feel better, if I could do that.'

'I'm sorry if you're upset, Harry.'

'Upset? It was me upset you. Damn fool that I am!'

They walked on, past the Scott Monument and the two great art galleries, making their way to the west gardens where there was space enough to get away from the crowds.

'No seats left, of course,' said Harry. 'Sometimes think the whole of Edinburgh comes here on a Sunday.'

'Their chance to see a garden.'

'Aye, it's true, no' many folk have got gardens in the city.' He glanced at Mae. 'Ireland must be different, eh?'

She laughed. 'I can tell you have never been to Dublin! But it's true, the Irish like their patch of land, even if it's the size of a pocket hankie.'

'Your folks have that?'

'There's just my da. He grows a few vegetables, but he's a fisherman. We live by the sea.'

'Now, that I'd miss!'

They halted a moment and Harry pointed through the trees at the swathes of daffodils, still flowering on the steep slope below the Castle Esplanade.

'There are your flowers, Mae. Nearly over – we're just in time, eh?'

'And I think I see a seat,' said Mae, shading her eyes with her hand. 'See, below the Castle?'

There they sat, looking down to Princes Street, and Harry, who had relaxed a little on the walk, was nervous again, turning his cap in his hands, never glancing at Mae.

'About what I said the other day – like I said, it was just a spur o' the moment thing,' he said at last. 'Just – came out.'

'I'd have been impressed, anyway, if you'd told me you were a lighting man. I can guess that that is an expert's job.'

'Aye, but I was never trying to impress you.' Harry finally raised his eyes to Mae's face. 'It was for maself I said it. Och, you'll no' understand. It's just that when you asked me if I was an actor, I said I was because it's all I've ever wanted to be.'

47

Oh, dear Lord! Mae looked away. He's just like Lottie. Who'd have thought it? A practical man like him! Why should he share her dreams?

'You'll think that funny,' he said, watching her. 'A fella like me, wanting something like that?'

'No, no.'

'Aye, you do. I can see it in your face. It's always in people's faces – that look – when I say what I want. Harry Alpin, lighting man. Lives in a tenement. Never studied Shakespeare. Speaks with a Scottish accent. Who does he think he is, then?'

'Look, you shouldn't care what some folk think, Harry. My da's a fisherman, but he likes to read. He has books. The quality folk are surprised. He never cares. He knows what he wants.'

'When you asked me if I was in *Hay Fever*, I could've laughed maself,' he said, scarcely listening. 'I mean – a Noel Coward play. Can you imagine me, doing the voice for that?'

'Actors can do any kind of voice. They're taught, they have special training.'

'I did an audition once. Got nowhere.'

'Oh, Harry!'

'Aye. I'm no' saying they laughed. They just said, "no".'

'But you shouldn't give up, Harry. If it's what you really want.'

'There's too much against it,' he said tiredly. 'I've made up ma mind to forget it. Concentrate on what I can do, and that's hard enough.'

'Sure, it must be. Lighting must be very important to a play.'

He reached across and took her hand. 'You're very understanding, Mae. I'm sorry if I upset you. You know I never meant to, eh?'

'I know that. And I'm sorry I made such a fuss about it.' Mae gently removed her hand from his. 'Perhaps we'd better go back now?'

'I thought we might have a cup of tea somewhere. Bound to be something open on a Sunday.'

'I think I should go home, Harry. I've things to do before tomorrow.'

'Poor lassie, you don't get much free time. That woman's no' working you too hard, is she? Ma says she's a slave driver.'

'So far, we're getting on well, she's been quite reasonable – let's me come a bit late on a Sunday morning, so I can go to the cathedral. I feel sorry for her daughter, though. She has all the time in the world, but none for what she really wants.'

'Under Ma's thumb, eh?' Harry laughed shortly. 'That's what mothers like.'

They walked slowly back, not talking much, each relieved that they had made their peace. At the top of the Row, however, Harry stopped and touched Mae's hand and she sensed at once that things had changed. He was as tense as before, his eyes anxious. He wants to see me again, she thought. What shall I say?

'Mae, I was wondering, would you like to go out with me some-time?' He spoke quickly, as though he must get the words out before his nerve failed.

She looked into his face. It was a handsome face, no doubt of that, and a good face. The face of a man she would like to see happy. Yet, even now another face was forming over it, one she knew so well. Handsome, in a different way. Casual, charming, and far away. Not from her mind, though.

'I'd like to, Harry,' she said at last. 'But not yet.'

'Not yet?'

'I still care for someone.'

'I see.' His eyes on her were cold, showing his hurt.

He didn't see, that was the point, but no words would come for her to be able to talk to him, as she had talked to Sandy. She didn't feel ready for that yet, any more than she felt ready to go out with him, or anyone.

'We'll leave it, then,' he said curtly. 'Thanks for listening to me, anyway.'

'I enjoyed our walk,' she said hastily. 'It was lovely for me to see a bit of Edinburgh with you.'

'Aye.' He put on his cap and turned from her. 'I'll away, then. Best of luck, Mae.'

It was a firm goodbye, one she should want, and yet, she wished, perversely, that he hadn't made it.

'Goodbye, Harry!' she called up the stair after him, but he did not look back.

'You've missed your tea, Uncle Harry!' his small nieces cried, running to him. 'And we had trifle!'

49

'Have tea out, did you?' asked Rona with interest. 'Where'd you find something open?'

'Never had any tea.'

'You've been out all this time and had no tea!' cried Emmy. 'Whatever were you thinking of?'

'Not of tea, that's for sure,' said Ben with a grin. 'That Irish girl's pretty, eh?'

'You needn't worry about her,' Harry said quietly. 'She doesn't want to go out with me.'

'You asked her?' Emmy went pale. 'Oh, Harry, I canna believe it!'

'I tell you, she doesn't want to go out with me. Not yet, anyway.'

'There you are, Emmy,' said Ben. 'No need to worry.'

'Not yet?' asked Emmy. 'What does she mean by that?'

'Don't think she meant anything. She was just letting me down lightly.'

'Lightly!' Emmy was filling the kettle to make Harry's tea. 'Why's she no' want to go out with you anyway? Who does she think she is?'

'Och, Emmy, you're hopeless!' said Ben. 'The lassie can do nothing right. If she goes out with Harry, she's wrong. If she doesn't go out with Harry, she's still wrong. There's no pleasing you.'

'No' where ma son's happiness is concerned.'

'For God's sake!' cried Harry 'Leave ma happiness to me, Ma!' He stood up and snatched his cap from its hook. 'Never mind about the tea. I'm going out to see ma mates.'

And when they heard the door bang and his feet go clattering down the stair, even Susie and Jannie didn't say a word.

Chapter Twelve

Some days later, when Mae was still feeling vaguely guilty over her rejection of Harry, two postcards arrived for her. While one had crossed the Atlantic, the other had only had to travel from a New Town post box to Mrs Beith's flat. That was the one Mae read first.

'Dear Mae,' ran the large round handwriting. 'Had my wee boy on Sunday. No trouble at all, would you credit it? His name is Finlay, weighed seven pounds, twelve ounces. Come soon. Love, Sandy.'

What a relief! Sandy seemed to be fine, the baby, too. Now, all she had to face was giving him away. Poor girl. Mae decided to visit her on Wednesday, which was her afternoon off.

The second card showed a picture of the Statue of Liberty in New York harbour. For some moments, she held it at arm's length. This was the one she didn't really want to read. Didn't want to be told that everything in New York was wonderful. That everything was working out just as planned, for Rosaleen and Kieran Connor.

Oh, but was that not mean-spirited? Showing green-eyed envy? Be generous, she told herself. Wish them well.

Mrs Fitzgerald had sent the card on from Cork, for of course Rosaleen didn't yet know that Mae had left Ireland. Must write to Mrs Fitzgerald, thought Mae, and Rosaleen, too. She had the penny bottle of ink and the paper she used for writing home to Da. How much would it cost to send a letter to America? Having put it off as long as she could, she read the card.

'Everything here is so exciting,' Rosaleen had written, in her flamboyant hand. 'New York must be the busiest city in the world!

Kieran's Uncle Nick is being very kind and next week we are moving into our own APARTMENT, that's what they call flats here. Just wish you could see it! I've put the address at the top of this card. Hope Da is well, and Annie, and you, too. Kieran sends his regards. All my love, your cousin, Rosaleen.'

Mae laid down the card, and for a moment let the tide of bitterness wash over her. It was wrong, of course, to give in to bad feelings, but there was no doubt, it helped. In the end, though, shame took over and she mentally shook herself. Enough of that! Wish them well. She had a life to live and must get on with it. Find her own happiness. And she would, too.

'Everything all right, dear?' asked Mrs Beith, as Mae came out of her room.

'It is. One of the girls at the hostel has sent news of her baby. A boy. I'll be going to see her on my afternoon off.'

'Oh, that's nice. A boy, eh? I suppose she's no' married?'

'Nobody's married at Adelaide House.' Mae smiled wryly, and passed over Rosaleen's card. 'But this one's from my cousin in New York. Now, she IS married.'

Mrs Beith put on her glasses to study the Statue of Liberty. 'Is that no' grand, eh? Are they no' lucky, then, to get to America?'

'Very lucky.' Mae, putting the postcards in her bag, did not fail to see the curiosity lighting Mrs Beith's pale-blue eyes, but made no effort to say more. If her landlady could make the connection between these cousins in New York and Mae's heartache, the best of luck to her. Mae was not going to make it clear.

'If you want a little present to take the babby, I've a wee matinée jacket you can have,' Mrs Beith said, rising. 'I always have a few bits and pieces in ma drawer, in case they come in.'

'Oh, I could not be taking this,' cried Mae, admiring the little white jacket Mrs Beith was showing her. 'It's beautiful, so it is, but it's your work, Mrs Beith.'

'Och, there's no new bairns on the horizon for me at the moment. You take it, Mae, and I'll find a bit o' paper to wrap it up.'

'If you'll let me give you something—'

'Whisht! What'd be the point? I made it ages ago. I've no idea now how much the wool was. Here's a bit o' tissue paper, anyway, will make a nice parcel. You give it to the poor girl, Mae, and wish her and the babby good luck, eh?'

She may be inquisitive, thought Mae, gratefully accepting the little package, but Mrs Beith's got a soft heart. Who said she was tough, then?

Chapter Thirteen

It was strange, returning to Adelaide House, on Wednesday afternoon. Everything so familiar, even to the smell of stew and cabbage in the hall, yet already seeming something from the distant past.

But I have not been gone give minutes, thought Mae, in light dress and jacket, for the spring weather had turned unusually warm. It's just that so much has happened since I moved into Victoria Row, I feel it's long ago that I was here.

And then Miss Thorburn was tapping down the stairs and greeting her and escorting her into the second house to find Sandy, and she had no more time to think about the past.

'Here we are,' said Miss Thorburn, opening the door on a roomful of women in nightgowns and shawls, some lying on their beds, some admiring their babies in cribs, some gossiping at the window. Though one or two were familiar to Mae, she could see no sign of Sandy.

She was still looking about her, when up leaped a stranger, a slim young girl, who came flying along to hug her. And of course it was Sandy, but a Sandy Mae had never known and couldn't at first believe in.

'Why, Sandy, look at you, then! Sure, you're half the size you were!'

'Aye, I've been lucky. The minute ma boy was born, there was me slim again, instead o' looking like a great sack o' tatties! Oh, Mae, it's good to see you. And so pretty in that dress and all. Is it summer outside, then? But come and see ma wee Finlay!'

'Ah, he's so beautiful!' cried Mae, looking down at the baby boy, snuffling and twisting in his sleep, tiny fists working away, his mop of dark hair damp on the sheet. Was it perhaps already hinting at his mother's colour of red? Mae was sure he was going to look like Sandy. 'How glad you must be, it's all over,' she murmured.

'You're right about that.' Sandy sat down on her bed, drawing her shawl around her. 'All went like clockwork. Never needed Dr Rick, I'm sorry to tell you, but Mrs Mennie wasnae too bad. She got me through without stitches, anyway, and soon as she showed me Finlay, all complete, I felt on top o' the world.'

'Here, I've brought you a little matinée jacket,' Mae handed over her package, glad to put off the moment of asking about the adoption. 'My landlady knitted it – I've not had time yet to make something myself.'

'Dinna apologise, this is perfect. And second size, too, that's grand.' Sandy held it up admiringly. 'I call him wee Finlay, you ken, but in no time at all, he'll be out o' what I've got for him. Canna wait to see him in this.'

Mae hesitated. 'Sandy, I hope you will not mind if I ask you—'

'About the adoption?' Sandy set her mouth in a straight, tight line. 'He's no' going to be adopted.'

'You've changed your mind? But what about the people who wanted him?'

'I feel bad for 'em, but what can I do? Soon as I saw Finlay, I knew I could never let him go.'

'I suppose they always knew you might have the second thoughts?'

'Aye, they knew. And they should've expected it, is what I say. I mean, it's different before the babby's born. You think you'd do anything, just to be free, be yourself again, and I never dreamed for a minute that I'd want to keep him.'

'It was hard for you,' Mae murmured. 'They will surely understand?'

Sandy was looking down at Finlay in his crib, her face softening with love and the new experience of caring that was now to be part of her life. 'They'll have to,' she whispered. 'I'm no' changing ma mind back.'

'But what will you do, Sandy? How will you manage?'

'Och, I'll be OK.' She shrugged. 'In fact, ma mother's going to help me.'

'Your mother? You've made it up? Sandy, that's wonderful! I am so pleased for you.'

'Aye, well, she came in to have a look at Finlay and she said if I mean to keep him, she'll mind him. 'Cos I'll be having to go to work.'

'And what'll you do? Domestic work like me?' Mae made a face and told Sandy something of her life at Mrs Cameron's. 'I would not be recommending it.'

'Och, no, I couldnae stand it! Being at some awfu' woman's beck and call. No, dinna worry, I'll find something. Mebbe in a shop. Some posh dress shop, eh?' She giggled. 'Can you no' see me, then, walking up and down like thae mannequins?'

'I'm keen to do sewing,' said Mae. 'I'm looking around.'

'Sewing? Did a bit o' that once. Worked for a dressmaker in Nicolson Street.' Sandy shook her head. 'No' for me. Stuck in a wee room, treadling a sewing machine all day. You fancy that?'

'I do.' Mae smiled. 'Sure, we're all different.'

'Aye. Just as well, eh?'

With young Finlay showing every sign of waking up and preparing for a good howl, Mae said she'd better go, but she'd come again soon. Sandy, however, was cagey about her plans.

'Dr Rick, he's no' one for making us lie in bed for ten days. He says it's bad for us and we should get moving, so I might be out o' here sooner than you think. Tell you what, I'll send you another card wi' Ma's address, eh?'

When Mae had stooped to touch Finlay's round cheek, she turned to Sandy and hugged her thin frame.

'Take care,' she said quietly. 'And keep in touch. I'll look out for that card.'

'I'll no' forget, I promise. Bye, Mae, and thanks again for the wee coat!'

'Bye, Mae,' shouted those women who recognised her, and from the door she turned to wave. Sandy, lifting Finlay from his crib, made to wave his little hand back, and grinned.

'How did you find Sandy, then?' asked Miss Thorburn, when Mae looked in on her in her office.

'She seems very happy.'

'She told you she'd rejected the adoption bid?' Miss Thorburn sighed. 'It was my job to tell the young couple, of course. They were devastated, even though they'd always known it could happen.'

'But Finlay is Sandy's. It's her right to bring him up, if she wants.'

Miss Thorburn fixed Mae with her dark intelligent eyes. 'They were well-to-do, the people who wanted him. He would have been given every advantage.'

'But they aren't his parents.'

'He will never know his real father, and his mother will be out working. It's his grandmother who will be bringing him up and she has four other children, all younger than Sandy, and lives in a crumbling tenement in the Old Town.'

Mae looked away. 'It's difficult,' she said after a pause. 'Who can say what is best?'

'We'll have to hope Sandy is.' Miss Thorburn came round from her desk and turned Mae's face to the light. 'You're looking tired, you know. Not being worked too hard, are you?'

'I'm all right, thanks.'

'If only you could have come to us.'

As Mae moved to the door, Miss Thorburn suddenly smiled.

'I forgot to tell you Dr Rick's good news. He's engaged. To a lovely young nurse – we're all so happy for him.'

'Happy?' Mae laughed. 'Sure the girls'll be wearing full mourning, if I know them!'

She had reached the Queen's on her way home and would have hurried past, not wanting to dwell on Harry Alpin, when she saw Lottie standing on the steps, reading the playbills.

'Lottie! What are you up to, then? Not booking a seat?'

Lottie jumped and coloured a little. 'Oh, Mae, it's you. No, of course I'm not booking a seat.' She looked round, as though expecting her mother to come running across the road to catch her. 'I'd like to – but I'm not.'

'What's the play this week, then?'

'Something by John Galsworthy. *The Silver Box*. It's a drama.'

Mae looked around, too. 'If your ma's at her bridge today, you could sneak in to the matinée.'

'It's nearly over.' Lottie put her hand to her mouth. 'But what are you saying, Mae? I'd never dare to do that. Oh, there'd be such a row, you've no idea!'

'How old are you, Lottie? Nineteen?'

'I'll be twenty in August.'

'Old enough to tell your ma you'd like to go to the theatre.'

'Next week it's J M Barrie's *Mary Rose*,' Lottie said in a low voice. 'I'd really like to see that.'

'There's your chance, then. Book a seat.'

'You're not really thinking I would?' Lottie hesitated. 'I suppose you don't want to see it, do you?'

'I might.' Mae's blue eyes were thoughtful. 'Wednesday is a matinée. Wednesday, your ma plays bridge. Wednesday is my afternoon off. I could come with you, if you liked.'

'Would you – do that?'

'I would.'

Lottie swallowed hard. 'Shall I book, then?'

'For the cheap seats. I will pay my own way.'

'I could pay for both of us.'

'No, we must pay separately.'

'I'll book for the gallery, then. That's the upper circle.' Lottie's voice was shaky. 'I think it costs ninepence.'

'I have it.' Mae counted out the coppers from her purse. 'Let's book together,' she said kindly. 'The girl in the box-office may not be able to hear you.'

'I'm terrified of hearing myself,' said Lottie.

When the deed was done, they came out of the theatre and looked at each other like Gunpowder Plot conspirators.

'Oh, Mae,' whispered Lottie. 'Will you keep the tickets?'

'Under lock and key.' Mae laughed. 'No, that's a joke. But I'll make sure nobody sees them.'

'Till next week, then.'

'Next week? I'll see you tomorrow.'

'Don't say anything, though. This is our secret.'

And I hope it stays that way, thought Mae, watching Lottie wavering away to cross the road. Maybe I should not be getting involved in this. On the other hand, maybe I should. Somebody's got to rescue Lottie.

Chapter Fourteen

They had a week to wait, and it was a long week. Mae at least remained outwardly calm, but pale Lottie could not control her fears, jumping every time her mother looked at her, sliding out of rooms as though the police were after her. It was only by good luck that Mrs Cameron did not appear to notice; but, then, she saw what she expected to see, which was her daughter being no more than her usual, self-effacing self.

'If you are really so worried, we needn't go to the matinée,' Mae told Lottie, as she dusted her bedroom. 'It's terrible, so it is, to see you looking so anxious.'

'Whatever happens, I am going,' Lottie declared, tidying the things from her dressing table in an effort to be helpful. 'It's a matter of principle. I can't give in.'

'Well, your ma may not go to her bridge.'

'She will not give up her bridge. She'd have to be running a fever before she'd do that. Maybe not even then.'

'She usually leaves at two o'clock?'

'And is back at half past five.'

'I'm thinking we'll be all right, then.' Mae dusted the dressing table and put back its glass tray and framed photograph of Mr and Mrs Cameron. 'We'll have plenty of time.'

'Fingers crossed,' said Lottie hollowly.

Lunch on Wednesday was a nightmare. First, Mrs Cameron seemed to take longer than usual to prepare it, and Mae had to keep asking what she could do to help, while keeping an eye on the clock and praying the meal would not be late.

'I've the washing up to do before we go,' she whispered to

Lottie, when it became clear that the lunch was not going to be ready on time. 'And I dare not be leaving that!'

'I'll help you, don't worry,' Lottie promised, twisting her thin hands together. 'As soon as Mummy leaves.'

But when would that be? At five minutes to two, the meal being finally over, she was still combing her hair and pressing in her water waves. At two o'clock, she was slowly putting on her coat and adjusting her hat, and Mae had still to finish the washing up alone, for Lottie couldn't help until her mother had gone.

It was not until ten minutes past two that Mrs Cameron at last called goodbye, with all her usual reminders to Lottie to lock the door and check round the house if she went out, and a final word to Mae that she would see her in the morning and it was to be hoped that she would enjoy her afternoon off. Then the door banged behind her, and Lottie leaped down to the kitchen.

'It's all right, she's gone! Quick, Mae, get changed and I'll finish off here. We've to be in our seats at half past two.'

'I'm ready,' Mae answered breathlessly. 'I've only to take this apron off. And everything's done. We've just to go.'

'Oh, Mae!' Lottie's eyes were glittering. 'Isn't it silly? All this for a matinée?'

'There's more than that at stake. Were you not saying so yourself? Come on, bring your keys. Let's lock the door and go.'

Mae had not been to a theatre since Mrs Fitzgerald had taken her to see Irish plays in Cork, when they'd had good seats in the stalls. Never had she had to climb up so many steps as at the Queen's, twisting round and round to reach the gallery, the Upper Circle as some called it, which was one above the Grand Circle, which in turn was one above the Dress Circle. And somewhere below that were the stalls on the ground floor, which you could only just see, if you didn't mind peering down and risking going over the brass rail edging the front row.

But Mae and Lottie could see the red velvet curtains of the stage, all right, opened at present to reveal the safety curtain, with the ornate boxes on either side, and the orchestra pit, in which there were no musicians that day. With the audience, now growing quiet, they watched, thrilled, as the safety curtain began to rise and the lights to dim, and quite forgot they'd ever felt anxious about their little adventure of coming to the Queen's.

'Oh, this is so marvellous,' whispered Lottie, opening their programme. 'Oh, don't you feel it, Mae? The magic? It's a different world, isn't it?'

'It is,' said Mae, but the thought came into her mind that this world was Harry Alpin's. Was he on duty somewhere close, helping to manage the lighting? How painful was it for him, to look down on that stage, now being revealed, as the velvet curtains came together and then parted again, and know he was excluded? Poor Harry. Her heart went out to him. Well, part of it.

'Act One, Scene One,' breathed Lottie. 'Oh, whatever it costs me, this has been worth while.'

'The seats only cost ninepence,' Mae whispered, smiling. But she knew only too well what Lottie meant.

The play itself, Barrie's famously eerie ghost drama, went down well with the audience, but the girls would have enjoyed anything. It was being in the theatre that counted; seeing actors on the stage, being taken out of their own lives for a little while and transported, as Lottie had said, to another world. When the lights went up for the interval and they looked at each other, blinking, it was hard for a moment or two to come back to themselves. Even when they queued for ices, they didn't speak; didn't want to spoil the magic.

But when the curtain went up and they prepared to lose themselves again, Mae's eyes went to the clock over the exit, and her heart sank. It was much later than she'd thought – well after four, with a whole act still to come. To be on the safe side, they'd decided they must be out by five, which meant they might have to leave early.

'Lottie,' she whispered, 'look at the clock.'

Dreamily, Lottie turned her head. 'What's wrong?' she mouthed.

'It's late. We may not see the end.'

'Oh, no!'

'Ssh!' cried a woman in front of them, turning round and frowning, and Lottie, shaking her head, subsided.

It was Mae who had to keep watching the clock, and Mae who took Lottie's arm some time before the end of the play and forced her to move. Mae, who also did the apologising as they squeezed past the other people in the row, and Mae who made Lottie run, round and round, down the steps from the gallery to the foyer, and out into the early evening sunshine.

'Oh, Mae, it's so awful, having to leave!' cried Lottie. 'I'm sure we could've just seen the end, I'm sure we wouldn't have been late.'

'Lottie, it's after five already. If your ma comes back early and sees you crossing from the theatre, what are you going to say?'

'Oh, Lord, I don't know! I'm just up there, in the air. I can't take it in, that I managed to get inside the Queen's after all this time!'

'Better get home now, though,' said Mae, feeling just a little resentful that she had to act as Lottie's older sister – mother, even – when she was no more than a year older. 'Run across the road and get yourself in your door. And watch the traffic!'

But Lottie was still havering. 'Mae, can we go to the theatre again, do you think? Everything's worked out so well, it shows we can do it. Shall I get tickets for the next play?'

'Yes, yes, just go!'

When Mae had watched Lottie's slight figure finally reach Number Thirty-Five, she breathed a long sigh of relief, for even if her mother was back at home, she wouldn't know where Lottie had been and all she had to do was say she'd been to the shops, or something of that sort. What a terrible thing it was, then, to be telling lies, but sometimes it was necessary. Folk should not attempt to rule other people's lives, whether parents, or not. Parents, especially, should not be unreasonable.

'Bye, Mae,' said a man's voice, and she swung round to see Harry Alpin walking away from her.

'Harry!' she called after him, but he only glanced back, touching his cap.

'Got to hurry. I'm meeting some o' the lads.'

The sight of his tall figure walking so resolutely into the distance quite spoiled the memory of her amazingly different afternoon. It was so sad to think he'd taken such offence he didn't even want to walk with her, but there was nothing she could do about it. She wasn't ready yet to forget Kieran Connor, although it did occur to her, as she made her way back to Number Eight, that she hadn't actually remembered him for the whole of that day.

Chapter Fifteen

The Queen's, once a variety theatre, now ran a repertory company, the Queen's Players, putting on a different play every week, with occasional musical shows for visiting companies in the summer and a pantomime every Christmas. The plays produced were of the kind to suit general audiences – nothing too unusual or high-brow, although the management prided itself on offering some Shakespeare and Bernard Shaw, making up on school audiences what they lost from the public.

Whatever was offered in the weeks following their first successful outing, Mae and Lottie went to it, gradually growing in confidence with every occasion that Lottie got safely home before her mother, and Mae returned to her lodgings without disaster.

'I never dreamed it could be so easy, doing what I want,' Lottie remarked. 'But I can't thank you enough, Mae, for supporting me. I'd never have managed it on my own.'

'We should not take risks, though. It only needs your ma to come back early one day and we'll be in trouble.'

'Oh, I know, I haven't forgotten. But, after all, what can she do?' Lottie shrugged. 'Stop my allowance? I expect I'd get it back.'

'It's very brave, you are now.' Mae laughed. 'For me, it would mean more than losing an allowance.'

'You really think my mother'd sack you? She wouldn't. You're too good at your job.'

'Let's hope we need never find out what your ma might do.'

Towards the end of June, they had a scare at an Oscar Wilde matinée when Mae, queueing with Lottie for ices in the interval, was recognised by Miss Dow from the hostel.

'Why, Mae!' cried Miss Dow, beaming. 'How nice to see you! I didn't realise you were a theatre-goer!'

'Just like to come to a matinée sometimes,' Mae mumbled. 'Er – this is Miss Cameron, a friend of mine. Lottie, this is Miss Dow from Adelaide House, where I was staying before I found my lodgings.'

Lottie and Miss Dow shook hands, Lottie immediately shrinking a little when the older woman asked pleasantly, 'And are you in service with Mae, dear?'

'No – I-I'm not working at the moment.'

Miss Dow, surprised at Lottie's accent, raised her eyebrows. 'Now, I wonder if I might know your mother? I believe I once played bridge at the Caledonian Ladies' Club with a Mrs Cameron.'

'That must have been someone else. I don't think my mother's a member.'

'Well, of course, it's true, there are lots of Mrs Camerons.' Miss Dow turned to Mae. 'And when are you going to come to see us again, Mae? We all miss you, though of course your friend Sandy's departed.'

'I was going to ask you about her, Miss Dow,' Mae said quickly. 'She was saying she'd send me her address, but never a line have I had. I hope she's all right.'

'Blooming, when she left, my dear. But I daresay she doesn't want you to call on her at her mother's.' Miss Dow shook her head. 'Not exactly the place to receive guests.'

'I'm a friend, not a guest. I'd like to see her.'

'Better leave it for now, I think.' Miss Dow moved a little away, 'Well, we'd better get our ices, or the curtain will be going up without us. So lovely to see you, Mae. Don't forget us. Goodbye, Miss Cameron – nice to have met you.'

'Oh, God, she knows my mother,' Lottie said desperately. 'She does, I can tell she does! And if she should see her—'

'Why would Miss Dow be seeing your mother? She spends most of her time at the hostel. Probably never plays bridge now.'

They bought their ices and ate them quickly, but when they returned to their seats, Lottie had lost her usual pleasure in her surroundings and would only stare gloomily at her programme while Mae tried to distract her.

'You might try doing some voluntary work at Adelaide House, Lottie. They'd be glad to have you, so they would, and your ma might approve.'

'Approve of me mixing with umarried mothers? I thought you knew her better than that.'

'Sure, they're not all unmarried mothers. Some have been ill-treated by their menfolk and need help to recover.'

Lottie shuddered a little. 'I don't think I'd be any good at that sort of work. They'd all hate me, anyway, for being lucky. I suppose they'd think me lucky?'

'Now you are feeling sorry for yourself. Of course, it's lucky you are, to them.'

Lottie gave a sheepish smile. 'Do I sound a selfish load of misery? I'm not, really, but I don't think I could do voluntary work just now. I'm learning my lines.'

'Lines?'

'For roles in auditions.'

'I see,' murmured Mae, amazed. 'You're really going to try for the stage?'

'Yes. Seeing all these plays has made me even more determined. I'm not going to let my mother stop me and that's that.'

'So, what roles are you learning, then?'

'Rosalind, in *As You Like It*. Ophelia, in *Hamlet*, and maybe something from Shaw or Somerset Maugham, to be modern. But there goes the bell for curtain up. We'd better not talk any more.'

Glued to the last act of *Lady Windermere's Fan*, Lottie was oblivious of the covert glances Mae was sending her, leaving Mae to marvel again at her moth-like air of fragility. So weak, she seemed, yet could surprise with sudden obstinacy. She was not going to let her mother stop her from being an actress, she had declared, and had sounded as though she meant it.

But even the thought of Miss Dow's telling her mother she'd seen her at the theatre, had been enough to send her into a state of terrible anxiety. Poor Lottie! As Mae's gaze moved to the clock, as it always did as the play neared its end, she knew, if it came to a contest between Lottie and her mother, there was no question of Lottie's winning.

*   *   *

As it happened, they left the theatre that afternoon with time in hand, and were able to stand on the steps, enjoying the summer sunshine.

'Let's see what's on next week,' said Lottie, turning to look at the playbills. 'We'll book anyway, shall we?'

But Mae made no reply, for she was facing straight ahead and looking into the clear, cold eyes of Mrs Cameron.

Chapter Sixteen

Bright red spots had appeared on Mrs Cameron's cheekbones and she was beginning to breathe fast. As she looked from Mae to the stricken Lottie, it seemed as though she might speak, but she only jerked her head in its brimmed felt hat and indicated that they were to cross the road. Back to Number Thirty-Five was the order, and they did not disobey; there was no point.

She interviewed them in the stuffy and over-furnished drawing room, for Mrs Ord was in the kitchen, cooking and singing, and the first words Mrs Cameron uttered when she found her voice were to tell Mae to close the door.

'No need to wash our dirty linen before others,' she declared. 'Mrs Ord will know soon enough what has happened.'

Mae was about to speak, then thought better of it, but did not lower her eyes from Mrs Cameron's face. Lottie, it seemed, was incapable of saying a word.

'First, I should like to know how long this has been going on,' Mrs Cameron said, not motioning to the girls to sit down, but taking a chair herself. 'Today wasn't the first time you'd disregarded my wishes, Charlotte, was it?'

'No,' Lottie managed to answer in a whisper.

'So, when did it begin? If you're not going to tell me, I'll tell you.' Mrs Cameron's eyes went to Mae. 'When Mae O'Donovan came to work for me. Isn't that right?'

'It was my idea, Mummy. Mae had nothing to do with it.'

'I saw nothing wrong in it,' said Mae. 'There is no harm in going to a theatre. I often went to the theatre in Cork with my previous employer.'

Mrs Cameron leaned forward, her eyes icy. 'And that gives you the right, does it, to decide what my daughter should or should not do? The fact that my husband and I do not approve does not come into it. You know best.'

As a great wave of colour suffused her face, the contrast between the heat of her cheeks and the coldness of her eyes was so alarming, it took all Mae's courage not to look away. But she would not give her employer the satisfaction of thinking she was afraid. Lottie she might tyrannise; she must not be allowed to think she could tyrannise Mae.

'The cheek of it!' Mrs Cameron was crying now, her voice trembling. 'The unutterable CHEEK, that you should come into my house and encourage my daughter to do what she knows is wrong! Oh I always knew I should never have taken on an Irish girl, who wouldn't know what's right, but I trusted Mrs Beith. I believed the references from that woman in Cork, who turns out to be no better than her own servant, going to theatres and heaven knows what—'

'Please not to speak of Mrs Fitzgerald in that way,' Mae interrupted. 'She is a lady, she is good, and educated and refined. I will not have her insulted.'

'You will not? You?' Mrs Cameron stood up. 'That's enough, Mae O'Donovan, that's more than enough. I will pay you a week's money in lieu of notice, but I wish you to leave my house now. Please take whatever is yours and go.'

'With pleasure,' retorted Mae. 'And there will be no need to pay me or worry about a reference. I shall manage without anything from you. Goodbye, Mrs Cameron.'

'Don't say goodbye to me,' said Lottie quietly, so pale now, she might have been ready to faint, except that some inner resolve seemed to be keeping her on her feet. 'Don't say goodbye, Mae – I'm coming with you.'

'Charlotte!' cried her mother. 'Whatever are you saying?'

'I'm saying, if Mae goes, I go too.'

'Have you taken leave of your senses? You have no money. Where will you go?' Mrs Cameron was wringing her hands and staring at Lottie as though she were a stranger. 'What's got into you? Are you ill? This is your home, I am your mother. You can't leave. I forbid you to leave.'

'I'm sorry, Mummy,' Lottie said tremulously. 'I can't stand by and let you be so unfair. You know Mae's done nothing wrong, you know we've neither of us done anything wrong. It was just something you didn't want us to do. We went against you, that was all.'

'The theatre is full of immorality,' said Mrs Cameron deliberately. 'Everyone knows those actors and actresses are not like good-living people. And the ones who write the plays are the same. You have been protected all your life, Charlotte, you probably have no idea what I'm talking about. But everything I've done has been for your sake. Can't you see that?'

'I'm grown up now. I have to make up my own mind about things.'

'Honour thy father and thy mother, Charlotte. That's what the Bible says. And in law, you are still a minor. Please to remember that.'

'I'm going, and you can't stop me. And I do have some money – you've forgotten my post office account. Mae, will you wait, while I pack a few things?'

'I'll help you,' said Mae blankly.

Still shocked by Lottie's sudden transformation, she followed her up to her room, where she found her throwing clothes into a suitcase, tears flowing down her cheeks.

'Don't worry, Mae, this won't take long. I can't take much, can I?'

'Lottie, listen.' Mae took her by the hands and made her sit down in a bedside chair. 'I am not wanting you to do this. There's no need. How will it help me, for you to leave home?'

'I have to do it. There's a principle at stake.'

'But are you ready to hurt your folks like this? You have to be sure what you are doing.'

'Honour thy father and thy mother,' Lottie said bitterly. She brushed the tears from her face and blew her nose. 'Is that what you want me to do, Mae? After the way my mother's behaved? She rules my life, I have no rights, no say in what I want to do.'

'That's true and it's wrong. I will admit, I was all for rescuing you, and I know you will have to leave home one day, but now I'm thinking, maybe not like this. Not in the heat of the moment, and for me.'

Lottie leaped up from the chair and snatched a dressing gown from the bed, which she stuffed into her suitcase. 'This is my chance to start a new life for myself, and I'm taking it.'

'But what will you do? You said you had no training for work.'

'I can take some sort of job, and I've the post office money; I can manage for a while.' Lottie closed her case and turned to face Mae. 'But first, I'm going to try for an audition.'

'Where? At the Queen's?'

'Yes! You know it's what I want to do. What I must do.'

'Well, I'd feel better if it was not just for me you were leaving.'

'It is for you, but me as well. What Mummy did to you, just made me find the will to leave, which I needed.' Lottie hesitated, looking at the photograph of her parents on her dressing table. With a sudden movement, she opened her suitcase and swept the photo inside. 'But I'm not going to forget them, you know. You needn't think that.'

'We'd better go,' Mae said softly. 'Give me your case.'

But Lottie was full of new independence and carried it herself; probably, thought Mae, smiling inwardly, for the first time in her life.

Downstairs, it seemed that Mrs Cameron had decided to play the dignified and injured parent, and made no move towards Lottie, who faced her with Mae at her side. Instead, she sighed and put her hand to her brow.

'If you want to hurt me this way, Charlotte, I can't prevent you. But it seems a strange return for all I've done for you, ever since you were born. I really don't know how your father will take this. He will be a broken man.'

Oh, Lord, she's clever, thought Mae. That's the way to touch Lottie's heart. Not by shouting and shaking the big fist, but by seeming damaged; by being the sad mother, hurt by an ungrateful child.

But though Lottie's eyes filled again with tears, it seemed she was not moved enough to change her mind.

'Mummy, I don't want to hurt you or Daddy, but I think it's time for me to go. I'd have gone one day, anyway, even without what happened. Please try to understand. I have to live my own life.'

A shudder ran through Mrs Cameron's small frame. Perhaps she knew she was facing defeat, but she had not yet surrendered.

'And what do I tell your father? That his only daughter has run away from home, heaven knows where?'

'Tell him, I'll be in touch, I promise. And I'll send an address, as soon as I get one.'

'When you change your mind and decide to come crawling back, do you expect to find the door open, Charlotte?'

Lottie bit her lip. 'That's – that's up to you.'

'I shouldn't count on it, then.'

Mother and daughter exchanged looks from eyes that could seem so much alike, except that Mrs Cameron's were as cold as winter, and Lottie's softly pleading.

'Goodbye,' she said quietly, but her mother made no reply.

'Hey, Mae, what's going on?' asked Mrs Ord appearing in the hall from the stairs to the kitchen. 'I thought I heard your voice. And Miss Charlotte, are you away, then?'

'My mother will tell you all about it,' said Lottie. 'Goodbye, Mrs Ord.'

'Shall I no' get you a taxi? You've got that case, eh?'

'No taxi,' said Mae. 'We're not going far.'

'Where are we going?' asked Lottie, when they were in the street.

'To my lodgings. Mrs Beith's a lovely woman. Sure, she'll take you in, you've no need to worry.'

Chapter Seventeen

'Well!' cried Mrs Beith, her chin wobbling, her whole face sagging a little, as she tried to take in this extraordinary happening. Miss Charlotte, out of her mother's house? Miss Charlotte, here, in Mrs Beith's flat, wanting lodgings? It was against all reason, so it was. Young ladies did not do that sort of thing. Mrs Beith looked away from Miss Charlotte's eyes, so anxious, and Mae's, so hopeful.

'Well, I dinna ken what to say,' she told the two young women. 'This has knocked ma breath away.'

'Ours, too,' said Mae. 'But I know you'll help us out, and let Lottie stay.'

'You mean Miss Charlotte?'

'Everyone calls me Lottie, Mrs Beith.' Lottie managed a smile. 'I hope you will, too.'

'Your ma never called you Lottie, if you dinna mind me saying so.' Mrs Beith pulled a chair from the table and sank into it. 'Seemingly, you've forgotten about her.'

'No, I haven't forgotten.' Lottie's smile died on her lips. 'I am thinking about her all the time.'

'But you've run away from her, eh?'

'I didn't exactly run. My mother was very unfair to Mae when she dismissed her. I couldn't stand by.'

Mrs Beith glanced at Mae, whose eyes were now no longer hopeful. 'Let me get this straight. When Mrs Cameron asked you no' to go to the theatre, the both of you still went?'

'I had a right to go to the theatre,' said Mae.

'Aye, but no' with Miss Charlotte. You went against your employer's wishes. Canna be right. And Miss Charlotte disobeyed

72

her ma. That's no' right, either. Honour thy father and thy mother, is what the good Book says.' Mrs Beith stood up. 'I'm sorry, Miss Charlotte, I canna give you lodgings.'

Mae flushed scarlet. 'You will not help her? Mrs Beith, I cannot believe it. This is not like you. You're always so kind, so understanding. We thought we could get another bed for my room, and then you'd have the extra money—'

'It's all right, Mae,' Lottie murmured. 'Don't say any more. I'll find somewhere else.'

'Time's getting on,' said Mrs Beith. 'I'll give you ma wee cupboard bed just for tonight, Miss Charlotte, but I canna go against your ma's wishes, you ken. I canna let you stay. If she was to hear I was offering you lodgings, what'd she think?'

'Are you worrying about the work she gives you?' asked Mae coldly.

'Well, I have to think o' that, Mae. It's convenient and Mrs Cameron's always been very nice to me. But, the truth is, I'm no' keen to be involved. You two are in the wrong, and I dinna want to be part of it. I'm sure you understand, eh?'

'We understand very well,' said Mae. 'Lottie, put your case in my room for tonight. We can decide what to do in the morning.'

In the morning, Mae told Mrs Beith she would be giving up her room. She and Lottie were going to look for somewhere else to stay.

'Oh, Mae, you're never going to leave me?' Mrs Beith, ladling out porridge, appeared upset, but also, to Mae's eyes, a little relieved. 'Still, if you think you'll be happier, you're best away.'

'And Mrs Cameron will be happier, too, if I'm away,' said Mae. 'And not with you.'

'Aye, she might. But, oh dear Lord, Mae, I'll miss you!' Mrs Beith shook her head. 'The only one to make me a cup o' tea, eh? And always that helpful.'

There was a silence, as Mae and Lottie tried to eat their porridge, and Mrs Beith sat with her hand round her teapot, staring into space.

'I dinna ken if this'll be what you're wanting,' she said at last, 'but I did hear that Freda Burns is flitting.'

'Freda Burns?' Mae repeated, instantly alert. 'From the ground floor, next to Rona Walker?'

'That's the one. Her man's got a job in Dundee, so she's away. There's just the two rooms in that flat – but you'd no' want more, eh? Else you'd pay more rent?'

'Can we see it?' cried Lottie, coming to life. 'Is it available?'

'Run down and find out from Freda, eh?' Mrs Beith cleared away the girls' plates. 'Did you two no' want your porridge, then?'

The girls made no answer. They were already out of the door.

Chapter Eighteen

Within a week, they were installed. Impressed by Lottie's manner and the girls' offer to pay rent in advance, the landlord had made no difficulties over their tenancy, and for a while at least, they knew they'd be able to manage from their savings. Jobs must be found, however, and quickly. Domestic work, probably, for Mae, though she'd have to use her old references and omit the fact that she'd already worked in Edinburgh, while for Lottie it would have to be anything she could find. Until, as she said hopefully, she became an actress, at which Mae tried to look encouraging.

After they'd hired some furniture and used their dwindling savings to buy one or two second-hand pieces, they set about cleaning and then transforming their new home, with Lottie trying her hand at painting, while Mae made curtains on Mrs Beith's sewing machine.

It might have been that Mrs Beith was suffering a little from conscience over being too hard on the girls. She had certainly not admitted to it, but apart from allowing Mae to use her machine, she had also agreed to let them stay for the week till Freda and her husband had moved out.

'She is not too bad, your Mrs Beith,' Lottie remarked one afternoon, putting her brush into turpentine while she took a break.

'Not too bad,' Mae agreed. 'Just not quite what I thought.'

'People are often like that, I find. But not you, Mae.'

'And not my old employer, and not Miss Thorburn at the hostel. You know where you are with them.' Mae finished putting hooks into one of the curtains she'd made and laid it to one side. 'You're looking weary, Lottie. Why not leave the painting for today? Let's have some tea.'

'I'm not tired. Just a bit low – I don't know why. I'm thrilled with the flat.'

'I know why. You are wondering if you've done the right thing. It's not surprising, is it?'

'It is surprising. I mean, I'm free, which is what I wanted.'

'It was a big decision you made, though. If you think it's wrong, you could go back.'

'I don't think it's wrong. I'll never go back. If I did, I'd never leave, I'd never do what I want to do.' Lottie sighed. 'But I can't help feeling sad, that's all, the way it happened. I wish I'd been able to say goodbye to my father.'

'You could visit him at the bank.'

'I think I will. Might make me feel better.'

'And we'll both feel better with some tea and Mrs Beith's soda scones. Then, tomorrow, we go out job hunting. We cannot live on our savings for ever.'

'I said I'd go to the theatre to ask about an audition.' Lottie shivered. 'But I'm so nervous! Mae, will you listen to my "Ophelia" again?'

'Dear Lord, you know it backwards!' groaned Mae, who, knowing nothing of Shakespeare, had still been persuaded to help Lottie rehearse her roles.

'Just to make sure of the words, though? I won't try to act, or anything—'

'Soon as we've had our tea,' sighed Mae.

'"There's rosemary, that's for remembrance".' Lottie was reciting in a curiously flat voice quite unlike her own, when a light knock came at their door. '"There's fennel for you, and columbines: there's rue for you: and here's some for me" – oh, damnation!' She halted in pacing the floor. 'Who can it be? I was just doing well—'

'I'll go.' Mae, putting down her copy of *Hamlet* with some relief, opened the door.

'Hello, Mae,' said Harry Alpin.

'Harry?' Her eyes lit up to see him, with a smile on his face, too. Maybe he'd forgiven her?

He took off his cap. 'I was wondering if I could have a word?'

'Indeed. Please to step inside. You know we've just moved in here?'

'Aye, I heard. Hope you're settling in well?'

'We're painting everything in sight. Lottie, this is Harry Alpin from the top flat. Harry, meet Lottie Cameron.'

'Sorry about the smell of the paint,' said Lottie, smiling as she shook Harry's hand.

'Och, nae bother. I'm used to it.'

'Like a cup of tea?' asked Mae. 'And a soda scone? Mrs Beith made them for us.'

'One o' Mrs Beith's scones? Thanks, I canna say no. But how come you've left her, Mae?'

'You were not hearing that, then? It's a long story. I'll just boil up the kettle. Sit down, if you can find a chair.'

'I'm on ma way to work, but a few minutes won't hurt.'

'Harry works at the theatre,' Mae told Lottie, as she made fresh tea, and watched her eyes shine.

'At the theatre? You're an actor? Oh, how wonderful!'

'I'm no' an actor,' he said at once, flushing. 'I'm a lighting man.'

'But that's still wonderful. You don't know how I envy you, Mr Alpin. I'd give anything to work at the theatre. Anything in the world!'

'Lottie wants to be an actress.' Mae poured Harry's tea and buttered a scone. 'She's going to ask for an audition.'

For some moments, he let his eyes rest on Lottie, their expression softening as he took in her slightness and her pallor. 'Bit of an ordeal, eh?'

'I don't even know if they'll agree to hear me.'

'Och, they will. They give regular auditions.'

'You think they'll give me one?'

'Aye, I do.' Harry bit into his scone and smiled in bliss. 'Good as ever, eh? Made a mistake, Mae, leaving a baker like Mrs B. You'll have to tell me about it later. Miss Cameron, if you like, I could ask the stage manager if he'd see you.'

'If I like!' Lottie's eyes were now starry. 'Oh, Mr Alpin, if you'd do that for me, I'd be so grateful! I was dreading having to go along myself.'

'I'll do ma best, then.' He finished his tea and gave a crooked grin. 'Funny thing is, though, it was Mae I came to see, about a job at the theatre.'

'Me?' Mae laughed. 'I'm not an actress, Harry.'

'But you said you liked sewing and dressmaking and that?'

'I did.' She had stopped laughing. 'Is there a sewing job at the theatre, then?'

'Assistant wardrobe mistress. The young lassie that was helping Mrs Ness is flitting to Cromarty. Just got wed, you ken. They're having interviews for her job next Tuesday.'

'Assistant wardrobe mistress,' Mae repeated slowly. 'I never was thinking of such a job, but I'd love it.' Her eyes met Harry's. 'But they'd never consider me. I have no experience of the theatre.'

'They'll no' expect it, from an assistant. You'd get training. Anyway, if you go along tomorrow and put your name forward, they'll put you on the list for the job.'

'Mae, you could do it!' cried Lottie. 'You'd be perfect. Look at the way you whipped up those curtains! I'd still be measuring the windows. Oh, you must go for it, you must!'

'But how do I know they'll put me on the list?'

'Dinna ken if I took a liberty, Mae,' said Harry hesitantly.

'What liberty?'

'Well, I told 'em about you. I said you'd be good.'

'Harry!' Her cheeks were scarlet, her eyes as bright as Lottie's. 'You said that? About me?'

'Did I do wrong? I remembered you were no' keen on domestic work.'

'You did no wrong,' she said softly. 'Sure, you're the kindest of men, to think of me, and I'm very grateful to you, so I am.'

'Me, too,' put in Lottie, gazing at him as though he were Father Christmas.

'I'd better be going,' he muttered, colouring furiously. 'I'll let you know soon as I can, Miss Cameron, what they say about an audition.'

'Thank you. You're very good.'

He bowed his head, turning to the door with a slight look of relief. It was clear he was a little overawed by Lottie – her fragility, her difference in social position – and uncertain of how to respond to her. Mae should have been easier, but when she slipped after him into the hall and gazed up at him with her Irish blue eyes, he looked away from her, too.

'I was just wanting to say, I'm glad we are still friends,' she told him.

He put on his cap. 'I'll always be friends with you, Mae.'

'You have been avoiding me, though.'

'No. Well, maybe.' He did not elaborate. 'But it's grand you've got your own place, eh? Even if it's with poor little Miss Cameron. You going to tell me what happened?'

She told him, briefly, and he softly whistled.

'You're well out of Victoria Place, then. And Mrs Beith's and all, if she's scared to keep you. Och, folk like Mrs Cameron think they own you, eh?'

'Certainly owned Lottie. Do your best for her, Harry.'

'Difficult for her, eh, having a ma like that?' He kept his eyes down.

She touched his hand. 'Thanks again, then.'

'You'll tell me how you get on?'

'Sure, I will. I know I owe this chance to you.'

'What a nice young man!' cried Lottie, when Mae returned. 'Half an hour ago, we'd nothing in sight, and now we have everything, thanks to him!'

'Best not to raise our hopes too high, all the same.'

'Ah, you're afraid of being disappointed. Well, I am, too, but at least we do have hope. And all due to Mr Alpin.'

As they cleared away their teacups, Lottie gave Mae a sideways look.

'Mind if I ask – is he your admirer?'

'Admirer? Sure, I couldn't say. He wanted me to go out with him once.'

'And did you go?'

'No.'

'Because there's someone else? Forgive me, Mae – I don't mean to pry.'

'It's all right. There is someone else. At least, there was. He married my cousin and he's in America.'

'I'm so sorry. But are you getting over him now?' Lottie laughed nervously. 'Do I make him sound like an illness?'

'Maybe he was.' Mae ran water from the kettle into the washing up bowl. 'Let's not talk about him. Are you keeping on with the painting? Or, are you wanting a rest?'

'No. I feel so much better, I think I'll carry on.'

'I'll give you a hand, then. Might as well just keep going. We'll never sleep tonight.'

And that was true. As each lay sleepless – Lottie in the pull-out bed in the living-room, Mae in the single bed in the one bedroom, the thought of the hurdles ahead of them churned in their minds the warm summer night through.

Will they really put me on their list at the theatre? Mae asked herself over and over again. Supposing they are after experience, in spite of what Harry thinks? Supposing this Mrs Ness says, 'And what gives you the idea, Miss O'Donovan, that you know how to make costumes? Next, please!'

'There's fennel for you, and rue for me,' sang Lottie in her mind. Oh, no, that's wrong. 'There's fennel for you and columbines for me ...' That's still wrong. Should I not do Ophelia? Maybe just Rosalind? Much more fun. Maybe I'll light the gas and study the lines again.

But the next thing she knew, the room was filled with sunlight and Mae was up and dressed and shaking her.

'Is it morning already! Oh, Mae, do you think Harry will call back today?'

'I don't know, but I'm going to the theatre this morning. Want to come?'

Chapter Nineteen

The receptionist in the theatre box-office had cropped dark hair and a cool dark gaze. When Mae gave her name and asked about the interview list, she showed interest.

'Miss O'Donovan? You're Harry's friend?'

'I know Mr Alpin.'

'He certainly gave you a good recommendation. Mrs Ness is looking forward to meeting you.'

'I will be honest,' Mae said, colouring. 'I've never worked in a theatre.'

'But she's very good with her needle,' Lottie put in quickly. 'She could sew anything.'

'That's all right, then, but everyone's going to be given a test, anyway. Come along on Tuesday, Miss O'Donovan, at eleven o'clock.'

'A test?' echoed Mae. 'What kind of test?'

'Oh, just something Mrs Ness has thought up. I shouldn't worry about it. Just be here on Tuesday.'

'Excuse me, could we have a peep into the auditorium?' asked Lottie. 'We wouldn't take long.'

The receptionist hesitated. 'I don't see why not. There's no rehearsal on. But be quick, eh?'

'Promise.'

'We've seen the theatre,' murmured Mae, preoccupied with the idea of a test. 'Why see it now?'

'I love to see a theatre any time. Come on.'

It was very quiet in the auditorium; hushed almost and airless. There was no one sitting in the rows of stalls, no one standing on

81

the stage, and it seemed to Mae that everything, seen without the excitement of performance, was a little worn, a little tawdry. The curtains that had seemed so magnificent were faded and filled with dust, the gilt on the ceiling and the boxes, dull. It was only when she looked up and saw the balcony circles rising high, that she felt again a certain awe. But she still missed the lights, the buzz of an audience, the magic.

Not so Lottie. She was standing at Mae's side, breathing hard, her face flushed.

'It's different, isn't it?' she whispered, grasping Mae's arm. 'But still something special? Not like anything outside?'

'It needs people—' Mae was beginning, when Lottie suddenly darted away towards the stage and to Mae's horror, ran up the steps at the side.

'Lottie, what are you doing? Come back!'

But Lottie was already centre stage, her arms flung out, as though to encompass everything about her.

'It's all right, Mae, there's no one here. I'm just getting the feel of things.'

'Lottie, someone will find you. Please, come down!'

'"All the world's a stage!"' cried Lottie. 'But that's not my speech. Shall I do my Rosalind?'

'Why not?' came a voice from the back of the theatre, and as Lottie stopped as though shot, a tall man with a bush of greying hair strode down the aisle towards the stage. 'If you're trying out for an audition, young lady, let's hear you, then.'

I'm not watching this, thought Mae, bending her head. I'm not hearing it. Oh, poor Lottie. Whatever will she do?

But Lottie seemed to be recovering. As the grey-haired man took a seat in the stalls, she stepped forward and looked down at him.

'This is from Act Four, Scene One, of *As You Like It*,' she announced clearly. 'Orlando has just told Rosalind that he will die in his own person, if she doesn't have him, and Rosalind says—'

'You don't need to tell me the plot,' came the voice from the stalls. 'Just speak your lines.'

Lottie moved back a little, stood still for a moment, then began.

'"No, faith, die by attorney. The poor world is almost six thousand years old, and in all this time, there was not any man died in his own person ..."'

82

Was that Lottie? Mae, taking her hands from her eyes, gazed at the figure on the stage, so slight, so frail, yet seeming tall, as Rosalind, Lottie'd once remarked, was supposed to be tall. And in command – Lottie'd said that, too. Always in command, in every scene in which she appeared, as Lottie here was also in command, and producing a strong, deep voice that Mae scarcely recognised. From where? But it must be reaching the back of the theatre, as voices were meant to do. Someone must be looking after her thought Mae, someone waving a wand. For if this wasn't magic, she didn't know what else it could be.

'"But these are all lies,"' Lottie was finishing. '"Men have died from time to time and worms have eaten them, but not for love."'

Her voice ceased and silence throbbed in the vast auditorium, until there was the sound of clapping from the stalls.

Wish I could clap too, thought Mae, but thought better of it.

'Got anything else?' asked the voice of the grey-haired man.

'Something from *The Circle* by Somerset Maugham. And some lines of Ophelia's.'

'Not the rosemary for remembrance speech?'

'I'm afraid so.'

'Let's hear it, anyhow.'

This time, Mae did not put her hands over her eyes or bend her head. She knew that Lottie was going to be all right. She would be Ophelia, as she had been Rosalind. As she had been in command as Rosalind, she would be drifting and singing, as poor mad Ophelia, and as you watched and listened, you would forget that she was Lottie, colourless as moonlight, and see only the person she had become.

I should have trusted her, Mae told herself, as the words she'd so often heard Lottie recite came echoing softly around the theatre.

'"There's rosemary, that's for remembrance ... and there is pansies, that's for thoughts. There's fennel for you, and columbines: there's rue for you: and here's some for me ..."'

Lottie always knew what she could do; always knew that she was born to act. But Mae had never believed her, any more than her mother believed her. And Harry hadn't believed her, either. He had called her 'poor little Miss Cameron'. But, as it had turned out, she wasn't poor Miss Cameron at all.

'Thank you,' said the man in the stalls, when Lottie's sweet piping as Ophelia had fallen silent. 'Don't move – I'll come up.'

Mae sat very still, trying to hear what the tall man was saying, after he'd leaped up on to the stage beside Lottie, but he was keeping his fine voice down now, and she was back to being herself – quiet, nervous, quite unsure. But when he indicated that they should walk off stage together, she was smiling. Looked hopeful – very hopeful. But where had they gone? Through some door at the side, it seemed, leaving Mae quite alone in the theatre.

'Mae!' came Harry's voice, and she jumped from her seat to run up the aisle towards him.

'Mae, what's going on? I spoke to the stage manager and he said he'd be willing to hear Miss Cameron next week. Then I see her going with Mr Standish into his office today!'

'Who's Mr Standish?'

'Only the theatre manager, the fellow that runs the place. What's been happening?'

'Sure, it was the strangest thing, Harry! Lottie was playing about on the stage, pretending to do her audition, when this man – he must've been Mr Standish – told her to say her lines for him.'

'And did she?' Harry asked woodenly.

'Yes, and she was wonderful! Never in this world was I thinking she could act like that. Made the tears come to your eye, so she did!'

'Shouldn't have thought she'd have the voice.'

'She has, though. She seems to have any voice that's needed. I never was so surprised—'

'Mae, I've got to go.' Harry's eyes were expressionless. 'All the best for your interview.'

'Harry!' She ran after him. 'Won't you show me where this office is? So that I can find Lottie?'

'Aye.' He shrugged. 'Might as well know how she got on.'

It was just as well she had a guide, Mae decided, as she followed Harry through the warren of passages, steps, ropes, hanging ladders, hampers, boxes, pieces of scenery, paint brushes, and fire buckets, that made up the backstage area of the Queen's. If she ever got to work here, how would she find her way around?

Everyone they met knew Harry, of course, and grinned at him and stared at Mae, but he strode on without speaking until they arrived at a closed door.

'We'll wait here,' he said over his shoulder to Mae.

They didn't have to wait long. After only a few minutes, the door opened and Lottie came out, closing it behind her. Her face was radiant.

'No need to tell us,' said Mae. 'He's given you a job.'

'Oh, Mae, I'm sorry I left you! And, Mr Alpin, thank you for everything.'

'Seemingly, you didn't need me,' said Harry. 'What's he offered, then?'

'I'm to be Assistant Stage Manager!' Lottie's hands were clasped, as though to stop them from trembling, but all of her small frame was trembling and shivering, and it was obvious she could hardly contain her joy. 'I can hardly believe it. I keep thinking I'm dreaming, because this is just what I've always dreamed might happen.'

'ASM's do everything,' said Harry shortly. 'You'll no' have to mind if you have to make the tea.'

'Oh, I know, I know! I'm to do all sorts of things, just make myself useful, but Mr Standish said I'll be given small parts and they'll train me. In fact, he's going to train me himself. I won't earn much, but it'll be enough for the rent, Mae, and the main thing is – I'm going to be an actress!'

'Lottie,' said Mae. 'You are an actress.'

Harry was standing a little apart, his face a blank, but as Mae looked at him, he seemed to rouse himself, relaxed, and found a smile.

'Well done, Miss Cameron. I wish you the best of luck at the Queen's.'

Well done, Harry, were Mae's unspoken words. Only she knew how much his congratulations to the successful Lottie had cost him, when his own dreams of becoming an actor had ended in failure.

'Let's hope Mae will be joining me,' said Lottie.

'Aye, you're next, Mae.' Harry had found a smile for her, too. 'Did you get your name on the list?'

'I did, but I have to have a test. I have to do some sewing or cutting out for this Mrs Ness and I'm worrying already.'

'You'll be all right. I told 'em you were the best.'

'Harry, that's why I'm worrying!'

That evening, Lottie said she would take Mae out for a meal. Yes, to a nice café. There was one near Holyrood she'd heard was very good.

'If we go to a café, we split the bill,' Mae said firmly. 'You can't afford to pay for me.'

'I can. I'm going to be earning. Oh, come on, Mae, we have to have a celebration!' Lottie hesitated. 'Or would you rather wait until after your interview?'

Mae thought for a moment. 'Maybe I would. But then we might have to have a wake instead.'

'Nonsense! We'll both be celebrating. I think we might invite Harry, too, don't you? As a thank you?'

Mae agreed, though she wasn't sure how much Harry would feel like celebrating.

Chapter Twenty

Apart from Mae, there were four applicants for the job of Assistant Wardrobe Mistress. All were in their twenties; all were nervous. In fact, one of them, a thin girl with glasses, asked if she might have a cigarette with the coffee they were offered when they first arrived. 'To settle maself,' she explained.

'Well, you could have one here,' Jackie, the receptionist, told her, waving a hand round the small room behind the box-office where they were sitting. 'But smoking's not allowed in the theatre. Risk of fire, you understand.'

They all nodded their heads sagely, and Greta, the girl with glasses, hastily said she'd do without her cigarette.

'Have there not been several fires on this site?' asked Mae, dressed in her usual blue. 'Someone told me that.'

'Four,' said Jackie. 'All back in the last century. Sometimes, the lead got melted on the houses in Victoria Row, and the cathedral was threatened. Sometimes, folk died.'

The candidates exchanged glances. 'Hope we'll be OK,' some-one muttered, but Jackie gave a superior smile, and they knew she was wondering why they were worrying. None of them had got the job yet.

'Hasn't been a fire since eighteen eighty-four; you'll be all right,' she said crisply. 'Now, if you've all finished your coffee, p'raps you'd like to follow me to Wardrobe?'

Wardrobe. Heavens, they'd seen nothing like it! There was a long trestle table for cutting out, and several sewing machines – these they had expected. But the rows and rows of costumes on rails, the piles of boxes and cartons, the hoops for crinolines, the papier mâché armour and cardboard swords, the dusty uniforms with faded epaulettes, the helmets, bonnets, togas, wigs – such a collection was quite outside their experience. Everywhere they looked, there was something to wear, or use. How did anyone keep track of it?

'Everything's labelled!' cried Mrs Ness, catching their expressions. 'Labelled and listed, as well as fixed in my memory!'

She was small and had perhaps been very pretty, before the weight went on; even now, with her double chin and roly-poly figure, she was still an attractive woman. Her dark hair was curly, her nose finely shaped, her brown eyes quick and sharp. When she had taken the names of the five candidates, that sharp gaze settled on Mae.

'So you're Miss O'Donovan, the Irish girl? Harry in Lighting tells me you're very good, though what he knows about sewing, I couldn't say.' As four pairs of eyes went to Mae, and Mae herself blushed, Mrs Ness added, 'And it's a funny thing, you know, but I've never thought of Irish girls being needlewomen. Don't know why.'

'And I'm not knowing why!' flashed Mae. 'Irish girls are taught by nuns and nuns are beautiful needlewomen, so they are.'

'Oh, well, you'll have to prove me wrong, then.' Mrs Ness smiled graciously. 'No offence intended.'

'None taken,' said Mae coldly.

After a short awkward silence, Mrs Ness waved a hand to the young women and shepherded them to the trestle table, where she told them to sit down.

'Here's where we do our cutting out and pattern making, and I'll be asking you in a minute just to do a bit of cutting and stitching for me, so's I can see what you can do. Nothing to worry about. Just basic garments. No need to look like that, ladies.'

'It's only nerves,' whispered Greta, rubbing her spectacles with a handkerchief.

'Nerves, is it? Well, my dear, you're in the right place for nerves in a theatre. Everybody lives on their nerves here, and they all end up in Wardrobe sooner or later, wanting this or that. Actors, of course, we have to dress, but then there's the stage manager and the stage crew and the lighting men – oh, we've to work with 'em all. And we've only a week to get a play on, remember, and then it's on with the next, so we're always ahead of ourselves, if we're no' behind!' Mrs Ness laughed merrily. 'But it's all exciting, eh? If you don't like excitement, don't come here!'

'Is a lot of the work alterations of what you've got?' one of the girls asked.

'It is, my dear, because we're always short of cash, and have to do what we can and improvise where possible. Then we have to try to keep everything looking nice and fresh, even if it's been on the rails for years, so we're always washing and mending and doing repairs as we go.'

'Still, you do sometimes have to start from scratch?' asked Mae. 'And then you have to find the money for the material?'

'Yes, but it's a last resort. And you always have to hope it's not for a costume play, where you need something that looks like velvet, or satin. "Looks like" are the key words here, remember. Nothing's real in the theatre, eh?'

Mrs Ness jumped to her feet. 'But let's be getting to work! I'll put what you need on the table. Scissors, tape-measures, pins, thread, paper. For material, there's calico. Can't afford anything better for this kind of pretend work, I'm afraid.'

'But who'll we measure?' asked Greta.

'Well, as we've no actors around, you'll have to use dressmaker's dummies – I've put 'em out for you at the back there. You can choose what you want to make – skirt, shirt, cloak, tunic – it doesn't matter. Just measure up, prepare your pattern, and start cutting. Everybody happy?'

'Yes, Mrs Ness,' they told her, trying to look confident, though under her eagle eye, it wasn't easy.

'What a caper, eh?' Greta whispered to Mae, as they began measuring dummy figures at the back of the room. 'Have you decided what to make.'

'A shirt,' Mae answered.

'Hen, there's a lot o' work in that. I'm going to do a skirt. Coupla half circles and waistband, and there you are!' She leaned closer. 'To tell you the truth, I dinna want this job. The sewing I can do, but who wants to be bothered with all these stage folk gettin' in your hair? I never thought there'd be so much to it.'

'I'd not mind that at all,' Mae whispered back. 'But I'm not going to get the job, anyway.'

'Because of what she said?' Greta jerked her head towards Mrs Ness, who was standing at the table some way off. 'It's unfair, that's for sure, if you don't get the job because you're Irish. But I suppose you have to accept it, eh? You're no' Scottish.'

'I am not accepting anything,' said Mae. She turned away. 'I've worked out that I need four yards of material with the full sleeves, so I might as well get on with the cutting out.'

Silence fell in the wardrobe department as the five hopefuls worked away, preparing patterns, cutting out pieces of calico, pinning, stitching, taking their turn for the sewing machines; at every stage, of course, being scrutinised by Mrs Ness.

'Now, I'm not expecting you to make complete garments in the time we have,' she called, as the clock ticked on. 'As long as you do enough to let me see how you shape up. And so far, you're all doing well.'

Quarter of an hour later, it was all over. The completed, or half-completed, garments were laid out for Mrs Ness's inspection. She put a label with the maker's name on each, shook each candidate by the hand and said she'd be 'letting them know'.

'Now, you can go and enjoy your dinner,' she told them with a smile. 'Well earned, eh?'

They thanked her, even Mae, who was still simmering over her remarks, and left the wardrobe department with some relief.

'Good luck, hen,' Greta called to Mae. 'Hope you get something else, then.'

'And you.'

'Yes, well, I'm no' taking this on, I can tell you. I like an easy life.'

'Mae!' cried Lottie, hurrying to greet her, followed by Harry. 'Oh, Mae, how did you get on?'

'Not well, I'm thinking.' Mae's mouth twisted a little. 'Mrs Ness is not one for the Irish.'

'Mrs Ness?' Harry stared. 'Oh, I canna believe that, Mae. She's the most easy-going woman you could wish to meet.'

Mae shrugged. 'Was after telling me that Irish girls can't sew.'

'What? That's disgraceful!' cried Lottie. 'And not true, either!'

'Maybe you've proved her wrong?' suggested Harry.

'She's one would never admit it,' Mae retorted, but as she spoke, the door to Wardrobe opened and Mrs Ness came out.

'Miss O'Donovan, you're still here? Now, that's lucky. Could I have a word, my dear?' She sent a smile to Harry and Lottie. 'I'll not keep her a minute.'

90

Mae, her face expressionless, followed the wardrobe mistress back into the department and watched her close the door. Now, what? she wondered.

'I'm glad I caught you,' Mrs Ness said cheerfully. 'First, I want to apologise for what I said earlier about Irish girls. Can't think why that popped out. That's me, though. For ever putting my foot in it!'

'That's all right, Mrs Ness.' Mae's tone was still cool.

'No, it was hurtful, and I'm sorry for it, particularly as I want you to be working with me, you see.'

'Working with you?' Mae's heart had begun to beat faster. 'But – you said you'd be letting us know.'

'Yes, well, I am. I'll be writing to the other girls, but I'm offering you the job now.' Mrs Ness clapped Mae on the shoulder. 'Your shirt was beautiful, but that's not the reason I picked you. I put you all to sewing when I knew you could all sew well, but I wanted to see how you'd set about it. Whether you'd be nice and calm, or get in a state because I was watching. Getting in a state's no good to me, you ken. We work under pressure here.'

'I understand that,' Mae murmured.

'And you came out best. I guessed you would, when you answered me back the way you did. I thought, this girl's got spirit – she'd be the one to enjoy working here. Am I right about that?'

'You are.' Mae was suddenly smiling. 'I want to work here, more than anything.'

'You accept, then? The money's not wonderful, but it'll be better than you were getting in service. You happy about it?'

'Very happy.'

'That's a relief. Well – they'll be sending you a formal letter, you understand, but will you shake my hand on it now?'

'I will.'

The two women exchanged long steady looks, then shook hands.

'Hope you can start soon, my dear,' Mrs Ness said, as she opened the door for Mae to leave her. 'I'm desperate for help, and that's no lie.'

'I can start any time you like.'

'I'll get the powers that be to fix a date, then. Goodbye, Miss O'Donovan. I'm looking forward to working with you.'

'Thank you, Mrs Ness.'

As the door closed behind her, Mae walked dazedly towards Harry and Lottie.

'Poor Mae,' whispered Lottie. 'Whatever did she say?'

'Never mind, you'll be sure to get another job,' Harry said comfortingly.

'As a matter of fact, I've got this one,' said Mae, and laughed as Lottie hugged her and Harry gave a long sigh of relief.

Chapter Twenty-One

They decided to go for something to eat to a nearby café much patronised by the theatre folk, where the girls had eggs on toast and Harry had cottage pie.

'Didn't we say we'd have a celebration?' asked Lottie. 'We must take you for a proper meal, Harry.' She looked at him bravely. 'You don't mind if I call you that?'

'Och, no.' He stared down at his plate. 'Everybody calls me Harry.'

'Well, most people call me Lottie.'

'How about your stage name?'

'I suppose that'll be Charlotte. I hadn't thought about it.'

'Have to think about the programmes.'

'Oh, yes.' Lottie's eyes glinted. 'Just fancy – me on a programme!'

Though he smiled at her pleasure, Mae guessed he was never going to be at his ease with her. Even now, though he seemed so happy for them both, she knew he was finding it hard to accept Lottie's success.

'Why would you want to take me for a meal?' he asked, when they had ordered apple tart for pudding. 'As though I'd let you, anyway.'

'Why, as a thank you!' cried Mae. 'I'd never have got my job without you, Harry.'

'And look how helpful you were to me,' said Lottie.

'You never needed me, Miss Cameron – I mean, Lottie.'

'That was just the way things worked out. I still appreciate what you did for me.'

'Nice o' you to say so. But – if we go out – I pay.'

'Let's leave it for now,' said Mae.

'I'm paying for this lot, anyway,' Harry declared. 'No arguments, eh?'

'You always like the last word?' asked Lottie, smiling.

'This is not the last word,' retorted Mae. 'We're just keeping Harry happy.'

'Quite right, too.' His smile was broad and he did seem, at that moment, to be as happy as Mae had ever seen him.

Still, he said he must get back to the theatre and fast; there was a lighting rehearsal for next week's play, he mustn't be late.

'We'll walk back with you,' Mae told him, but Lottie said she was intending to visit her father at the bank.

'I feel so bad,' she murmured. 'I should have gone before.'

'It's not been easy for you.' As Harry tactfully stood aside, Mae put her hand on Lottie's shoulder. 'Your da will understand.'

'But now I've been taken on at the Queen's, I want to tell him about it, and I want him to tell my mother. If she thinks I could be successful, she might see things differently.'

'But we know her views on the theatre.'

'I want her to be told, anyway, about my job.'

'Best of luck, then.' Mae gave an encouraging smile.

'We've been lucky, already. Wouldn't you say?'

The afternoon was warm, with heat striking up from the pavements as city workers mingled outside offices, and no hint of the usual Edinburgh wind.

'Too hot to hurry,' gasped Mae, taking off her hat and fanning herself with it. 'But you mustn't be late, Harry. Mustn't get into trouble.'

'I'll be there in time.' He looked down at her flushed face; at her rich black hair curling damply round her brow. 'It's grand you've got that job, Mae. I canna tell you how pleased I am for you.'

'For Lottie, too? She's so happy.'

'Aye, she's the lucky one,' he said, after a moment or two.

'Because Mr Standish gave her the job? You're not thinking she doesn't deserve it?'

'No, seemingly she does deserve it – that's why she's lucky.' He laughed shortly. 'She wants to be an actress and she's got the talent.'

'Harry—'

Mae suddenly stopped and stood staring into the distance.

'Sandy!' she cried. 'Sandy, wait!'

But the slim young woman hurrying ahead did not look back. Was it Sandy? Mae, shielding her eyes from the sun with her hand, tried to be sure. Had the girl ginger hair? It wasn't possible to see, she was wearing a close-fitting summer hat, and all that Mae now was the back view of her fast-receding figure.

'It's no good,' she murmured. 'She's gone.'

'Who? Who did you see?'

'I thought it was a girl I met at Adelaide House, the hostel where I was staying for a bit.' Mae shook her head. 'But it couldn't have been her, because she would have stopped when I called.'

'Easy to make a mistake.'

'Yes.' They began to walk on. 'I wish I had seen her, though. We said we'd keep in touch, but she was never sending me her address.'

'Folk are like that, sometimes.'

'I'm sorry, Harry, I think I was going to say something to you. Was it about Lottie?'

'Aye, you were going to tell me to be nice to her and no' be bitter.'

'Harry, I was not!'

'Look, nae bother. You're right. I'm just showing the green eye, eh?' He smiled down at her and she thought how handsome he was when he let himself be happy, and how there was still that look of Kieran Connor about him, except that he was so completely himself.

'Thank you again,' she murmured, as they came to the theatre. 'I was wanting a new life, and I've found it. All due to you.'

'No, Mae, I told you about the job, but you got it. I'm no' taking any credit.'

He looked down into her face, his hazel eyes golden in the sunlight, and if she had been seeking another difference between him and Kieran, there it was, for Kieran's eyes were dark green, often glittering, never golden. Would the day come, as Mrs Beith had predicted, that she would no longer remember Kieran's looks? Perhaps. She could almost imagine it; not quite.

'Penny for 'em?' asked Harry softly. 'You're miles away, Mae.'

'No, no.' To deflect his interest, she spoke again of her new life; of how things were so different for her now.

'I have a new job, Harry, and a new place to live, even new friends. Everything is changed.'

'Even new friends?' He raised his fair brows. 'Did you no' expect to make new friends here, then?'

'Well, this is Scotland. Some Scots are not fond of the Irish.'

'I'm a Scot. I'm your friend.'

'And I'm yours.'

'Don't forget that, when all the young actors come after you in Wardrobe.'

'Oh, Harry!' She laughed. 'You'd better go to work, or there'll be no lighting rehearsal.'

'Aye.' He drew away. 'You'll let me know when they want you to start your job?'

'Sure, I will. But you're not forgetting that Lottie is planning a celebration for us some time?'

'For the three of us?'

'The three of us. And we'll argue about the bill when it comes.'

It was his turn to laugh, before he finally left her.

New job, new place to live, new friends. As she crossed into the Row, Mae was still reflecting on the changes in her life. There'd been so much hurt, so much bitterness, back in Ireland. Here in Scotland, too, there'd been trouble and anxiety, not only for herself, but for Lottie. Rain, you might say, constantly falling.

But now, there was sunshine. For her, for Lottie, even for Harry, if he would settle for friendship, as he seemed willing to do.

Ah, she could almost feel the warmth of it, that sunshine, just as she felt the real afternoon sun beating down on her head and shoulders. Long might it last!

She took a last look across to the Queen's, and thought of Harry, with his spotlights and beams; of Lottie, on the stage; of herself, in Wardrobe, cutting and fitting and creating marvels on a shoe-string. What would the future hold for them? A silly question, with no answer, for she had no crystal ball.

But, as she let herself into Number Eight, for the first time that she could remember, she felt no fear of what lay ahead. And as she threw aside her hat and filled the kettle for tea, she found herself singing.

Part Two

Chapter Twenty-Two

Christmas was over, Hogmanay was over, and at the end of January 1929, Mrs Ness was glad the Queen's Theatre pantomime season was over, too.

'Thank the Lord!' she cried, as she ate a cheese and pickle sandwich at her desk in Wardrobe. 'Oh, I hate *Aladdin*, Mae, don't you?'

Trying on a bonnet she had just trimmed with feathers and veiling, Mae raised her dark brows and laughed.

'Now, why ever would you be saying that, Mrs Ness? The audiences love it, so they do.'

'True, but they don't have to stick on all the pigtails, eh? And mend all the lampshade hats!'

Mrs Ness finished her sandwich and took out a small pork pie. 'I wouldn't mind, if it was our company we were working for, but these visiting folk doing the panto, I tell you, they're nothing but trouble. Supposed to bring their own wardrobe mistress, but they never do, and then it's just you and me to run around after 'em, trying to make 'em look respectable.'

'I was happy doing that,' said Mae, rising. 'My first pantomime – I enjoyed it.'

'Wait till you've dressed as many as me, then you'll be just as glad to get back to normal.' Mrs Ness ate her little pie with evident enjoyment and swept crumbs into the bin. 'Want to go for your dinner, Mae? I'd better get on. I've Primmie's dress to finish for *The Rivals*. Is that her hat? You've made a good job of it. Oh, my word, though – have you seen that snow?'

'I'm looking,' called Mae from the window where she was watching the softly falling snow. 'Now this we never see in Traynore!'

'Good job you've no got far to run home, dear. Wrap up well.'

'I'm not going home'. Mae was buttoning on Mrs Fitzgerald's old coat and pulling her winter hat over her brow. 'I'm meeting Lottie and some of the others. We're going to the café. A little celebration.'

'Because the company's back?' Mrs Ness laughed lightly as she washed her hands at the corner sink. 'They'll be full of them-selves. Always are, when they've been on tour – and when they've not been on tour, come to that. Off you go, then. Enjoy yourself.'

Enjoy herself? That wouldn't be difficult, thought Mae, making her way to the stage door. Ever since she'd begun work at the Queen's, she'd enjoyed herself. Though she knew well enough that things rarely worked out the way you'd planned, her new life was turning out to be just what she'd wanted.

Of course, it wasn't easy. Nobody could say that. Mrs Ness was a wonderful character, but also a strict task mistress, and their work by its very nature kept wardrobe staff on their toes. As soon as one play was finished, there was another to dress and mend and launder for, and another one looming soon after that. Not to men-tion hunting for props, keeping the actors happy and pleasing Mr Standish, the theatre manager.

Now there was a man who drove his company hard and woe betide you if you failed to measure up. He seemed to know the capability of every member of the theatre staff – not just the actors – and demanded the best from them, day in and day out, with such force of personality, all they wanted to do was give it to him.

Even Mae, who thanked her lucky stars she did not have to appear on stage before him, felt his dynamism, while Lottie had suffered so much from his criticism in the early days, she'd felt like giving up before she'd even begun.

'I thought I was good,' she wailed to Mae. 'He said I was good. Now he tells me I can't breathe properly, I can't speak, I can't move, I can't do anything right! Why did he take me on, if I'm so hopeless?'

'They say it's his way,' Mae said comfortingly. 'If you're any good, he's terrible hard. He'd not be bothering with you, if he wasn't wanting you to stay.'

Others in the company had said the same. Though Mae some-times had the feeling that they were wary of Lottie, suspecting that she might turn out to be someone special, they were kind enough to encourage her. They'd all had to go through what she was going through, they reminded her. They'd all had to learn their art, and so would she. Old Standish was a devil, but he knew what he was doing; she must just have faith.

'Faith?' repeated Lottie. 'If only I had faith in myself, the way I used to have.'

'That'll come,' they assured her.

'You won't always be making the tea and buying the props,' a young actor named Brett Lester added, with a melting look. 'You'll get the parts, even when you're still learning.'

And so Lottie did. Small parts, of course. Maids, heroines' sisters, young women who had a line or two to set a scene. What did it matter? She was on stage. She was on her way. Mae was happy for her, as she was happy for herself. Things were working out.

Peering out at the snow that January lunchtime, Mae shivered and drew back, stamped her feet up and down and wished the others would come.

But it was Harry Alpin who joined her at the open door.

Chapter Twenty-Three

He was wearing a long rough coat with the collar turned up, and a cap that covered the blond hair that had first reminded her of Kieran Connor.

Ah, but at that time, everything had reminded her of Kieran; she had seen him everywhere, his image bright as sunshine. Now, it was as though a mist had arisen, shrouding him, shrouding Rosaleen, even though she had Rosaleen's letter in her bag. Even though Kieran's baby was on the way. Was it wicked she was, to picture the baby shrouded in mist as well?

But Harry was here beside her, with not a scrap of mist obscuring his handsome face. She could have put out her hand and touched his cold cheek, only of course she wouldn't do that. Whatever he'd felt for her once, she didn't know what he felt for her now. Except that he was friendly and pleasant. Always polite and raising his cap when they met. Always willing to help with any little job she and Lottie needed in the flat, explaining things about the theatre, or what his own work in lighting entailed. But that was all. Harry, her admirer, seemed to have given up his role.

Perhaps he had a girlfriend now? That must be it.

'Hello, Harry,' she said, smiling to cover her slight confusion. ''Tis missing you've been for days. What have you been doing?'

He shrugged. 'Working. Pantos need lighting, just like other plays.'

'I mean, you've not been near Wardrobe.'

'You'll have been busy yourselves.'

'Rushed off our feet.' Her eyes were bright. 'Listen, we're going to treat ourselves. Have lunch out. Will you not come with us?'

'You mean you and Lottie?'

'And some of the others. To celebrate being back at the Queen's, after Glasgow and Aberdeen.'

'Nothing wrong with Glasgow and Aberdeen.'

'But terrible cold in Aberdeen,' Lottie said. 'The lodgings were freezing and the landlady wouldn't let them have any extra coal. Will you be coming with us, then?'

He shook his head, touching his cap. 'Thanks, but I'll say no. Ma'll have ma dinner ready at home.'

'You never come, Harry. Why is that? We'd like you to be with us.'

'I don't think so.'

Mae coloured deeply. 'You think we don't want you?'

'I'm a lighting man, remember? No' an actor.'

'Harry, I make costumes, and the actors seem happy with me. Why not with you?'

'You're a pretty girl – who wouldn't want you? But I've got ma own interests, and they've got theirs. I've nothing in common with them.'

'Lottie's coming. You like Lottie, Harry.'

'She's an actress. Will you excuse me, Mae? I have to go.' He gave a quick smile. 'Got to face that weather. Take care, then.'

She stood aside, her expression troubled, and he swung away from her, striding through the snow. How often he seemed to be doing that, she thought: moving away from her. A few minutes later, the actors joined her.

Lottie and the tall, slim figure of Brett Lester. Black-haired Gareth Paget, leading man. Primmie Day, leading lady. Thea Reynolds, character actress. Vivvy Bryce, young and bouncy, who had been assistant stage manager before Lottie. Later, as she looked around their faces in the Rowan Tree Café, it seemed strange to Mae that Harry should not regard these people as friends, as she did.

Did they really make a distinction between those who were actors and those who were not? She, after all, was a girl from Wardrobe. A girl who not so long ago had been a real maid, not one of the dramatic creations Lottie was so pleased to play. Was she only tolerated because she was pretty?

She didn't believe it. Sure, the young men of the company, as soon as they'd set eyes on her, had been keen to hurry along to

103

Wardrobe, to be measured and pinned up for their costumes, and that was probably because she was pretty. But they'd never treated her as though she were different in some way. Nor had the actresses.

Harry had got it wrong, seeing things that weren't there, because he had failed in becoming an actor himself. Once again, her heart went out to him, but what could she do? What could anyone do, for Harry? She gave a little sigh and let her uncomfortable thoughts go, as the voices of the young people around her flowed unceasingly over the soup and sausages, cottage pie and hot rolls. She was content again.

'Everybody got over Aberdeen?' asked Gareth, working his way through sausages and mash.

'I shall never get over Aberdeen!' cried Primmie Day, fair and pretty as her namesake flower of primrose. 'Nothing against the city, but, oh my God, those digs we had! I thought I'd die at night, I'm not joking.'

'It's not exactly warm here,' said Thea, an attractive, rather overweight young woman with a cloud of hair that was at present red, but might easily become something else next week.

'Oh, what would Mummy say if she could see Thea?' Lottie had asked Mae in the early days. 'She'd say she was just what she'd expected an actress to be, because she dyes her hair – as though that matters tuppence!'

But Mrs Cameron was not likely to see Thea, or to say anything at all. She had not acknowledged Lottie's Christmas present or communicated with her in any way, and only her father's continued, though secret, interest made Lottie feel she was not an orphan. She had paid a high price to get what she wanted, she admitted to Mae, but Mae had stoutly told her she'd done the right thing.

'Oh, I know!' Lottie had cried. 'Of course I have!'

'There may be snow on the ground,' Primmie was saying now, as the waitress brought her an omelette, 'but my lodgings are as warm as toast and that's all I care about. That, and you getting me a nice costume, Mae, for when I play Lydia Languish. Now, have you sorted anything out?'

'Mrs Ness has it all in hand,' Mae said grandly. 'And I've trimmed your bonnet. You'll look beautiful.'

'And how about me as Mrs Malaprop?' asked Thea. 'I look anything but beautiful in that grey wig Mrs Ness's given me.'

'You're not meant to be beautiful,' Primmie told her sweetly. 'Doesn't somebody in the play call you an old weather-beaten she-dragon?'

'Cheek!' cried Thea, smiling, and would have thrown a bread pellet at Primmie, had not Gareth caught her hand and reminded her she had the best part anyway.

'You get the laughs, don't forget.'

'That's true. Everybody remembers *The Rivals* for Mrs Malaprop.'

'I should've been playing Julia,' Vivvy said moodily. 'Why'd Tim Powell pick Sally Anderson then?'

Tim Powell, the stage manager, was Lottie's immediate boss and worked with Mr Standish on casting. He never joined the actors for lunch. Never needed to eat, was the joke, he being so skinny, though he liked to say he couldn't spare the time to go out like the rest of them.

But where was Sally Anderson, then? Brett, taking his eyes from Lottie for a moment, asked after the young actress who had recently joined the company from a repertory theatre in Yorkshire.

'Gone shopping again.' Vivvy nodded. 'That's all she thinks about. She'll never make an actress. I'd have made a far better Julia.'

'Lottie, would you have made a good Julia,' said Brett, returning his gaze to Lottie, who blushed.

'Lottie?' Vivvy's eyes flashed. 'She's lucky to have got the maid's part. Now that's quite a big part with plenty to do. It would have been perfect for me. Why did Tim pick you, Lottie? Was that Standish's idea?'

'Oh, for heaven's sake, get on with your lunch and stop moaning!' cried Primmie. 'Next thing, you'll be saying you could have been Lydia Languish!'

'I could, too,' retorted Vivvy, then had the grace to laugh at herself and began to eat her lunch.

All this arguing and backbiting, it's not real, thought Mae, sorting out coins to pay for her lunch. Means nothing, but somehow they can't be doing without it. For herself, she found it fascinating. Reminded her of home, where everybody had to get their part in a conversation or feel they'd missed out. No cries here to the good Lord, or naming of favourite saints, of course, but sure these folk could've been Irish.

105

'Back to work!' cried Gareth, rising, conscious that one or two people in the café had recognised him and were whispering his name. He couldn't help holding his dark head a little higher and setting his determined chin. 'Shall I pay the bill and then you pay me?'

Chapter Twenty-Four

After lunch there were rehearsals for the company and more work on the costumes for Sheridan's *Rivals* for Mae. She didn't know the play, but Lottie had said Sheridan had been born in Dublin, so if he was an Irishman, it was bound to be hilarious, or else tragic; there were never any in-betweens for the Irish. It was hilarious, Lottie told her, and her own part of Lucy, maid to Lydia Languish, was the best she'd had yet.

'Oh, she's such a little minx, Mae! I'll have such fun with her. I'm so lucky Tim Powell gave me the part.'

'Sure, you'll be right for it, whatever Vivvy thinks,' said Mae.

A shadow crossed Lottie's pale brow. 'I'm sorry Vivvy's disappointed, of course, but what can I do? The part is mine, there's no more to be said.'

'You'd better be coming in and let me measure you for this maid's dress you're wanting,' Mae said after a pause. There had been a steely edge to Lottie's tone she'd never heard before, which was a little surprising. But, as Harry had said, she was an actress. Parts mattered, more than anything else.

'Will you be coming back to the flat for your tea?' she asked, as she measured up Lottie's slender frame, while Mrs Ness at a distance rummaged through a cupboard looking for swords. 'You're not in the play tonight, are you?'

'No, but I'll be needed, anyway. Don't worry about me – I'll have a sandwich, or something.' Lottie was still frowning a little. 'You know, I should have had a part in tonight's play. I mean, it's the opener for the new season – it's important. But they're doing an old Barrie thing, and everybody but me knows it backwards. I suppose that's why Tim didn't give me anything. I'm a quick study, though, I could have managed.'

'Remember you are being Lucy next week,' Mae said cheerfully. 'Now, I think you'd fit a costume in the store that might be just right. I looked it out while you were away.'

'A costume in the store? Couldn't you make me something new?'

'New, Lottie dear?' came Mrs Ness's crisp tones. 'That's not a word we use here, if we can help it!'

'You'll look perfect in this, I guarantee it,' said Mae. 'And there's a muslin apron and cap to match – just need a stitch or two.'

'Found me a sword yet, Mrs Ness?' asked Gareth, appearing in the doorway. 'I need it for the rehearsal. I'm Captain Absolute, you know.'

'Oh, la, Captain, haven't I got one in my hand?' cried Mrs Ness, advancing towards him and cutting the air with the replica sword she had just taken from the cupboard. As he laughed and bowed, Lottie and Mae laughed too.

Is this not a grand job? thought Mae. Sure, I'd not be so happy anywhere else. If only poor Harry felt the same.

It was Mrs Ness's turn to be on hand for the evening performance, which meant Mae could go home early. As she crossed through the slush into the Row, she thought again of Harry, who might have been hurrying back at that time for his tea break, but she saw no sign of him. The snow had ceased now, though the roofs were still white, but underfoot pavements were treacherous. Once or twice Mae almost slipped, and also narrowly missed being hit by a snowball hurled by one of the children of the Row.

'Sorry, Miss!' cried Susie Walker racing by, rosy-cheeked. 'Kenny didnae mean it!'

'Sorry, Mae!' echoed Jannie, as young Kenny, Maggie Sims's son, giggled and hid in a doorway.

'Miss O'Donovan,' corrected Susie. 'That's what Mammie says you have to say.'

'That's all right,' said Mae, laughing, as she let herself in to Number Eight. 'Kenny missed me, anyway.'

'Och, it's no' ma bairns causing trouble again, is it?' asked

Rona Walker appearing at her door. 'Mae, you've no idea how I dread the snow!'

'They're doing no harm,' Mae told her, taking pleasure in Rona's friendliness. She knew it was partly due to the fact that she and Harry were not after all going out together, and partly to the kindness she herself showed to Rona's girls, making dresses for their dolls and always taking an interest in them. All this seemed not to make any difference to Harry's mother, who was never more than coldly polite, or to the other women of Number Eight, who thought Mae and Lottie very strange folk anyway.

Why was Mae not taking herself back to Ireland? Mae knew they whispered. Why was Miss Cameron not going back to her parents? Och, these modern lassies, eh? Only Mrs Beith remained truly friendly, in spite of her disapproval of Lottie's behaviour, and of course her new lodger, Pauline King, a young woman who worked in some office, knew nothing about anyone at Number Eight and kept herself to herself.

'No' the help to me that you were, dear,' Mrs Beith had sighed to Mae after her new lodger's arrival. 'Och, she never so much as lifts a cup from the table. Spends all her time listening to ma wireless. If ma laddie signs himself out o' the army, and comes back home, I'd no' be sorry to see her go.'

'Miss Cameron no' with you tonight?' asked Rona now, and it didn't seem strange to her or to Mae, that Mae should be Mae but that Lottie should be Miss Cameron.

'No, she's still busy at the theatre.'

'Is she really an actress? We never saw her in the pantomime. Harry got us tickets, you ken.'

'The pantomime was done by a visiting company. The Queen's Players were on tour in Aberdeen and Glasgow. But Lottie's an actress, and a very good one, too.' Mae put her key in the lock of her door. 'She's in a play next week, in fact.'

'Fancy. What's she going to be?'

'A maid,' Mae answered reluctantly. 'But she has a lot of lines.'

'A maid!' Rona burst into laughter. 'Why, you could've played that, Mae. I'd say you'd make a grand actress, with your looks and all.'

'Me?' Mae, smiling, slid into her flat. 'Sure, I'd die of fright if I ever set foot on a stage.'

'But Miss Cameron's that quiet, eh? You'd think she'd be the one to be scared.'

'Ah, but you see she can overcome it. There's the difference.'

It was late when Lottie finally arrived home, and Mae, listening out, thought she'd already heard Harry's tread as he passed their door. She had made the flat warm and welcoming by then, with the kettle singing on the range and a pan of soup ready to heat up, if Lottie wanted it.

'Oh, I'm too tired to eat,' she said at first, but enjoyed the soup anyway. Apparently, the play had gone very well. Just *The Admirable Crichton* that everybody knew, with Gareth of course in the lead, but the audiences had seemed appreciative and glad to see the company back after its travels.

'I have some news,' Mae said, pouring tea. 'My cousin's expecting.'

Lottie's eyes grew large, then wary. 'Rosaleen? Oh, well, that's lovely. When's the baby due?'

'The end of June. It's all right, Lottie, I'm happy about it. Why should I not be, after all?'

'No reason. I was just thinking—'

'That it is Kieran's baby? I knew they'd have a family one day.' Mae drank her tea. 'But 'tis true what I said, I'm happy for them.'

Lottie sat back, relaxing. 'You know something, Mae? I think you're over Kieran.'

'You know something, Lottie? I believe I am.'

'You should tell Harry.'

Mae hesitated. 'He could ask me first.'

'You made it pretty clear, didn't you, that you weren't interested because you still cared for someone else?'

'That was some time ago. If we are talking of interest, maybe he's lost his.'

'No, no. I'm sure not.'

'I'm thinking he must have found someone else.' Mae sprang up and took their cups to the sink. 'Let's leave this for now, Lottie. I must write to Rosaleen.'

'Afterwards, maybe you'd hear my lines as Lucy?'

'Oh, Lottie! 'Tis word-perfect you are.'

'You don't know that.'

'I know you, Lottie,' said Mae.

Perhaps not as well as she'd thought, though.

Chapter Twenty-Five

When she could spare the time on Sundays, Mae would go back to Adelaide House to do what she could to help Miss Thorburn and Miss Dow. Sometimes she had her dinner with the girls, braving the usual cabbage and tough beef, and afterwards would show anyone who could be made to listen how to set about dressmaking.

'Thank heavens nobody here disapproves of working on a Sunday!' cried Miss Thorburn. 'Or, where would we all be?'

'When I was a girl, we did nothing on Sundays except go to the kirk and read the Bible,' said Miss Dow. 'But of course, I have to say, our maid still cooked our meals.'

'Sewing is not work to me,' declared Mae. 'Though I suppose what I do is useful.'

'You're absolutely right about that,' Miss Thorburn told her fervently. '"The better the day, the better the deed" – isn't that what they say? I can't tell you how grateful I am, Mae, that you're helping these girls to help themselves. If they can learn to make nice clothes cheaply, think how better they will feel!'

That was the theory, but practice is never the same as theory, and Mae usually found it uphill work to persuade the girls that sewing was worthwhile. Or, that they didn't really need to swear every time they tried to work the ancient sewing-machines, or drop cigarette ash over the material Miss Thorburn had found for them at knock-down prices.

'Och, Mae, it's all right for you,' the girls would groan. 'You're the clever one, eh? And you've no' got a great bump to cover up, either!'

'What's the point o' making nice clothes if we've to wear these horrible smocks?' was another favourite question.

'The clothes are for later, when you've had your babies,' Mae would explain patiently. 'And once you know how to sew, you can make anything, any time. Things for the baby, too.'

That made sense, the girls would grudgingly agree, but working out patterns still gave them headaches, and trying and failing to thread the bloody needles – och, they could scream, so they could.

Still, there were those who were thrilled to achieve a finished garment and came to enjoy sewing for its own sake, while the older women, who'd left brutal husbands, felt quite different in the new clothes they made themselves.

'He never saw me in this skirt, you ken,' one who called herself Pat said hoarsely. 'This blouse, neither. I'm me when I wear these, no' his.' The smoke from her cigarette rose over her damaged face and she gave the familiar smoker's cough. 'Aye, and I'm goin' tae keep on makin' ma own things till I've nothing left that was bought wi' his money. If you'll help me, eh?'

'I'll help you,' said Mae.

'Thanks, then. Thanks for iverything.'

Thanks such as these were so sincere, they strengthened Mae's resolve to keep going with her voluntary work, though Lottie expressed amazement and Mrs Beith said, 'Och, Mae, you're a fool, though a sweet one, eh?'

'One day, Mae, I see you here,' Miss Thorburn murmured once. 'You'd be a natural to make a career of this kind of work, you know.'

'No, no!' cried Miss Dow. 'One day I see Mae married, with a lovely family. Isn't there some young man in the offing?'

'There's no young man, Miss Dow.'

'What a shame, then. But what of that nice little friend of yours? The one I saw you with at the theatre that time?'

'Lottie? Why, she's an actress at the Queen's, where I'm in Wardrobe. She's doing very well.'

'Really? Anita, we must book ourselves seats at the Queen's. Look out for Mae's costumes. See that young girl on the stage.'

'When do I have time to go to the theatre?' asked Miss Thorburn with a laugh.

Later that same day, Mae asked Miss Thorburn privately if she might have a word.

'I know you are not happy giving out addresses, Miss Thorburn, but I've a little outfit for Sandy's baby. Could you not be telling me where her mother lives?'

Miss Thorburn's face went blank. 'You're still looking for Sandy, Mae? Don't you think that if she'd wanted to keep in touch, she would have done?'

'I have this feeling – 'tis hard to explain – that I could help her.'

'Mae, you can't help everybody in this world.'

'You try to, Miss Thorburn.'

'I've learned the hard way, that some folk you must just leave alone to get on with their lives as they want.'

'Sure, it'd do no harm for you to give me Mrs Corrie's address.'

Miss Thorburn sighed. 'What a persistent girl you are, Mae, aren't you?' She turned to her filing cabinet and pulled out a card. 'Here's the address, then – it's a tenement in the Cowgate – but whether you'll find Sandy there, I couldn't say.'

'If the baby's there, so will she be,' said Mae. 'Thank you, Miss Thorburn. I am obliged to you.'

'When are you planning to go? Not today? It'll soon be dark. I don't want you wandering round the Cowgate on your own after dusk.'

'Thursday is my half-day. I'll try then.' Mae smiled. 'No need to look so worried, Miss Thorburn. I know how the poor live – no one better.'

'Yes, well just don't mind what you find, Mae. Remember what I told you about leaving people alone.'

'I can always see little Finlay and give him my present.'

'Yes,' Miss Thorburn agreed wearily. 'You can do that.'

Chapter Twenty-Six

'February fill-dyke' was how some folk described February, and Mae, struggling along the Cowgate on the following Thursday afternoon could see why. The amount of rain falling on her umbrella would have been enough to fill any dyke, so it would, and hadn't she been a fool ever to try to find Mrs Corrie's on such a day? No matter. It would be a good thing to get the visit over. Sandy had been on her conscience for far too long.

She had left the tram, filled with damp humanity, with some relief, and was now below the South Bridge, from which people could look down into the Cowgate. And, from what Mae had heard, that was as much as respectable folk wanted to do, for this old thoroughfare, once the home of the quality, had sunk pretty low.

'Aye, rag and bone men's what you'll find there now,' Mrs Beith, meeting Mae on her way out, had told her. 'And folk with only one thought in their heads and that's to find money for drink. Och, keep away from the public houses, Mae, whatever you do!'

'It is the afternoon,' said Mae. 'I should be all right.'

'Afternoon, evening – any time'll do, dear. Even if the pubs are no' open, there'll be folk hanging about. Now, are you sure you want to go? You'll likely get soaked.'

'I'll be all right,' said Mae again.

But now that she had reached her destination, the dilapidated old houses of the long street depressed her. She remembered how Sandy had talked of sea and sky. 'Never see the sky from a tenement, you ken.' Not from these tenements, anyway, and it was in one of these that Sandy had been brought up, and where young Finlay would be brought up, too.

I'm glad I came, thought Mae, as the water cascaded from her umbrella, and her hands in their wet gloves stiffened round her bag containing the baby's present. I can see how things are.

Women in shawls watched as she fumbled with the note of Mrs Corrie's address and looked up at the ancient façades, searching for numbers. Were there any numbers? Did any postmen ever come with letters to such houses as these? Nothing was clear.

'Who you lookin' for, hen?' a young woman asked, eyeing bedraggled Mae, who gave her the number of the house she wanted.

'That's a coupla doors frae here,' the woman said. 'You're no far away, pet. Got a smoke on you, then?'

Mae, giving her a sixpence to keep her happy and hoping no one else expected one, thanked her and hurried away through the rain, aware that the women's eyes were following her. She couldn't help feeling nervous.

Mrs Corrie's house was numbered as Ten, though it was hard to distinguish the figures on the scuffed and open door that led to a familiar Edinburgh stair. Oh, dear Lord, though, no one ever washed this one, thought Mae, standing looking about her, until an old man with no teeth mumblingly asked her who she wanted.

'Mrs Corrie?' she ventured, folding her umbrella.

'Who wants me?' came a voice from the stair, and a thin, ginger-haired woman stood looking down at her. She was wearing a collarless black dress, much marked, and her bare legs were darkly veined and blue with cold.

Sandy's mother. Mae felt she would have recognised her anywhere, simply from knowing Sandy; even the truculent expression was the same.

'I'm Mae O'Donovan, Mrs Corrie. I knew Sandy at Adelaide House and I was thinking I'd see how she was.'

'Mae O'Donovan? I canna remember your name.' Mrs Corrie descended the stairs, her bedroom slippers slapping on every step. 'Were you a patient, then?'

'No,' Mae answered with a smile. 'Just staying for a few days. But could I see Sandy, then?'

'She's doing ma messages. You're welcome to come in and wait, eh? This way, hen.'

*   *   *

115

The room into which Mrs Corrie showed Mae might once have been a large, elegant reception room, with a high ceiling and long windows, except that, like the Cowgate, it had fallen on hard times. The windows were clouded with dirt, the ceiling blackened, and the state of the kitchen range, which gave out very little heat, would have thrown Mrs Cameron into hysterics.

There were a few chairs and a deal table so piled high with odds and ends, it would not have been possible to add one more item, while in the corners of the room lay several mattresses and old coats. It was on one of these coats that three small children, all with red hair, sat together, staring at Mae.

As Mae, fascinated, returned their stares, Mrs Corrie swept a few clothes from a chair and invited her to sit down.

'You'd like a cuppa tea? The kettle's on the boil.'

'No, no, thanks very much. I had one not long ago.'

'Lassie, you're wet through. Come on, you could do wi' a hot drink, eh?' Mrs Corrie, striking a match, lit a cigarette and taking down a canister, spooned tea into a large brown teapot. 'Like a smoke?'

Mae, refusing, loosened her coat and undid her bag. 'Is that Finlay there, Mrs Corrie? I have something for him.'

'Aye, that's Finlay, the wean. And that's ma Shona and Johnny. Twins, you ken, and ma man'd walked oot by the time they came along. Canna say it's been easy.'

'No, indeed!' cried Mae.

'Aye, and there's ma Terry and ma Georgie, as well – they're away to school. Hope they are, anyway.' Mrs Corrie laughed hoarsely. 'Dinna aye turn up, you ken. Then it's me gets the blame, eh?'

'Could I hold Finlay?' asked Mae, nervously watching Mrs Corrie pouring strong black tea into a couple of suspect cups. 'I am wanting to see if the romper suit I've made fits him.'

'Romper suit?' Mrs Corrie laughed again. 'He's no' much for romping, but it's very kind o' you, hen. Very kind indeed. Pick him up if you like, but he'll be a bit damp, you ken.'

It was while Mae was holding the truly damp and wriggling Finlay that she heard a door bang and steps quickly approaching.

'There's Sandy,' said her mother. 'I'll get her a cup. Sandy, Sandy, you've a visitor!'

'A visitor?' echoed Sandy from the doorway. 'Oh, my God, it's Mae!'

116

Chapter Twenty-Seven

Standing in her mother's doorway, holding two bags of groceries, Sandy seemed much the same young girl Mae remembered from the hostel, open and easy. But as soon as she recognised Mae, wariness replaced the easiness, and her gaze wavered. Still, she found a smile, as she set down her shopping.

'Mae, what a surprise! Fancy you finding me out.'

'Finding me,' said Mrs Corrie, sorting through the groceries. 'Did you get ma cigs, then?'

'Top o' that bag.' As Finlay, spotting his mother, began to cry to go to her, Sandy took him from Mae and held him close. 'Och, Ma, he's soakin'! Have you no' changed him?'

'I was jist goin' to, only Mae's got a wee suit for him, eh? Might as well try that on.'

'A suit? Oh, Mae, you shouldnae bother – here, let's put him down.'

Flinging aside her coat, Sandy quickly found a home-made nappy from a pile on a chair, changed the wailing Finlay and dressed him in the new blue suit Mae had made for him, while his small uncle and aunt watched silently from their corner.

'Oh, it's grand, it's perfect!' cried Sandy, turning to Mae and hugging her. 'Oh, will you look at him! Mae, you're a genius, so you are.'

'For making a romper suit?' Mae asked, laughing. She loosened herself from Sandy's embrace and took some chocolate from her bag. 'Look, I knew there were other children. Can they have this?'

'Can they have it? I should say so. Shona – Johnny – see what the kind lady's brought you. What d'you say, eh?'

Their eyes widening and glistening, the two children crept up to

Mae, snatched the chocolate she held out and ran back to their haven, where they tore off the paper and blissfully began to eat.

'Manners!' shrieked Mrs Corrie, but Mae told her not to worry them, as she put sweets for the older boys into her hand.

'Fancy you thinkin' o' the bairns, then! Wait till they see these. Want some more tea, hen? Have another cup wi' Sandy, eh?'

'I really should be going,' Mae answered quickly, hoping that Mrs Corrie had not noticed she hadn't drunk her first cup. 'This is my half day and I always do my washing and cleaning.'

'You still in service?' asked Sandy, who was watching Finlay crawling purposefully towards the children with the chocolate.

'No, 'tis costumes I'm making now, at the Queen's Theatre. I've rooms in Victoria Row. How about you, Sandy? Where are you working now?'

'Oh, here and there,' said Sandy. As Mae looked at her enquiringly, she added, after a pause. 'At the Art School and places. Do a bit o' cleaning.'

'I see,' said Mae, who didn't. Sandy doing cleaning? She'd sworn she never would. 'Well, now we've met, maybe we can meet again? You were after sending me a card, weren't you? But you never did.'

'Slipped ma mind,' Sandy said smoothly. 'Look, tell you what, I'll walk you to your tram, eh? Ma, keep an eye on Finlay.'

'As though I do onything else! Be sharp back, mind, and gi' me a hond wi' the tea.'

Mrs Corrie shook hands with Mae and thanked her for her kindness. 'Och, it's no' many'll take the trouble to seek oot folk like us, eh? Come again, ony time. I'm aye here wi' the bairns, though Sandy's not. But she does a' she can, you ken, and I'm the first to say it. Might be a devil when she likes, but she's good at heart, and that's the truth.'

'Mae doesnae want to listen to all that nonsense, Ma,' said Sandy, putting on her coat. 'Come on, then, let's away.'

''Twas nice meeting you, Mrs Corrie,' said Mae, taking up her wet umbrella and hastily following Sandy towards the stair. 'Goodbye, then.'

'Bye!' cried Shona and Johnny suddenly appearing and waving, and at their cautious little smiles, Mae felt her eyes prick with tears. Poor little uncle and aunt. Could not something be done for them?

'It's stopped raining,' Sandy cried from the front door. 'One piece o' luck, anyway.'

At the tram stop, she glanced sharply at Mae, and then lowered her eyes, pushing her hair under her close-fitting hat.

'Well, I suppose you've guessed I dinna do cleaning at the Art School?'

Mae stared fixedly at the rainwater rushing past them along the gutter. 'I know you said you'd never be a domestic servant,' she answered after a pause.

'You're right about that. So, modelling pays better. I'm a life-model, you ken. I pose.'

'Pose?'

'Aye, for the artists.' Sandy tossed her head. 'But dinna forget that I've a bairn to keep and money to find for Ma. Who'd you think paid for thae messages? They'd all be living on bread and dripping, if it wasnae for me.'

'I'm not criticising, Sandy. If it's what you want—'

'It's no' what I want. I'm no' keen to take ma clothes off and sit about for all thae students and folk, but I did it before till I fell for the babby, and when they wanted me back, I said yes. I work for other artists, too. Anybody who pays.'

'Is Finlay's father an artist?' asked Mae, suddenly fitting things into place.

'He is.' Sandy smiled coldly. 'I thought he was goin' to marry me, but he went off to London. I never hear a word.'

'Oh, Sandy!'

'Dinna worry, I'll no' make that mistake again. There'll be no more love affairs.'

Mae hesitated. 'There are other jobs, you know. What about that idea you had of working in a smart shop?'

'A smart shop?' Sandy laughed, and as other people waiting at the tram stop looked interested, motioned Mae to move a little away. 'Can you see me in Logie's?' she whispered. 'Or, Jenner's, or somewhere? They'd never have taken me on. And how much would I get in a factory?'

'Well, what about the sewing you used to do? Just lately, I've been teaching some of the girls at Adelaide House to sew—'

'Never!' cried Sandy, smiling for the first time since she'd left her mother's house. 'Och, that's a laugh, Mae. I canna see 'em even holding a needle.'

'Some have done very well. Some could earn money now, with what I've taught them. You could anyway, Sandy – you've already had some training. If you took a job like mine, it'd bring in enough for what you need. Plenty of women manage like that.'

'It's kind o' you, Mae, to think o' me, but no, it'd never do. I'm no' the type, you ken. Some o' the professional artists pay me pretty well and I'm planning to find a girl to help Ma. I'm lucky to have her, but she's too much to do and canna look after Finlay the way I want.'

'At least, you made your peace with her.'

'Och, it was never Ma I fell out with, Mae. Just a fella she'd let move in who fancied me as well as her. When I heard he'd moved out, I moved back.'

'Oh, dear Lord, what a time you've had,' groaned Mae, as the rain began to fall again and pattered on her hat.

Sandy gave a gallant smile. 'I'm all right. And when I get this girl to help, things'll be better for us all.'

'You'll keep in touch? Promise?'

'Your tram's coming, Mae. Better no' miss it.'

'I'll come and see you again.'

'Just leave it for now, eh? We'll be fine, dinna worry.'

As she climbed on to the tram, Mae felt she was moving like a tired old lady, and when she looked out at Sandy standing on the wet pavement, such a cloud of depression rolled over her, she could have burst into tears. She smiled, though, and waved, as the tram clanked away, and Sandy smiled back, and raised her hand. Then Mae was on her own.

Until a man's voice said, quietly, 'Mae, will you no' sit next to me?' And she found herself looking into Harry's wondering eyes.

Chapter Twenty-Eight

They sat together on the slatted wooden seat, Harry's gaze still fixed on Mae's face, she leaning against his shoulder, as though needing his support.

'Oh, Harry, 'tis good to see you,' she murmured so fervently his eyes lit up.

'Mae, where've you been? You look exhausted.'

'Seeing a friend.'

'That girl who was at the tram stop? She's the one you were seeking?'

'She is. I found her. I thought I could help her.'

'Looks to me like she can take care of herself.'

'She can, after a fashion. But she is not happy.'

Harry took Mae's hand and rubbed it between his own. 'And you've found out you couldn't wave a magic wand?'

''Tis true.' Mae gave a long deep sigh. 'Maybe Miss Thorburn at the hostel was right. Some people you must leave alone.'

'Most people,' muttered Harry.

They sat in silence, while passengers opposite stared across and the tram rattled on its way. Already, the sky was darkening, the short day nearly over.

'So, where have you been, Harry?' Mae asked at last. 'Is this free time for you?'

'My afternoon off – do you no' remember? I've been visiting a fella lives near here. One of the stage crew – had a bad fall. I looked in to see how he was.'

'That was kind. You see, you try to help, too.'

'Took him a magazine and some oranges. No' exactly putting maself out.'

She smiled, leaving her hand in his.

'You're awful cold, Mae. Chilled through.'

'I'll be all right, once I get home.'

'Can I do anything for you? Lottie'll be at the theatre, eh? Never does much anyway, does she?'

'Lottie works very hard, Harry.'

'Aye, for herself. I bet you do all the cooking.'

'We take it in turns.'

'Mae!' At his smile, she tossed her head a little.

'When she can manage it, I mean.'

'Let's no' talk about Lottie. Can I come in and give you a hand?'

''Tis kind of you, but your mother will be expecting you.'

'No, I told her I'd be going on to see some pals. But I can see them anytime.'

'If you're sure, then.'

'I'm sure,' he said quietly.

When she had let him into the flat and lit the gas, he stood for a moment looking round.

'Everything as neat as a pin,' he murmured. 'How'd you do it, Mae? With a job as well?'

'Training, I suppose.' She took off her hat and her damp coat, opened her umbrella and put it to dry. 'Spent a lot of my life tidying for other folk. Now I do it for myself. Give me your coat and I'll hang it up for you.'

Slipping into the little bedroom, she changed into a dry skirt and ran a comb through her hair, while Harry opened up the range and set the kettle to boil.

'Now, what are you going to eat?' he asked. 'You need something hot, eh?'

'I've a stew to reheat. Would you like some?'

He hesitated. 'It's a wee bit early—'

'For me, too.' She knew he was thinking of the meal his mother would be cooking for him, whether he was seeing his friends or not. 'Lottie's coming back before the performance – we can have it then. Let's just have the tea and shortbread.'

'You sit down. I'll make the tea.' As he fussed about finding what he needed, he grinned, pushing his damp blond hair from his brow. 'Think I canna do it? One thing I can make is tea.'

122

'You're like Lottie. She can make coffee.'

'Ah, now we're getting the truth of it!'

'Now you are teasing, Harry.'

'Now I'm making you look better. My God, you were so pale when I saw you on the tram, I thought you were ill.'

'Not ill. Just – sad.'

'Seeing this girl upset you.'

'It was the family . . . the children . . . how they live.' Mae shivered. 'You feel so bad – that folk should have to live like that. 'Tis the same back home.'

'Thought things had improved a bit in Ireland?'

'True, they have.' She watched Harry shake tea into the teapot and pour in boiling water. 'But there's a long way to go.'

'We've no' even started here.' He gave the pot a stir. 'Och, that's no' fair. We're no' throwing the slops out of the windows, eh? No' still living in the eighteenth century. But, like you say, we've a long way to go. Where are the cups, Mae?'

Chapter Twenty-Nine

When they'd finished the tea and eaten the shortbread, for which Mae had apologised because it was not home-made, (Harry had better not tell his mother), they held hands together on the second-hand sofa.

'Do I look better now?' Mae whisered.

'You look beautiful,' Harry said huskily.

''Twas when I saw you on the tram that I began to feel better.'

'That true?' He smoothed her hair from her brow. 'Why was that, then?'

'Because I needed you, and you were there. Made the world seem good again.'

'You really thought that? About me?'

'I did.'

A silence fell as their eyes met, a silence that seemed to be saying things they were afraid to put into words. Moments were so fragile, so fleeting. All they wanted to do was keep this one, this moment when doubt between them finally melted away.

'Mae,' Harry said at last, drawing her to him. Then again, just her name. 'Mae.'

She knew he was going to kiss her, and that she wanted him to. Everything was clear now, about her feelings and his, for love was what they had. Perhaps had always had, or the promise of it, from that first meeting on the stair. Now was the reality.

The kiss when it came was long and sweet, and was followed by others, deeper and stronger, until they pulled away, still gazing into each other's eyes.

'I canna believe this is happening,' Harry said softly. 'I never dreamed it could.'

She put her fingers over his lips, asking him not to speak.

'I have to speak, Mae. I have to ask you about – about him.'

No name. Harry had never known his name.

'I've forgotten him,' she said simply.

'When? When did you forget him?'

'Sure, I cannot say exactly. He just – faded.'

'Why didn't you tell me?'

'You never asked me. I was thinking there was someone else.'

'Someone else? For me? There was never anyone else. Why did you think that?'

'You seemed different – towards me.'

'I was never different, I always loved you.'

'Loved me?' Here were words, then. 'You always loved me, Harry?'

'You know I did.'

'You seemed changed.'

'I was just trying no' to let you see how I felt, because I thought you still cared for him. Whoever he is.' Harry's gaze meeting hers was sombre. 'Will you tell me about him?'

'He's not important now.'

'Tell me, Mae. Please.'

After a long pause, she braced herself. 'He was just a boy from the village, Harry. He never said he loved me, though I was thinking he did.' She shrugged. 'I was the foolish one, you see. Anyway, he married my cousin, Rosaleen. I was her bridesmaid.'

'Poor lassie.' Harry gently touched her hand. 'Must've been hard.'

'He is in America now, and far away. You need never think of him.'

'I'll always think of him.'

'No.' She kissed him on the lips. 'Just think of me.'

Time was hurrying by. She said he must go. Lottie would soon be back.

'We needn't worry about Lottie.'

''Tis only that I want to say goodnight to you on our own.'

'I don't want to say goodnight at all.' As he put on the coat she had fetched for him, he looked intently into her face. 'When can I see you again, Mae?'

'Tomorrow. You can cross the road with me to work.'

125

'You ken fine what I mean. When can we go out together? Be on our own?'

She sighed. 'You work most evenings, Harry, and I work some. We've only Thursdays.'

'And Sundays. No work on Sundays.'

'We could go out on Sunday evenings.'

'Only evenings? What's wrong with daytime?'

'Well, the thing is, I like to go to Adelaide House, to help out.' At the look on his face, she said quickly, 'Not every Sunday, of course.'

'You put the girls there before me?'

'No! I m just not wanting to let them down.'

He was silent, his fair brows drawn together; then his expression relaxed and he shrugged.

'OK, as long as I see you some time, Mae. You're the boss. But, listen – tomorrow, shall we go out for one of the lunches you're keen on? Just the two of us?'

'That would be lovely, Harry. But be sure to tell your mother you will not be going home.'

'Of course, I'll tell her,' he said at once.

She looked at him for a moment, then took his hands in hers, as though reassuring him. Of what? That she was not going to cause trouble?

I am trouble, she thought. He knows it. But it wasn't right that she should be, and he knew that too.

'One more kiss, before I go?' he asked, when she had released his hands.

'As though you need to be asking!'

But when they had kissed, with something of the desperation of goodbye, Harry did not let Mae go. His look was sombre.

'What is it?' she asked quickly. 'Why are you looking at me like that?'

'I told you I loved you, Mae. But you never said you loved me.'

'Never said?' She laughed a little. 'Sure, you must know!'

'I want you to say it.'

'Ah, sweetheart, I'm sorry.' He wanted words, as she had wanted words, of course he did. She held him close. 'I'll say it, Harry. I want to say it. I love you.'

'For a long time, you didn't. You still thought of him. You said so.'

'Yes, but then I told you I had forgotten him.'

'So, when did you begin to love me?'

'I think I was always drawn to you, Harry. I think there was always love there for you, but I had to be free of Kieran Connor first.'

'Kieran Connor? So, that's his name.'

'What does it matter about his name? Forget him, Harry.'

'Makes him seem more real, somehow. Knowing his name.'

'Harry, don't be spoiling what we have,' she said quietly, and his gaze on her melted.

'I'm sorry, Mae, I'm sorry. You're right, I shouldn't be talking about him. It's natural, though, eh?'

'Is there anyone for me to talk about, then?' she asked lightly. 'Any old flames from your past?'

'Old flames?' His tone too was light, his smile sunny. 'Canna even remember 'em. Let's see, now – there was a lassie at school – she's married now – I think I went to her wedding – oh, Mae, why'd we have to say goodnight?'

When they had kissed again, long and passionately, for yet another 'last time', they looked out of Mae's door, up and down the passageway and up the stair, but there was no one to see Harry leaving the Irish girl's flat.

'All clear,' she whispered, and he smiled uncertainly and walked away, along the passage, up the stair, waving as if he were going far away. Which, perhaps, in a way, he was.

Alone in the flat, Mae felt suddenly weak. The change in her fortunes seemed to have come so quickly, her head was spinning.

Only a few hours ago, she'd been weighed down with misery for Sandy and her family, and all the Sandys and their families in the world. Everything had seemed so dark, so hopeless, and perhaps would seem so again when she thought of Sandy, but now, after all the years of longing for the wrong man, she had another love, and a true one. One that was shared. Harry had declared his love for her; she had discovered her love for him. These were the thoughts that sent her mind reeling.

She couldn't sit still and moved around the room, picking up things and putting them down, wondering if she should start peeling the potatoes, or wait for Lottie; deciding she would wait for

Lottie. At one point, she looked in the mirror by the door and studied the wild-eyed girl who looked back at her.

You wasted time, she told her. You could have accepted Harry's love long ago.

Well, I've accepted it now, the girl seemed to be replying. Sure, I'll be wasting no more time.

But if she and Harry wasted no more time, if their love moved straight on to marriage, how did they overcome the one great barrier that faced them? One they hadn't yet discussed?

Even to the girl in the mirror, Mae did not give that barrier a name.

'Oh, I'm so pleased for you!' Lottie cried later. 'I knew it would happen. I knew you were over the Irish fellow.'

''Tis an idiot I've been,' declared Mae. 'Harry was waiting for me all the time, and I couldn't see it.'

Lottie gave her a hug. 'Well, I hope you'll both be very happy. You deserve it.'

'Anyone would think we were getting married tomorrow. Nothing's been arranged.'

'There will be. I can tell, by the way you look tonight. You will be getting married, and quickly, too. Why wait?'

'I think I'd better start our supper,' Mae said after a pause. 'Want to give me a hand?'

'Why, of course,' Lottie answered cheerfully. 'You know I'm always ready to help.'

Neither of the young women mentioned Harry's family up the stair.

Chapter Thirty

'Where's Mae?' asked Gareth as the actors gathered at the Rowan Tree the following day.

'Saw her going off with Harry Alpin,' Thea told him, and, at his blank look, added, 'You know – Gerry's assistant.'

'Oh, the lighting man.' Gareth frowned. 'Why him?'

'He's good-looking, dear,' said Primmie. 'Haven't you noticed his lovely hair?'

'Haven't noticed him at all. Except when he doesn't get my spotlight right.'

'I don't think he's particularly good-looking,' said Brett Lester. 'Isn't he one of your neighbours, Lottie?'

Lottie, next to him, went rather pink. 'Lives in one of the top flats. Actually, he's been very helpful to Mae and me. Mending things, and so on.'

'Ah, got his feet under the table, has he?' asked Thea.

'Not Lottie's table, I hope!' cried Brett.

'Must be Mae's, then. Well, she's a very pretty girl.'

'Very pretty,' Gareth agreed. 'Hope we're not going to lose her from Wardrobe.'

'Why, she's only gone out to lunch with this fellow, hasn't she?' asked Brett. 'Are we marrying her off already?'

'Can you catch the waitress's eye?' Lottie asked quickly. 'I'd like some coffee.'

In a different café across the town, Mae and Harry were having steak pies and gazing into each other's eyes.

'Happy?' asked Harry in a low voice.

'I am. I've never been happier.'

'Not missing the nobs?'

'Nobs? You mean the actors?' Mae laughed. 'They're not nobs. They're just like you and me.'

'Like you, maybe. No' like me.'

'Let's not talk about them.' Mae leaned forward a little and laid her hand over his. 'I've been thinking, Harry, that if you want to, we could go out together this Sunday afternoon.'

His eyes lit up. 'Thought you were planning to go to the hostel?'

'This Sunday, I'd like to be with you.'

'Mae, that's grand! I thought I'd have to wait till evening to see you. Where shall we go?' He gave a rueful grin. 'No' much open, you ken.'

'We can walk somewhere.'

'I know where I'd like to walk. Princes Street Gardens. Where we first went together – do you remember?'

'I remember.'

How long ago it seemed; how things had changed for her since then. Yet, this same man who was with her now, had been at her side then. She knew now that he hadn't changed.

'Shan't see the daffodils today,' she said softly. ''Tis too early.'

'Mae, I'll have 'em bloom just for you.'

As they held hands and laughed, and ordered a pot of tea, life to them seemed very good.

When Sunday afternoon came, it was almost a repeat of their first Sunday together, when they walked about the city, scarcely knowing each other at all. Mae wore the same blue hat she had worn then, with her same second-hand coat, and Harry wore his same jacket and cap and had his fair hair plastered down in the same way. This time, though, he had not told his mother where he was going.

'Just going out to see the lads,' he had said jauntily.

'You're taking awful trouble, just to see the lads,' she had remarked.

'Got a secret lady-friend, I expect,' said his father, at which Harry's heart had jolted so hard in his chest, he'd crazily thought somebody would see.

But his mother had only smiled. No lady-friend of Harry's could have been a secret from her. Or, so she believed.

130

As they passed the Scott monument again, on their way to the west gardens, Harry put his parents from his mind. With Mae's blue eyes looking at him from under the turned back brim of her blue hat, he found it easy enough.

It was true, there were no daffodils flowering yet on the slopes of the Mound, but the bench below the Castle where they'd sat before was still there and empty. Of course, it was not the weather for sitting on seats outside. Only a pair of lovers would have braved the wind and sat huddled together; only a pair of lovers would have been perfectly happy, even when a chill rain began to fall.

''Tis all right, I have my umbrella,' said Mae, putting it up. 'We are used to rain in Ireland.'

'Pretty used to it here, too, but I suppose we canna stay.' Harry bent his head to share the umbrella. 'You got soaked the other day, you ken, and I was worried then, you'd get pneumonia.'

'What an idea! I am never ill. But I think maybe you are right, we should move on.'

When they were sheltering in the wide doorway of Logie's department store, the driving rain peppering them with drops, Harry said they should find a place for tea. There was bound to be somewhere open.

'We could always go back to the flat,' said Mae. 'I still have some shortbread.'

'Will Lottie be there?'

'I think Brett Lester was coming round. They were going to learn lines together.'

'Learning lines,' Harry said contemptuously. 'Och, I canna stand that Lester fella.'

'He's nice, Harry. Very fond of Lottie.'

'They'll no' want us barging in.' Harry put his hand outside their shelter. 'I think it's fairing up, anyway. Tell you what, we could go to one of the hotels. They always do teas.'

'Harry, are you crazy? We cannot afford hotels!'

'I'm no' talking about the North British. Just one of the smaller places. Come on, it'll only cost a few bob.' He smiled down at her. 'And I feel rich today.'

But they never went to any hotel, for as they left the doorway of

131

Logie's, a childish voice cried, 'Look, there's Mae! Mammie, it's Uncle Harry and Mae!'

'Say Miss O'Donovan, Jannie,' corrected another young voice, 'Mammie, do you no' see Miss O'Donovan and Uncle Harry?'

'I see them,' said Rona. She took her arm from her husband's and stood foursquare in the middle of the pavement, while her little girls jumped from one foot to the other at her side. 'Hello, Harry. Hello, Mae.'

Chapter Thirty-One

'Fancy meeting you.' Rona's eyes – a darker hazel than Harry's – burned with interest. 'What you up to, then?'

'Might ask you the same question,' Harry replied, holding Mae's arm.

'Just getting a wee breath of air. Stuck in the house all day of a Sunday, it's bad for the bairns.'

'True,' agreed Jake, looking mournful under his cap. His face was so long and thin, his eyes so drooping, he usually looked like he was going to a funeral, was Harry's thought. But then it couldn't be any bed of roses, being married to Rona.

'We're just going to get a cup of tea,' Harry murmured, trying to manoeuvre Mae away down the pavement. 'If we can find one.'

'Why, there's that wee café bottom of Frederick Street – that's always open.' Rona's eyes were fixed now on Mae. 'But we're going back to Ma's. Why'd you no' come with us?'

'Yes, yes, come with us!' cried the children. 'Miss O'Donovan – come back with us!'

'Not today,' she said with a smile. 'And I think it's time you were calling me Mae. Who is this Miss O'Donovan?'

'There you are!' shrieked Jannie. 'I said we could call her Mae, I did, I did!'

'I think we'll no' bother Ma just now,' said Harry, still edging away. 'She'll have enough to do with you folks.'

'There's always plenty – nae bother.'

'No' today, Rona.'

'I'm sure Ma said you were out with the lads. I'll tell her I've seen you, then, shall I?'

'If you want.' Harry's eyes were steady on his sister's face. 'Though you needn't.'

Rona, taking Jake's arm again, called to the girls that they were going. 'Just as you like, Harry. I needn't say a word.'

'Damn Rona,' said Harry, after a waitress in the Frederick Street café had brought them tea and cakes.

'Harry!' cried Mae.

'Well, of all the folk in Edinburgh, we had to meet her. Who plans these things, eh?'

'You're worried she will tell your mother you were with me?'

'I wouldn't say worried. That's the wrong word. Just annoyed. I wanted to tell the folks maself – about you and me.'

'You will have to talk to your ma anyway.'

'Aye, but if Rona's got in first, it'll look bad. Like I was keeping you a secret.' Harry looked down at his plate. 'As a matter of fact, I did say I was seeing the lads today, instead of you.' He raised his eyes to Mae's. 'Think I'm a great jessie, eh?'

'Jessie?' Mae poured tea. 'What's that?'

'A man who acts like a lassie. A man like me – scared to talk to his own mother.'

'Well, that is not you, Harry. You were just not wanting to upset her.'

'That's it. I didn't want a row before I went to meet you.' Harry drank his tea. 'Thing is, Mae, there should be no row just because we want to see each other.'

'I am an Irish girl. What more is there to say?'

'They've nothing against you,' he said quickly. 'Never think that. It's just that when you've had certain beliefs all your life, you're no' going to change overnight.'

'There are plenty in Ireland who are the same. Only with views the other way round – 'tis the way people are.'

'Your dad, for instance, he'd no' want me for you, I suppose?'

'My da is different. He's a tolerant man.'

'I'd like to meet him.'

'Maybe you will.'

'Mae, you do see us going forward, eh? Staying together?'

'I do, Harry.'

'It's what you want?'

'All I want.'

134

She glanced around at the crowded teashop, at the tired waitresses carrying trays, the damp customers, the fractious children, and as Harry's gaze followed hers, he laughed a little.

'No' very romantic sort o' place, you're thinking?'

'I'm thinking it's lovely.'

'You seeing it through one of ma special coloured lights?'

'I'm seeing it with you.'

'Ah, Mae, you've a sweet way of talking, eh?'

'Comes of being Irish. Some advantages, you see.'

They gave themselves up to happiness for a little while, but then Harry sighed and put up his hand for the bill.

'Better be getting back,' he said quietly.

'You are going to see your folks?'

'Aye. See what big-mouth Rona's been up to.'

'She may have said nothing.'

'I've got to say something, anyway.'

'Shall I come with you?'

'No, sweetheart, it'd be easier for me on ma own.'

'I shall not mind what they say.' Mae shrugged. 'I know what it will be.'

'Leave it to me for now. You'll see 'em soon enough.'

Outside, it was already dusk, the street lights glistening on still wet pavements as they walked slowly back to Number Eight and stood staring at the door.

'Oh, God, why do people have to make life so difficult?' asked Harry, as they moved into the house.

'People have been asking that for a very long time.'

'Aye, and no one's been answering.'

'Want to come in for a bit, Harry? It's still early.'

'No, I think I'd rather talk to ma folks. Get it over with. Besides, Lottie'll be there.'

'She might have gone out with Brett by now.'

Harry shook his head. 'I'll come down later.'

'I'll be here.'

They kissed briefly, this being no time for passion.

'Shall I wish you luck?' asked Mae.

'We shouldn't need luck,' snapped Harry. 'I'll make ma own.'

She watched him mount the stair and halfway turn to wave, as she had watched before, then saw him disappear from her view.

135

I should say a little prayer, she thought. But, then, why should she? There should be no need of prayers, any more than luck, for Harry's people to accept her. She was a good-living girl, she had done nothing to hurt them, or anyone. But she knew in her heart that they would not accept her and all that lay ahead for her and Harry were stormy seas. Even shipwreck.

On the table in her flat lay a note from Lottie.

Dear Mae, Just gone out with Brett for a break. See you soon, Love, Lottie.

Thank God, for that, thought Mae and sat down to wait.

Chapter Thirty-Two

They'd finished tea, his family. That was good, thought Harry. Now Rona and her family should get off home. He didn't want an audience when he spoke to his mother.

Emmy Alpin was fussing about, putting tea things away, with her granddaughters supposedly helping. 'I'll carry the milk jug, Jannie, you might drop it.' 'No, no, Susie, I'll carry it, I'll be careful, I'll no' drop it!'

'Girls, girls, be quiet!' Rona, at the door, was putting her coat round her shoulders. 'Jake, will you get thae lassies to come now, so we can get home some time, eh?'

'Why, here's Harry!' said Ben Alpin, looking up from lighting his pipe. 'Had a good time, then?'

'You weren't out long,' called Emmy, closing the cupboard doors. 'What happened to your pals, then?'

Harry's eyes met Rona's. So, she hadn't told their mother. He gave a small sigh and nodded very slightly, at which she gave a frown and put back her blonde hair.

'Jake!' she cried. 'Let's away.'

'And now, I suppose, you'll be wanting your tea?' Emmy asked Harry, when the Walkers had departed.

'I've had ma tea, thanks.' He took off his raincoat and hung it on the door.

'Why, where'd you go?'

'That little teashop in Frederick Street.'

'Canna see you lads in a teashop,' said Ben, puffing on his pipe.

'I didn't go with the lads.' Harry sat down near his father. 'I went with Mae O'Donovan.'

There was the silence he expected. His father took his pipe from

137

his mouth and looked at once to Emmy. Harry looked at her, too, and saw her face change; become mask-like; the skin stretched over brow and cheekbones, the lips losing all colour.

'Mae O'Donovan,' she repeated. 'You took her out today?'

'Aye, I did.'

'So, when you said you were seeing your pals, that was a lie?'

'I'm sorry. I just didn't want to stop and argue.'

Emmy sank down at the kitchen table and put her hand to her brow. 'Tell me the truth now, then. How long have you been seeing her?'

'No' counting a couple o' walks early on, we've been out twice on our own.'

'That's no' much,' Ben said eagerly. 'He's no' been keeping much from us, Emmy.'

'Oh, yes he has!' she cried. 'He's been keeping everything from us. He's been sweet on that girl the whole time she's been here and she's never bothered with him till now. Is that no' true, Harry?'

His face was red and there was a line of sweat on his brow. 'It's true I've loved Mae since I first met her.'

'And you asked her out and she wouldn't go, would she? Little Miss Hoity-Toity had someone else in tow and never wanted you. Now she's changed her mind and you've come running. Oh, Harry, can you no' see what she is?'

'I'll tell you what she is, Ma. She's a fine, good-living girl. She tries to help others – does voluntary work at Adelaide House – teaches 'em sewing. Just last week, she was moving heaven and earth to find some girl from the hostel she wanted to help – went all the way to the Cowgate to look for her. Miss Hoity-Toity?' he laughed harshly. 'Shows you don't know her at all, to call her that!'

'I know this, then,' cried his mother. 'She's Irish! She's from a country that's never been anything but a load of trouble since time began, full of folk going round shooting and blowing things up. They canna get on with each other or anyone, they drink and pick fights, and they've no sense in their heads. And you have the nerve to tell me you want to take out a girl who's one of them?'

'I've the nerve to tell you that I'm going to marry her,' Harry said with dangerous calm.

It was his bombshell, one he had not been planning to use until later, but his mother's tirade had pushed him to the edge and he

138

aimed it now. 'Bullseye!' he might have cried, if he had not been ready to weep at the way things were going. If his mother had not looked so stricken.

'Marry,' she whispered. 'Och, no, it's no' possible, Harry, you canna marry an Irish girl.'

'Nothing against her, you ken,' Ben put in hastily. 'Seems she's a nice, kind lassie, but no' from the kirk, that's the thing. You couldn't take her on, Harry. Put her right out of your mind.'

'Right out of your mind,' Emmy repeated with trembling lips. 'Or you're right out of this house. Make your choice, Harry.'

Harry sat like stone, his handsome face so stern as he looked at his parents, he was like a stranger to them. Their flesh and blood, yet no one they knew. How could he look at them so? Very quietly, his mother began to cry, and Ben rose and put his arm around her shoulders.

'Now you've upset your mother,' he muttered. 'Have to think of your folks, Harry.'

'All ma life, I've hated injustice,' Harry said after a long silence, during which his mother continued to sob. 'And Ma, you've been unjust to Mae and her country. Aye, there are plenty o' wild Irish like you said, and some Scots as well. But no' all Irish folk are like that, and neither is Mae. Her dad's a fisherman who's tolerant and good and he's brought her up to be the same. If I got Mae, I tell you, I'd be a lucky man.'

'She's still no' your religion,' said his father heavily. 'You'd never be able to work things out between you. Folk have to have things in common to get on, and if you marry a girl who's different, you'll find that out.'

Again, a silence fell. Emmy stopped crying and blew her nose. Ben sat down and fiddled with his pipe. Harry stayed very still.

'Did you mean what you said?' he asked at last. 'Did you say I'd have to go, if I wanted to marry Mae?'

Emmy and Ben looked at each other.

'We'd never want you to go, son,' said Ben. 'But you see how it is? We canna accept that lassie as one of the family.'

'You were sympathetic about her once.'

'Aye. I'm still sympathetic. I think she's a nice girl – pretty and clever – but no' for you.'

'So, I move out, unless I stop talking about getting wed?'

Emmy sniffed and dabbed at her eyes. 'Maybe I was a bit

hasty, eh? Saying that? It'd break ma heart, to see you go, Harry.'

He looked at her and smiled wryly, as he read her thoughts. Let him go, and she'd have lost completely. Let him stay, and who knew? She might persuade him to change his mind. And though he felt like walking out of the door without even packing a bag, he knew that he would stay. Who knew? He might be the one to do the persuading.

'I needn't go, then?'

His mother darted another glance at Ben, who shrugged.

'It's up to you, Emmy. You decide.'

'Stay, then, Harry.' She rose and went to him, putting her arm around him. 'Let's no' split the family, eh?'

'Ma feelings exactly.' He moved from her embrace and stood up. 'Now, I'm away.'

'To see her?' cried Emmy. 'Oh, Harry!'

'She's waiting for me. Did you no' think she'd want to know what you folks said?'

'Look, tell her we're sorry you canna give her good news,' said Ben. 'But that's the way things are.'

'She won't be expecting good news,' said Harry. 'She knows the way things are.'

Chapter Thirty-Three

As soon as she opened her door to him, Mae told him that Lottie was out, and he gave a great sigh and held her close.

'The one bit o' good news,' he whispered, kissing her, and she drew back.

'Was it bad, Harry?'

'Terrible. At one point, they were going to throw me out.'

'Oh, dear Lord, they'd never be after doing that?'

'Changed their minds. Only because they think I'll change mine.' He sank onto the sofa. 'They've got another think coming there. Come here and sit on ma knee, Mae.'

For some time, she rested against him, her hand on his chest, her face against his, and he lay with his eyes shut, recovering, as he put it.

'Aye, I feel I've been in a fight, Mae. And what's worse than fighting your own folks? But they've got closed minds. It'd need dynamite to open 'em up.'

'I was never expecting anything else. I knew they'd never accept me.'

'Ma's the one,' Harry said quietly. 'I think Dad likes you, to be honest, but he goes along with Ma in this. He did say to tell you they were sorry about everything – but if they'd meant it, we'd no' be having any trouble.'

'Harry, what shall we do?'

He straightened up, opening his eyes and searching her face. 'There's no question, is there? We get wed, as planned. You've no' been put off, have you?'

'I have not! You're all that matters to me, Harry.'

'So, we arrange things without ma folks. First, I buy you a ring.

I've a bit saved up, so don't think I canna afford it. Next afternoon off, we go up to the Royal Mile – got some good shops there – and you pick one out.'

'Harry, there are things I want more than a ring. Why waste money?'

'A ring means something, Mae. Means we are serious about each other and that we want other folk to know. It'll no' be just an ordinary ring.' He gave a sudden grin. 'Come, you'd like one, eh? All girls like a ring.'

'I would, then,' she agreed, smiling with him, and as she flung her arms around him, he thought of his mother's hopes, and of how they would come to nothing.

'Are you hungry?' asked Mae, a little later.

'I am, I'm starving,' answered Harry. 'Got anything in the larder?'

'Ham and eggs be all right?'

'For ham and eggs, I'd sell ma soul.'

'You sit there, then, and I'll get things ready.'

'Will you always look after me like this?'

'No promises.' She tied on an apron and turned to smile at him. 'In Ireland, men are brought up to do nothing at all in the house. They'd die of starvation, if there was no woman around to cook for them. Is that right, d'you think?'

'Och, yes,' Harry said solemnly. 'We men have our principles, eh?'

Then he burst out laughing and said if Mae trusted him, he'd take a cookery lesson then and there, but she said he could wait till they were married. At which they grew serious; they were still so very far away from reaching that happy ending.

'Do you no' sometimes wish we could just run away to Gretna Green?' Harry asked, attacking his ham and eggs. 'Get married over the blacksmith's anvil?'

'Sure, I'd never think it a marriage at all,' cried Mae.

'Legal, though. As good as a registry office wedding.'

'I could never be married in a registry office, either.'

Harry raised his fair brows. 'I was thinking that's how we would be wed. I'm no great kirk-goer, but I canna see maself in your cathedral. I mean, the priest'd never marry us, would he?'

Mae was looking troubled. 'He could. It would be a very simple service, but that would not matter. A lot of fuss would not suit us, anyway.'

'But the registry office'd be simplest of all. Could we no' just have that?'

When she did not reply, Harry put down his knife and fork.

'Would you no' be happy about it, Mae?'

'I would be happier in church.' She raised her eyes to his. 'But I want you to feel right about it. I want us both to feel right.'

'Canna really hope for that, the way we're placed. One of us'll have to try to please the other.' Harry began to eat again. 'And I think it'll be me. Nae bother, Mae. We'll get married in your church.'

'Are you sure, though?'

'Aye. You're the church-goer, and I'm not. Means more to you than me, where we get wed, eh? All I want is to BE wed. To you.'

'Oh, this is good of you, Harry. I appreciate it.' Mae leaned over and kissed his cheek. 'I'm afraid your parents will not come, though.'

'They'll no' come to ma wedding wherever it is.'

'Your wedding to me,' Mae said quietly.

'Their loss, eh? Now, shall I make some tea?'

'We have coffee. Want to make coffee?'

'Och, too difficult. Need Lottie for that.'

And Lottie they had, for the flat door was already opening and Lottie and Brett came rushing in, making theatrical entrances, crying how cold it was, and asking what was that delicious smell?

How different she looks these days, thought Mae, eyeing Lottie as she took off her coat and threw her hat on a peg. Once so colourless, she had seemed pale as moonlight. Now, her light was different. Bright and hard. Starlight, perhaps. Small parts or not, she was making for the top. Everyone at the theatre felt it, not just the admiring Brett. Harry felt it, too, but then Harry had always felt it. As he stood up at Lottie's entrance, Mae sensed he was distancing himself in the way he did with the actors; moving back into his shell.

'We've been having ham and eggs,' Mae told Lottie. 'We were going to make coffee.'

'Ham and eggs! Oh, lovely! What a pity we've had supper. Brett, wouldn't you have liked ham and eggs?'

'Yes, but now I couldn't eat a thing,' he answered cheerfully. 'Wouldn't say no to coffee, though.'

'I'll make it,' said Lottie. 'My party trick. Coffee for everyone, is it?'

'I've got to go,' said Harry.

'Oh, look – have we broken things up?' asked Brett, conscience-stricken. 'Lottie, we came back too early.'

'I was going anyway.' Harry moved to the door. 'See you folks in the morning. Goodnight.'

'Harry!' cried Mae, following him as he let himself out. 'Harry, why are you leaving like this?'

They stood in the passage, their faces strained and shadowed under the gaslight; Mae's eyes appealing, Harry's expressionless.

'Why d'you think?' he whispered. 'We were so happy, then they have to come in, spoiling everything.'

'They meant no harm. They wouldn't even have known you were here.'

'Och, I'm just too on edge, I suppose. Canna be patient. Especially when I lose out on kissing you.'

'You need not lose out on that,' she told him, and his eyes softened, as they clung together, kissing long and passionately.

'See you tomorrow,' Harry said, catching his breath. 'And we'll set all the wheels in motion, eh? Towards getting wed?'

'Towards getting wed,' she repeated, and once again watched him mount the stair and pause to wave.

Chapter Thirty-Four

'I'm so sorry, Mae, I should have realised Harry might be here,' Lottie murmured. 'I expect he hates us, doesn't he?'

'We both share the flat, Lottie. You have a right to come home. But, listen – I have some news for you. Harry and I are engaged.'

'Engaged? Why, that's wonderful! Now didn't I say you'd be getting married, and soon?' Lottie flung her thin arms around Mae. 'Oh, congratulations! Why didn't you tell me when Harry was here?'

'What's up?' cried Brett, coming over from the sofa. 'Is it Mae's birthday?'

'No, she's engaged. To Harry!'

'Oh, God. No wonder he looked like a thundercloud when we come in. I'm surprised he didn't chuck us out.'

'If only we had some champagne, or, wine, or something, to drink a toast,' sighed Lottie. 'All we've got is coffee. When I make it.'

'Really ought to keep a few bottles in, Lottie,' said Brett. 'Never know when you might need it.'

'Just in case somebody else gets engaged, I suppose?'

'Well, it could happen.'

Lottie smiled and touched his cheek. 'I don't think so, Brett, but it's a nice thought.'

As the two of them stood close, Lottie measuring out the coffee, Brett watching Lottie, Mae suddenly wished herself away. Didn't know where. Anywhere, where she could be alone and take in what was happening. Were she and Harry really engaged? And without his parents' blessing? Her head was aching. If only she could be somewhere quiet. If only Brett would go.

In fact, he didn't stay long, perhaps sensing Mae's weariness. When they'd finished their coffee, he rose and kissed her on the cheek. 'I wish you all the happiness in the world,' he told her, 'and Harry, too. Now, I'd better be on my way. See you girls tomorrow.'

'I'll see you out,' said Lottie. 'Make sure you're word-perfect for rehearsal, Algernon.'

'Algernon?' asked Mae, when Lottie returned.

'Brett's playing Algernon in *The Importance of Being Earnest*, and I'm Cicely. Primmie, of course, is Gwendolen and Gareth is Jack. And guess who's Lady Bracknell?'

Mae shook her head dizzily.

'Thea! It's all worked out beautifully. Poor old Vivvy has to be Miss Prism. But, oh, Mae, you look ready to drop! Poor girl – you get to bed and I'll clear up. Has it been too much for you?'

When Mae made no answer, Lottie hesitated.

'I don't want to pry, but – is anything wrong?'

'Just Harry's folks. They cannot accept me.'

'Oh, Mae!'

'I was prepared for it. I was thinking I wouldn't mind. But, now it's happened – I mind, Lottie.'

'I should think so! Why, that's terrible. So insulting. Why should they not accept you?'

'You know why. I'm Irish and a different religion. I wouldn't fit in.'

'Of all the nonsense!'

'No, 'tis something they believe. Really believe. They were even going to make Harry leave home over it.'

'They threatened that?' Lottie stood very still, and suddenly looked her old pale self, her brightness fading. 'He was going to have to leave home?'

'In the end, they said he could stay, but they will not see me, I'm thinking. They will not come to the wedding.'

Lottie went to Mae and hugged her hard.

'I'm so sorry. I know what this must mean to you, and I know what Harry's going through. Even if you think your parents are wrong, it's hard, when there's conflict.' She smiled briefly. 'I speak from experience, as you know.'

'I do. But you were brave. You knew what you had to do.'

'And you must be brave, Mae. Fight for Harry. Don't let his parents win.'

'I am not thinking of winning or losing. I just want them to be fair to me, and they are not being fair.' Mae's eyes were glittering, her breath coming quickly. 'They have turned me down without even knowing me. How can that be right?'

'It's not right, but I can't think what you can do.'

'I must make them see that Harry and I can be happy together, whatever the difficulties. That is my aim.'

Lottie began to clear away the coffee cups. 'Maybe they'll come round anyway. Sometimes, people do.'

'Sometimes. I'm not hoping for it.'

'Well, Mummy never has, I'll have to admit.' Lottie shook her head. 'Why do people have to make life so difficult, I wonder?'

'Harry's exact words,' said Mae.

In spite of her fatigue, sleep did not come easily to her. Too much had happened. Too much was moving round and round in her head. On the one hand, she had been offered true love; on the other, she'd been rejected. The love was all that really mattered, but she knew she could not live without trying to overcome the rejection. As she had told Lottie, it was unfair. It must not be let to stand.

Harry would help. Harry was on her side and saw things as she did. Was she not the lucky one, then? A smile curved her lips in the darkness, and gradually – gradually – she slept.

In the morning, of course, everything seemed better. By the time she'd washed and dressed and snatched some breakfast, Lottie was telling her she looked herself again.

'Fighting fit,' agreed Mae, as she put on her hat, and smiled. 'A manner of speaking, only.'

'You'll need to be fit this morning, anyway.'

'This morning?'

'For all the congratulations at the Queen's, of course! Haven't you just got engaged?'

'You think folk will be interested?'

'Of course they will! You're very popular, Mae, everyone will be wishing you well.'

'And Harry, too.'

'Harry, too. Goes without saying.' Lottie hesitated. 'Mae, it's early days, I suppose, but have you thought about where you're going to live?'

147

Mae's eyes widened and she put her hand to her lips.

'Sure, I'd not thought of it at all! What a strange pair we are, then, Harry and me, not to have discussed it.'

'You've had a lot on your minds. The thing is – if you did want to stay on here, I could move out, you know. No, it's all right, I could, easily. Thea was saying the other day she wouldn't mind having someone to share, her rent being pretty high. But then, you'd probably want to get away from here, wouldn't you?' Lottie shivered a little. 'I would, if I were you.'

'Maybe I'd rather stay,' Mae answered slowly. 'Maybe I'd rather not – run away.'

'But the atmosphere, Mae? Always having to avoid the Alpins. You'd hate it.'

'I want to win them round, Lottie. Can't do that if I am not here.'

'Win them round? That's crazy. You'll never win them round.'

'Maybe not. I'll see what Harry thinks.' Mae gave a sudden quick smile. 'But, thanks, Lottie, for the offer. I appreciate it, I really do.'

'Mae, I want to make things as easy as possible for you. Don't I know what it's like, when they're not?'

Chapter Thirty-Five

While Mae and Harry at the theatre faced the showers of good wishes Lottie had predicted, the news of their engagement buzzed round Number Eight like a swarm of bees. Or, wasps.

Oh, what a thing to happen, eh? Harry Alpin engaged to the Irish girl! He'd always had his eye on her, everybody knew that, though Emmy would never believe it, and she'd thought she was safe anyway, when the lassie would no' go out with him. Now, the worst had happened. She'd have an Irish daughter-in-law – aye, and Irish grandchildren and all, probably. Whatever would she do? And Rona, come to that? She'd never want that lassie for a sister-in-law, even if she did give the wee girls sweeties and dress their dolls.

Of course, Clara Beith was all for taking Mae O'Donovan's part. Saying she was a nice girl, and all of that. Well, she might be, but she'd already had a row over in Victoria Place, and got that foolish Miss Cameron to leave home, eh? And then didn't the pair o' them go and land jobs at the theatre? Poor Emmy! She'd never stood a chance, with Harry seeing Mae every day, and you could say what you liked, she was a lovely girl, just the sort to turn a fella's head.

Now, if he'd only taken a fancy to Clara's lodger, what a difference there'd have been. She'd no' got Mae's looks, but she was a nice steady girl and a kirk-goer, too. Just what Emmy could've done with for a daughter-in-law. What a shame, eh? The way things turn out.

Still, you never knew. There was many a slip twixt cup and lip, and Harry might change his mind. Might all be too much for him, struggling with the difficulties. That was what Emmy must be hoping, though she was never saying a word when she went out for her messages with a face like thunder, flinging her shopping basket around like it had done her an injury.

Och, but the storm clouds were poised over Number Eight, eh? If that Irish girl had any sense, she'd head straight back to County Cork and give up life in Scotland. But then folk in love never show any sense, and she must be in love with Harry to take on Emmy, eh?

Over at the Queen's, Mae had been deeply touched by the interest being taking in her engagement. It was not just the actors, but Gerry Ames, Harry's boss, and Tim Powell, the stage manager, as well as the carpenters, the flymen and box-office girls – all were wanting to shake her hand and wish her luck. And even Mr Standish himself had put his head into Wardrobe and had boomed his congratulations in that wonderful carrying voice of his, that was as rich as plum cake with brandy.

'Who would have thought folk would care so much?' Mae asked Mrs Ness. 'I never even realised they all knew who I was!'

'Why, Mae, you're an important part of this theatre. How'd they put a show on without costumes? And don't forget, you're easy to remember.'

'Being Irish?'

'Being good to look at.' Mrs Ness's eyes on Mae were thoughtful. 'Being Irish doesn't come into things here. Theatre folk don't care about differences, my dear – like some outside might do.'

Mae, who was threading one of the sewing machines, made no reply, and Mrs Ness put her hand to her lips.

'Oh, Lord – you're not remembering that time I said something about Irish girls not being good at sewing? Will I ever live that down? Of course, I didn't mean it. And you're one of the best needlewomen I know, anyway.'

'That was not in my mind at all, Mrs Ness. And the theatre folk have always accepted me.'

'Something's on your mind, though. Is it Harry's folks, then? Are they making difficulties?'

'You might say so.'

'Take no notice. Just ignore them. And if there's anything I can do to help, just let me know.' Mrs Ness suddenly clapped her hands. 'I'll tell you what, I'll make your wedding dress! Yes, it'll

150

be my present to you. You're always sewing for other people – this'll be my chance to give you something you've not had to make yourself. What do you think?'

'Mrs Ness – I am bowled over! Sure, 'tis the kindest thing in the world.' Mae left her machine and made to shake Mrs Ness's hand, only her boss gave her a hug instead.

'That's settled, then. We'll start looking at patterns this very day.'

'I will not be wearing a formal dress,' Mae said hesitantly. 'The wedding will be very quiet.'

'I understand. You'll make a lovely bride, anyway. Though it's my loss you're going to be one, anyway. What am I going to do without you?'

'You need not be doing without me. I plan to keep working, if that's all right?'

'Not many women work after marriage, Mae. Of course, in the Civil Service and such, you're not allowed to – keeping a man out of a job is the reasoning. But not many men want to work in Wardrobe.' Mrs Ness laughed. 'I'd be thrilled if you'd stay on. Until the family comes, anyway.'

'Oh, yes,' agreed Mae, blushing. 'I'd have to give up work then.'

'Do different work, my dear. From what I've heard of folk with children, life's not exactly a holiday. Still, you're not even wed yet. Needn't look too far ahead.'

''Tis never wise,' said Mae.

Later, when she and Harry were having a frugal lunch together at the café, she told him how much it had meant to her that the theatre folk had been so kind.

'Were you not surprised, that they'd take such interest, Harry? I never thought we'd matter to them so much.'

He shrugged. 'Think it's you they're interested in, Mae. No' me.'

'Ah, now that is just not true! Why will you never admit that people here are good hearted? And they like you. Sure, they admire you!'

He permitted himself to smile. 'OK, they admire me. First I've heard of it, but I'll no' argue. And, yes, they've been nice about the engagement. I'm just being the usual grump.'

'Makes a difference to me,' she said quietly. 'To have folk caring about us.'

They were silent, thinking of those who were not caring about Mae.

'Have you thought any more about Lottie's offer?' she asked at last, wondering why he'd not mentioned it again after she'd first raised it with him.

'Och, I'm just no' sure what to say, Mae.' He ran his hand over his brow. 'Do we really want to be staying on in the Row?'

'Would be the easiest thing.'

'Easiest? To live near ma folks? We'd be better away.'

'If we move away, we shall never make it up with them, I know it.'

He fixed her with a long sad gaze. 'You still think we can make things up with them?'

'If we stay on at Number Eight, we shall have a chance, Harry. If we move away, there'll be none.' Mae leaned forward to take his hand. 'And I am not wanting you to be estranged from your parents all your life. That'd be too much of a burden for me to be carrying.'

'Ah, Mae, we should think of ourselves!'

'I know, but I want to let them see that I am right for you and should be a part of the family.' Mae lowered her eyes. 'This is very important to me, Harry – I must get the chance for it.'

He took her left hand, smoothing her still ringless third finger. 'You'll have it,' he whispered. 'We'll stay on at Number Eight. Now – you haven't forgotten we have to get the ring on Thursday?'

'I have not!' Her expression brightened, as she pressed his hand in return. 'But we've a lot to do on our afternoon off. I want to take you to the hostel, to meet Miss Thorburn and Miss Dow.'

'And the girls?' he asked with a hunted expression. 'Mae, I hope I'm no coward, but I canna face them.'

'Sure, it will please them so much to meet you, Harry.' Mae was laughing. 'Oh, if you could see your face!'

Shortly afterwards, they left to walk back to work, relieved that they had made a big decision, neither mentioning what they still had to do, which was to arrange their marriage at the cathedral.

If there are any problems, thought Mae, we shall have to have the civil ceremony. Am I selfish, not to agree to that anyway? She dreaded upsetting Harry, but then he had agreed to do this for her. It gave her a wonderfully warm feeling to think that he would.

Chapter Thirty-Six

'Are the angels above looking after you?' her father wrote to Mae a week or so before her wedding in July.

Sure, it seems everything has worked out well for you, even though you'd difficulties like thorns to be cut before you could wed. But now it is all arranged, and a grand day to look forward to, with me there in spirit and thinking of you. Such a fine man, your Harry looks, from the photograph you sent. You can be sure, when you are over for your honeymoon, I'll be looking forward to meeting him.

Annie wishes to be remembered and has made you a grand present. Ah, now, was that a secret? Be sure to be looking surprised when you get it.

Take care, dear girl, and may there be blessings on you and your man on your wedding day,

Your loving father, Joseph O'Donovan.

P.S. By the time you are reading this, might I be a great-uncle? I cannot think of Rosaleen as a mother. She is always six years old to me, yourself being eight.

Are the angels looking after me? Mae had smiled when she'd read that. It was certain they'd been looking after Rosaleen, for the news had already come that she'd had the most perfect baby in the world. A daughter, fair as a lily, to be named Mary Clare and known as Molly. Oh, what a relief! And Rosaleen had dashed off a note for Mae, to hurry up and have a baby too, soon as she had wed this handsome Harry she'd found. Then she would be as happy as Rosaleen herself. And Kieran!

Ah, but Mae was happy already, as long as she didn't think about the Alpins, and she'd had her share of luck from the angels, or somebody, for as her da had said, things had worked out in the end for her wedding. Not that he knew all the thorns she'd had to face, for of course she had not told him.

Yes, he knew Harry's family were not approving of the marriage, but not of their refusal even to speak to her. Or of Rona's snatching away her little girls when they ran to Mae, smiling, as they'd always done. Or of how much that had hurt.

Nor did he know of Harry's arguments with the priest across at the cathedral, and of how hard Mae'd had to work to try to achieve co-operation, while trying to see everybody's point of view. It had come at last and a date had been fixed for the very quiet wedding in July, thank heavens. Or, should that be, thank the angels? It was fixed, anyway.

Then there'd just been the little reception at some café to think about, with Harry saying he would pay, and Mae declaring it was her responsibility, she was the bride. Whoever heard of a bridegroom organising a wedding?

'Neither of you is organising it,' declared Mrs Ness. 'You've no mother, Mae, and Harry's people are out of it, so we're all clubbing together here, to give you a good send-off. No arguments, it's all arranged.'

All arranged? Mae and Harry couldn't believe it. After the morning wedding, everyone would assemble on the stage of the Queen's, with food, drink, and a cake provided by the company. There was even a fiddler and accordionist booked to play for dancing, and everybody was going to have the time of their lives and not give a thought to the evening performance.

'Aye, thank the Lord, there's no matinée that Saturday,' said Mrs Ness laughing. 'That'll give us time to tidy up. But you folks'll be away to Ireland by then, for your honeymoon, eh? Ah, now, Mae, what are you crying for? Not a wake we're planning, is it?'

'It's just that I'm so happy,' murmured Mae, dabbing her eyes, and turning to Harry. 'Oh, why is everyone being so good to us?'

He might have answered that some were not, but in truth was as touched and surprised as Mae herself by the theatricals' thought for them, and for once had no words of complaint. All he had to worry about now, he said with a somewhat forced laugh, was his visit to Adelaide House.

'Poor Harry,' Mrs Ness had said, laughing with him. 'Those girls'll eat you alive.'

But the visit to the hostel went better than expected. While Miss Thorburn and Miss Dow were clearly impressed by Harry, the girls were so much in awe of Mae's luck in finding him, they'd really been quite subdued.

'Och, Mae, will you look at the lovely man?' they whispered, as they gathered in the dining-room for cups of tea and hard scones somebody'd had a go at making the day before. 'Is he no' a dream-boat? Where'd you find him, then? How about finding one for us?'

When everyone had admired Mae's elegant, old-fashioned ring, there were presentations. Silver spoons from Miss Thorburn, Miss Dow, Mrs Mennie and Dr Rick, who'd looked in briefly to wish Mae and Harry all the best, and a cake stand from the girls, which deeply touched Mae's heart, for she knew how little they had.

There was only one difficult moment, when one of the girls suddenly gave a cry, as Mae was making her thanks, and squealed out, 'Och, would you credit it? I think the babby's coming! Jist when I was havin' a good time, eh?'

But though people went running and Harry closed his eyes and said they should go, the panic ended when stout Mrs Mennie stepped up and smoothly removed her patient, and Miss Thorburn smiled and said it was all in a day's work, who was for more tea?

'He's a good man, your Harry,' the woman called Pat told Mae, drawing her to one side. She was moving to a secret address the following day, and looking so much better, Mae hardly recognised her. 'You'll be all right wi' him, I can tell.'

'And you'll be all right now,' Mae answered. 'You've a new life beginning – just like me.'

'I wish I could've invited all the girls to the reception,' she told Harry on the way back to the Row. 'But there'd have been too many.'

'Far too many,' he agreed at once.

'Ah, now, they weren't so bad, were they? Gave us a lovely present they couldn't afford, and let you off lightly, too.'

'Think so? Ma face is still as red as a beetroot. I mean, they talked about me as if I wasn't there.' He looked down at Mae and smiled. 'But I guess you're right. They're no' so bad. And the two ladies'll be coming, eh? How about your friend, Sandy?'

Mae shook her head. 'I asked her, but I am sure she will not come.'

'She'll miss a good party, then.' A shadow crossed Harry's face. 'No' the only one.'

Mae sighed. 'We can't be making your folks come, Harry. I wish we could.'

'Well, I'm going to ask 'em again – at least, to come to the theatre. If they still say no, I'm moving out to Gordon's. I'll go to the wedding from his place.'

'I suppose he is your best man,' Mae said with a sigh.

'Aye. So, I'll speak to them now, soon as we get in. Will you take these presents, then? No point in me taking 'em up the stair.'

He expected nothing and was not surprised when he received nothing. Once again, his parents told him they would not be attending the wedding or reception, and nor would Rona. How could they, in view of the circumstances?

'I'm sorry, son,' said Ben, along with Harry who was packing his things. 'I am – and that's the truth.'

'The offer's still open if you want to come, Dad.'

'You ken fine we canna come.'

'All you've got to do is walk across the road.'

Ben's eyes fell. 'Better no' upset your ma, talking about it.'

'I'm talking to you, Dad. All I'm asking is that you come over and have a drink. Wish me well.'

Ben began to move towards the door. 'I do wish you well, Harry, and Mae and all. Maybe it will work out for you, eh? That's ma hope.'

After his father had left him, Harry went on packing, keeping himself calm. When he had closed up his cases, he gave a last look round at the tiny room that had been his, and felt a dull pain in his chest. He was saying goodbye, and no ordinary goodbye. A farewell to boyhood and a farewell to the two people who'd once meant so much to him. His folks. Couldn't just cut them out of his life, could he? Yes, it was what he had to do. Give them up, as they were prepared to give up him. Mae still hoped for reconciliation, but he faced facts. He'd been given a choice to make and he'd made it.

He picked up the cases and walked from the room.

'Goodbye, then,' he said to his parents, sitting by the range. 'I'm away to Gordon's.'

His mother put down the sock she'd been pretending to darn. 'You've taken all your things?' she whispered.

'Not all. I'll come back for the rest later.'

'You are moving into the lassie's flat?' asked Ben. 'I mean – afterwards?'

'Aye. When we come back from Ireland.'

'Ireland.'

His mother closed her eyes. She did not speak again and neither did Ben. Harry quietly let himself out of the door and went down the stair. Out of their door, out of their lives, he thought. But he would see Mae before he went on to Gordon's, and his heavy heart lifted. In a few days' time, they would be married. Everything would be different then.

Chapter Thirty-Seven

At first, they didn't feel any different. The simple ceremony was so short, it seemed to be over almost before it had begun.

'That's it?' Harry asked himself, watching Lottie and Gordon Kinnon, the witnesses, signing the register. 'We're married?'

'We're married?' As her thoughts echoed his, Mae's great blue eyes were bewildered, but then she looked down at her finger and there it was – the wedding ring. She was Mrs Harry Alpin, and the priest was smiling at her, and so were Lottie and Gordon. She was the bride, Harry was the groom. It was time to walk together out into the sunshine.

The cathedral might have been empty of spectators, but outside there was a crowd. Mae, hanging on to Harry's slightly trembling arm, stopped short at the sight of so many faces and would have bent her head in its brimmed white hat, had not Lottie whispered to her to look up and SMILE.

'Smile, Mae, smile! For the photographer. Oh, you look so beautiful. Harry, doesn't she look the perfect bride?'

'Perfect,' he said hoarsely. 'But where on earth have these folk come from?'

There were theatricals and girls from the hostel. There were Harry's old friends. There were Miss Thorburn and Miss Dow. There was Mrs Beith, who'd been invited to the reception, and Tilda Tamsin and Maggie Sims, who had not. There were women from other tenements in the Row, and passers-by; there were children waiting for coppers, and the inquisitive woman from the newsagent's. There was even Dr Rick, but he was carrying his bag and must have been on his way to a patient.

He waved, though, and shouted 'Good luck' with the rest of the crowd, and Mae, now wreathed in smiles which were not just for the photographer, whispered to Harry that she could not believe so many people had come along just to see them wed.

'You're the attraction, sweetheart,' he whispered back. 'You're the prettiest bride ever.'

It was true, for though she was not wearing the traditional bridal gown with veil, the white two-piece Mrs Ness had made for her, with its elaborately stitched top and fashionable longer skirt, was in itself a perfect wedding outfit. She felt right in it, she knew she looked her best, and what more could a bride be wanting? Sure, when she'd put on her white hat and pinned on her white carnations, she'd even forgotten Harry's people. This was her special day, and his, and nothing would be allowed to spoil it.

'Get going, Harry, lad,' said Gordon, his heavily-built old schoolfriend. 'It's time for the party, eh?'

'And we haven't far to go!' cried Lottie, who was looking elegant in grey silk with a great picture hat that would have not have been out of place at a Holyrood garden-party. 'Isn't it lucky, having the theatre so close to the cathedral?'

'Always did wonder why they built it next-door,' said Harry, smiling and throwing handfuls of coins for the children to run after. Then, to the accompaniment of cheers from the crowd, taking Mae's hand, he led the little wedding party into the Queen's.

Two people were late for the reception. They didn't know each other, but when Stan Morris, the doorkeeper, asked if they were for the wedding party, the young red-haired woman and the middle-aged man both exchanged hesitant smiles. 'Oh, yes,' they replied.

'Expected, then?'

'I was invited,' said the young woman.

'So was I,' said the man. 'No' sure I'm expected though.'

Sam raised his eyebrows, but motioned them through the vestibule. 'Straight through the auditorium and you'll see 'em all on the stage,' he told them.

'On the stage,' they repeated, moving slowly away together.

What a strange thing it seemed, to see so many people standing with plates of food and glasses of wine on the stage of the Queen's! The music had not yet begun for the dancing, but there

160

was enough noise coming from the wedding guests to fill the theatre anyway, and under its cover, the two latecomers moved down the aisle.

If anyone had been watching, they might have given the impression that they didn't want to be seen, but for some time no one paid them any attention anyway. Until Gareth suddenly spotted the two figures standing at the foot of the steps to the stage, and he came bounding down.

'Hello, there! Come to join us?' His dark gaze moved from the man to the young woman where it stayed. 'No formality, no announcing, but shall I tell Harry and Mae you're here?'

They didn't answer; didn't need to, for Harry had come running, followed by Mae, and they had taken the newcomers' hands and were crying their names.

'Dad? You came, then!' gasped Harry. 'I canna believe it, just canna believe it!'

'Sandy?' whispered Mae. 'Oh, I'm so glad to see you! I never thought I would. And Mr Alpin?' She turned to Harry's father and took his hand. 'Thank you. Thank you for coming. You cannot know what this means to us.'

He shook his handsome head and cleared his throat.

'Och, I thought to maself, whatever Emmy says, whatever Rona says – I'll see ma son on his wedding day, so I will. And here I am.'

'Me, too,' said Sandy. 'I knew I had to come, and I'm that glad I did. Mae, you look so lovely. And is this your Harry, then?'

'I've seen you before,' he told her. 'On a very special day.'

'Where?'

'At a tram stop.' He grinned. 'Never mind, it's a long story. But meet ma dad, eh? Dad, this is Sandy.'

'And may I be introduced to Sandy?' asked Gareth, bringing forward glasses of wine. 'Come and have something to eat before the speeches.'

'Aye, Dad,' Harry said fondly. 'Come with me, eh? Just come with me.'

The cake was cut and passed around. Mr Standish's speech in praise of the young couple was short but witty, and Harry's words of thanks were short but heartfelt. He and Mae would never forget the kindness of those from the theatre – and here he glanced at

161

Mae and asked her to stand so that they could drink their own toast.

'To all at the Queen's,' they said together and drank their sparkling wine.

'Very nice!' cried Mrs Ness. 'But it's us should be drinking a toast to you. Come on, then, everybody – be upstanding for the bride and groom!'

'The bride and groom,' rang out the voices, including Ben Alpin's, as Mae gave a radiant smile and Harry put his arm around her.

'Are you no' ready for the dancing?' asked the fiddler, deciding to get these folks on with what mattered. 'Shall we start oor playing noo?'

'Aye, come on, lads!' cried a sceneshifter. 'Let's get to work.'

With practised ease, the men cleared the stage and when the transformation was complete, Harry was told by Mrs Ness to take Mae's hand and open the dancing.

'Our wedding waltz,' he whispered, looking down at her with such love in his eyes, the onlookers sighed. 'Ah Mae, I'm so happy.'

And as he led her on to the cleared stage, his gaze went to his watching father and he smiled.

They could not stay dancing long, they had to catch their train for Liverpool, the first stop on the journey to Cork, where they were to spend a night at Mrs Fitzgerald's, before travelling on to Traynore. Soon, they had to say their goodbyes and make their thanks. There was a flurry of embraces and kisses, tears and handshakes, as a taxi waited for them at the stage door, and then there was only Ben to hug again.

'Take care, Dad,' said Harry huskily. 'We'll no' be gone that long, you ken.'

'Aye.' Ben lowered his eyes. 'You'll no' expect—' He stopped.

'I'll no' expect anything. It's just good that you came. That's what we'll remember.'

'All we'll remember,' said Mae.

She kissed Ben's cheek, Harry shook his hand, and then they were in the moving taxi with confetti raining around them, and people laughing and running to cry goodbye.

'Good luck, good luck!' Miss Thorburn was calling, and Lottie, her picture hat askew, was waving, as Mrs Ness, surprisingly ran the fastest after the taxi, until Sandy caught her up and became the last face they saw before being borne away.

'It's over,' Harry said in a low voice. 'We're wed. How are you feeling, sweetheart?'

'You're asking?' Mae smiled and pressed his hand. 'You know how I am feeling.'

'I should,' he agreed. 'I feel the same.'

'Waverley, eh?' asked the taxi-driver. As though he didn't know. 'Better get rid o' that confetti, eh? Before you catch the train.'

'Och, no,' said Harry, with a grin. 'We like it. We like being newly-weds.'

'Make the most o' that feeling, then,' the driver laughed. 'Doesnae last long.'

How could he say that? The way they felt then was the way they would feel for the rest of their lives. Of that, they could not have been more certain.

Chapter Thirty-Eight

Maybe a lumpy bed in a Liverpool boarding house was not the best way to begin a honeymoon, but neither Mae nor Harry had much idea what the bed was like, except that it was a place where they could make love.

'Thank God, I need never leave you again,' Harry said softly, as Mae lay against him. 'Remember how I used to have to go up the stair and leave you at your door? You'll never know what that cost me, sweetheart.'

'Sure, and you're wrong about that,' she whispered, running her hand down his body so close to hers. 'Cost me as much, so it did.'

'And you a prim little Irish girl! I never thought you'd any idea.'

'Everybody has an idea, I'm thinking.'

'Ideas, though, they're no' the same, eh?' He was a little worried and trying not to show it. 'I mean, as the real thing. You were no' disappointed, Mae? It meant so much to me, I wanted it to be the same for you.'

She was silent, thinking about her first experience of love. Harry had been so sweet, so careful; she had been so excited. Had it been the same for her as for him? Maybe not, but it would be. It would be.

And in the nights that followed, so it was.

Harry loved Ireland. True, it was very different from Scotland, but there was its charm. He'd been told there was Georgian architecture in Dublin, not unlike the buildings of Edinburgh's New Town, and certainly Cork, where Mrs Fitzgerald had made them

164

so welcome, was a fine city like many another. But the country-side, as far as he could tell, was special to Ireland.

A land in miniature, the cabins and whitewashed cottages so low and small; the bright green fields a patchwork of pocket handkerchiefs, as Mae had once described them. There were the isolated 'big' houses of the quality and, of course, the churches, but even the hills seemed softer, less rugged than Scottish hills, and there were no hills round Traynore, anyway. Only the sea, creaming along the shore, looking so innocent, although of course Harry knew of its power.

He couldn't get over the number of pubs in the village, in one of which Mae's da had booked them a room. Sure, Joseph O'Donovan had said, his little house was no place for a honey-moon couple – well, not with him in it, anyway, and where would he have gone?

'To Annie's?' Mae had asked demurely, but he'd laughed and said was it shaming him in front of his son-in-law she was after? One of these days, he and Annie would be man and wife, but the truth of it was that they'd not got round to the service yet. So, Mae and Harry'd be better off at Joe Durkin's, where Peg Durkin had made them up a bed with the best sheets and bits of lavender, he'd been told, and she'd cook them grand meals, for wasn't she taking in paying guests these days and knew just what to do?

It was in the lavender-smelling sheets, then, that Mae and Harry spent their wonderful nights, and by day, toured the countryside in a pony and cart, meeting Mae's old friends, visiting Skibbereen, Baltimore, and Roaring Water Bay, taking boat trips to Sherkin Island where they walked on white sand and collected shells, or circled Cape Clear and the Fastnet Rock.

'This is all so grand, Mae, how come you could leave it?' asked Harry, then bit his lip, for he knew why she had left it, and had promised himself he would never mention Kieran Connor, or even think of him. Even when he'd seen the name Connor on one of the pubs, he'd managed not to ask if that was Kieran's father's pub, and Mae had kept silent.

She said nothing of Kieran Connor now, but she did tell Harry gently that what he saw was what the tourists saw. Beauty, yes, but a fine covering over hardship, and in Skibbereen, for instance, the

165

covering was thin, for the children had no shoes and the women in shawls had the faces of the poor.

'Still, you've got your independence, eh? Maybe the fellas in charge'll get something done, one of these days.' Harry gave a wry smile. 'They say our new Labour government's got great plans for clearing slums, but I bet you they'll be in London, eh?'

'I thought you were after telling me there'd been progress in Edinburgh?'

'Some, but slow. Awful slow.'

'Ah, and isn't Ireland the same?' Mae shook her head. 'But we can be thanking God the troubles are over. Peace is a grand thing, so it is.'

Folk in the village were complimentary about Harry, even though he was 'from away' and didn't go to Mass, and as for Annie next door, she thought him a dream.

'Sure, and he's a lovely man,' she told Mae. 'And steady, I'm thinking. 'Tis the sense you've found at last, Mae, to put that Connor boy out of your mind and take a man that'll be no worry to you.'

More important, though, to Mae was what her father was thinking.

'You like him, Da?' she asked one evening, as they sat outside the cottage in the summer dusk, while Harry made himself useful, mending a lamp for Annie next door.

''Tis a fine man, he is,' Joseph answered gravely. 'A man to be trusted.'

Mae's eyes rested on her father's face. His words were what she wanted to hear; his eyes, though, were looking away, towards the line of the sea.

'And you like him?' she persisted.

'I do. I'll be saying nothing against him.' He paused. 'But, there's a little darkness there, mavourneen. For himself, I'm meaning. Not you.'

'A darkness? What sort of darkness?'

'A little discontent, maybe, with this life.'

'Discontent? No, Da.' Mae hesitated. ''Tis true, he was wanting to be an actor one time, but he never speaks of that now. He has forgotten it.'

166

'Because he is happy with you?' Joseph smiled and shrugged. 'Maybe I am wrong, then.'

'Yes, Da, you are mistaken. There is no darkness in Harry. He is happy. He has never been so happy.'

'Sure, a man on his honeymoon should be happy.' Joseph plucked a flower from the fuchsias that grew wild about the cottage. 'Take care, though, Mae. Look after him.'

'Look after him?' She laughed uneasily. 'I'm thinking we'll look after each other.'

'That's the way,' he agreed, after a pause. 'Man and wife, is what you are. And lucky.'

She laid her hand on his, knowing he was thinking of her mother, dead for so long. He had Annie, and Annie was sweet and generous – hadn't she looked after him all these years? And look at the beautiful embroidered tablecloth she had given Mae for a wedding present! But she wasn't his Katie, any more than he was her Liam, lost at sea, they both knew that.

At Mae's touch, he smiled now, with a shake of his head, and pressed the fuchsia flower into his buttonhole.

'Here comes your man,' he whispered. 'And Annie is pleased with him – see her smile. 'Twas me supposed to be mending that lamp, I am ashamed to tell you.'

'Such a marvel you have here, Mae!' cried Annie, bustling up, with Harry smiling self-consciously at her side. 'Has himself not fixed that lamp for me, and set the leg on my chair and the handle on my cupboard?'

'Was a pleasure,' Harry murmured, taking Mae's hands and pulling her to her feet. 'And didn't take five minutes. Shall we be walking back, Mae?'

She looked into his dear face, then glanced quickly at her father. No darkness, her look said. Where is the darkness, Da? As Joseph said nothing, she put her hand into Harry's arm.

'Let's go back,' she agreed. 'The evening's nearly gone.'

'Soon have to be going home,' Harry murmured, as they lay together in their lavender sheets after making love. 'Will you be sorry, sweetheart?'

'Sorry? No! Why would I be sorry to be going home with you?'

'Well, this is your home, too. Here, where your dad is, and all you remember.' He played with her dark hair. 'You might be homesick.'

'I'll be sorry to leave my da, but I am over being homesick.' She hugged him close. 'My home's with you now, Harry.'

He lay staring into the darkness. 'Just want you to be happy in Victoria Row,' he said after a silence. 'Just hope it'll be all right, eh?'

''Twill be all right,' she said firmly. 'We'll make it so.'

'Aye.'

But for some time, they lay awake, thinking of how they might make it all right, hoping they could. In the morning, in the sunlight, they felt better.

'Strange, how problems melt away in the daylight,' said Mae, finding a fresh white blouse to wear.

'What problems?' asked Harry. 'Ah, Mae, do you have to put those clothes on, eh?'

'Can you see Peg Durkin serving me my breakfast without them?'

They fell into each other's arms, laughing, and were late for Peg's breakfast, anyway.

Chapter Thirty-Nine

It was raining when they returned home, which allowed Mae to blame her low spirits on the weather, though in truth she knew she was apprehensive about seeing Harry's family again. Back in Ireland, she had declared that everything would be all right at Victoria Row, she and Harry would make it so – and she'd meant it. Yet coming back now, all that was in her mind was the memory of Emmy's pinched little face, and Rona's hard stare. Supposing the two of them were waiting, when she and Harry came in the door?

Ah, now, that was a foolish thought, for why should they be waiting? In fact, the only person waiting when Harry carried their cases into the hall, was Kenny Sims, who was batting a ball up and down the stair.

'Where've you been?' he cried, running down. 'What's in thae cases?'

'We've been on holiday,' said Harry. 'Our clothes are in the cases. Folk have to take clothes on holiday, eh?'

'Never have a holiday,' Kenny retorted, bouncing his ball. 'Did you bring us onything back?'

'Here's a penny for you, if you'll run back up home, eh?'

Kenny didn't hesitate. He snatched the penny and made off up the stair, leaving Mae to smile and ask why Harry had wanted him out of the way.

'Can you no' guess?' Harry, turning the key in the lock of the flat, swung her into his arms and carried her into the flat. 'Have you no' heard that the bridegroom has to carry the bride over the threshold into their house?'

'Ah, 'tis a lovely idea,' she said breathlessly, as he set her down. 'But I'm glad no one was here.'

They stood together, looking round their home, which had been left beautifully and surprisingly tidy by Lottie, and which now seemed such a haven, Mae felt a rush of relief.

'There's just the two of us here,' she whispered. 'Is it not the best thing in the world?'

'Aye, I've dreamed of it. Being alone with you, in our own home.'

They held each other quietly, thinking of it, then Mae broke free and began to walk about her domain, which was so familiar and yet new, because now it was Harry's, too.

'Oh, look, Lottie's left us groceries!' she cried, finding a box of food on the kitchen table, together with two bottles of milk. 'And a note!'

Dear Newlyweds, (Lottie had written in her small hand.) Welcome back! I've done my best to leave everything in apple-pie order, and hope it's all right for you. Some things to keep you going are in the box on the table, and I've put sheets on your bed. Now I'm installed in Thea's flat, so, please, please, let me know if you need anything. Poor darlings, do you really have to come back to work tomorrow? Can't wait to see you. All my love, Lottie.

'Oh, she is so sweet!' cried Mae, passing the letter to Harry, who frowned.

'Och, typical Lottie,' he muttered. 'Typical actress's style, eh?'

''Tis a nice style, though?'

'Who else in the world would ever call me "poor darling"? I ask you?'

'Why, I might! Are we not poor darlings, then, having to end our honeymoon?'

Harry's brow cleared and he laughed. 'What gave you the idea our honeymoon's ending?'

With more hugs and kisses to exchange, it was some time before they could unpack their cases, put together a meal, and inspect the bed with its crisp sheets newly laundered at Lottie's expense.

'But no going to bed yet,' said Mae firmly. 'First, I must wash up and leave everything tidy. As Lottie said, we've to go to work tomorrow.'

170

'Are you sure you're happy about that?' asked Harry. 'I mean, going to work? Married women usually stay at home.'

'Sure, we've discussed it often enough, Harry. What would I do all day in this little flat? Mrs Ness wants me to stay on and I want to stay on, too.'

'As long as you're happy, that's fine with me.' Harry gazed into her eyes, long and significantly. 'Might have to give up work anyway, one of these days.'

'One of these days, I will.'

'Because I want a wee lassie, just like you.'

'What if I want a little boy just like you?'

'We'll have twins, eh? One of each.'

'Sounds so easy.' Mae laughed and took up an empty milk bottle. 'I'll just put this out for tomorrow morning – tell the milkman what we need.'

Standing on the step, she took a deep breath of the fresh, damp air. The rain had stopped and there was a faint late sunlight gilding the Queen's opposite, and the taller, blackened buildings of the cathedral beyond. What an age it seemed since her wedding. Since she'd stood on the stage of the theatre and welcomed so many people come to wish her and Harry well. Sandy had been one and her arrival had been a lovely surprise, just like Harry's father's. Surely, his coming was a good omen? Harry had said not to expect too much, but Mae could not help hoping.

She sighed and turned to go back to Harry, smiling as she moved into the house; then her smile faded. Rona was coming out.

'Same idea, I see,' said Mae, clearing her throat.

'What?' Rona's dark hazel eyes were expressionless.

'Putting your milk bottles out. Like me.'

Rona took a step forward. 'If you'll let me get by?'

'We've just come home. We are settling in.'

'I'm no' interested.'

'Rona, can we not be friends? You were friendly before – can things not be the same between us again?'

'Just let me put ma bottles out, please.'

Mae put her hand on Rona's arm. 'Will you be telling me what I've done, then? Apart from marrying your brother?'

'That's what you've done.' Rona, pushing past Mae, thumped her bottles to the step outside, and came back. 'Can you no' see that that's what's wrong? Aye, we were friendly enough before, but no' now. Never again.'

For some time, Mae stood quite still, staring at Rona's door through which she'd vanished, banging it behind her. It was only when Harry came to call her that she smiled, straightened her shoulders, and returned to the flat.

'What's up?' asked Harry. 'Did I hear you talking out there?'

'To Rona.'

His lips tightened. 'And what did she say?'

Mae shrugged. 'Nothing new.'

'Doesn't want to be friends?'

'Seems so.'

Harry put his arms round her. 'As you say, nothing new. We weren't expecting anything good from Rona.'

'I was, in a way. Because of your dad, you see.'

'I told you what he did would make no difference to the others.'

'I am still hoping you are wrong.'

'Even after what happened just now? You might have to wait a long time, my darling.'

'I'll wait, then.'

He held her at arm's length, studying her face, then relaxed, and let her go.

'Come to bed,' he said softly. 'We can wash first – I'm boiling kettles for the bath. How'd you like to scrub ma back?'

'Think we'll ever have a bathroom like Mrs Beith?' Mae asked as they washed in the tub, each taking a turn, because, however much they wished it, they couldn't fit in together.

'Certainly! I'm due for a rise next month. We could afford a bit more rent, move somewhere bigger, if you like, and maybe have a bathroom.'

'We said we'd stay here.'

'If it's what you want.'

'For now, anyway.'

He sighed deeply, knowing what was in her mind, then leaped out of the bath, sending a rush of water over the mat, and wrapped himself in the towel Mae had laid ready.

'Come on, beauty – let's get to those lovely sheets, eh?'

Oh, but the lovely, crackling sheets were cold! Even after their lovemaking, they were still shivering and could not sleep.

172

'Should've put a hot bottle in,' said Mae. 'These sheets need airing.'

'Why are women always talking about airing?' asked Harry drowsily. 'Nae bother, we'll be warm in a minute.'

They lay quietly for some moments, then Mae said into the darkness.

'I said we'd make things all right in Victoria Row, Harry, and we will. I am not one to be giving in.'

'I knew you were thinking of that. Come on, try to sleep. It's our first night in our own home, remember.'

'In the meantime, we have each other,' she went on, not listening.

'All that matters. Goodnight, sweetheart.'

'Goodnight, dear Harry.'

Suddenly, wonderfully, they were warm, content, and ready to sleep. And slept.

Chapter Forty

'Poor darlings' that they were, they managed to get themselves back to work the following morning, feeling that they'd been away for ever. Yet, nothing had changed. The same highly charged atmosphere of backstage theatre was there to surround them; the same noises – hammerings and banging, laughter and arguments – greeted them.

Lottie's welcome, of course, was extravagant, and everyone wanted to know, with jokes and grins, if they'd enjoyed Ireland, and had a 'good time', while Vivvy Bryce and Sally Anderson, trying on costumes, kept giving Mae strange looks, which she quite understood.

She was a married woman now. How had it been, then, on the honeymoon? They were dying to ask, but with Mrs Ness pinning and cutting around them and her knowing eyes gleaming, didn't dare to get the words out. Mae, much amused, didn't help them. Anyway, she'd too much to do.

'What a pile of work I've saved for you, dear,' Mrs Ness had exclaimed as she'd walked through the door, and unlike young Vivvy and Sally, had not needed to ask how Mae had fared on honeymoon.

'Anyone can see you and Harry have been up there in the sky, floating, eh? What a shame, you've to come down to earth, but, there it is, happens to us all. Now, they're doing that *Vanity Fair* adaptation week after next, so there's a load of old dresses here to sort through and mend, and then we can start fitting the girls when they've a minute.'

When Vivvy and Sally had taken themselves off, Gareth came in, supposedly needing sleeve alterations to his costume, but actually wanting to talk to Mae. Mrs Ness had just gone up to have a word with Tim Powell, and as Gareth bent his head over Mae, she did wonder if he'd been waiting until he could find her alone. As soon as he asked, keeping his voice down, for her friend's address, she knew she was right.

'Which friend are you meaning, then?' she asked, looking at him with her limpid blue gaze.

'Ah, you know the one I mean – that pretty red-haired girl who came to your reception. I danced with her a couple of times, as a matter of fact, and she told me her name was Sandy, but that was all.'

'Sandy,' Mae repeated and looked down at the jacket he had given her.

'Yes, and I tried to find her at the end of the dancing, but she'd gone. I thought you'd know where she lives.'

'You were wanting to ask her out?'

He gave a self-conscious grin. 'Why not? She's a very attractive girl.'

'Would you like to try these sleeves, Gareth? Then I can check the length for you.'

'You're not answering my question, Mae. Where does Sandy live? And what's her other name?'

'She's a very private sort of girl,' Mae answered slowly, as she studied his sleeves. 'I'm thinking I should ask her first, before I tell you her address.'

'I'm a perfectly respectable character, you know.' His dark eyes were flashing. 'All I want is to give her dinner, perhaps go dancing. Where's the harm?'

'I will see what she says, and let you know.'

He stared at her for a moment, then shrugged. 'All right, then. But do your best. I really want to see her again.'

'Now Gareth Paget, what are you doing here?' cried Mrs Ness, sweeping back into Wardrobe. 'Not those sleeves again, is it? They fit perfectly well and you know it. Mae, you've enough to do without making unnecessary alterations.'

'OK, forget it.' Gareth, snatching back his jacket and flinging up his dark head, made a stormy, theatrical exit, at which Mrs Ness laughed.

'What's he up to, I wonder? You can never tell what these folk have got into their heads.'

But Mae, hurriedly beginning work on a dress for *Vanity Fair*, did not tell Mrs Ness what Gareth Paget had in his head. She was already worried about it.

'What should I do?' she asked Harry, when they went home at the end of the morning for a sandwich.

'About Gareth Paget, you mean?' Harry had already heard the story of what Gareth wanted. 'Nothing, is my advice. You canna put him in touch with Sandy, Mae. That'd never do.'

Mae, slicing ham left by Lottie, flushed a little. 'You are saying she is not suitable?'

'Of course she's no' suitable. Can you see Gareth calling at the Cowgate? With thae children, you told me about, and one of 'em hers?'

''Tis a snobbish way of looking at things, Harry.'

'OK, maybe Gareth could put up with the Cowgate. But no' with the wee laddie.' Harry took the sandwich Mae passed him and looked inside. 'Any mustard? Nae bother – maybe you could get some, eh? What I'm saying is, that no' many fellas want to take on another man's son, specially when the mother was no' married to his father. Be sensible, Mae.'

'She might not want to be involved with Gareth, anyway. Sandy is proud.'

'No' too proud to earn her living stripping off for artists.'

'I should not have told you about that. But she is thinking of her family.'

'You can make excuses for her if you like, just don't give Gareth her address, eh?'

Mae slowly ate her sandwich. 'I might just write to her and tell her about him. Is it for us to decide what they want to do?'

'Suit yourself, then, but I'd stay out of it. Shall I make the tea? I have to be getting back.'

'I want to get in touch, anyway. Sandy did come to the reception, and I think that's a sign she wants to see me again.'

'Shouldn't bet on it. At least she's taken your mind off troubles at Number Eight, eh?'

'I am not thinking of any troubles.'

'That's the way.'

After Harry had left, Mae, who had a little more time, quickly dashed off a note to Sandy and put it into the pillar box on her way back to work. Would it ever be delivered to that shabby door in the Cowgate? She could only hope for the best.

Days went by, and Mae never set eyes on Emmy Alpin, or Rona, though Ben, going out to work one morning, had given her a sheepish grin, and sometimes Rona's little girls, leaving for school, would smile like their grandfather, but never speak. Would things always be this way?

To please Harry, she no longer talked about her hopes for reconciliation, especially after he'd swallowed his pride and gone up to see his mother, only to be met with frost as cold as Christmas, as he put it. He had married the Irish girl and made his choice, Emmy had declared; he need not expect to be a part of his family as he had been before.

'I told you,' he muttered to Mae. 'She'll no' come round.'

''Tis early days,' was all the comfort she could find.

Neither of them had said any more, and Mae had worked hard to put the Alpins from her mind for the time being and think of other things. Sandy's failure to reply to Mae's letter, for instance. Had she ever received it? Meanwhile, Gareth Paget kept making excuses to come into Wardrobe and give Mae dark looks, until Mrs Ness said he was getting on her nerves and pushed him out.

Chapter Forty-One

It was a relief, one humid August day, when Sam, the doorman, came round to tell Mae she had a visitor and she guessed at once who it was. Aye, a ginger-haired lassie, Sam said, didnae give her name. Mae's eyes flew to Mrs Ness, who raised her eyebrows.

'That redhead who came to your reception?' she asked. 'Looks like she lives on fresh air? Better see her, Mae, before she fades away like the Cheshire cat.'

'Oh, Mae!' cried Sandy, stamping out her cigarette at the stage door, when she saw Mae hurrying towards her. 'Och, I'm glad you could come, eh? I thought you'd mebbe be too busy.'

'You had my letter?' asked Mae, noting Sandy's anxious eyes.

'Aye, it's why I wanted to see you.' Sandy was looking about her with such unease, Mae drew her away from the theatre and along to a bench in front of the cathedral.

'Let's sit here a minute, and tell me what's the matter. No need to worry about Gareth Paget. He's rehearsing, he's nowhere near.'

'Thank God for that. I dinna want to see him, Mae, I dinna want to be involved. No offence, but there it is. Promise me, you'll no' tell him where I live?'

'Sure, I'll never tell him at all, if that's what you want.' Mae hesitated. 'He's a nice fellow, Sandy.'

'I ken fine what he's like.' Sandy shrugged. 'Just tell him I'm no' interested, eh?'

'I will, but he'll be very disappointed. Being so attracted to you.'

'If I went out with him, there'd only be trouble.' Sandy stood up. 'I'd better let you go, Mae. Dinna want you to be getting wrong, because o' me.' She gave a sudden smile. 'Feel better, now I've seen you. I know I can trust you.'

'Always.' Mae hesitated. 'Listen, forgive me for asking again, but will you not reconsider my idea?'

'What idea?'

'That you'd go back to sewing. Dressmaking, or maybe tailoring. I could help you.'

Sandy sighed. 'I know you mean well, Mae, and I'm grateful, but it's no' for me just now. I've got the lassie I wanted to help Ma, and things are better. We're managing fine.'

'You could go to evening classes, you know. Maybe spare an hour or two to brush up on the tailoring?'

'Evenings are no' ma best time. Let's leave this, eh?'

'I'm hoping to get my own machine soon,' Mae pressed on. 'You could come and practise sometimes.'

'Aye, and what'd your Harry'd think o' me taking up your time? That reminds me, Mae, I never asked you about your honeymoon and going to Ireland. I can tell it was lovely, you look so well. Pretty as a picture.'

How smoothly she has changed the subject, thought Mae. Miss Thorburn was right, she's one to leave alone.

All the same she could not resist catching Sandy's arm as they said goodbye.

'Sandy, if you ever need me – you will call on me?'

'Now, why are you worrying? I can take care o' maself.' Sandy laughed shortly. 'Folk like me have to, you ken.'

'You promise, though?'

'I promise.' Sandy moved briskly away, looking back only once. 'Keep in touch, eh?'

'Everything all right with Copperknob?' Mrs Ness asked with interest, when Mae returned to Wardrobe.

'Sure, she's fine.'

'What's she wanting you to do for her?'

'Nothing,' Mae answered, with truth.

'I can believe that. She looks the type to go her own way. Didn't I see Gareth Paget dancing with her at your wedding? Seemed a bit smitten.'

Mae made no reply. She was wondering how smitten Gareth would take the news she had to give him.

'Just not interested?' he repeated, giving her the full power of the

179

smouldering dark eyes that transfixed the gallery. 'That's all she said? She wasn't interested?'

'I was telling you, you know, that she's a very private person,' Mae answered, doing her best to make him feel better. 'I'm sure she likes you—'

'Did she say so?'

'Well, no, but—'

'But nothing. She didn't think me attractive enough, even to have dinner with, eh?' Gareth laughed. 'That cuts me down to size. Heartthrob Gareth, that's me, I don't think. Looks like I'd better start playing character roles from now on.'

''Tis a lot you're making of this, Gareth,' Mae was driven to say at last, and his eyes flashed.

'All right, I'll say no more about it. If she's not interested, she's not interested. I daresay I'll survive, if one girl doesn't want to go out with me.'

He was dramatising the situation, of course, as actors always did, but his hurt was none the less real for that. Mae longed to reach out, take his hand and give him Sandy's address, but never in the world would she do it.

Poor Gareth. Poor Sandy. When Harry came to collect her at teatime, Mae hugged him hard in front of Mrs Ness, and when they were walking across the street, whispered in his ear.

'Oh Harry, are we not the lucky ones? To have found each other?'

'Hey, what's brought this on?' he asked, laughing, but pleased.

'I just feel so glad that nothing came between us and that we are wed.'

'You mean, we didn't let anything come between us, eh?'

They had reached the door of Number Eight, where usually Mae braced herself, in case there were those in the hall she might not want to see. Or, who might not want to see her. Tonight, though, she walked in proudly, willing to meet anyone. This was her place. Harry was her husband. And, as she had said, they were the lucky ones, whatever was thought up the stair.

'Quick, now, Harry, and be letting us in,' she told him, and he smiled as he opened the door to the flat.

'Want me to carry you over the threshold again, Mae?'

'I cannot say I am still a bride, Harry.'

'You'll always be a bride to me, sweetheart.'

'A wife, I'm thinking.'

'Even better, then. More settled, eh?'

'Settled. 'Tis a grand word, that.'

'Why are we standing here, talking?' Harry took her hand and together they went into the flat that was their home, and closed the door.

Part Three

Chapter Forty-Two

On a bright April day in 1931, Mae and Harry were at home, having something to eat at lunchtime and sharing the newspaper. Its headlines made a contrast with the weather.

'Three million unemployed,' Harry read aloud. He lowered his sheet of the paper and looked at Mae. 'My God, what's happening?'

In fact, he knew what was happening, and had been happening ever since the New York stock market crashed in October 1929. No country had been left untouched by the catastrophe. Businesses had failed across the world; markets for goods had disappeared; all the great industries – shipbuilding, coal, manufacturing – were suffering.

In Britain, gaunt-faced men with no jobs to go to gathered on street corners, while desperate women at home tried to care for their families with no money coming in. Charities were doing what they could, but the lack of action from the government was already embittering those who only wanted the right to work.

'Oh, I feel so guilty,' murmured Mae, rising to clear away their plates. 'We have our wages, Harry. We are not being touched by this cold wind.'

'Aye, seems we're in the right job.' Harry tossed his paper aside and lit a cigarette. 'Folk have to have some relief, eh? We give it to 'em. They come to the theatre to forget their troubles. Same as going to the pictures.' He hesitated. 'Dad's no' in the right job, though.'

'Your father?' Mae looked stricken. 'He is out of work?'

'Laid off last week. Nobody wants electrical parts these days.' Harry drew on his cigarette. 'He's trying for a night-watchman's job, and Jake's doing short time at the brewery. Ma's in a state, so's Rona.'

'Your father was telling you this?'

'Aye. Had a pint together.'

Mae, without speaking, brought the kettle to the boil and made the tea. She knew that Harry and his father met from time to time, and was glad of it, but there was no sign of softening in Emmy's attitude, or Rona's. Even if the children still seemed willing to give Mae a smile, whenever she met their mother or grandmother, eyes were kept down and nothing was said.

She felt she was like a stone being worn away by something she could not change. Why not just give in, then? Abandon the idea of making herself part of Harry's family? She still could not accept that that might be best.

'Is the tea ready?' asked Harry, putting out his cigarette. 'Got to go in a minute.'

'Me, too.'

They drank the tea standing up with their jackets on, Harry eyeing Mae over the rim of his cup, she looking away, knowing what he would ask.

'No news, I suppose?' He set down the cup.

'You know there is not. And I'd have said, anyway.'

'Well, you might no' have been sure. Might be waiting, to say.'

'There is nothing to say.'

He gave a long sigh. 'You'd have thought we'd have started a bairn by now.'

'We've not been married long at all.'

'Most folk have one in the first year.'

'Most, but not everyone.' Mae put on her hat. 'Look, Harry, now is not the time to be worrying. A child will come. We must just be patient.'

He put their cups in the sink, his brow darkening. 'Some might say we were better off no' bringing children into a world like this, but I canna agree. Every man wants a son – it's natural.'

'I thought you were wanting a lassie like me,' Mae said, trying to lighten his mood. 'Seems now it's a son you are after.'

Harry did manage a grin and caught her to him. 'Aye, but a wee lassie'd do. Let's hope we're lucky soon, eh?'

'We are already lucky,' she answered, as they left the house.

* * *

186

Mrs Ness was not in Wardrobe when Mae returned, but Lottie, who was walking about the room with a nervous spring in her step, said she'd just had a telephone call and gone out.

'Which is fine,' Lottie added, 'because I wanted to talk to you, Mae.'

'Something to alter, is it?'

'No, nothing like that. It's – well – I've some news. I'm going down to London, for an audition.'

'London?' Mae stared. 'What audition?'

'For RADA. You know, the Royal Academy of Dramatic Art.' Lottie clasped her hands together and looked soulful. 'I'm not even hoping, but, oh, it would be so wonderful if I were accepted.'

'This is the place that teaches you how to act? But, Lottie, you can act already. What is there for you to learn?'

Lottie burst into laughter. 'Oh, Mae! I shall be learning all my life! No, it was Mr Standish's idea. He told me I was doing very well here and he could give me better roles, but I've the chance to get to the top and RADA could help me. If they take me, of course.'

'Sure, they'll take you! Isn't everyone certain you are going to be a star?'

'I wouldn't say that. Just keep your fingers crossed for me at the audition on Tuesday week.'

'But if you leave us, what will we do without you? Specially Brett?'

'Oh, Brett will probably leave as well. He's keen to try his luck in London.'

'Keen to follow you.'

Lottie shrugged. 'Maybe, but we have our careers to think about. I'd better go. Don't want to get into trouble with Mrs Ness for wasting your time.'

'I wonder where she went?' asked Mae.'

'I've no idea, but she'll catch me loitering, if I don't go now.'

Another half hour passed before Mrs Ness came back, her face rather flushed and her eyes very bright.

'So sorry, dear,' she said to Mae, breathing hard, her double chin quivering. 'You must've been wondering what'd happened to me.'

'Lottie said you'd had a telephone call. Not bad news, is it?'

'Oh, no, not at all!' Mrs Ness, perching on a stool at her work-table, fanned herself with her hat. 'An old friend has just arrived back in Edinburgh from what you call foreign parts. Rangoon, to be exact. Had the nerve to ask me to run out and have a drink with him at the station.' She laughed. 'Naturally, I said yes, but don't you dare split on me to Mr Standish, Mae!'

'Mrs Ness, as though I would!'

'Of course not. Well, I wasn't away long, was I? And I must say it was nice to see old Ronnie again. Used to be a friend of my poor husband's, you know.'

Mrs Ness stood up and began to search in her bag until she came up with a peppermint. 'Better have one of these, in case any-body wants to confer about something. Oh, dear, I feel quite light-headed! I'll have to leave any cutting out to you, Mae – daren't trust myself with the scissors. Anybody been in while I was away?'

'Only Lottie, as I was saying.'

'Dear Lottie.' Mrs Ness sucked on her peppermint. 'Our name in lights girl. I heard a rumour she was trying for a RADA audition – don't know if it's true. Ah, you're not saying, so it is. Well, she'll probably get it, and then Brett Lester will leave with her, and that'll be three of 'em taking wing from the Queen's, counting Gareth Paget.'

'So many changes,' Mae murmured, narrowing her eyes as she threaded a needle.

'Always changes in a company like this, Mae. And Gareth was long enough dying to get away, wasn't he?'

'Was he?'

'Oh, yes, he was awful blue till he got the job at the Old Vic. I sometimes used to wonder what was up with him.' Mrs Ness slid off her stool and yawned and stretched. 'Must get on, I suppose. Talking of changes, though, the new man's lovely, eh? Such a strong jaw! No wonder the gallery's queuing at the stage door every night!'

The new man, Antony Vincent, was certainly an asset, thought Mae, stitching away at a doublet, but she rather missed Gareth's brooding heart to hearts about Sandy, and still brooded herself on her failure to bring those two together.

So, it was unrealistic, but Mae was never one to give up on the hopeless, which was why she still had her dreams of winning

188

round the Alpins. Sandy, however, had defeated her. There was nothing to be done for her, and indeed Mae had given up trying; they had not met for some time. As for Gareth, he had done the best thing for himself, by departing.

'Fresh woods and pastures new for me,' he had announced to Mae. 'There's nothing like London for giving a fellow a new lease of life.'

'You'll be missed,' she had told him.

'Missed? Don't you believe it. There's always somebody waiting in the wings.'

Brett Lester, thought Mae. But it had turned out to be the square-jawed Tony Vincent, who had stepped into Gareth's shoes.

'Ah, well, that's the way things are in this business,' Thea had said, when Brett moaned as though he were another Vivvy Bryce.

A hard business, thought Mae.

'Mae, are you listening to me?' she heard Mrs Ness's voice close by and gave a start.

'Sorry, Mrs Ness. Sure, I was dreaming there.'

'I was only asking – don't mean to pry – but you're not planning to leave me, are you?'

Mae, keeping her eyes on her work, snipped off a thread. 'No, I'm not planning to leave.'

'Had no luck, dear?'

'Not in the way you mean, Mrs Ness.'

'Plenty of time. No need to worry.'

'That's what I'm thinking.'

'There you are, then. Now, why don't you put our little kettle on and make us a cup of tea? Can't say why, but alcohol always makes me feel as parched as the desert sand. And shall we see if there are any biscuits in our tin? That's another thing about drinking – makes me so peckish!'

Chapter Forty-Three

'"Change and decay in all around I see".' Sang Mrs Beith, sweeping the stair two weeks later, until she saw Mae and Harry leaving to go to work, when she hurried down.

'Just a wee word,' she whispered, her eyes making the usual, covert scan of Mae's figure. 'Never seem to see you folk these days. All right, eh?'

'Very well, thanks,' said Harry, before Mae could speak. 'We're both very well. Just got to rush, you ken.'

'Lucky, then, you've somewhere to go. Did you see in the paper – three million unemployed we've got now? Ma laddie would've been out o' the army by now, if he could've found a job, but looks like he'll have to stay in. Canna wait till he gets some leave.' Mrs Beith leaned on her broom, shaking her head. 'But where I'll put Pauline when he does, I dinna ken, because he'll want his room, eh?'

'Nice talking to you, Mrs Beith,' Harry said, firmly steering Mae towards the door. 'We have to go, or we'll be late.'

'I'll come and see you one day, Mrs Beith,' Mae said quickly. 'I promise.'

She felt bad as she said the words, for she had said the same to Miss Thorburn, when she'd promised to look in on the hostel any time she could, but Harry had not made that easy; she had only rarely been back.

Now here was Harry standing on the pavement, almost pawing the ground, but Mrs Beith still held Mae's attention with a deeply sympathetic gaze.

'Things no better with Emmy, then?' she asked in a low voice. 'What a way to behave, eh? And Rona, and all? There's enough misery in the world, without them adding to it, I say, what with Jake on short time and Ben a night-watchman. And him a qualified electrician – is it no' a disgrace?'

'Mae!' called Harry, and Mae, smiling apologetically, pressed Mrs Beith's hand and ran.

'What a chatterbox,' Harry muttered, striding along. 'She'd keep you all day, if she could, eh?'

'She's lonely, Harry. Her lodger's at work, she never sees any-one.'

'Och, she sees the neighbours, ma mother for one.' Harry smiled wryly. 'Of course, they spend their time arguing, that's ten-ement life for you. But when Mrs B's laddie comes home, she'll be OK. The sun shines for him, you ken.'

'"Change and decay all around I see",' sang Mae, as they reached the theatre. 'Is that not a very gloomy hymn she was singing, though?'

'Sums up the world at the moment, I guess.'

'And the Queen's – the change, I'm meaning, not the decay.' Mae kissed Harry's cheek as he prepared to depart for Lighting and she for Wardrobe. 'Wonder if Lottie will be making changes? She should have heard by now.'

'Heard what?'

'About her audition.' Mae paused, and as she realised her mis-take, a little coldness crept around her heart. 'You know – for RADA. In London.'

'I didn't know. You never mentioned it. How was I to know?'

'Everyone knew. Sure, I was thinking you'd been told.'

'I tell you I wasn't told. I didn't know Lottie'd gone for an audition.'

Harry's voice had roughened; his eyes on Mae seemed filled with strange light. She looked away.

''Tis not important, Harry. Not important at all.'

'Did I say it was important?'

'No, but the way you are looking—'

People were coming in through the stage door, greeting them, stepping round them. Mae, touching Harry's hand, said they should move.

'You will call for me at lunch-time?'

He nodded, taking off his cap and running his hand through his fair hair.

'You might have told me,' he said softly. 'You didn't want to, did you?'

'I never thought of it, believe me.'

Was it true? At one time, she would not have risked bringing up Lottie's acting success, knowing that it pained him, reminding him of his own failure. But as she had told her father in Traynore, he seemed to have forgotten his old ambitions; there should have been no need to worry what she told him. Something, though, had held her back from saying, oh so casually, 'By the way, Lottie's trying for RADA ...'

'I'm sorry,' she murmured, raising her blue eyes to his. 'But Lottie might not have got in, anyway.'

'Oh, she'll have got in.' He laughed. 'I'd take bets on it.'

As he marched off, she realised that the coldness round her heart had not gone away.

And of course, Lottie had got in to RADA. She wasn't due to be at the theatre before the afternoon rehearsal, but came dancing in halfway through the morning, specially to tell Mae – or anyone else around – that she'd just received her letter of acceptance. She was to start at the Academy in September and would be moving to London in August, to give herself time to find somewhere to live.

'Honestly, I'm amazed,' she told Mae and Mrs Ness in Wardrobe. 'I mean, I did a terrible audition. Dried up twice in *Lear*, lost my voice in *St Joan* – how they ever accepted me, I simply don't know.'

'Sure, they could tell you were good,' said Mae, and Mrs Ness echoed dryly, 'Sure, they could.'

'Now, I feel so strange,' Lottie went on. 'Here, and not here, if you know what I mean. Happy, and not happy. I'm thrilled to be going to London, but I'll be so sad to leave the Queen's. Oh, Mae, think of saying goodbye!'

'And how's Brett going to say goodbye?' asked Mrs Ness, busily pinning a collar to a shirt.

'He's not. At the moment he's asking Mr Standish to help him find a London agent.'

'Poor Brett,' said Mrs Ness.

'He might as well try for London. Now that Tony's come, he thinks he's no chance of the big parts.'

'As I said, poor Brett. Well, congratulations, Lottie, but we must get on. You know what it's like here – everything has to be ready by yesterday.'

'Oh, yes, sorry.' Lottie flushed. 'But, listen, won't you both come out and have lunch at the Rowan Tree today? My treat. I have to have a celebration of some sort. Tell Harry, Mae, won't you?'

But Mrs Ness said she really couldn't spare the time, she would just have a sandwich at her table, and Mae, though she would have given a great deal to go, made an excuse. She knew there was no point in asking Harry to celebrate with Lottie.

'I told you, didn't I?' he asked, on the way home, when Mae had valiantly given him Lottie's news. 'Och, it was a foregone conclusion. I knew they'd want her.'

'She was never sure of that herself.'

'All an act. She acts all the time, on and off the stage. Just like the rest of 'em.'

'Would you not have been the same? If you had been an actor?'

He shrugged. 'We'll never know, eh? I stayed a lighting man.'

'And a very good one too. Why not take pride in that?'

He shrugged and as they reached the flat, turned aside. 'Think I feel like a drink, Mae. D'you mind? I'll just pop up the road to the pub. See you back at the theatre.'

Mae's eyes sparkled and her colour rose. 'Sure, I made a mistake, then, not going to the Rowan Tree with Lottie! I knew you would not want to go, and preferred to be with you. Now, it's drinking you're after, and I can sit at home alone?'

'You can still go to the Rowan Tree,' Harry said coldly. 'Quick, get yourself along to join in the applause.'

'All right, then, and I will!'

For a long moment, their eyes locked, then Mae, swallowing tears, dropped her gaze and left him, and Harry, his face set with misery, went his own way.

It was their first real quarrel. Mae, walking in a daze, knew she couldn't join Lottie at the café. To sit with someone so happy, to join in all the lighthearted banter – no, it wasn't possible. Maybe she'd just turn and go home, try to eat something. But she found herself at the cathedral and pushed open the great door.

There was the familiar smell, of candlegrease and musty prayer books, flowers and old oak. It was very quiet, with only one or two people sitting with bowed heads in the pews, and a woman in an apron dusting the altar rails. All so peaceful.

After a few moments, Mae sat down, letting the peace take hold, trying to calm her thoughts to match, but she was still angry. It was true what her da had said, that there was a dark side to Harry.

'And look after him,' he had added. But maybe she didn't feel like looking after him, when he showed his envy and mean spirit. Of course, she was sorry for him; he had to stand by while others achieved what he wanted and couldn't reach. But that didn't excuse his ungenerous attitude. It didn't excuse his wanting to go off and drink, when he knew she couldn't join him.

Gradually, her thoughts ceased churning and she sat quietly, her hands folded, wondering what to do. She did love Harry so. Somehow, she must try to patch things up, make him see he would be happier himself, if he could accept his life as it was. And he still had her. Wasn't she enough? The dear Lord knew, Harry was enough for her.

She knelt to say a prayer, then rose, sensing someone behind her, and swinging round looked into Harry's sad hazel eyes.

'Oh, Mae, I'm sorry.' He took her hands. 'So sorry. Can we go home?'

'I was not expecting to see you,' she murmured, when they had embraced and kissed outside the cathedral, disregarding any passers-by, scarcely even seeing them. 'Weren't you going for a drink?'

'I never went to the pub. I just stood and watched you.'

'And I never went to the café.'

'You went to St Mary's. I saw you go in.'

''Twas peaceful.'

'Aye, I guessed you wanted peace away from me.'

'Harry, I'm saying sorry, too. I was angry.'

'You'd every right to be.' He looked away. 'I know I'm at fault, Mae. I know what I should do. Just canna do it, that's all. I want to be glad for Lottie, but sometimes when I try to say the words, it comes over me, that's she's had it so easy, and got talent and all, and it just seems that everything's loaded for her sort, and no' for mine.'

'Lottie's had her troubles, Harry.'

'I tell you, she's been lucky.' His voice shook. 'All of 'em are lucky in the company. They can do what they want to do. Might have troubles – who hasn't? But they'd never envy me, would they?' He grasped Mae's hand. 'It's me has to envy them. That's what I canna take.'

''Tis too late to go home,' Mae said after a pause. 'I'm not hungry, anyway.'

'Nor me.'

'Let's go back to the theatre, then.'

At the stage door, she turned to look up at him.

'You know, Harry, I am different from you. I have no envy of anyone, because I have you.'

A flush rose to his brow and he lowered his eyes.

'Oh, God, Mae, that cuts me. Do you think you're no' the most important thing in ma life? You're all that matters, and that's the truth!'

'And the acting? That is not important?'

'No' compared with you.'

'You mean that?'

'I do.'

As their eyes met again, hers filled with doubt, his earnestly pleading, Sam Morris appeared and with much hilarity tried to get his stout frame around them.

'Come on, you two lovebirds, then! Should be trying for *Romeo and Juliet*, eh, the way you're making sheep's eyes at each other?'

Were they Romeo and Juliet? They laughed, and the tension melted.

'There's nothing keeping us apart,' said Harry.

'Nothing,' echoed Mae.

Chapter Forty-Four

Early in August, Lottie arranged a farewell luncheon for herself and Brett at one of the hotels.

'Daddy's paying,' she told Mae. 'I didn't want him to, because he's already paying my RADA fees, but he insisted, and I'm going to need all my savings for living expenses. As for Brett, he hasn't a bean. And no job, either.'

'He's still going to London?'

'Oh, yes, but separately from me.' Lottie's limpid eyes rested on Mae's face. 'Listen, Mae, would you like to help me?'

'If I can.'

'If you will.' Lottie laughed nervously. 'I want you to come with me to say goodbye to my mother.'

Mae's face reddened. She swallowed hard. 'Oh, Lottie, what are you saying? I am the last person your mother would want to be seeing!'

'She threw us both out, and I want her to accept us both. That's my plan. Look, where's the harm? If she won't see us, well, we'll have done our best. Come on, Mae, say you'll support me.'

'From a distance, Lottie. I'm thinking it's a grand idea for you to make it up with your ma before you leave, but you'd be better off without me. Sure, I'd be spoiling the whole thing, so I would.'

Lottie was drooping, as she so easily did. 'The point is, I'll never get there without you. I'll never even ring the bell.'

'Will your da not go with you?'

'Daddy? He'd never dare! No, it's you and me, or neither of us.'

Mae sighed. 'All right, I will go with you to the door and see you ring the bell.' She raised her hand. 'But no more. 'Tis all I can do.'

'All right, then. When shall we go?' Lottie's spirits had not yet rallied. 'Before the lunch? If I fail, I can drown my sorrows, can't I? Oh, Lord, I think I could do with a drink now!'

The day of the lunch party was warm and humid, and Mae, changing into a thin blue dress after the morning in Wardrobe, felt sticky and ill at ease even before Lottie came to collect her. Harry, in his best suit, had already left to wait for her at the hotel, keeping his thoughts on Lottie's plan to himself, though Mae could tell he didn't approve. But he had been very careful of late to say nothing against Lottie, and had in fact contributed more than he could afford to her leaving present.

Oh, how I wish this meeting was over, thought Mae, when Mrs Ness, in bright pink, had left her. And where is Lottie? She's cutting it fine, but if she's given up the idea of us both going over the road, it will not be me complaining.

Lottie, though, had not given up the idea. Just as Mae was about to leave for the hotel without her, she slid through the door, wearing a pale-green two-piece and matching hat, and looking so strung up, she might have been facing a command performance. Even so, she smiled when she saw Mae.

'Come on, let's go,' she whispered. 'Over the top, then.'

The maid who opened Mrs Cameron's front door was middle-aged, with a frizz of grey curls beneath her cap and a sour expression.

'I will see if Madam is at home,' she said, looking coldly from Lottie to Mae, who was standing a little apart. Perhaps she'd seen photographs, thought Mae. Perhaps she knew who Lottie was. She would not know Mae, of course, but then Mae was not going in.

'That's all right. I'm Mrs Cameron's daughter,' Lottie said quickly. 'I'll find her myself.'

'No, Miss, I'll tell Madam you're here,' the maid insisted. 'Please to wait.'

'No, I will not wait, and neither will Mrs Alpin, here. We are coming in now. Will you please excuse us?'

Us? echoed Mae. Oh, Lottie, I might have known, you'd get me in.

'Who is it, Agnes?' came Mrs Cameron's high-pitched voice, and a moment later, she was herself in the hall, her water-clear eyes going from Lottie to Mae, her face darkening. 'What is the meaning of this?' she whispered.

'Mummy, may I speak to you?' asked Lottie, suddenly standing straight and using her best carrying voice. 'Just for a moment?'

Mrs Cameron glanced at the maid who was standing impassively waiting for orders.

'That will be all, Agnes.'

'Very good, ma'am.'

When the maid had withdrawn, Mrs Cameron turned back to Lottie, then let her eyes go to Mae, who with a great effort of will, met her gaze full on.

'We really have nothing to say,' Mrs Cameron said, after a pause. 'I don't understand why you have come here, Charlotte, or why you've brought Mae O'Donovan with you.'

'Mae is married now, Mummy. Her name is Mrs Alpin. And she isn't a maid any more – she works on the costumes at the Queen's theatre. I think you know I've been working there, too.'

'I am not interested in what Mae does. Or what you do, Charlotte, if it has to do with the theatre. I think you'd better go now.'

But Mrs Cameron's lower lip was trembling and she seemed not to be in command of her feelings, which had never been a problem for her in the past. Poor soul, thought Mae, amazed to be feeling sympathy for her old employer. She wants to give in, she's dying to give in, but she will not do it, she will not let herself weaken. Sure, she'll send Lottie away, then go and have a good cry, and her chance will be missed. There is nothing we can do.

But someone was opening the front door to come quietly into the hall, and Lottie gave a cry.

'It's Daddy!'

'John?' Mrs Cameron's gaze on him was astonished. 'What are you doing home from the bank at this hour?'

'I'm going to Charlotte's farewell luncheon,' he answered, taking off his hat and endeavouring to appear calm. 'She's leaving Edinburgh, Ada. Going down to London, to study at the Royal Academy of Dramatic Art.'

'To study? Whatever is there to study about acting? And what's all this about a luncheon?'

'I was talking to Hector Standish, the theatre manager of the Queen's, at the New Club the other day. He's a pretty knowledge-

198

able fellow, and he told me that Charlotte – well, he called her Lottie, seems they all do – has the makings of a very good actress. A star, in fact. He said we should be proud of her.' Mr Cameron's hands on his hat were moving constantly, but his voice was firm. 'He specifically said that you must be proud, Ada – being her mother.'

There was a silence. Mrs Cameron sat down heavily on a hall chair and lowered her eyes. 'You know my views on the theatre, John.'

'There's nothing wrong with the theatre. Would a respectable man like Standish be involved in it, if there were?'

'I don't know this Mr Standish.'

'You must have heard of him. He's an eminent chap. A gentleman of the old school, I'd say, and very well thought of by everyone I know.'

Mrs Cameron slightly tossed her head. 'You certainly seem impressed.'

'I am. So will you be, when you meet him.'

John Cameron put his hand on his wife's shoulder.

'Come along, then, let bygones be bygones, get your hat, and come with us to the hotel. There's a decent buffet laid on, and we can say goodbye to our daughter together. All she wants is to have your approval again.'

'All I want,' Lottie said in a low voice.

'They both disobeyed me,' Mrs Cameron murmured, still trying to mount a rearguard action. 'Charlotte and Mae. I had to ask them to go.'

'Well, that was some time ago, Ada. Think about now. Think about coming over and meeting Hector Standish and the company, and having lunch with Charlotte. Being a family again, for a little while.'

Another silence followed, with Mr Cameron breathing hard and Lottie scarcely breathing at all, while Mae stood very still and waited. Finally, Mrs Cameron rose.

'I shall not go to the luncheon,' she murmured. 'But I'll wish you well, Charlotte. If that life is what you want, so be it. It's your decision. I will not stand in your way.'

Lottie immediately looked at her father, who moved forward and took his wife's arm.

'No, Ada, that won't do,' he said gently. 'I'm not going to the

199

hotel on my own. You're coming with me. Our daughter needs us both.'

'I have my bridge,' Mrs Cameron murmured. 'It's arranged.'

'Cancel it. We have a telephone.'

'I'd need to change.'

'No, just get your hat.'

'But I should look smart—'

'Mummy, you look absolutely right,' Lottie told her tremulously.

'Perfect,' agreed Mr Cameron. 'Right, let's go, before the guests have eaten everything.'

It all seemed wonderful on the surface, but below the relieved smiles and trembling handshakes, lay, as they all knew, the deep chasm of pride and regret, old resentments and fears. It would take time to build over, but a start had been made, they could be happy about that, and as Lottie dreamily introduced her parents to everyone from the Queen's, Mae experienced a great rush of relief. Why, Mrs Cameron had even looked her in the eye again and said she was pleased to hear she was doing well, and married, too.

'This is your husband?' She had given tall, handsome Harry a quick appraising glance. 'So what do you do, Mr Alpin?'

'I look after the theatre lighting,' he had answered politely.

'I'm sure that that must be a very interesting job.'

'Indeed, ma'am.'

When she had moved on to talk to Primmie, averting her gaze from Thea's hair, now raven black, Harry mopped his brow.

'Och, it was like talking to Queen Mary,' he said in a whisper. 'Think I should have bowed?'

'Oh, Mae, I'm so happy,' Lottie told her later. 'It was so good of you to come with me, I'll always remember it.'

'Sure, you left me no choice. And you were not needing me, you know.'

'Yes, for moral support!'

'But then your father came, after all. Were you not proud of him?'

'Mae, more proud than you'll ever know. He's never stood up to Mummy in his life before. I still don't know how it happened.'

Mrs Cameron was ready for it to happen, was Mae's opinion.

She had probably been trying to find a way of taking Lottie back for months, and suddenly Mr Cameron gave it to her. Ah, how lucky they all were!

'I thought, you know, when I left home,' Lottie was continuing, 'that I'd be free. But the funny thing is, I only feel really free now, when my mother has accepted what I do.' Lottie laughed a little. 'Silly, isn't it?'

''Tis true, everyone likes to please their parents. But you had to leave when you did. You had to lead your own life.'

'I know. But now it's as though the clouds have moved away from me.' Lottie laughed again. 'Does that sound theatrical?'

'No,' Mae answered quietly. 'I know about the clouds. Nobody better.'

'Ah, Mae, Harry's people will come round eventually. If Mummy can, anyone can!'

'Your mother wanted to – that's the difference.'

The excellent buffet lunch gradually came to an end and the guests began to queue to say goodbye to Lottie, who would not be returning to the theatre. Brett was appearing in the play that evening and would travel to London later in the week, but she was to go down on the night train. This, therefore, was her final performance.

With her parents at her side, she made it a good one, shedding a few tears, making promises to keep in touch; giving Mr Standish a last handshake and her friends a last smile.

When it came to Harry's turn to say goodbye, he gave a fine performance, too, wishing Lottie luck, laughing lightly as she kissed his cheek. All his feelings were well and truly under control; corked up tight as a bottle of whisky and only Mae knew what they were.

As for Mae herself, Lottie hugged her fervently and whispered that she must come down and visit her, as soon as she found a place to live. They'd a special bond, they must never lose touch, and Mae, returning her hug, agreed. But somehow, she couldn't picture herself visiting Lottie in London. Somehow she felt that this was truly goodbye for them. Mae, like everyone at the Queen's, was vanishing into Lottie's past, and Lottie herself was looking towards the future.

'That's the way things are,' Thea might have said.

It was the way of the world, anyway.

Chapter Forty-Five

It was business as usual back at the theatre after Lottie's departure, with a read-through of a new play for the actors, and usual duties for everyone else before the evening performance.

'All a bit of a let-down, eh?' said Mrs Ness. 'Can't seem to settle. Especially after the wine.' She laughed. 'Told you how alcohol affects me!'

''Tis so hot,' sighed Mae, who was still wearing her best dress because it was coolest, but was not feeling at all cool. 'Thundery.'

'Due for a storm, I should think.' Mrs Ness yawned and stretched. 'At least you can go home this evening. Now, I've got to sit and watch all those folk larking about in *Rookery Nook*, haven't I? What's the betting I fall asleep?'

'Harry's working, too.' Mae washed her sticky hands and made an effort to begin work. 'I'll be having a nice quiet evening.'

After his large lunch, Harry said he wouldn't bother going back for tea, and at the end of the day, Mae went home alone, walking slowly through the humid air. There was a feeling of expectancy, as though the city was waiting, poised for the storm. Women, standing outside their doors were scarcely talking, and the children, playing, seemed subdued, their cries blanketed by the heat.

'Och, is it no' funny weather?' Mae heard one of the women murmur. 'We're no' used to it, eh?'

'Always get one or two days like this in August,' her neighbour replied. 'Then comes the storm, and that's the end o' summer!'

'Aye, make the most o' being warm, then!'

The end of summer, echoed Mae, letting herself into her flat. Was that not a depressing thought? But as she took off her dress and washed in cold water, she knew she was feeling a little depressed, anyway. As Mrs Ness had put it, those left after Lottie set off for her new life, were experiencing a bit of a let-down. The party was over.

But not for me, Mae told herself, putting on a cotton blouse and skirt. Heavens, she was not complaining. She had all she wanted. Harry, and work she liked, and surely a family to come some time in the future. Unlike Lottie's mother, the Alpins had not 'come round' – that could not be denied. But there was time even for that.

As she made herself tea and sat quietly in her chair, she decided it was just the oppressiveness of the air that was getting her down. A good old downpour would clear the city and her spirits, and sure, any minute now she would be hearing the rattle of thunder.

But the thunder that came was from a knock on her door. A hammering so loud, it sent her leaping from her chair and her teacup crashing to the floor.

'Mother of God!' She had her hand to her heart. 'Who is it? Oh, not Harry? Please God, something has not happened to Harry?'

'Harry, are you there?' cried a voice, and it was Rona's. 'Harry, open up, for God's sake, open up!'

Mae, her feet crunching the remains of her cup, ran to the door and wrenched it open, to find Rona, deathly pale and wild-eyed, standing outside.

'Harry? Where's Harry?' she gasped. 'I need him, I need him.'

'Oh, Rona, he's at work, he's at the theatre.' Mae seized Rona's clammy hands. 'What is it? Tell me. What's wrong?'

'It's Jannie. She's bad. She's terrible bad. I dinna ken what to do.' Rona flung back the damp strings of her hair. 'She's got the diphtheria.'

'Oh, Rona, no! Are you sure? Has the doctor come?'

'Tilda went for him, but he lives way off and she's no' come back. But oh, it's the diphtheria, Mae. You can tell, you can tell!'

'Let me see her, Rona. I've seen cases before, in Ireland. Maybe I can help.'

'For God's sake, come, then.'

Jannie was on a couch in the living-room, propped up against a cushion, her face colourless, except for blood around her nostrils, her eyes terrified. Standing beside her, with her arm round the softly crying Susie, was Emmy Alpin; her eyes, too, were filled with fear.

'Has he come?' she cried. 'Has Harry come?'

'Mae's come,' said Rona. 'Harry's at work.'

Emmy looked at Mae as though she didn't recognise her. 'They're all at work,' she whispered. 'Ben. Jake. Harry. There's nobody, eh? No doctor. Nobody.'

'There's me,' said Mae.

She knelt beside Jannie, smiling and murmuring soothingly, gently touching her swollen throat.

'Will you let me see inside your mouth, Jannie?'

With a moan, the child opened her mouth, revealing what Mae had dreaded to see – the yellowish, parchment-like membrane that was the characteristic symptom of diphtheria. Oh, God, there it was, covering almost all the back of her throat. Without treatment, it could kill, as Mae knew, for children in the village at home had choked to death. And Rona knew it too, for when Mae looked up from Jannie, she read the knowledge in the mother's eyes.

'It all come up so sudden,' Rona whispered. 'Jannie was no' well, but I thought it was just a sore throat, you ken, and Jake went off to night shift. And then I saw the terrible thing in her mouth and I ran for ma folks, but Dad had gone to work and Ma went to pieces. Tilda said she'd fetch the doctor, but she's no' come back and Harry's no' here. I thought he could cut that thing out, but he's no' here, and I daren't do it, I daren't. Mae, what'll we do? She'll no' die, will she?'

'She will not,' said Mae, rising to her feet. 'Sure, we'll get her to the hospital. If we try to cut that membrane, we might do damage. The only thing is to get her to the doctors so they can do an operation.'

'An operation? Oh, God!'

''Tis just a hole they make in the windpipe, so she will not choke. There was a child in Cork had it done and was right as rain. But we must go now. We must lose no time. Quick, let's wrap her in a sheet and take her now.'

'You canna run all the way to the hospital with a bairn in a sheet!' cried Emmy. 'It's miles away!'

'Not to the hospital. Only to the theatre.' Mae glanced at the clock over Rona's range. 'The play will be starting soon. There will be taxis arriving. We will take one.'

The two women stared at Mae as though mesmerised, until she called again for a sheet and when Rona fetched one, wrapped it round Jannie and ran to the door.

'You are coming?' she cried to Rona.

'Oh, God, yes! Ma, you stay with Susie, and tell Jake where we've gone when he comes in – the doctor and all, if you see him. Susie, pet, be a good girl, eh? Stay with Gran and I'll be back soon.'

'No, no, I want you, Mammie!' Susie began to wail. 'I want Jannie. I dinna want her to die!'

'She is not going to die,' Mae told her. 'She is going to the hospital where they will make her better. Now, be good, and take care of your grandmother.'

'Is that you, Rona?' came a voice from the door and Tilda Tamsin came bursting in, her hat falling from her head and her breath coming in great gasps. 'Listen, I've no' got the doctor, he's away to a confinement, they dinna ken when he'll be back. What'll we do?'

'Mae and me's going to the hospital,' said Rona. 'We have to go now. Will you help Ma?'

'You and Mae?' Tilda's eyes followed Mae, who was running into her own flat for her purse. 'Well, 'course, I'll help Emmy. I'll make her a cup o' tea.'

How strange it was, to see another world outside theirs continuing just as usual. People arriving at the theatre, laughing and talking, checking on their tickets, looking forward to their evening out. All so carefree, so unconcerned.

But all that concerned Mae was that she'd been right about the taxis. Thank God, there they were, lining up as they deposited their passengers, who were stepping out with such obvious pleasure.

'Taxi!' she cried, and a driver swung up and opened the door.

'Where to, Missus?'

'The Royal Infirmary. Quick as you can, please.'

And as they sank with Jannie on to the back seat and the taxi roared away, thunder sounded overhead, and the first raindrops began to fall.

Chapter Forty-Six

'Now, you're not to worry,' said the nurse in the casualty department, as a young doctor took Jannie in his arms and sped away where Rona and Mae could not follow. 'It'll all be over in no time and when we've made your wee girl comfortable, you'll be able to see her.'

'I want to see her now!' cried Rona, tightly clasping her hands in front of her, as though she was having difficulty in keeping them off the calm-faced nurse. 'How'd you like to have an operation and no mother with you?'

'It's a very simple procedure, dear,' the nurse replied, unmoved by Rona's threatening stance. 'All they do is make an incision in the windpipe for a tube to make a new airway, so the lassie can breathe. Now, you sit down and let your friend get you some tea.'

'Tea? Why's everybody keep offering folk bloody tea?' Rona swept the nurse's hand from her arm. 'I dinna want any tea, and I'm no' sitting anywhere till I see ma Jannie!'

'Suit yourself, Mrs Walker, but now I have to get on.' The nurse straightened her starched cap and began to move away. 'I know this is very difficult for you, but could you please not make so much noise? You're upsetting the other patients waiting.'

'And there's plenty o' them,' muttered Rona, finally allowing Mae to lead her to a bench, and tossing her head at the eyes watching her. 'All they ever do in these places is make you wait.'

She sat down, shuddering, and put her hand to her brow. 'Och, I'm no' being fair, eh? I ken fine they're doing their best for Jannie, but they should've let me go with her. That was all I wanted, eh? To be near ma bairn and stop her being frightened. You understand, Mae?'

'Sure, I understand,' Mae said soothingly. ''Tis only that the doctor probably thinks he can get on better if you're not there.'

'Aye, maybe.' Rona sat quietly for a moment, listening to the sound of the thunder still rolling around outside, then suddenly gave a wrenching sob. 'Oh, God, when'll they come for us, Mae?'

'Think I will be getting you some tea, anyway,' said Mae, rising. ''Twill maybe steady you.'

'You're the one to steady me.' Rona put up a restraining hand. 'Never mind about the tea. Sit down, eh?' For a long moment, she looked into Mae's face. 'You're awful pale, you ken. Do you no' want to go on home?'

'I'll stay till they let you see Jannie.'

'That's good o' you. Why've you been so good to us? We've no' been good to you.'

Mae moved uneasily. 'No need to talk of that now, Rona.'

'Never gave you much of a chance, did we? Ma and me? Had our ideas, you ken. Just want to say this – there's no' many would've done what you did for me tonight.'

'Sure, they would.'

'No.' Rona smiled grimly. 'I know plenty who'd have left me to get on with it.'

'Rona,' Mae said quietly, 'the nurse is back.'

The tracheotomy had been successful. With the new airway she had been given, Jannie was out of immediate danger, and would not choke over the membrane in her throat. Unfortunately, that could not be removed without leaving a very painful, ulcerated surface, but it would eventually come away itself, and though she was still very ill and would need careful nursing, her prospects of recovery were good.

'A grand little patient, too,' commented the nurse cheerfully. 'All right, Mrs Walker?'

Rona's mouth opened, she seemed to be searching for words, then burst into tears and collapsed into the nurse's arms.

'Now, I did say not to worry, didn't I?' The nurse patted Rona's heaving shoulders. 'Come on, dry those tears and I'll take you up to see your wee lassie. She'll not be wanting to see you bawling your eyes out, will she?'

'I'm that sorry, that sorry!' Rona whimpered, as she was led away, still looking back. 'Oh, but Mae – will you tell Ma what's happened, tell her no' to worry? And Mae—'

'Yes, Rona?'

'Thanks, eh?'

Chapter Forty-Seven

'Tell Ma what's happened,' Rona had said. But first, Mae had to tell Harry.

The storm was over, the thunder gone and the night air cool and fresh, as she ran from the tram and caught him as he left the theatre.

'Oh, Harry!' She fell into his arms as he stared down at her, instantly afraid.

'Mae, what's wrong? Why've you come over?'

''Tis all right, dearest, 'tis all right!'

But of course he knew, just seeing her there, in his arms, instead of at home, that things had been at some point all wrong, and wouldn't move until she'd told him everything. And then his face paled in the late dusk and he let her go, staring across at Victoria Row, murmuring Jannie's name.

'Wee Jannie so ill, and I never knew,' he muttered. 'Diphtheria . . . my God, Mae, it's a killer. A lad I knew at school died – only ill three days. And then there was a flyman here – he died – caught it from his daughter.' His eyes glittering in the shadows, Harry caught Mae to him. 'Why'd you no' come for me, then? I could've taken Jannie to the hospital. Why'd you no' come?'

'There was no time, Harry. We were so afraid that the membrane would go down into her throat and choke her. To be finding you, would have taken too long.'

'So, you managed yourself. With Rona.' Harry shook his head. 'What the hell did ma folks think of that? You doing all that for 'em? What did Rona say?'

'Sure, she thanked me.' Mae put her arm into Harry's, as they began to walk towards the Row. 'I'm thinking, maybe, things'll be

209

all right between us.' Her eyes, though, as she looked into Harry's face, showed no pleasure. 'But I never would've wanted this to happen because of Jannie, you understand—'

'Goes without saying, but Rona should've done the right thing, anyway. Did you say she wanted you to see Ma?'

'To tell her Jannie is out of danger. For now.'

'For now.' Harry shivered. 'Don't say that. Don't say "for now".'

'I am just being careful, because 'tis true she's very ill. But her prospects of getting better are good. 'Twas what the nurse told us, and the doctor had said it.'

'Still ...' He looked back at the cathedral, standing square and solid next to the theatre. 'Are you no' going in there, then, to say a prayer? If I was a kirk-goer, I'd be saying one maself.'

'Tomorrow.' Mae took a deep breath. 'Tonight, we see your mother.'

Emmy Alpin opened Rona's door and silently beckoned them in. She had thrown a shawl around her shoulders and looked cold; chilled to the bone, as though it were winter outside, instead of high summer. But then, thought Mae, to live with great fear, was to be in a kind of winter, anyway.

Everything was quiet in Rona's living-room. Quiet and tidy. No doubt, Emmy had spent time tidying. Something to do, once Susie had gone to bed.

Still no words were said, as Emmy turned her empty eyes on their faces, until Harry put his arm around her and said, 'Ma, Jannie's all right. She's no' in any danger. Mae's brought the message from Rona.'

'All right?' Emmy pulled away, her face curiously dissolving from its frozen state into fleeting expressions of hope and wonder. 'Oh, God, is it true? I canna believe it, I've no' even dared to think—' She turned to Mae. 'Is it true? Is it true what ma Rona says? Jannie's been saved?'

''Tis true, Mrs Alpin. The treatment has been successful.' Mae's voice was shaking, but she kept her gaze steady, meeting the older woman's desperate stare with all the reassurance she could bring. 'Jannie will not choke now, but she will need careful nursing.'

'But in no danger?'

'No danger.' Mae's eyes went to Harry's, but she did not add the words that had sent him talking of prayer. She did not say, 'For now'. The doctors had expressed hope. Jannie's grandmother must be allowed hope, too.

For a moment, Emmy did not speak. She sat down by the stove, pulling her shawl close, then looked up at Mae.

'Sit down, eh? Get warm.'

'It's no' cold tonight, Ma,' said Harry.

'Is it not? I feel it is.' Emmy shivered. 'Aye, I feel nithered. Soon as I got poor Susie to bed, I'd to go up for ma shawl. Open the damper, Harry. Get the kettle to boil.'

'Where's Jake?' asked Harry, busying himself with the stove and the kettle. 'Thought he'd be back by now.'

'Back and gone, up to the hospital. Flew out o' here like a man possessed. And what a time I had wi' Susie! She wanted to go with him and was greetin' and greetin', and would no' be comforted, whatever I did.'

'Ah, poor Susie!' cried Mae.

'She's asleep now, though?' asked Harry, pouring tea into three thick cups and stirring in sugar.

'Aye, she was too tired to keep up any longer. But when'll Rona be coming back? She canna stay at the infirmary all night, eh?'

'As soon as Jannie's settled, she will come home,' Mae told her confidently, and Emmy fixed her with a long considering stare over the rim of her cup.

'You were good, to take 'em in a taxi,' she said at last. 'I can pay you back, you ken.'

'No need,' cut in Harry. 'Mae doesn't want paying back.'

'No, indeed!' cried Mae. ''Twas my pleasure, to do that for Rona and Jannie.'

'For Rona, as well as Jannie?' Emmy shook her head. 'Why'd you want to do anything for Rona?'

'Who would not have helped Rona tonight? With her little girl the way she was?'

Emmy set down her cup. 'You did, and I'll say thank you, anyway. Aye, I will, no matter what.'

'Of course you will, Ma,' Harry said in a low voice. 'You finished that tea?'

He took her cup and she sat staring down at her knee and pleating a fold of her shawl, until at a signal from Harry, Mae rose to her feet.

'Better be on our way,' he said, putting on a show of heartiness.

211

'Will you be all right, Ma? Till Rona and Jake come back? We can stay if you like.'

'Och, no. You need your sleep, you've work tomorrow.'

Suddenly, amazingly, she smiled, and seemed to Mae a different person, for she had never seen Emmy look anything but grim, or, of late, sad. 'I feel better,' she told them. 'I feel grand. Since you brought me that message, Mae. A few words, and I'm no' cold any more. Is that no' strange?'

'No' strange to me,' said Harry, kissing her cheek. 'Well, if you're sure, Ma, we'll be away. But we're just next door. Remember that.'

'I will.' Trailing her shawl from her arm, Emmy went with them to the door. 'Goodnight, then.'

'Goodnight, Ma.'

'Goodnight, Mrs Alpin,' said Mae.

There was an awkward pause. Should I take her hand? wondered Mae. But the other woman made no move and Harry was opening the door. As Mae moved to follow him, Emmy cleared her throat.

'When Jannie comes home,' she began, and stopped.

'Yes, Ma?' asked Harry.

'When Jannie's better,' she began again, 'you must come up the stair, Mae.'

'Up the stair?' Mae repeated, her head throbbing.

'Aye, for your tea.' Emmy's pale eyes gleamed. 'If you want to, of course.'

'Sure, I want to, Mrs Alpin. Thank you very much.'

Mrs Alpin. The name hung between them, but it was no surprise to Mae that her mother-in-law did not say now, 'Call me Ma'. Many women kept the formalities going all their married lives. It was the way things were. And even had it not been, Mae could not imagine Emmy letting down the barricades so easily. It was enough that she had made her great concession. She had invited Mae to tea. Up the stair.

It was no wonder that Mae felt herself inwardly reeling, as she and Harry stepped out of Rona's door and through their own. Or, that, as she looked back at Emmy, watching, she should faintly smile.

* * *

Back at home, her eyes went to the remains of the smashed cup still lying on the floor. There it was, a reminder of that terrible moment when Rona had thundered on her door.

'I'll just sweep this up,' she told Harry. 'Then I'll get us something to eat.'

'I'm no' hungry.'

'Bread and cheese, then?'

'Fine. And I'll have a beer.'

He took the top from a bottle and filled a glass.

'Thank God this day is over, eh?'

'Sure, it feels like a hundred years since this morning.' Mae set out their bread and cheese and they ate a little. 'Was it today we said goodbye to Lottie?'

He shrugged. 'Canna think of anything but Jannie.'

'She is going to get well, Harry.'

'Aye, but why's she got to suffer? Why's any bairn got to go through thae terrible illnesses? I mean, where's the point?'

''Tis hard to understand.'

'Hard? It's impossible.'

'Some say there's a pattern. One we're too close to see.'

Harry stared disbelievingly, then put down his glass and lit a cigarette.

'There's no pattern, Mae. Nothing but accidents. Random happenings.'

'I'd not be happy, thinking that.'

'Aye, well, you've got your church, eh? Makes things easier for you.'

'You said you'd like to pray for Jannie yourself, Harry.'

'I said, if I'd been a kirk-goer, I'd have prayed. But I'm not.' Harry ground out his cigarette and stood up. 'You look weary, Mae – let's go to bed.'

She went to him and took his hand. 'Harry, good things happen as well as bad. Jannie's going to get better. Rona and your ma have accepted me. Can you not be taking comfort there?'

He stooped to kiss her lips. 'Maybe. Well, of course I'm glad about Jannie, and if you're pleased about Ma and Rona doing what they should have done before, well, OK – I'll be pleased too. But I'm no' changing ma views. This world's no' worth a bent penny, and that's all there is to it.'

213

Mae sighed, and turned away. 'Let's get to bed,' she agreed. 'Maybe things will look better in the morning.'

But as they lay in bed, too tired to sleep, morning seemed very far away.

Chapter Forty-Eight

On a grey day in early November, after long weeks in the isolation hospital at Colinton, Jannie finally came home.

'Och, I never thought to see this day!' Rona cried to Mae, as Jake, followed by Ben, carried her proudly from the ambulance. 'Are we no' lucky, eh? And all thanks to you, Mae.'

All the neighbours had gathered on the stair and clapped and cheered, while Emmy wept and Susie stared, saucer-eyed, at her little sister. For fear of infection, she had not been allowed to visit the isolation hospital with her mother, and now saw Jannie's cropped head for the first time.

'Where's all her hair?' she cried. 'It's like a boy's!'

'Aye, like mine!' cried Kenny Sims, whose mother pulled him away and told him not to put his spoke in, eh?

'Dinna want to upset her,' said Ben hoarsely, but Jannie, pale and listless, only lay on the couch and closed her eyes.

'They cut her hair in the hospital,' Rona explained. 'Keep it short when there's a fever, you see.'

'She's a shadow,' said Jake, gazing down at her. 'A wee shadow of herself, eh?'

'Now she's home, she will come up like a flower,' Mae told him. 'Every day, she'll gather strength, you'll see, and then she'll be running about with Susie here.'

'Oh, I wish she would,' sighed Susie. 'I've been on ma own for so long, 'cos she got sick. I'll no' get sick, will I?'

'Please God, no!' cried Rona, throwing her arms around her.

In a low voice, she whispered to those around that Susie had been what they called immunised. Would it do any good? Rona had no idea, but anything that saved bairns going through what

Jannie'd gone through would be worth trying. Aye, you had to hand it to the doctors, eh? Always coming up with something new. But in the end, you sometimes just had to pray.

'Let's have ma cake,' said Emmy, who had been saving to buy the ingredients to make it, money being as tight as ever. 'Mae, you'll be staying, eh?'

But Mae had to go back to the theatre.

'I'll tell Harry all about Jannie,' she promised. 'Sure, if it hadn't been matinée day, he'd have come over with me.'

'Aye, he would,' Emmy agreed. 'He's aye been fond of Rona's lassies.'

There was just the smallest of pauses, as the thought floated from head to head that it was time Harry had a lassie – or a boy – of his own but no word, of course, was said. No one wanted to upset Mae. From being an outcast, she had become a favourite, and nothing to her could be stranger.

Now she took from her bag two small dolls in crinolines, both exquisitely dressed from scraps of material by Mae herself, and giving one to Susie, put the other into Jannie's wasted hand.

'Oh!' cried Susie. 'Oh, Mammie, look! Is she no' bonny? Thank you, Mae, thank you!'

'Jannie, what d'you say?' asked Rona anxiously.

There was a long moment while the onlookers thought even the lovely doll would not stir their weary Jannie, but slowly her heavy eyes opened as her fingers felt the doll's soft little ringlets, and she sat up.

'See what Mae's given you?' asked Jake, kneeling beside the couch. 'Is she no' a grand wee dollie, then?'

Jannie's dark-rimmed eyes went to Mae. 'Pretty,' she whispered. 'This is – ma prettiest doll. Has Susie got one?'

'Aye, I have!' cried Susie. 'Shall we play with 'em, or keep 'em safe?'

'Keep 'em safe,' said Jannie.

'Oh, I had better be going,' Mae murmured, dabbing at her eyes. 'I will see you later.'

'Aye, come for your cake,' called Emmy. 'And tell Harry to come and all. We never see him these days, eh?'

Who did see Harry? He had become as elusive as in the old days, before he and Mae were married, either working late for no particular reason, or spending time in the pub, or, if at home, sitting without talking, seeming far away.

'What's wrong?' Mae would ask. 'Tell me, if there's something wrong.'

But he always said there was nothing wrong. Just a bit out of sorts, maybe. Not to worry, he'd snap out of it. So far, he had not done that, even though Jannie had recovered; even though they'd had the date for her coming home.

Sure, though, he'll cheer up when I tell him she's back, thought Mae, and was hurrying out of the front door when she almost collided with Mrs Beith and her son, Norrie, who had at last arrived home on leave.

'Oh, Mae!' cried Mrs Beith. 'Is Jannie home, then?'

'She is, and she's fairly well, though weak.'

'Ah, the poor wee soul! I'll have to pop in and see her. But have you met ma Norrie, then?' Mrs Beith gave a beaming smile, as she turned to her son. 'Mae's married to Harry Alpin, Norrie – stays in Freda Burns's old flat here.'

Norrie, though in civilian clothes, still looked exactly like his photograph, and like his mother, too. When he shook Mae's hand, he gave a wide smile that showed his good strong teeth.

'Heard a lot about you, in Ma's letters,' he told her. 'Said you were a grand lodger.'

'Better than some I could mention,' his mother remarked coldly, and Norrie shook his head in mock disapproval.

'Och, Ma, Pauline's OK. What've you got against her?'

'Nothing, except she thinks she's a lady, eh? To be waited on hand and foot.'

'Well, she pays her way. Canna forget that.'

'And that's why you let her keep your room, I suppose?'

'Could hardly expect her to sleep by the stove, Ma.'

Norrie, turning to Mae, touched his cap. 'Nice to meet you, Mrs Alpin. Give ma best to Harry. Used to play kick the can with him, when we were lads. He always won, and all. Lucky fella, eh?'

As he left them, leaping up the stairs two at a time, Mrs Beith sighed heavily.

'He's already taken Pauline to the pictures,' she whispered. 'And her as plain as the day, eh? Mae, if only it'd been you!'

Mae, smiling politely as Mrs Beith made her own slow way up the stair, was pondering on Norrie's words. Lucky fella? Harry?

She wished it were true.

Chapter Forty-Nine

A letter came for Mae a few days later. It bore American stamps, but was not from Rosaleen.

''Tis from Kieran,' she told Harry. 'His name's on the back.'

'Oh?' Harry, watching as she opened it, saw her face change. 'No' bad news, is it?'

Mae laid the letter down and looked unseeingly into his eyes. 'Their little girl has died. Mary Clare. They always called her Molly.'

'Oh, God.' Harry pushed aside the toast he'd been eating. 'Ah, Mae, I'm sorry. What happened?'

''Twas only a cold.' Mae's voice was thickening with tears. 'Turned to pneumonia. She was two and a half years old.'

'Canna imagine how they're feeling.' He shuddered and came round the table to take Mae in his arms. 'Did I no' tell you this world's a rotten place? Where's that pattern you told me about?'

She shook her head, as she released herself. 'I cannot say. Let's go to work, Harry.'

'You needn't go in today. You're upset.'

'I'm all right. It's Rosaleen I'm thinking about.'

Mrs Ness agreed with Harry; Mae needn't have come in to work that day.

'Are you sure you're all right?' she asked. 'I can manage, you know.'

'It's very kind of you, Mrs Ness, but I'm only thinking of my cousin, Rosaleen. She is not used to trouble at all and will not know how to bear it.'

'Everyone has to learn, sooner or later.'

'I just wish there was something I could do. But I'm so far away.'

'If you were on her doorstep, Mae, there'd be nothing you could do.'

Mae bowed her head. ''Tis true. She must get through this herself.'

'As her husband will. They'll both have to face this in their own way.'

But Mae couldn't think what Kieran Connor's way would be. He was another who'd never been touched before by adversity's cold wind.

Emmy and Rona were made desolate by Mae's news. Hadn't they been to the edge of the abyss themselves, and almost hurtled over? That poor lassie in America – what must she be suffering?

But Harry, like Mrs Ness, was remembering Kieran.

'Are you no' thinking o' the father here?' he asked sharply. 'Is he no' suffering, too?'

Mae coloured and looked down, but did not speak. No one spoke. They all knew Harry was putting himself in the place of the father of the dead child, though he wasn't a father, and perhaps might never be. What could anyone say about that?

As the days moved slowly by and November turned to December, Mae's anxiety for Harry began to move to the foreground of her mind. Rosaleen was always there, of course, and she had managed to write to her, somehow finding words of comfort, but she knew she could not put off for ever trying to help Harry.

Her father had written of his sadness on the death of little Molly, and thinking of him and his sympathy, she had been reminded again of his warning concerning Harry on her honeymoon.

'There's a little darkness there, mavourneen . . . take care, look after him . . .'

She had seen no darkness then, but now it was like the clouds in a storm, rising and covering their sky, and she must try to do what she could to bring back the light.

'Look after him,' her da had said, and she had laughed and said they should look after each other. Maybe, in those early days, she had thought that possible, and that they could be truly happy. But there had always been something fragile about Harry's hold on happiness. Hadn't she known that, in her heart?

She left it till they were going to bed one night to say what was in her mind.

'I could speak to the doctor, Harry – he might give us advice.'

'Advice? What about?'

'You know what about.'

He climbed into bed and lay with his arms folded over his chest. 'I don't want you going to the doctor's. I'll not have all our private affairs spread out in the open for other folk to see.'

'Other folk? A doctor is not "other folk"! He's like a priest. You can tell him anything and it will go nowhere at all.'

'I don't want you to go, Mae. Is that no' enough?'

'Then go yourself. Sure, if we want a family, 'tis a small price to pay, to see if anyone can help us.'

Harry's face was scarlet. 'I canna believe you're talking like this, Mae. These are private matters, eh? I could never see maself telling a stranger about you and me. Anyway, what could they do? It'd all be for nothing.'

'Let's leave it, then.' She put on her nightdress and, turning off the light, lay beside him. ''Tis early days, anyway, in my opinion.'

He was silent for a long moment.

'Truth is, you blame me,' he said quietly. 'I ken that, I feel it. You think I canna give you children.'

'No, Harry, that is not true. It could be me who cannot have them. That's why I was suggesting I see the doctor, in case he could tell me.' Mae leaned over him, her eyes wide on his face.

'And if it's no' you, it must be me.' Harry put his arms around her and held her close. 'If that's what they found, Mae, I'd never be able to accept it.'

'Harry, we don't know that they could tell us anything, but it's no disgrace, not to be able to have children. And supposing they could help us – think how we'd feel!'

'No, you were right before. It's early days yet. Let's leave it, eh? Besides, after what's happened to your cousins, do we want to risk all that sorrow?'

'We do,' she answered promptly. 'Risk is part of life. We cannot say no and hide away.'

'Well, shall we say we'll agree to leave things for the time being?' He slipped her nightdress over her head. 'We've still got this, eh?'

Making love, yes, they still had that, but even as they shared their joy, Mae sensed Harry's fear that it was not enough, that somehow they had failed each other. All her efforts to help had been in vain, and they must continue as they were, hoping for a miracle. And if it was true that Jannie's recovery had been something of a miracle, as Rosaleen and Kieran knew only too well, miracles were not for everyone.

Chapter Fifty

Christmas arrived and was celebrated by some and avoided by others. For many people across the world, 1931 wasn't a time to be happy, or even pretending to be happy. If there'd been jobs, now, in the Christmas stockings, that would have been cause for celebration. But there were no jobs, in or out of stockings.

Mae, like the rest of Harry's family, had given thanks that little Jannie was with them, to find an orange and an apple and a bright new penny in her own stocking, as well as the few toys folk had managed to buy for her and Susie. Yet, Mae could only feel glad when Christmas was over. Rosaleen's sad letter that had followed Kieran's had made her heart ache. Harry's inclination to drink more than ever before, using the season as an excuse, had made her anxiety rise. But what could she do?

When Gerry Ames had taken her to one side and asked her to have a word with Harry, as no lighting man could afford to drink on the job, she had refused. Things were 'difficult', she'd said, and Gerry had been sympathetic.

'Only thought your word might carry more weight than mine,' he'd told her.

She had no hope that that was true.

After Christmas, it was pantomime time again at the Queen's, with the official company away on tour, and the visiting company putting on *Puss in Boots* and annoying Mrs Ness as usual.

'To tell you the truth, this could be worse than *Aladdin*,' she murmured to Mae, two days after Boxing Day when the pantomime had opened. 'I mean, look at that cat suit moulting all over the place! I ask you, how are we expected to patch it up? And if I hear one more of those daft songs they make everybody sing, I think I'll go barmy!'

'Ah, but the children love it,' said Mae. 'Were you after seeing Harry's nieces when he brought them in? They thought they'd been to paradise, so they did!'

Mrs Ness's expression softened. 'Yes, did my heart good, especially to see the little invalid looking so grand. Something to be grateful for, eh?'

''Tis the best thing that's happened.' Mae bent her dark head, not wanting to think of the worst thing, and Mrs Ness patted her shoulder.

'All the same,' she sighed, 'I'll be glad when the panto's over again. It'll no' bother me, not to have to look after another one.'

Mae looked up. 'Sure, you will be looking after another one, Mrs Ness?'

'Tra-la!' cried Mrs Ness, rising and singing, and rooting for something in one of her cupboards. 'Just talking, my dear, just talking. Tell me, did you see little Miss RADA over Christmas then?'

'No, she wrote to me, though.'

'How kind. Thought she'd have come up to see her folks.'

'They went down to stay with her. Now, why are you always so critical of Lottie, Mrs Ness?'

'Just natural cattiness, my dear. But she's a taker, you know, like all successful people. When's she opening in the West End, then?'

'Ah, now, you know she is still studying!' Mae was laughing, when the door opened and Sam put his head round. 'Someone to see you, Mae.'

'Oh, God, not Copperknob again, is it?' asked Mrs Ness.

Sam grinned. 'It's a lady, then. Name of Dow.'

'Miss Dow!' Mae, trying not to show her fear that something must be wrong, hurried down the cramped passageway. 'How nice to see you! I'm so sorry I've not been to the hostel for so long.'

'Don't talk of that, my dear, we understand.' Miss Dow, her calm manner just as usual, her plump face well powdered, stretched out a gloved hand to take Mae's. 'I'm the one to apologise, intruding on you at work, but I thought perhaps I should.'

'Is anything wrong?' asked Mae. 'It's not Miss Thorburn?'

'Oh, no!' Miss Dow smiled. 'Now, when is anything ever wrong with Anita?' Her smile died. 'It's – well, it's Sandy.'

'Sandy?' Mae swallowed hard. 'She's not at Adelaide House, is she?'

'She is, dear, that's the thing. We had to take her in. From the hospital, you see. She's not in any danger, but she needs looking after, and you know what things are like at home.'

'She's been taken ill?'

Miss Dow's eyes flickered. 'Not exactly. To be honest, she's been attacked. One of her employers, I'm afraid. Lost his temper.'

'Oh, dear God!'

'There's no permanent damage, but she will need time to heal, you see, and you being her friend, I knew you'd want to be told. She doesn't know I've come, of course, but Anita and I decided it would be for the best.'

Miss Dow stopped and rested her blue eyes on Mae's face with a hopeful expression.

'Will you come, Mae?'

'I will. Tonight, in fact. I'll come tonight. I'm not on duty.'

'That would be wonderful.' Miss Dow gave a relieved smile. 'Come for supper, if you like. You'd be very welcome.'

'No, I'd better make it a little later.' Mae gave Miss Dow a quick embrace. 'But, sure, I'll be there.'

'We're so grateful, dear. You're bound to cheer her up, poor girl. She's always set great store by you, you know.'

Up to a point, thought Mae.

'So, you're going down to the hostel tonight?' asked Harry. He'd finished his tea and was standing up, smoking a cigarette. 'Honestly, Mae, you're like a puppet on a string. Folk pull you wherever they want you to go.'

'You are saying I should not see Sandy, when she's in trouble?'

'No, but it gets to me, that you're always ready to rush down to that hostel whenever they call. And whatever has happened to Sandy, she's brought it on herself.'

'I want to see her,' Mae only said obstinately. 'And I am going to see her. It was Miss Dow who asked me to go, not Sandy. She knows nothing about it at all.'

'May not even want to see you, then.'

Mae put on her winter hat and the tweed coat that had finally replaced Mrs Fitzgerald's hand-me-down, and at the weary look on her face, Harry's heart smote him and he put his arms around her.

'Sorry, Mae, sorry. Of course, you have to see her. Take no notice of me.'

The light in her eyes that renewed Mae's beauty was his reward.

'Oh, Harry, you make yourself out to be so hard!' She laughed and kissed him. 'But you're as soft as anyone inside!'

'Aye, nearly as soft as you.'

They walked arm-in-arm to the theatre, where they parted like lovers, Harry going in the stage door, Mae continuing on her way to the hostel. For a little while, she walked on air, because Harry had been like his old self, but as her thoughts turned to what she might find at the Adelaide, her feet were well and truly on the ground and faltering. By the time she'd reached the familiar door, it took all her courage to ring the bell.

Chapter Fifty-One

There was a row going on somewhere in the background. Wasn't there always? But Mae, hearing the voices raised over the clatter of dishes, tried to smile, when Miss Thorburn appeared.

'More trouble?' she asked.

Miss Thorburn laughed and kissed her cheek.

'Happy New Year, Mae. Oh, it's just the usual. Someone's accidentally pulled down someone else's paper chains. Heavens, you should have been here for our Christmas dinner! Fur was flying then, not to mention gravy. But thank you for coming, my dear. I knew you'd want us to let you know what had happened.'

'I am grateful, Miss Thorburn.' Mae hesitated. 'How – how bad is Sandy?'

'She's better than she was. But come into my office for a moment, where we can have a word.'

The details were soon told. Apparently, the man who had assaulted Sandy had been one of the artists she regularly posed for, one known for passionate and difficult behaviour and a heavy drinker. When things had not gone right with his work, he had suddenly 'made advances', as Miss Thorburn delicately put it, and when Sandy had fought him off, had lost his temper and attacked her. There were facial injuries and damage to her head, which had so shocked him he had called an ambulance himself, after which he'd disappeared.

'The injuries are not serious,' Miss Thorburn added hastily, seeing Mae's expression. 'But of course not pleasant to see. As soon as her mother saw her, she used a public telephone to tell me. As you might guess, Sandy would not have told me herself.'

'But she agreed to come here in the end?'

'I think in the end she wanted to. Wanted to bury herself somewhere for a while.' Miss Thorburn sighed. 'By the time I offered to put her up, she was really quite keen, poor girl.'

'You've been very good,' Mae murmured, rising. 'Always so good. Can I see her, then?'

'I'll take you up. She'll be in the dormitory by now. On her own, I hope – you remember the girls like to go to the recreation room after tea?'

It was the same dormitory where Mae and Sandy had slept before, and here was Sandy back again, but looking – oh, dear Lord – so different. She was dressed and lying on her bed and turning the pages of a magazine, but when she saw Mae, she threw aside the magazine and gave a groan.

'Oh, no, Mae, what you doing here, then? I never wanted you to see me like this.'

Her voice was slurred, because her mouth, which had been stitched, was swollen. Her face too was swollen, with bruises in a mass of colours, and there was a bandage over her head where her hair had been cut back. There were more bandages over her hands and a plaster covered her nose, but as Mae sank on to the bed and gazed at Sandy without flinching, she was surprisingly relieved.

Yes, Sandy looked different and terrible, but she was still, in spite of what had happened to her, the same Sandy. And she would heal, Mae was sure of it. She had seen plenty of battered women in her time – in Cork, in the hostel. Sandy was no worse; might even be rather better.

'Oh, Sandy, you knew I would be wanting to see you!' she cried, as Miss Thorburn moved quietly away.

'Like this?' asked Sandy, her eyes, almost hidden beneath purple swellings, still managing to flash. 'I dinna think so.'

'Ah, 'tis terrible what has happened, but you're still the same Sandy, that's the thing. And all this'll soon pass – sure, it will!'

'Easy to say. You see what I look like. But how do I feel inside?'

Mae bit her lip. She stretched out her hand and pressed Sandy's. 'I can imagine. Oh, how could that fellow do this to you?'

'Never mind him.' Sandy's head moved restlessly against her pillow. 'To tell you the truth, I think he was sorry, soon as he'd done it.'

'Are you not going to tell the police about him?'

227

'No! No, I dinna want them involved.'

'He could attack some other woman, you know.'

But Sandy only moved her head slowly from side to side. 'All I know is that I'm never going to put maself in that kind o' situation again. I've learned ma lesson now, Mae. I should've listened to you. I'd have been better off with a sewing machine, eh?'

'You thought you were doing the right thing.'

'Aye, well, I made a mistake.'

Mae hesitated. 'What will you do, then?'

'Work in a shop.' Sandy attempted a smile. 'Did I no' say I would? Forget Logie's, though. They'd never take me, even if I got ma looks back. But I've been lying here, thinking – what about John Johnson's up the bridges? They're a big store. They might have a vacancy for somebody like me.'

'Why, Sandy, that sounds a grand idea!'

'I ken there's no' many jobs around at the moment, and even if I get one, it'll no' be well paid, but soon as I stop frightening folk wi' how I look, I'll go up and see if there's anything going.'

Sandy shivered and looked down at her bandaged hands. 'See these? Got damaged when I tried to save maself.' She raised her eyes to Mae's. 'Och, it's me for a quiet life from now on. I'm no' risking maself, or ma family.'

'Where do the children think you are now?'

'Well, Ma told 'em I was infectious and might be in the hospital a long time, but Finlay, of course, canna understand. I'll have to get back soon as I can.'

Sandy sighed deeply. 'At least the hospital did a good job, though. Sewed me up, fixed ma nose – och, I was lucky, eh?'

'Sort of.' Mae shook her head. 'Look, I was too late to get you some flowers, so I've brought chocolates instead.'

'Chocolates?'

'They're from the theatre shop.' Mae laid a colourful box on the bed. 'Jackie found 'em for me. Hope they're all right.'

'All right? Mae, they're the best thing I've set eyes on since I came in here!' With renewed energy, Sandy sat up. 'Let's have one now, eh? Come on, then, open 'em up!'

'Harriet was right,' Miss Thorburn remarked when she came back a little later. 'She said Mae would cheer you up, Sandy, and so she has.'

'I think Sandy's cheering herself up,' Mae murmured, rising and putting on her hat. 'Is that not right?'

'I do feel better,' Sandy admitted. 'As though I might get back to normal one o' these days. Mae, will you come again?'

'I will.' Mae pressed her hand. 'And soon.'

'Give ma best to Harry, then.'

'How'd you find Sandy, then?' Harry asked, when he came home.

'She's in a bad way, but she'll recover. And we are all so relieved she's going to look for other work. Maybe a job in a shop.'

'About time.' Harry yawned and said he'd turn in early. Lighting the pantomime was tricky – lots of changes, spots, cues, and all the rest of it. He was weary.

Mae said nothing. She could smell the alcohol on his breath; knew he'd been to the pub. At least he'd gone after work and not before. It was on the tip of her tongue to tell him what Gerry had said, but she held back, not wanting to spoil his mood which still seemed good.

'Not long to New Year,' she said brightly. 'Rona wants us all to go to her. I said I'd make something. She hasn't the money, at all.'

'Aye, that'll be nice.' Harry stood up. 'Roll on nineteen thirty-two, I say.' His eyes rested on Mae. 'Our lucky year, eh?'

'Lucky? Maybe. Wasn't Norrie Beith saying you always had the luck.'

'Norrie Beith?' Harry shrugged. 'He's just never forgiven me for beating him at kick the can in the old days. Puts it all down to luck, you ken, instead of ma wonderful skill.'

'I think we are both lucky,' said Mae. 'To have each other.'

As he kissed her quickly, saying she was right, she couldn't help wishing he'd been the one to say it.

Chapter Fifty-Two

Their lucky year? Not so far, thought Mae, when 1932 had advanced to spring. There had been no changes for her and Harry, or for their world, still in the grip of the Great Depression, which showed no sign of slackening. In some ways, it was like living through a war, with no hope of beating the enemy. Poverty and want were worse to fight than men, it seemed.

On the other hand, life was happier for some. Jannie had recovered so well she was back at school, and Rona and Jake looked like themselves again. Sandy too, had recovered, wonderfully well.

It had been a source of great satisfaction to Mae and Miss Thorburn, when her true looks began to emerge from the damage they had suffered. One by one, the bruises had faded, her hands and mouth healed, and her nose, thank God, had returned to its normal shape. Soon, only the wide scar above her brow remained.

'And in time that will fade, too,' Dr Rick told her, when she was due to go home. 'Might have to grow a fringe, but maybe that's fashionable.' He'd laughed. 'My wife would know, but I couldn't say.'

'Dr Rick's nice, eh?' Sandy commented later, when Mae came to visit her. 'The only man I'd ever say that about. And his wife's the same. Sweet as they come.'

'Any children?' asked Mae, pulling Finlay, now three years old, out of the coal scuttle and wiping his hands.

'Still waiting, Miss Thorburn said.'

'Like me, then. And please don't be telling me I have plenty of time.'

'But it's true!' Sandy's eyes, restored to their former beauty, were full of sympathy. 'What you have to do, Mae, is just stop thinking about it. Then before you know it, you'll have fallen for a babby, just like other folk.'

'It's Harry I'm thinking about. He seems to think he has failed me somehow.'

'Aye, there are fellas like that. Take it as a personal insult if they canna have a bairn. And if they get a lassie, then they want a son.'

'Harry would settle for either.' Mae rose to go, as Sandy's mother came in with Finlay's little uncle and aunt she had been meeting from school. 'Me, too.'

'Have you lassies finished all the tea?' cried Mrs Corrie. 'And here's me gaspin', eh?'

'The kettle's on, Ma,' Sandy told her. 'And see – Mae's brought us a cake.'

'Mae, you didnae! Och, you spoil us!'

'A little spoiling will not hurt,' said Mae. 'Come here, now, Shona, mavourneen, and let me do your hair.'

'Edie never did ma hair!' shrieked Shona.

'Never give us cake, either,' said Johnny, hastily backing away all the same, in case Mae tried to turn her comb on him.

'Canna afford Edie now,' said Sandy. 'But we'll get by, nae bother. Mae, it's true, you spoil us, but we dinna mind.'

It was shortly after her return home that Sandy applied to John Johnson's, the department store on the North Bridge, for a job in dress sales, and was given an interview.

'Och, you'll never guess what happened!' she told Mae and Harry, who'd invited her to the Rowan Tree for a meal. 'Talk about a laugh.'

'What is it, then?' asked Mae, as Harry stolidly ate steak and kidney pie. 'Do not be keeping us in suspense.'

'After all I've said about no sewing, I'm going to be working in Alterations! Would you credit it? They asked me if I'd any experience in that line, and when I said I'd plenty – I'd worked at a dressmaker's, made a lot of it, you ken – they said would I be interested in sewing for them?'

Sandy drank coffee and grinned. 'Turned out I had to be interested, anyway, because the sales job had gone and Alterations was all they could offer. So, I said yes, you bet, I'd do the sewing, and that's me, then. I start on Monday. On a month's trial.'

'Sandy, I am speechless,' cried Mae. 'How strange it is, the way things turn out.'

'Think you'll enjoy it?' asked Harry.

Sandy turned a defiant gaze on him. She knew he didn't approve of her. Perhaps thought she couldn't settle down to the life of an ordinary working girl. As though she wasn't desperate to do just that.

'I'll enjoy it,' she told him coldly, and turned back to Mae.

'So, the other thing is, I've signed up for some evening classes in September, but, I was wondering, Mae – it's awful cheek – but if you still want to give me a hand, I'd no' mind taking you up on it.'

'Sure, I'll be glad to help!' cried Mae. 'When would you be wanting to come round?'

Sandy coughed and looked embarrassed. 'Before I start work, if that's OK? Just to give me a few tips, eh? I mean, I can turn up hems and all that kind o' thing, but, it's true, I'm a wee bit out o' practice.' She coughed again and kept her eyes from Harry. 'I'd be that grateful, Mae.'

'Sandy, 'tis the very thing I was going to suggest,' said Mae. 'I am doing what you might call alterations all the time. I can give you all the tips you want. So, come round as soon as you like.' She glanced at Harry. 'When you're at work, Harry, of course.'

'Aye, seeing as sewing's no' ma line.' He finally managed to smile at Sandy, who somewhat frostily smiled back. 'Make it Friday, then.'

'I'm that grateful,' Sandy said again.

'Hope all goes well for you.' Harry waved to the waitress for the bill. 'And congratulations on getting the job – takes some doing these days. Mae, we'd better be on our way.'

'You're always so hard on her,' Mae told him, when Sandy had left them and they were back at the Queen's. 'She's made mistakes, but she's always put her family first. And now she's got this new job, I am thinking she'll do well.'

'Who says I'm hard on her? I was polite, eh?'

'She knows what you think.'

'Canna help that. How am I supposed to stop thinking?' Harry

232

laughed shortly. 'Now, I'm supposed to be on stage with Mrs Ness this afternoon. She wants me to check the colours of some materials under the filters.'

''Tis strange, the way the lights can make the colours look what they are not,' said Mae.

'Nobody ever tell you, the theatre's all illusion? If I'd ever got to be an actor, maybe I'd be an illusion and all.'

'No, Harry, no!' Mae didn't know why, but the light-hearted remark sent something cold running down her spine. ''Tis not right at all to be talking like that!'

'Why, what's got into you?' he asked teasingly. 'I was just making a joke.'

He opened the door of Wardrobe. 'No Mrs Ness?'

'She is not back from her lunch.'

'Seems to be going out to lunch quite a lot these days. Got an admirer, eh? I've seen her arm-in-arm with an old codger.'

'Somebody who used to know her husband,' said Mae. She was still shivering, though feeling foolish about it. 'Maybe I'll come up on stage with you.'

But Mrs Ness came hurrying in, her face flushed as it always was when she'd been out for lunch, and with the faintest smell of alcohol on her breath.

'Oh, dear, late, as usual,' she said without any obvious regret. 'There you are, Harry – waiting for me, are you? Just give me a minute to find those samples – Mae, where did I put them?'

'Here, Mrs Ness.' Mae found the pieces of material in a box and handed them across.

'Aye, we're spending money, making from scratch with these,' said Mrs Ness. 'So, I want to get the colours right. Let's get started, then.'

'Take care,' called Mae, and when they turned to look at her in surprise, blushed scarlet.

'We're not planning on taking any risks,' Mrs Ness said wryly.

'She's joking,' said Harry. 'We're all joking today.'

And Mae could not explain that just for a little while she had felt afraid.

'Listen, was that Copperknob I saw you with, when I went out earlier?' Mrs Ness asked when she came back from the stage. 'What's she up to these days?'

'Sewing,' answered Mae with a smile. 'She's been taken on at John Johnson's for dress alterations.'

'Never! You do surprise me.' Mrs Ness laughed. 'No offence, dear, I know she's your friend, but she's always looked like a bit of a baggage to me. Still, if she's turned into a needlewoman, can't be bad, eh?'

Chapter Fifty-Three

It didn't take long for Mae to realise, when Sandy came round to practise her sewing, that she was going to be all right. She was so quick and skilful with her stitching and cutting and using Mae's second-hand sewing machine; so casual and unworried, talking and laughing, and biting off thread, that Mae could only open her blue eyes in surprise.

'Sure, you are not needing me at all, then, Sandy!' she exclaimed. 'Have you been practising already?'

'Och, no, but it's all coming back to me, you ken.' Sandy was laughing again, pleased with herself, and clearly relieved. 'Just like riding a bike, eh?'

'But if you were so good with your needle, why were you not wanting to keep on with it? 'Tis hard to understand.'

'Och, I wasnae much more than a bairn! Just out o' school. Stitching, or machining, day in, day out, it wasnae for me.' Sandy shrugged. 'Now, it's all I want.'

'I think you'll do well. You've no need to worry about your work at all.'

'Only thing is, I'm no' sure about fitting folk. Have you got one o' thae dummies, then?'

'No, but we can go over to Wardrobe at the theatre and use one there. Quick, now, Sandy, get your hat.'

'But are you sure it'll be OK for me to go? I'm no wanting to get you into trouble.'

'There'll be no trouble.' Mae was putting on her own hat at her mirror. 'Mrs Ness will not mind at all, but I'll speak to her any-way.'

Sandy still seemed to be hesitating.

'And that fella – the actor – Gareth something. He'll no' be there?'

'Gareth Paget's gone.' Mae looked with interest at the Sandy she could see in the mirror. 'He went down to London some time ago.'

'That's all right, then.' Sandy pulled on her small, brimmed hat. 'Shall we go?'

'Still interested?' asked Mae softly.

'I was never interested! I'm no' interested in men at all, as a matter of fact.'

''Tis understandable, but it'd be a shame to let what has happened spoil your life, Sandy.'

'Let's no' talk about it. I just want to see this dummy o' yours, Mae.'

They slipped in at the stage door, where Sam looked at Sandy with interest, and Sandy appeared fascinated by just being backstage.

'Och, what a warren, eh? How d'you find your way around? And where are all the actors?'

'Acting, o' course,' said Sam. 'You can hear their voices from here. They're doing a Scottish play tonight – *Rob Roy*.'

'Can I go up and watch from the sides?'

'The wings,' said Mae. 'We'd better not, might get in the way. But look – here is Wardrobe.'

'Oh, my lord!' cried Sandy, charmed, as Mae had been at interview, by the rows of costumes, wigs and props, the whole Aladdin's cave of bits and bobs and who knew what treasures. She stood in the centre of the long room, looking around with her hands clasped, and gave a long whistling sigh. 'What a grand place to work, Mae! Are you no' the lucky one?'

'I am.' Mae, smiling at Sandy's enthusiasm, showed her the dressmaker's dummy she was to practise on. 'Now, if you'll just be having a look at that, I will speak to Mrs Ness.'

But a voice calling her name made Mae jump and stare. Heavens, here was Mrs Ness herself, then, coming through the door, when she should be up by the stage!

She was accompanied by a middle-aged man wearing a trilby hat and a dark suit with a white carnation in his buttonhole. Though his tan was fading and his greying hair thinning, he was handsome in his way and clearly had once been a charmer. Might be one still, as far as Mrs Ness was concerned, for this was surely her admirer, the 'old codger', Ronnie.

'Whatever are you doing here, Mae?' asked Mrs Ness, raising her eyebrows. 'And with your friend?'

'Oh, Mrs Ness, sure I was just coming up to find you, to see if 'twas all right.' Mae was blushing a little, but Sandy was keeping quiet, simply standing beside the dummy and ignoring Ronnie's interested gaze.

'All right for what?' asked Mrs Ness. 'Running up a costume, or two?'

Hastily introducing Sandy, Mae explained that they had just come to Wardrobe so that Sandy could do a practice fitting on the dummy. She was starting her new sewing job on Monday.

'Oh yes, I think you told me.' Mrs Ness introduced Ronnie as 'her friend, Mr Abercromby'. 'I just came down for my coat,' she added. 'I don't think they need me up there, so we're going out for a bite of supper. You crack on, girls, and the best of luck, Miss Corrie, in your new job.'

'Yes, best of luck,' Ronnie echoed in gravelly tones. 'Nice to have met you two young ladies.' He tipped his hat and turned to help Mrs Ness into her coat. 'Perhaps we'll meet again?'

'Come along, Ronnie.' With a last look back to Mae, Mrs Ness took Mr Abercromby's arm and left.

Mae and Sandy exchanged glances.

'So, that's your boss?' asked Sandy. 'Different, eh? Never met anyone like her before.' She picked up a tape-measure and began to measure the dummy. 'And the old friend – who's he?'

'Somebody her husband knew. She's a widow.'

'Maybe there'll be wedding bells.'

Mae smiled. 'They're middle-aged, you know.'

'What of it? You can get married any time.'

'Sure, I'm always wanting my da to marry again. But I cannot see Mrs Ness getting married, somehow.'

'Most folk like being married.'

'Except you, Sandy?'

'Mebbe I'm different, too.'

They worked on for some time, with Mae demonstrating how to measure up the pretend client, how to drape material, how to pin and cut and make the necessary alterations, and Sandy following suit. Then Mae boiled the kettle on Mrs Ness's little gas ring and made tea, and they looked in the box and found a couple of digestive biscuits.

'Isn't this nice?' asked Sandy. 'So peaceful?'

''Tis not usually peaceful. Wait till all the actors are needing new costumes at the same time!'

'I bet you manage well, Mae. Cool as a cucumber, eh?'

And you would manage, too, thought Mae.

But then Harry arrived and said the play was over. Whatever were they doing in Wardrobe at that time of night?

'Enjoying ourselves,' said Sandy coolly.

'Working,' said Mae.

He looked from one to the other. 'Time to go home, anyway. Sam's locking up.'

They went out into the spring night and Sandy, turning up her collar, thanked Mae and promised to let her know how she got on.

'If I do OK, it'll be because of you. You're good at teaching folk like me.'

'You're a natural,' Mae told her. 'I am taking no credit.'

When Sandy had departed for her tram, Mae took Harry's arm.

'Guess who we saw tonight? Mrs Ness's admirer, Mr Abercromby. She brought him in, while she got her coat.'

He didn't seem interested and made no reply.

'Sandy thinks they might get married. I cannot believe they would. If they did, though, and Mrs Ness left, I might get her job.'

Harry looked down into Mae's upturned face. 'And work for ever?' he asked coldly.

'Well—' she was faltering under his gaze '—unless something happened.'

'Nothing is going to happen,' he told her, and opened their door.

Chapter Fifty-Four

Summer came, then autumn, and it was true, that for Harry and Mae 'nothing happened'. Things were happening elsewhere, though. A new political party was making news in Germany, and some said there could be trouble. Then there really was trouble nearer home, when hunger marchers rioted in London. But all of that simmered down, with no gains made for the poor starving folk, and there seemed no end to their misery.

The Queen's decided to put on a charity production of *Peter Pan* before Christmas, to benefit the children whose fathers were on the dole. What a wonderful idea, thought the company, until Mr Standish spoiled everything by asking Lottie to return as a visiting star to play Peter.

'Visiting star!' cried Primmie in fury. 'She's still at RADA! Now, I could play Peter perfectly well!'

'And I could,' chimed Vivvy, 'I'm small enough.'

But Mr Standish decreed that Lottie was so slight and ethereal, she was a natural for the flying role of Peter, so that was that.

'What he says, goes,' said Tony Vincent. 'I must say, it doesn't seem fair.'

'Just hope no one casts me for Tinker Bell,' Thea remarked.

'I'd settle for Tinker Bell,' cried Vivvy. 'Unless, of course, I'm Wendy.'

'Not a hope,' snapped Primmie. 'If I'm not going to be Peter, I'm certainly going to be Wendy, or I resign.'

'Oh, will you listen to them?' Mrs Ness asked testily. 'They're like a load of bairns arguing in the playground. I shall not be sorry to be out of this, Mae, I'm telling you!'

Mae raised her eyes. 'If I am not speaking out of turn, when are you going to be out of it, Mrs Ness?'

Mrs Ness flushed a little and made no reply.

'I am asking because you often say you might be leaving,' Mae pressed, surprised at her own boldness. 'I was thinking that I'd like to know where I stand.'

'I'm sorry, Mae, I should have put you in the picture before, but you know how it is.' Mrs Ness laughed and put her hand to her hair. 'I'm a bit self-conscious, discussing it, me being no chicken—'

Mae waited, scarcely breathing.

'And neither is Ronnie, of course, but the fact is, we've had an understanding for some time. Now, we think we might as well get wed. You probably think it's crazy? Getting married at our age?'

'No, I am thinking 'tis wonderful.' Mae stood up and throwing her arms around Mrs Ness, hugged her hard. 'Sure, you are doing the right thing and I am very glad for you. I wish you all the best.'

'Ah, you're a sweet girl, Mae, and I'm going to miss you when I'm away.' Mrs Ness sat down at the trestle table and put her hand-kerchief to her eyes. 'Oh, I'm shaking like a jelly. Can you believe it? Me behaving like a seventeen year old?'

'I'll make you some tea,' said Mae. 'Would you be having a biscuit, at all?'

'Couldn't eat a thing, dear. But, you know what, you'll be in line for my job. I've already told Mr Standish he'd never get any-one better, and he agreed.' Mrs Ness, looking in the biscuit tin, took out a shortbread. 'Might as well have this, just with my tea. So, there you are, Mae, it'll be promotion for you, and no one deserves it more. I'll be leaving in the New Year.'

'I cannot take it in,' said Mae faintly, as she poured out their tea. 'I am needing this as much as you, Mrs Ness.'

'It's late in the day, but call me Bernice, dear. I hope we'll always keep in touch.'

Mae was hesitating, looking over the rim of her cup.

'If I do get the job—'

'You will, Mae, you will.'

'I'll need an assistant.'

'Aha!' Mrs Ness. 'I know what's in your mind. You want your friend Sandy to take your place, eh?'

'I was thinking that,' Mae admitted. 'She's done so well at John

240

Johnson's, you see, and she really is good. I know she'd like to work here, she's said so, and I was thinking, maybe I could put her name forward?'

'She's a bright lassie, and no mistake, but I daresay she'd have to have an interview.' Mrs Ness crunched on her shortbread. 'Why don't you have a word with Mr Standish?'

'After I have been appointed myself,' said Mae with a smile.

'Well, yes, dear, better wait for that.'

Chapter Fifty-Five

Amazement greeted Mrs Ness's announcement of her engagement to the company. Mrs Ness, getting married again! At her age? And going abroad, too, for Ronnie Abercromby, it seemed, could not take the Scottish climate after his years in Burma and would be removing with his bride to the south of France.

'The south of France?' cried the actors, almost turning green.

'Aye, we're going to live in a pension in Nice and look around for an apartment,' Mrs Ness told them triumphantly. 'Ooh-la-la – here I come!'

Well, of course, she was wished the best of luck and heartily congratulated. In fact, there were congratulations all round, for there was general delight that Mae had been appointed to Mrs Ness's job. Couldn't be a better choice, was everyone's opinion, and Lottie, up for the rehearsals of *Peter Pan*, said she was quite over the moon.

Even when she was flinging her arms round Mae and seeming just her old self, it seemed to Mae that in some subtle way she had changed. The steel that had always been there was just a little more apparent, and where confidence had never been her strong point unless she was actually on stage, it was now a part of her. Oh, it was true – Lottie might be still a student – but she was, as Mr Standish had declared, an obvious star.

'And how's Brett?' asked Mae. 'Doing well?'

'He's getting some parts, but to be honest I don't see him so much these days. We've – you know – grown apart.' Lottie sighed. 'Mummy's always wanting me to marry and settle down, but she understands now that I'm married already.'

'To your work.'

'Right, as usual, Mae! But, tell me, how's Harry?'

How was Harry? Very well, of course, Mae answered. Fine. And if Lottie saw the shadow that crossed her face at the mention of his name, she was too tactful to mention it.

But Mae had found much to grieve over since her appointment had been announced. Congratulations all round, yes, except from the one who mattered most.

'It's just like I said,' he'd muttered when she'd told him her news. 'You'll be working for ever.'

'You've never minded me working, Harry. Why should you not be pleased if I get promotion?'

'Can you no' understand, Mae? Makes it clear that your job's no' just temporary till the bairns come. They'd never have given it to you if they'd thought you might be leaving any time.' He'd laughed shortly. 'Lets everybody see what our situation is, eh?'

'You are making it sound as though we should be ashamed of not having children.'

He'd made no reply, but she knew it was true of him. Harry was ashamed. Took it as a personal insult, as Sandy had put it, that he had not been able to father a child, and would not seek help. 'If they found out it was me, I'd never be able to accept it,' he'd said. But, then, he had scarcely been able to accept his failure to become an actor.

If only she could help him, Mae thought, as she had so often thought before. But there was nothing she could do.

On a day in December, Sandy, having sailed through the interview, was appointed as Mae's assistant, to the enthusiastic approval of the males of the company. A redhead in Wardrobe? No disrespect to Mrs Ness, of course, who'd always done well, but with the lovely Mae in charge, and Copperknob as her assistant, things were looking up, no doubt about it.

'We should have a little celebration,' suggested Lottie, on the day of the charity performance of *Peter Pan*. 'Just our usual at the dear old Rowan Tree. It will take our minds off opening night.'

'Surely, you are not nervous?' asked Primmie.'

'I am always nervous.'

'All good actors are nervous,' declared Tony Vincent. 'I'm a bag of nerves myself, and I'm only Captain Hook.'

243

'Of course, I'm nervous, too,' Primmie said quickly. 'So, it's a good idea to go out for lunch and think of something else.'

'I'm the nervous one,' Sandy whispered to Mae. 'I mean, being with all thae toffs. What'll I say?'

'Toffs?' Harry interrupted. 'They're actors, not toffs. No different from you or me, that's what Mae told me once. So, you just be yourself, Sandy, and you'll be fine.'

She looked at him, surprised, and gave him a grateful smile. 'You're coming, Harry, eh?'

'No, I've things to do. Canna manage it.'

'Oh, Harry!' cried Mae. 'Please, come.'

He stood firm, however, and in the end they went to the Rowan Tree without him.

They were late back, and so was Harry, from wherever he had been. The pub, thought Mae, her heart sinking, as she met him in the stage door passageway and smelled his breath. As the actors went on to prepare for a last rehearsal later that afternoon, Mae caught at Harry's arm.

'You were not doing anything, were you?' she asked him quietly. 'You could have come with us.'

'Got plenty to do now, anyway. There's a spotlight bulb to change before tonight's performance.'

'A spotlight bulb? Who's helping you? It's dangerous to try to work on a ladder on your own.'

'You trying to tell me ma job, Mae? I know I need somebody to foot the ladder.'

'You will be sure to find someone, Harry?'

'I've said, haven't I?' His face softened as he took in her expression. 'No need to look so worried, sweetheart. I'm experienced, remember?'

Sure, he was, yet she could not control the sudden fear that was sending again a trickle of coldness down her spine.

'Harry, I've been thinking,' she said quickly. 'If you are not wanting me to do this job, I need not do it. What is a job? It should not come between us.'

He bent to kiss her. 'Ah, Mae, that's good of you. I know how much it means to you.'

'I mean it. I can give it up.'

'I don't want you to do that. There'd be no point, eh? Let's just keep going and see what happens.'

'You are sure, Harry?'

'Aye, I'm sure.'

They kissed again, and then he left her, heading for the upper circle, while Mae went into Wardrobe and sat down in the empty room. Mrs Ness was still out with Ronnie. She'd been asked to join them at the Rowan Tree, but had said some other time. Everybody knew, of course, that she'd be going with Ronnie to the Caledonian – his favourite watering hole, as he called it.

Mae, looking out at the dark December afternoon, was glad to be on her own; she did not at all want to talk. In fact, she was feeling strange; on edge, as though waiting for a storm, though no storm was brewing on that winter's day. Perhaps in her head? Something was beating, there. Throbbing. Pulsing. Suddenly, it seemed to her that she knew what she must do.

'Harry!' she cried, leaping to her feet. 'Harry, I am coming!'

But she was too late. Mr Standish was at the door, Mrs Ness behind him, still wearing her hat and coat, her eyes on Mae so wide and dark.

'Mae, my dear,' Mr Standish was whispering. 'Oh, Mae – will you come with me?'

'Is it Harry?' she asked, her face very calm. A mask.

It was Harry.

Chapter Fifty-Six

He was lying where he had fallen, at the foot of his ladder beneath the bar that held the spotlight. He looked very young, very peaceful, and as though he were sleeping. As though he could wake at any moment. Open his hazel eyes and spring to his feet, and say, 'Why, Mae, what's wrong? Why are you looking like that?'

As she knelt beside him and put her face to his, those with her looked away. Of course, they knew she couldn't be taking in that he was dead. It was too much; too much of a shock, and she was keeping far too calm.

Let it go, dear, Mrs Ness told her silently. Cry. You must cry.

But for long moments, her mask stayed in place. Then she kissed him on his still warm cheek, and the tears came.

'What happened?' she asked shakily, as they helped her up and held her.

He had fallen from the ladder, they said, though Gerry Ames was holding it. But why had he fallen? Oh, not because of his drinking, thought Mae, twisting her hands in anguish, please God let no one speak of that. But Gerry, with tears in his eyes, said he didn't know why Harry had fallen.

Everything had seemed secure. Harry had done all that he should have done, disconnected the power just as he always did, and replaced the bulb. But then, after he'd done that, Gerry had looked away, only for an instant, down to the stage where some actors were gathering, and the next thing he saw was Harry falling. Somehow, coming down, he'd missed his footing. Gerry had rushed to save him, to hold him, but he was too late. Harry had hit the floor. Harry was dead.

It was the way he had fallen, they murmured, just bad luck. He had broken his neck. All over in a moment. Gone.

'Oh, my God,' Gerry kept saying brokenly. 'Oh, my God, there he was, there he was – I couldn't believe it, Mae – I couldn't believe it!'

But Mae, with dread, was asking Mr Standish, 'Has anyone told Harry's mother?'

Oh, poor Emmy! There was no mask for her. She came apart immediately, as they'd known she would, and though Rona and Mae herself supported her, she could not contain her grief. Even when the doctor came, followed by the police, for of course there would have to be a fatal accident inquiry, she would not leave Harry and had to be prised away. It wasn't till Ben and Jake arrived that she allowed herself to be parted from her son, be given tea she didn't want and cling to those who were left.

'I'll give her something,' the doctor murmured. 'What about you, Mrs Alpin?'

But Mae didn't want anything. Except for the mists surrounding her to clear, so that she could think about her Harry and try to understand.

'Come home, Mae,' Lottie whispered. 'Let us take you home.'

'I want to see Harry again,' said Mae.

Yes, one last look and one last kiss, but still she didn't go home. She went to Emmy and put her arms around her, and together the Alpins went back to the Row, while Lottie and Sandy and everyone else stood aside. This was family grief; they would not intrude.

'What shall we do about the performance?' the company asked Mr Standish. 'Will you cancel?'

'In the ordinary way, I would have done.' He sighed and ran his hand over his ashen face. 'But think of the children.'

'Harry wouldn't have wanted it cancelled,' said Gerry thickly. 'Those bairns have been looking forward to this for weeks.'

'I vote we go ahead,' declared Thea. 'Mae wouldn't want to disappoint the children, either.'

'Shall we speak to Mae?' asked Primmie.

But no one wanted to speak to Mae. The decision was taken to go ahead with the charity performance, and if it was the hardest work the company had ever done, their reward was to know they had enchanted their audience.

'Oh, those poor little kids,' said Thea, watching them rushing for free ice creams in the interval. 'Thank God they don't know what's happened.'

'Aye, they're in Never-Never Land for once in their lives,' said Tim Powell, the stage-manager. 'No point letting reality in.'

No point telling them that a man had died who would have been glad to see them happy. Or, that his family across the way was trying to face a reality of their own, which was grief.

Chapter Fifty-Seven

Doing what had to be done after a death helped Mae and the Alpins through the days that followed, although Emmy could not be comforted whatever she did. It was his family's wish, even if Harry himself had been no kirk-goer, that his service should be held in the kirk, and Mae had agreed. She would say her own prayers, light her own candle, but come to the kirk to make her last goodbye.

Everyone was so kind, but she liked to spend time alone, reliving her life with Harry, rethinking their last day, when they had parted with such sweetness; seeing him again, as she had seen him where he lay, as though asleep. A troubled man, at peace at last.

After the funeral, she said she planned to go to Ireland. Spend Christmas with her da. Yes, that would be best, everyone agreed, then she could decide what to do.

She had asked, what was there to decide?

Well, where she wanted to stay. In Edinburgh, she was a long way from home.

Her look had been surprised. Why, her home was here, where Harry's had been. There would be no change. She would continue her work at the theatre. What else?

'Just take one day at a time, dear,' Mrs Ness advised. 'That's the way.'

Perhaps she was right. It wasn't possible, thought Mae, to contemplate a whole lifetime ahead without Harry. First, she must get through the funeral.

In a terrible way, it was a repeat performance of the wedding. On a hard, cold December afternoon, the same people came, but this time to the kirk. Apart from his family, all Harry's friends were there, including Gordon Kinnon, who had been his best man, as well as the neighbours from the Row, Mrs Beith's son and Pauline, her lodger, and everyone from the Queen's. Miss Thorburn came, and Miss Dow, Dr Rick and Sandy, and even, again, the woman from the newsagent's where Harry had bought his paper. Oh, yes, it was a grand turnout, the Alpins said, Harry would have been proud.

After the service, folk were invited back, not to the theatre, but to a café off Princes Street, for tea and sandwiches, while the family made their tragic journey to the cemetery. The Alpins had been worried that they couldn't afford to pay for the refreshments, but Mae had a little money from an insurance policy Harry had left and told them she could afford it.

'Ah, you're a good lassie,' Ben had murmured. 'And you were a good wife, too,' he added in a low voice. 'Did all you could for Harry.'

She made no reply to that.

Some days later, she left for Ireland, pale and subdued in her black, but finding a smile for Susie and Jannie, whose eyes on her were huge and who clung to her with thin determined arms.

'You'll be coming back, eh?' they asked her. 'Promise, Mae?'

'Sure, I'm coming back. I promise you.'

'Aye, they'll be looking out for you,' said Rona, standing ready to wave. 'Canna lose you as well.' Her lip trembled and she gathered the children to her.

'They will not be losing me.' Mae gave them all quick hugs. 'Take care, then, Rona. Take care of your ma.'

They thought of Emmy in the flat up the stair, which she now rarely left, and knew that no amount of care would restore her soon to health.

'Time's the thing,' said Mrs Beith arriving with a bag that she pushed into Mae's hand. 'Aye, time's the healer. There's a few o' ma scones for the journey, Mae. Dinna say no. You've to keep well, you ken. Eat what you can.'

And then Mae was away to the station, in the taxi Mr Standish had booked for her, and the last thing those on the step saw was her white hand waving, as the cab turned the corner and left the Row.

Chapter Fifty-Eight

Joseph O'Donovan met Mae at Cork. He was wearing a black tie and his ancient black suit, and as soon as he put his arm round her and let her cry, she felt comforted, as she had never felt comforted since Harry's death.

'Poor girl, poor Mae,' he said softly. ''Tis a terrible thing to be losing your man so young – against all nature, can only be said. But I'm thanking God that you've come home.'

'For a little while, Da. I have to go back.' Mae wiped her eyes. 'Is there time for a cup of tea before our train?'

'Sure, there is.' Joseph carefully took a leather purse from his waistcoat pocket and examined his coins. 'All the time in the world.'

Over her mug of strong sweet tea in the station buffet that was decorated for Christmas and full of Christmas travellers, Mae raised drenched eyes to Joseph's face.

'What is it?' he asked swiftly. 'Mae, what is troubling you? 'Tis more than grief.'

''Tis regret, Da. Was it my fault?'

'Your fault Harry fell?'

'My fault he was not happy.'

'Ah, mavourneen, these thoughts always come after death. 'Tis so final, is all. No chance ever again to make the loved one happy. But you made Harry happy in life.' Joseph stretched out his hand to hers. 'I know it. And he was knowing it, I am telling you.'

'There was the darkness in him, Da, you were seeing it yourself. Should I not have saved him from it?' Mae's face was working with emotion. 'Should I not have helped him more?'

'Put these regrets away, Mae. Your conscience is clear. Harry was a difficult man, not made for happiness, but as sure as I am looking at you now, I know you both loved each other and that you made him as happy as you could. Thanks be to God for that, my dear girl. As the time goes by, the clouds will clear and you will remember it.' Joseph smiled, in reminiscence of his own happiness. 'And think of the good times.'

'Think of the good times,' Mae whispered. 'Da, I will. I will.'

'Drink up your tea, then, and we'll go for the train. There's a surprise for you, waiting at home.'

'A surprise? You mean, a present?'

'Not a present. A person.' Joseph smiled. ''Tis Rosaleen.'

She was as lovely as ever, though thinner, and in her violet eyes, as Mae recognised, was the knowledge of sorrow. Still, she was ready with her smiles when Mae arrived, and though never close, the two cousins, after the long years apart, held each other in shared sympathy.

'Oh, Mae, I was so sorry to hear from Uncle Joseph about your Harry,' Rosaleen said in her soft voice that had taken on a slight American accent. 'You poor, poor girl . . . I had no idea.'

'I sent a letter, but they take so long – you can never have received it.'

'No, it's some time since I left. Shall I be taking up your bag?' Rosaleen put back her black hair that she had kept unfashionably long, and laughed a little. 'We'll be up in our old place, Mae. How many years since we slept up there?'

But Joseph took up Mae's bag and Annie Morragh came bustling in to fold Mae in her arms and shed a few tears.

'Oh, 'tis too hard,' she declared. 'A loss like this you should not be bearing. Such a lovely man to be taken – 'tis too hard, so it is.'

And Mae knew she was remembering Harry on his honeymoon, mending her lamp and her chair, just as she herself was remembering him. Remembering Harry, in those early days when he had been happy.

They had tea and soda bread, and Mae unpacked her few clothes up in the old loft room she was to share with Rosaleen. Weary as she was, when she came down, she said she'd like to walk by the sea.

'Are you not wanting to rest?' asked Rosaleen. 'Such a long journey as you've had?'

'The air will clear my head,' Mae answered, and the two cousins put on their coats, tied scarves around their black hair and went out together.

The sky was darkening over the sea that was beating fiercely on the shore, and there were no fishing boats to be seen. This was Traynore in winter – bleak, comfortless – but familiar. Just another aspect of home, and what the cousins sought, for there they were, home again.

'Want to walk on to the harbour?' asked Rosaleen. 'There'll be no activity today.'

'No, I'll go tomorrow.' Mae glanced at her cousin's delicate profile. 'Rosaleen, might I be asking, but where is Kieran?'

'Kieran? In New York, of course. Working.'

'He wasn't wanting to come with you?'

'No, this trip is for me alone.'

There was a spot above the tidemark where someone had placed a rough bench, and Rosaleen drew Mae towards it.

'Shall we sit here for a while?' She took off her scarf and let her hair blow freely. 'If you are wondering how I paid for it, I borrowed the money from Kieran's uncle. He's always been very kind to me.'

'I was never thinking of it,' said Mae.

'No, though 'tis something to think about, crossing the Atlantic.' Rosaleen smiled. 'But I shall not be needing a return ticket.'

'Rosaleen!' Mae's eyes widened. 'What are you saying?'

'I have left Kieran.'

'But that's not possible. You are married. You can't stop being married.'

'In Ireland, maybe not. But in America, yes, you can.'

'You are not – you are not talking of divorce?'

'Not yet. But really our marriage is over.'

Mae looked out to sea, her face shadowed and troubled. 'I always believed you to be happy,' she said after a pause.

'We have never been happy since Molly died. It was as though what we had – went with her.'

'Oh, Rosaleen, I'm so sorry.' Mae caught at her cousin's hand. 'So very sorry. And for Kieran, too.'

253

'Yes, it's hard.' Rosaleen shrugged. 'But these things happen. Life's hard for us all.'

'What will you do, then? Stay here, in Ireland?'

'I'm not sure. I am thinking I might go to London. Find a job in a hotel, or something. Not as a chambermaid.' Rosaleen's lovely mouth turned down. 'No more service for me. Maybe, receptionist, something like that.'

'I cannot think what to say,' Mae said after a long silence. 'This is such a surprise. What does Da say?'

'Oh, you know your da. He never judges.' Rosaleen stood up and retied her scarf. 'But Annie's looking down her nose at me, when she's a fine one to talk, and all. Shall we go home, Mae? Will soon be dark.'

At the door of the cottage, Mae looked back at the way they had come. Already, in the short time it had taken them to return, night had fallen. It wasn't possible to see the sea, or anything, in the soft, Irish darkness, but she felt a part of it. Knew she would, for a time. Perhaps for a long time, would cherish the dark, before she looked for the light again.

'Come in, come in,' Annie was calling to her. 'See where your da's lit us a lovely fire?'

And Mae went in and put her hands to the blaze, and felt at peace.

Part Four

Chapter Fifty-Nine

Another season of pantomime had ended. Another *Aladdin*, in fact, for the Queen's hadn't produced it since the winter of 1928/9, and it was worth repeating. Everyone liked it, that was the thing. Except Mrs Ness. But, then, Mrs Ness was in the south of France, and had been for four years. No more complaining about mending lampshade hats for her!

Four years. Had it been so long since Mrs Ness married? And Harry died? For Mae, waving to the departing company with Sandy at her side, watching them pack their costume hampers into their van, lampshade hats and all, the answer was yes. Yes, it had been so long. A lifetime. It was only now that she felt she was coming out of that life into another. Only now, in February 1936, was the pain of loss easing away.

'Thank goodness that lot's gone,' said Sandy, shivering as she came back from the stage door. 'Och, I dinna care for visiting companies. I'm looking forward to our folk coming back.'

There had been changes, though, amongst the Queen's Players. Changes everywhere, Mae reflected. Even a new king had been proclaimed, for George V had died in January, and the Queen's had had to close for a while out of respect. How would the Prince of Wales, the darling of the people, take to being king? Didn't matter as much to Mae as the changes nearer home.

Only two years after Harry's death, Emmy had died in her sleep. Heart, the doctor said, but everyone knew that Emmy had never wanted to wake up in the mornings.

'Aye, poor Emmy, never could face anything,' Ben had sighed. 'Like Henry, you ken. I always used to think he took after his ma.'

But Rona had said, 'Poor Dad', and with her family had moved up the stair to look after him.

'He canna boil a tatty,' she'd told Mae. 'Ma spoiled him, like she spoiled Harry. Too late for him to learn now, eh? But why do you no' take on my flat, Mae? It's got a wee bedroom you could make into a bathroom, same as Mrs Beith's.'

At first, Mae had protested that she could never leave her own little place where she and Harry had been so happy; at least, in the early days. But then the idea began to appeal, for Harry was with her wherever she went, and she'd always longed for a bathroom. In the end, she did make the move next door and after borrowing the money from the landlord, put in the longed-for bathroom.

Oh, joy! But then had come another change, for who should move into her old flat, but Norrie Beith, who had left the army, found a job at the Council offices, and married Pauline King.

'Aye, she'll have to stir herself now,' Mrs Beith had commented. 'She'll no' have me to wait on her, and Norrie'll be out at work. There's a babby on the way as well, so watch out for bawlin', Mae.'

'I shan't mind,' Mae had said bleakly, and Mrs Beith had pressed her hand.

But she was content in her new home, and happy in her work, with Sandy as her capable assistant. Some things worked out for the best, then.

'Waiting for anyone special?' she asked Sandy, who gave her a sharp look.

'Now, who would that be? And dinna say Brett Lester!'

There was a change for you, thought Mae. Brett Lester back at the Queen's, but not as an actor. No, he'd been given Tim Powell's old job as stage manager, Tim having gone to New York, and would be doubling up as designer.

'It's essential now, everyone says, to have a proper designer,' he'd told Mae, on his return. 'And I've done a course for it, which impressed Mr Standish. Must have done, seeing as he gave me Tim's job.'

A little older now, and somehow more attractive for it, Brett was still his easy, friendly self. Seeing his eyes stray to Sandy, busy with wigs at the long table, Mae wondered if he was taken with her and had forgotten Lottie. All the same, she asked him about Lottie.

'Lottie?' He smiled wryly. 'She's too grand for me these days. I hardly ever see her.'

'I'm sorry about that.' Mae did not mention that she only heard from Lottie at Christmas herself. ''Tis good she's doing well, though.'

'Oh, yes, even had her name in lights on Shaftesbury Avenue. Thea saw her lately – said the offers were rolling in. Always knew they would.'

''Tis good that Thea is still with us,' Mae said after a pause. 'Too many have gone.'

Among them, Tony Vincent and Primmie Day who'd not only gone to London but married as well – who'd have thought it? And Vivvy Bruce was now training as a mannequin and out of acting altogether.

'Showing sense at last,' Brett remarked. 'And I'm glad I'm out of it, too. When I see all these new guys here, for instance, angling round for the best parts, I think, thank God that's not me!'

'You mean, Roderick, Lance and Desmond?' asked Mae laughing, and glancing at Sandy. 'Sure, they're more in Wardrobe than on the stage.'

'I bet they are,' said Brett.

But Sandy wasn't interested, in Roderick, Lance, or Desmond. Or in Brett himself, it seemed. Certainly didn't care to discuss him, that wintry February afternoon, when Mae was gently teasing. No doubt, one of these days, she would really forget the bad times and fall for someone, as Mae had done herself. Meantime, she was doing well; looking after her mother and the family as before, and if she had less money to spend on them since she'd given up her modelling work, at least she was happier.

And she was not alone in being short of money. The economic situation was no better. There was still talk of hunger marches.

'Aye, we'll be no better off till there's a war,' some folk were saying, but Mae couldn't bear to think of that. Surely, anything would be better than enduring another war?

Chapter Sixty

A day came when Brett looked in at Wardrobe with a message. Mr Standish wanted to see everyone at eleven o'clock. On stage.

'Wants to see us?' Sandy stared. 'What for?'

'Never said. Just wants everyone there, on stage, at eleven o'clock this morning.'

Mae and Sandy exchanged glances.

'He must be going to make an announcement,' said Mae slowly. 'Bad news, would it be?'

'The theatre's closing?' asked Brett, with a grin that quickly died. 'I say, you don't really think that could be it?'

'Why would he want to speak to everyone?' asked Sandy, who had turned pale. 'Och, this is a terrible world, eh? Everything collapsing around us?'

'Sure, we're only guessing here,' said Mae. 'No need to worry yet.'

All the same, she looked worried.

'I've other people to see,' said Brett, glancing at his watch. 'Typical of old Standish to give us scarcely any notice. Or, maybe that was planned? Doesn't want us to speculate.'

'Let's go up now,' Sandy said nervously. 'It's no' far off eleven. Dinna want to be late.'

'Indeed, no,' Mae agreed. 'Best not keep himself waiting.'

They hurried up the tortuous route from Wardrobe to the stage, where they found members of the company already gathering, together with the rest of the theatre staff, all looking nervous.

'Morning, Mae,' said Gerry Ames. 'What's all this about, then?'

'Who knows?' She smiled, but when her eyes and those of Gerry's companion met, she looked away and so did he.

'Hello, Mae,' said Euan MacKail, the young man who had replaced Harry in Lighting, and also moved in as Mrs Beith's new lodger, on Mae's recommendation. He would certainly be able to knock in nails and do Mrs B's odd jobs, she had reasoned, yet she was glad she didn't often see him at Number Eight.

'Hello, Euan,' she replied.

After an awkward moment, he moved off.

It was always that way when they met, Mae and Euan, for when she saw him, she realised her loss afresh, and when he saw her, he remembered what had happened to his predecessor. Both were relieved to turn away to others.

On the stroke of eleven, however, Mr Standish appeared, and those on the stage fell silent.

Chapter Sixty-One

'You are probably wondering why I've asked you to come here this morning,' the theatre manager began, in his splendid voice. 'Let me put your minds at rest. The theatre is not going to close. The Queen's Players are not going to be disbanded.'

A murmur of relief ran through his audience, at which he held up his hand.

'So, what do I want to say, then?' He paused, playing his audience along, like the good actor he had been. 'Something to be expected, maybe. Or, maybe not. It's this, anyway. After many happy years at the Queen's, I have to tell you, ladies and gentlemen—' he bowed his head '—that I am planning to retire.' After a moment, he looked up and smiled. 'No applause, please.'

The murmur that rose up then swelled into a chorus of sighs, groans, cries of 'No!' 'Impossible!' 'But why?' until Mr Standish, still smiling, had to call for silence.

'"Why?" did I hear you ask?' He flung out his hands. 'Because I want a little time for myself. To play golf, or travel, maybe. To go to America with my dear wife to see our daughter. Or, maybe just to hand over the reins to someone else. You'll be pleased to know that I've found that someone, and my recommendation for the appointment has been accepted by the Board of Directors.'

More murmurs, whispers, and exchanging of looks, which Mr Standish allowed to continue for a moment or two, before again holding up his hand.

'Who is he? Someone you'll remember – at least, some of you.' He ran his eye over the watching faces. 'Ah, now, I can see you looking puzzled – who can it be? Well, here's a clue. Some years ago, he played most of the leading roles for this company. Any clearer?'

'For God's sake, will he stop teasing,' muttered Brett, as Thea kicked his ankle to warn him to shut up. 'Who the devil is it?'

'You'll forgive me my little bit of showmanship.' Mr Standish was walking towards the wings. 'Because you all understand, of course, that it's my job to be a showman. I've been one all my life. So, ladies and gentlemen, I give you my successor as theatre manager of the Queen's. Here he is – fresh from his triumphs at the London Old Vic—'

And as Mr Standish waved his hand, out from the wings stepped a tall, black-haired man, known indeed to many of those present.

'No!' whispered Sandy, grasping Mae's arm. 'Oh, no!'

'Mr Gareth Paget, in person!' cried Mr Standish, and it was Gareth's turn to bow.

'Stage direction – pandemonium,' Brett said acidly, as there was a rush from the company to surround Gareth and Mr Standish, who was proudly watching his successor as though he were a schoolmaster admiring a favourite pupil.

'Now, now, green-eyes,' Thea whispered with a laugh. 'It's no skin off your nose to have Gareth appointed – you're too young to have got the job.'

'Oh, God, though – we knew him as one of us!'

'He's been away, he'll be different. Come on, look happy, let's join in the congrats.'

As Brett was hauled away, Sandy was edging from the crowd round Gareth and staring at Mae.

'Oh, Mae, what a thing, eh? Him coming back? I canna believe it. I thought he'd gone for good.'

'You've no need to worry about him,' Mae whispered comfortingly. ''Tis years since he was here.'

'You mean, he'll have forgotten me?' Sandy smiled crookedly. 'Aye, I'm sure you're right. Think I've a big head, then? Why should he remember me, eh?'

'We will not be seeing much of him, I'm thinking, he being top man.'

'And probably married, anyway.' Sandy shrugged. 'Hope he is.'

'Let's go over to say hello.' Mae took Sandy's arm. 'Come on, get it over with. You'll have to see him some time.'

With the reluctant Sandy in tow, Mae inserted herself into the crowd of well-wishers and added her congratulations.

'Why, Mae, thank you!' cried Gareth, shaking her hand. 'I'm so glad to see you. I want to tell you how very sad I was to hear about Harry, and how sorry I was to miss the funeral. I did mean to write, in fact—'

'I understand, Gareth,' she told him gently. 'No need to speak of it.'

'You're sure?' Gareth was turning his head toward Sandy, who was staring down at the stage boards. 'But it's grand you're still here. Is Mrs Ness with you?'

'Mrs Ness has married again and is living abroad, but I have her job now, and Sandy here is my assistant. You remember Sandy Corrie?'

'Miss Corrie?' Gareth smiled coolly. 'Yes, of course. Didn't we meet at the wedding? How are you, then? How amazing that you're working in Wardrobe.'

'Gareth!' cried Mr Standish, coming up and clapping him on the shoulder. 'Come and have a drink – I've ordered wine for everyone. Excuse us, Mae, won't you? But have some wine yourself. You, too, Sandy.'

'Well, seemingly you got it right, I needn't worry about him,' Sandy said flatly, watching Gareth's tall figure move away. 'If he does remember me, he's no' keen about it. Gone up in the world, eh?'

'You refused to go out with him,' Mae reminded her, as hired waitresses brought round wine. 'Perhaps he is remembering that.'

'Och, he can tell I'd no' be right for him, anyway.' Sandy drank deeply. 'Apart from anything else, I'm no' his class, eh?'

'Ah, now, Sandy, that's no way to be talking.'

'And he's a married man an' all.' Sandy tossed her head. 'Believe me, he's got the look.'

But Sandy was wrong about that, for Sally Anderson, trying on a dress in Wardrobe, reported with pleasure that Gareth Paget was still a bachelor.

'Very eligible,' commented Thea.

'Available,' said Sally.

Sandy, stitching with concentration, made no comment.

Chapter Sixty-Two

Mae had prophesied that they would not see much of Gareth, now that he was top man, or Director, as he now styled himself, and at first this was true. He was a new broom, he had to start sweeping, and spent much of his time closeted with Brett, mapping out future plans for the Queen's.

'Not that they're anything startling,' Brett told Mae, for unlike Gareth, Brett frequently dropped in on Wardrobe from his little office next door. Always said he found it 'peaceful'. 'That a joke?' was Sandy's laughing question.

'What sort of thing, then?' Mae asked now.

'Oh, just wanting to involve everybody more. Letting 'em put forward their views and such. Liaising, as he calls it.'

'Not a bad idea?'

'No, and pretty modern, as a matter of fact. I agree, you have to move with the times.' Brent shrugged. 'I've worked in London, I know what's new. But then he wants to widen the theatre's appeal. Get poor folk interested, which I can tell him now is a complete waste of time, unless he gives 'em the price of the tickets.'

'When they have no food on the table, they are not going to be able to afford the theatre.' Mae sighed. 'I wish they could, though.'

'Wish we lived in an ideal world.'

'At least Gareth's heart is in the right place.'

'Couldn't say where his heart is.' Brett slid off the table where he had been sitting, swinging his long legs. 'But I'd better get back – he'll be looking for me. Sandy not in?'

'Out buying some thread we need.' Mae looked towards the door. 'Or, was. I think she's coming in now.'

'Hey, where's the fire?' asked Brett, laughing, as Sandy, her face flushed, came hurrying in. 'You look as though you're on the run.'

'What a piece o' nonsense!' She took off her coat and hat, and tidied her hair. 'What are you doing here, anyway?'

'Chatting to Mae about our dear Director. Which reminds me, I'd better go and see if he wants to – ahem – liaise with me.'

'He's just come in,' said Sandy, then lowered her eyes as fresh colour flooded her face. 'I mean, I saw him at the stage door.'

For some moments, Brett and Mae gazed at her, then Mae began to examine the contents of the package she had laid on the table, and Brett moved away.

'So, he will be looking for me,' he said jauntily, and slid out of the door.

'Damn,' said Sandy. 'Damn, damn, damn. And a lot more words I'll no' say out loud. Och, it'll be all over the theatre now, that I've been talking to Gareth.'

'Have you?' asked Mae.

Sandy put her hands to her scarlet cheeks.

'Oh, Mae, it's so crazy – he's asked me out.'

It took patient questioning and two cups of tea before Mae could find out how this had come about. Only a meeting at the stage door, apparently, where Gareth had been having a quick smoke when Sandy had rushed in with her shopping. Sam not being there, they had talked together, easily and without the coolness of their previous encounter, and – well – they'd ended up arranging to go out the next night for dinner.

'Dinner,' echoed Mae, smiling. 'Just what Gareth wanted to give you all those years ago! You see, he has not forgotten you, Sandy.'

But Sandy, now quite pale, was not looking happy.

'It sounds OK, Mae, but the truth is, I should have said no, like I did before. I mean, what's changed?'

'Why, a lot has changed. You are here, Sandy. 'Tis a huge difference.'

'I canna change what I used to do.' Sandy's voice was low. 'And I canna change having ma boy, and dinna want to.'

Mae was silent. She held up the new threads, examining their shades in the light, then laid them down.

'Just what we wanted,' she murmured. 'Thanks, Sandy.'

'I notice you're no' finding anything to say, Mae. You ken as well as me, I shouldnae be going out with Gareth Paget. I mean, what do I tell him?'

'Nothing, when you're just going out for a meal.'

'It might no' be just this one dinner.' Sandy shook her head.

'Still, you need not tell him straight away.'

'No. But it'll be hanging over ma head until I do.' Sandy shivered a little. 'Oh, God, will he understand? I mean, it's no disgrace to work for artists, eh? It doesnae mean anything. And then, I did think Finlay's dad loved me. I thought we'd be married.'

'And you were very young. You should not be blamed.'

'So, he might understand?'

'He might. I mean, he will. But leave it for a while. Until he knows you better, and you know him.'

'I think you're right, Mae. That's what I'll do.'

Heavens, how Sandy is changing, thought Mae, taking my advice.

No more was said until the end of the day, when Sandy, who was on duty that evening, watched Mae getting ready to leave.

'Mae,' she said quietly, 'D'you mind if I ask – would you no' like to meet someone again?'

Mae, putting on her hat, smiled.

'I'm happy as I am, Sandy.'

'But it's been a few years now, since Harry went, and you're young, you deserve some happiness again.'

'No need to worry about me, I'm all right. And don't worry about Gareth, either. Everything will work out, I feel it.'

'I dinna ken what I feel,' sighed Sandy.

Am I happy as I am? Mae asked herself, as she left by the stage door. Probably it was more true to say she'd just grown used to her life without a man. Maybe it had its advantages. If you didn't mind being lonely sometimes. If you didn't mind doing without love.

Chapter Sixty-Three

In spite of Sandy's fears, Brett had apparently spread no gossip about her, for no one at the theatre teased her, and no one even seemed to suspect that she and Gareth were meeting. Of course, they were very careful. It was the last thing either of them wanted, that anyone should know of their relationship, for Gareth had his position to think of, and Sandy had her own reasons for keeping things quiet.

'Gareth's so new to his job, he feels it wouldnae look right,' she told Mae. 'I mean, to be starting a love affair at the same time.'

'This is really a love affair, then?'

Sandy looked down. 'Seems to be,' she said huskily. 'But I'm no' keen to have it all out in the open, because – well, you ken why. I've things in ma life I want to keep secret.'

'So, you've not said anything yet to Gareth?'

'No' yet.'

Mae's eyes on Sandy were steady.

'I believe Gareth cares for you,' she said quietly. 'And the time is right to tell him about Finlay and your modelling work.'

'It's like I said, ma work never meant anything. I never slept with the men who painted me. And there were women artists an' all, you ken.'

'Tell him, then. As we've said, he'll understand.'

'But mebbe no' about Finlay. I mean, some men just dinna want another man's bairn. Specially a laddie. They want their own laddies, like them.'

Mae was silent, thinking of Harry. Finally, she said she wished she could help. Just wished there was something she could do.

'Nobody can help. I've to do this maself.'

For some time, Sandy sat in thought. 'Tell you what you could do, though,' she said at last. 'If you wouldnae mind? You could help me get our place ready one Sunday. I think it's time Gareth met Ma and the bairns.'

'Sure, I'll help, I'd love it!' cried Mae, thrilled at the idea of getting to grips with Mrs Corrie's flat. 'And I think 'tis good you are taking Gareth to meet your family. Maybe Gareth will be taking you to see his?'

'Och, they live down south. His dad's a lawyer.' Sandy rolled her eyes. 'I dinna ken what Gareth'll make o' Ma, but I want her to meet him and I want Finlay to get to know him and all. 'Course, Terry and Georgie will no' be there – they've joined the army – but the twins'll be larkin' about. My Lord, they've changed!'

Mae's eyes were suddenly sparkling.

'Sandy, shall we make your ma and the children some new clothes? They needn't cost much and it'd make such a difference. When can we start?'

By the time the Sunday tea was on the horizon, they had run up the new clothes for the family, mainly from cut-price materials – Mae had her sources – and were ready for the grand spring-clean of Mrs Corrie's flat. This they could do on Saturday, as there was no matinée.

'Lucky,' said Mae.

'Dinna know about that,' groaned Sandy. 'Wait till you see how much there is to do.'

But Mae was not to be daunted and arrived at the flat with her own cloths and dusters, carbolic soap, tins of cleaning powder and blacklead, and even a large broom that caused some problems on the tram.

'I am really looking forward to this,' she told Mrs Corrie, who was standing with the apprehensive-looking twins, now tall twelve year olds, and young Finlay, who was almost eight and the image of his mother. 'Spring-cleaning can be satisfying, because you can see what you have done.'

'Aye,' Mrs Corrie agreed, taking out her cigarettes, and sighing when Sandy's hand closed over the packet.

'Outside, Ma, if you want to smoke. There's enough nicotine on this ceiling as it is. Why d'you no' take the bairns out somewhere and let us get on?'

269

'I'll take 'em round to Ruby's next door, eh?'

'Och, no!' cried Johnny. 'I'm no' going there – we can play in the street, eh?'

'Aye, let's away,' said Shona.

'Take Finlay with you!' shouted Sandy. 'And look after him, eh?'

'I dinna need looking after!' cried Finlay. 'And I want to stay wi' Auntie Mae.'

'Away you go,' said Sandy. 'Or, you'll be helping wi' the cleaning, I'm telling you!'

As he scuttled away, with the chocolate Mae pressed into his hand, telling him to share it with his uncle and aunt, Mrs Corrie said hastily, 'I'll still go to Ruby's, eh? You'll no' want me around, gettin' in your way?'

As soon as they were alone, Mae and Sandy, their hair tied up in dusters, set to work. They moved furniture and took down and beat curtains. They shook ancient mats and washed and scrubbed walls and floors; cleaned windows, cleaned paintwork, black-leaded the stove; removed years of accumulated sticky finger-prints from every surface they could see. And finally, when they'd rehung the curtains and put everything back, they sank on to still damp chairs and had a cup of tea.

'Och, talk about transformation!' cried Sandy. 'This is like the last scene of the pantomime, eh?'

'Ceiling's still yellow,' sighed Mae, undoing the duster from her hair. 'But, sure, the room looks different.'

She looked around at the long, shining windows, the mats which now showed they had colour again, the scrubbed table and chairs and the highly polished range, and she smiled with satisfaction.

'Just ha' to keep it this way till tomorrow,' said Sandy. 'Oh, Mae, I'm so nervous, eh?'

'Everything will go well, Sandy, I promise you, because Gareth will want it to. He's not going to be finding fault.'

'Mebbe.' Sandy sneezed and ran her hands through her hair. 'Meantime, can I come down on the tram and have a bath at your place, Mae? I think I'll never see the end o' this dust.'

'Sure, you can. Bring the family, if you like. I'll make potato cakes and fry some bacon – we can have high tea.'

'If we're talking about pantomimes, you're the fairy godmother,' Sandy said with a laugh. 'Just bring your wand tomorrow.'

But Mae said she wouldn't come tomorrow. It would be better if there was just the family present for Gareth's visit. She had a promised cake for them, though, and a few soda scones, which Sandy could collect.

'Oh, Mae, I feel bad, letting you do so much!'

'To tell the truth, I cheated,' Mae said with a laugh. 'I asked Mrs Beith to do the baking. She's better at it than me.'

'Didnae cheat, doing all this cleaning. I couldnae be more grateful. If things dinna go well tomorrow, it'll no' be your fault!'

'I've told you, Sandy, they will!'

But some twenty-four hours later, Sandy was knocking at Mae's door, her face chalk-white and her eyes filled with unshed tears.

Chapter Sixty-Four

Mae drew her in, sat her down, and made the inevitable tea, while she said nothing; only looked as though she'd reached the end of the world.

'Now, tell me,' ordered Mae, as Sandy took a sip of the tea and with shaking fingers lit a cigarette. 'Tell me what has happened.'

'Just what I thought would happen. Soon as I told him about maself, he gave me up.'

'I cannot believe it.' Mae sank back in her chair. 'When did you tell him?'

'After we'd had our tea. It seemed right, because the tea'd gone so well. Och, I was that pleased!' Tears began to slide down Sandy's cheeks. 'Everything was looking so grand, wi' Ma and the bairns all smart and the place so clean and tidy, and Gareth had brought chocolates and flowers, and gave the bairns half a crown. I thought, it's OK, he's no' minding how we live, and we were all easy and happy, and talking like nobody's business—'

As Sandy's voice died away and she wiped her eyes with a damp handkerchief, Mae, her heart a great solid burden in her chest, poured more tea.

'Go on,' she whispered.

'Well, Gareth had his little Morris, you ken, and he says, why not us go for a wee drive up Calton Hill, and Ma says, all relieved, aye, you do that, and the bairns and me'll wash up. So, out we went, and it was a lovely night, and I felt that happy. I just thought it'd be right to tell him everything. I told him about ma posing. I said it'd never meant anything, just like I told you. And then I told him about Finlay. He'd no idea, you ken. He thought all the bairns were Ma's.'

Again, Sandy paused, and drawing fiercely on her cigarette, raised her eyes to Mae's.

'I waited for him to say something, but he didnae. He just sat like a stone, looking down at the view, and there were all the lights coming on and a few cars, but being Sunday, it was quiet, you ken. I said, will you no' speak to me, Gareth? And he said there was nothing he could say.'

'Oh, Sandy, Sandy—'

'I said, are you worrying about me posing, and he said of course he was. I said again, it never meant anything, and he said, well, it meant something to him.'

'Oh, dear Lord.' Mae put her hand to her brow. 'And Finlay? What did he say about Finlay?'

'Said it'd been a shock. Said I should've told him before. I asked him, if I had, would he have gone out wi' me, and he never answered. So, I knew it was the end. I opened the car door and I got out, but he said, no, get back in, I'll take you home. I didnae, though. I wasnae that far from you and I just kept running till I got here. I think he called ma name, but he didnae follow. Och no!' Sandy ground out her cigarette. 'He'll never follow me anywhere again, eh?'

There seemed no more to be said. Mae offered to make more tea, but Sandy shook her head and lay back in her chair, her tears drying on her cheeks. Very quietly Mae removed their cups and carried them away.

The thought occurred – might Sandy want to leave the Queen's? She might, and who could blame her? She wouldn't want to risk seeing Gareth Paget every time she went into work.

Mae sat down by her bed and picked up a letter she had received from her father the day before. He made no complaint, but it was on her conscience that she had only been back home once, since the time she'd been newly widowed and Rosaleen had just parted from Kieran.

Now Rosaleen was divorced, though the fact was never to be whispered in Traynore, and working as a hotel receptionist in London. The divorce had been an American one and quick, but so far neither she nor Kieran seemed to have made plans to marry again. Perhaps, like Mae, they were content to live alone, but Mae couldn't see Rosaleen staying single forever. Hadn't she, on her

273

one visit to Edinburgh, turned every male head backstage at the theatre?

Ah, but I should be going back to see Da, thought Mae, deciding to return to Ireland as soon as possible. She had enough in her savings now to pay for the trip, but of course, if Sandy left, she would not be able to go; someone must look after Wardrobe. Still, she wouldn't try to persuade her to stay.

After a while, she crept back into her living-room and found Sandy still lying, motionless, in her chair. Poor girl, how raw the wound must be! How she must wish she could just drift into sleep and not face the pain. Mae sat down near her, wondering what she could say, when a knock came at her door and she leaped to her feet.

'What is it?' asked Sandy, struggling up.

'Someone at the door. 'Tis late for anyone to come calling on a Sunday night.'

But already her heart was thumping with ridiculous hope. Ah, now, it wouldn't be . . .

It was, though. It was Gareth Paget. Leaning against the doorpost, as though his strength were spent. Face very white. Eyes so dark, they were like coals against the pallor.

'Is Sandy there?' he asked hoarsely.

'She is, then. Come in, Gareth.'

'No. No, thank you. But could I see her?'

'I'll tell her,' said Mae, but there was no need. Sandy was flying to the door.

She called his name; he took her in his arms, then they left, together, and Mae closed her door.

What passed between them, out there in the April night, Mae was never told, but when they came back to her, it was clear that, whatever it cost him, Gareth had chosen not to let Sandy go. Perhaps he could do nothing else; couldn't live without her, even though he had lived without her in London. Since then, though, there'd been their love affair. Things, it seemed, were different now.

Different, surely, for Sandy, whose life had been turned upside down and suddenly, amazingly, righted. It was easy to see that she could scarcely believe it. Could scarcely believe that the burden she had been carrying for so long had been lifted from her shoulders. Am I free to love you? she seemed to be asking, as she kept turning to look into Gareth's face, and pressing his hand. The answer must have been yes, for though Mae couldn't see Gareth's expression, Sandy still looked happy.

When they had left her, Mae sighed with relief. Thank God, for the present, at least, she needn't worry about Sandy, or, who would look after Wardrobe when she was away.

As she began to rub her arms and neck that were stiff after so much cleaning yesterday, she found herself longing to see her da again, to be back in Ireland, to have time of her own. So much of her life lately seemed to have been lived through other people's. Was this what happened to single women? She gave a wry smile as she began to prepare for bed. Maybe she did need a man in her life, then? She put the thought from her.

Chapter Sixty-Five

It was good to be back. Mae, her conscience somewhat eased by being home again, was still wishing she'd come before.

True, it wasn't easy to make the trip often; the cost of the sea passage had to be found, and her annual holiday was short. She would not, however, leave it so long again, for it had seemed to her that her da was looking older. As Annie said, however, all fishermen looked older than their years, sea spray and the wind not being kind to faces.

Walking down Traynore's one straggling street, swinging Annie's shopping basket, Mae found herself enjoying meeting again so many people she knew. Everyone was asking, how was she, then? How was the big city, and all? When was she coming home to live?

'Ah, now, what would I be living on?' asked Mae. 'It'd be back to Cork for me.'

'So it would,' they agreed. There were no jobs in Traynore for clever girls like Mae.

She made a few purchases for Annie at Bridie O'Mally's shop, where the dry goods were usually pretty damp, and there was not much of what you could call choice. But, sure, you could have a grand conversation while Bridie was getting things for you, and she never made mistakes in the change.

Then it was out into the fresh air again and a wander round the small harbour to look at the yachts of the folk from away, for the fishing boats, including Joseph O'Donovan's, were all out on this fine late spring morning.

Mae sat for a while, basking in the sunshine, then stirred herself to take home Annie's shopping. Ah, what a treat it was, then, not to have to hurry to finish a piece of work, or worry about something or somebody! All she need do was please herself – a novelty, indeed.

Folk always said that Irish villages were full of pubs and in Traynore, small as it was, there were several. The one just ahead of her, as she retraced her steps, was Connor's, and though at one time it had been painful for her even to look at it, now, of course, it held no threat. On she went, full of sunny confidence. And stopped. A young man, carrying a barrel, had just come out of the pub.

He wore a collarless shirt and rough trousers, and a cap over his fair hair. His features were good; strong and regular, and known to her. Even so, the name she whispered to herself was:

'Harry?'

Of course, she was being foolish, and knew that, too. But she had confused this face with Harry's once before.

'Mae?' asked Kieran Connor, setting down his barrel. 'Mae, is it you?'

He stepped forward, shook her hand, then brushed her cheek in a cousinly kiss, the first he had given her since his wedding.

'I never realised you were here,' he murmured, standing back to look at her and taking off his cap. His voice, soft as she remembered it, had lost some of its Irishness for a touch of American twang. 'Why have I not seen you?'

'I'm just over to visit my da.' Mae's eyes were roving everywhere except on Kieran's face, though she had already noted that he was the handsome man she remembered, if seeming just a little older. Well, the years had gone by. No doubt she looked older, too.

'It's wonderful to see you,' he told her. 'But for a second there, I took you for Rosaleen.'

Mae, naturally not willing to tell him she'd crazily seen him as Harry, gave a nervous smile. 'And she in London, Kieran?'

'Ah, she might have come over. Never can tell what Rosaleen will do. Had you heard she was receptionist in some grand hotel? Typing, and all?' He laughed. 'Got the job on her looks, I'm thinking. When did she ever learn the typing?'

Mae took a step or two past him, as though she must be on her way. 'You over on holiday. Kieran?'

'I have taken unpaid compassionate leave. Da's not well.'

'I'm sorry to hear that. What's the trouble?'

'Heart.' Kieran knocked the barrel with the toe of his boot. 'Things are getting too much for him. In fact, he wants me to take on the pub.'

'And will you?'

'I have not decided.' He put out his hand to touch her arm. 'But, Mae, I want to tell you how sorry I was, to hear about your loss. A tragedy, indeed.'

'Thank you.' She hesitated. 'You will know how grieved I was about Molly.'

At her mention of the name, his green eyes grew blank and he nodded, but did not speak.

'And Rosaleen,' Mae said after a pause. 'So sad, you are parted.'

Again, he nodded. 'Let me walk back with you to your da's,' he said quietly. 'How is he, then? And Annie Morragh?'

When she saw Kieran, Annie, standing at the door of Joseph's cottage, tightened her lips.

''Tis you, then, Kieran Connor,' she said coldly. 'I was hearing you were back from America.'

'To help ma da, he not being well,' he told her smoothly. 'And how are you keeping yourself, Mrs Morragh?'

'Thank you, I am fine.' Annie fixed her gaze on Mae. 'Best come in, Mae. I've a stew ready.'

'I won't stay,' Kieran said politely. 'Mae, it was good to see you. Maybe you will look in and say hello to my folks?' He touched his cap. 'Mrs Morragh.'

'Short shrift for Kieran, Annie?' Mae murmured, when he had left them.

'Short shrift for him, indeed.' Annie, moving into the cottage, began to unpack the basket Mae had brought her. 'How he has the nerve to show his face here, I cannot believe. Separating from Rosaleen! Letting her live on her own in London, of all places! There's no one in Traynore with a good word to say for him, I'm telling you.'

'His father is ill, he is doing his best.'

'Always a wild one, he was, like his brothers – but they're away to Liverpool and God knows where. So 'twill be Kieran running the pub, and that's bad news.' Annie, having emptied the basket, snatched up a spoon and stirred the stew over the fire. 'You keep out o' his way, now, Mae, for 'twill only stir up old memories, if he comes charming you again.'

Mae's cheeks went red. 'Annie, I am not the foolish girl I was. Kieran means nothing to me.'

'Tis glad I am to hear it.' Annie shook her head. 'But keep out o' his way, is my advice, and I am a lot older than you, so do not mind taking it.'

'Good advice, Annie,' Mae retorted. 'But, thank you, I am not needing it.'

At night, up in the room her da had made her take again, she told herself again that it was true; she was needing no advice to keep out of Kieran's way. But was it true he meant nothing to her? If he meant nothing, it would not matter if they met.

She lay in her old bed and stared at her square of window, pale in the darkness, as something disquieting churned in her breast. As soon as she'd seen him, stepping out of his father's pub, a sort of dread had descended on her. A fear of long-forgotten feelings stirring; a fear of old pain.

'Harry,' she whispered. 'If only you were with me, how different it would be.'

But Harry was not with her, and never would be again. She was alone and vulnerable, and the only thing to do, until she went back to the safety of Edinburgh, was to take heed of Annie's warning. Keep out of Kieran's way.

Chapter Sixty-Six

But Traynore was small. It was not easy to keep out of anyone's way, and if one person wanted to meet another, sure, they would.

So it appeared, for everywhere Mae went, she seemed to see Kieran. Walking on the shore, shopping at Bridie's, waiting for the bus to Skibbereen – he always seemed to be in her sights, his eyes brightening as he came up and took her arm. But while he took obvious pleasure in their meetings, her own heart sank.

Why didn't she make excuses to walk away? Why let him look at her the way he did? Because she seemed to be powerless in his presence. A doll that moved to his pulling of the strings.

Sometimes he was playful and ready to tease. At other times, quite serious. Once, when they were walking together at the edge of the village, away from watching eyes, he talked of little Molly, and of how their grief for her had formed a barrier between himself and Rosaleen.

There were those who could come together over something like that, but he and Rosaleen had moved farther apart. Now their marriage was over, without regret on either side. But when Mae tried to express her own regret, he put his finger over her lips, and would not speak of it again.

Another time, he told her how much it had meant to him, to have her company in Traynore.

'You can have no idea what it is like for me back here, Mae. Everyone treating me like a criminal, for separating from Rosaleen.' He gave a grim smile. 'And they not knowing the truth of it.'

'Have you not even told your folks you are divorced?'

'Dare not do it, Mae. They'd collapse on me, I'm telling you. My mother writes anyway to Rosaleen, asking her to come back.' Kieran shook his head. 'A waste of time, as I keep saying, if she will only listen. But tell me this – why should two people who want to part have to stay married? Where's the sense in it?'

'I suppose, you have taken vows,' Mae said, after a pause.

'Well, why be taking vows? Why not just have a civil ceremony?'

'Some people do.'

'And for the best, in my view. Anyway, I am a free man in the eyes of the law.' He fixed her with a direct gaze. 'That is what counts.'

As Mae made no reply, he took her hand.

'You are like your da,' he said softly. 'Not one for judging. Has Rosaleen told him about us?'

'She has, in secret, but he has never spoken of it to me.'

'He has not told Annie?'

'I'm sure he has not.'

'And I'm sure, too!' Kieran laughed. 'Or, she'd have forbidden you to see me.'

'She has advised against it, anyway.'

'She has? And you have disobeyed her. Ah, Mae, that's good, that's cheering. Sure, I still have one friend left in Traynore, then!'

'Of course, I'm your friend,' she said hastily. 'And I am your cousin, too.'

'Forget being my cousin. Being my friend is what matters to me.' He suddenly stooped and kissed her hand, then let it go. 'So, shall I be seeing you at the Saturday dance, then? Would you dare to go with me?'

'The Saturday dance?' She was staring at her hand. 'I have not been thinking about it.'

'Always went in the old days. You and me.'

'And Rosaleen.'

'Rosaleen is not here. Shall we go, Mae?'

'Are we not a little old? We are not eighteen any more.'

'You remember the dances. Everybody goes, old and young. You can dance with anyone, not just me.'

'I will go,' she said, after a long moment, and despised herself for her weakness.

* * *

281

The dance was held in the church hall. The band consisted of an accordionist and a couple of fiddlers, who sat on a platform surrounded by glasses of beer, smiling and nodding, as they went through their repertoire, while, as Kieran said, what seemed to be the whole village of Traynore occupied the floor.

Old, young, and even the infirm, would do what they could, while, seeing that things did not 'get out of hand' as he called it, was tall, gaunt Father Cassidy, who had a word of welcome for everyone, except, of course, out-of-favour Kieran Connor.

'Sure, I am the skeleton at the feast,' Kieran murmured, as he came up to greet Mae at the door, for she had insisted on arriving separately from him and, worse still, in his eyes, was accompanied by Annie. But she was looking so lovely in a dark-blue dress, he immediately forgave her and before Annie could say a word, weren't the two of them on the floor, doing their fancy footwork as though they were the young ones again?

Annie's face was a study in thunder, as she sat down for a moment to watch, then was up on the floor herself with Albert Murphy, the butcher, and showing off her own footwork, while still trying to keep an eye on Mae with Kieran.

'Anybody'd think she was your chaperone,' said Kieran in Mae's ear, as the music changed from an Irish jig to an old-fashioned waltz. 'Please say you are not going home with her, mavourneen.'

'Going home? We have only just arrived.'

'But I am planning ahead. And meantime, I am relying on you to give me a good name with old Father Cassidy and the rest of 'em. If they see you being nice to me, they'll think I can't be all bad.'

'Ah, now stop the teasing,' said Mae, smiling yet feeling her usual unease. 'Perhaps you will be taking your mother home, anyway.'

He was serious then, saying his mother had not come, she preferred to stay with his da.

'He is not so well?'

'He is never well.'

The evening wore on, with the younger dancers growing hotter and sweatier, and the older ones dropping out. Several fellows Mae had known in the past came up to dance with her, and Kieran did his duty by dancing with Annie.

282

Though she steadfastly refused to succumb to his charm, others who followed pursed their lips as he led them on to the floor, but always ended by graciously smiling. True, they might shake their heads over that 'Connor boy', when they returned to their husbands, but as Mae told him when he claimed her again, he was no skeleton at the feast.

'There are some will always forgive you,' she said with a smile.

'Will you?' he asked.

'What have I to forgive?'

'Maybe, what might have been.'

It was Annie who saved Mae from having to answer, when she came up saying she was going home and wasn't Mae coming with her? Her dad had been all on his own the whole of the evening, so he had.

Mae's eyes went to Kieran, who said quickly. 'Ah, Mrs Morragh, we've not even had our cup of tea!'

'Mae can have tea at home.'

Go, Mae told herself. Go with Annie. Now.

'Annie, I think I will be staying a while,' she murmured. ''Tis early, yet.'

'Please yourself, then.' Annie, her eyes full of meaning, tossed her head. 'But your da will not be wanting you to be late.'

'As though you were sixteen,' said Kieran, as Annie stomped away. 'Sure, it's all you look, of course.'

Chapter Sixty-Seven

Though it was not quite dark when they left the dance, by the time they reached the harbour wall on the way home, the sky was velvet black and the moon was rising.

'A lovely night,' remarked Kieran, putting his arm round Mae, as they looked down at the boats rocking on the water. 'A perfect night for lovers.'

'There are no lovers here,' Mae answered, slipping from the circle of his arm. 'I must be getting back, Kieran.'

'No lovers? Sure, there's one. There's me.'

'Oh—' She moved impatiently. '—You are always the one for talking nonsense.'

'It's no nonsense to say I've fallen in love with you, Mae. Soon as I saw you again – there was the arrow.' He was smiling at her, in the moonlight. 'Straight to the heart.'

'Kieran, I can't be listening to this. I'm going home.'

As she turned, determined to leave him, he caught her back, holding her easily, bringing his face close to hers.

'You must have realised, Mae. Folk always realise. What is it they say? "Love and a cough cannot be hid". I knew when you loved me once.'

A great wave of colour she hoped he couldn't see swept over her face, as, breaking free from his grasp again, she hurried – almost ran – away from him. Up the cobbled slope from the harbour and into the village street, with Kieran following and catching her before she reached his father's pub. Holding her close, as they both breathed hard.

'Mae, don't be upset. I knew it was just a girl's fancy. Still, if I had not been the fool I was, it might have been me you married.'

'I married Harry, Kieran. I loved Harry.'

'I know, I know, and I married Rosaleen, and I loved her. But that's over now, and I am free and you are free. This is our chance, mavourneen, for a new happiness.' His eyes, colourless in the pale light, were shining. 'Can you not see that, Mae?'

'I am going back to Edinburgh very soon, Kieran. There's no place for you in my life, and I could never fit into yours.' She pressed his hand quickly. 'Goodnight. Don't be following me now.'

For answer, he kissed her. It was a long, passionate, and expert kiss that left her speechless, her gaze falling before his when it was over, so that he shouldn't see the feelings he had roused. Perhaps he saw them anyway, but he showed no triumph. Just stroked her cheek and took her arm.

'I'll walk you back to your da's, Mae. No need to worry – it's not late.'

At her father's door, everything was still. The little house, ghostly in the moonlight, showed one light, but there were no voices. No breeze. Only the murmur of the sea, washing the shore.

They exchanged looks and one last kiss, quiet this time; no passion.

'Shall I see you tomorrow?' asked Kieran. 'I could take an hour or two off in the afternoon.'

'No, 'twould be better not. We are being foolish.'

'You'll see me, though?'

Though she slipped through the cottage door without a word, she knew he was confident she would see him. She would prove him wrong, she would! If only she could.

Joseph was in his chair, glasses on the end of his nose, his book ready to fall from his knee when he caught it as Mae came in.

'Good, was it?' he asked. 'The dance?'

'Fine.' She looked around. 'Where's Annie, then?'

'Gone to her house. Terrible headache, she said she had.'

''Twas hot in the hall.' Mae sat down. 'Tiring for her, maybe.'

'And tiring for you?'

'I am looking tired?'

'Troubled.' Joseph put his book aside. 'Is it Kieran Connor, then, who's troubling you?'

'Was Annie saying?'

He gave a guilty smile. 'Sure, you know Annie. She worries about you.'

'I worry about myself.'

'Kieran is turning to you. Is that it?'

'And I am wanting him to, Da. You remember, I cared for him once.'

Joseph was staring into his peat fire, rubbing his chin. 'Well, you are free, Mae. And so is he, I suppose. If you are not thinking of the Church.'

'I am thinking of Rosaleen,' Mae said in a low voice. 'Da, I still think of her as his wife.'

'Seems she is not thinking that.'

''Tis true, she thinks of herself as free, and so does Kieran. But I am afraid, Da. I am afraid of loving him again.'

'Is he saying he loves you?'

'He is, but it has all been too quick. Too quick for me.'

'Can happen that way. Sure, I was taking no time to love your mother.'

'But it was not me Kieran loved before.'

'Is it not you now, though?'

Mae looked for a long time into her father's eyes.

'I don't know what to do, Da. Tell me what to do.'

He shook his head. 'I can't be telling you that. You must decide what you want.'

As she bent her head, sighing, he put his hand on her shoulder.

'I'll say this, then. Go home and be taking your time to know what is right for you. Maybe you know already.'

She raised her head. 'I think I do. Sure, you're a wonderful man, Da.'

As he took off his glasses and raised himself slowly from his chair, she flung her arms around him.

'You'll take care of yourself, when I am gone?'

'Ah, now, I leave that to Annie.'

'Well, you will be doing what she says?' Her eyes, so like her mother's, searched his face. 'And I will not be leaving it so long this time, before I come back again.'

That was a promise she would keep.

Chapter Sixty-Eight

Back in Edinburgh, she was proud of herself. Somehow, for the remainder of her holiday, she had managed not to be alone with Kieran – except for the time when he insisted on accompanying her to the station in Cork, but that didn't count. She was going home then, and he knew he had lost his battle.

At first, he had been astonished, that she had not wanted to see him; then, quite genuinely upset.

'But, why?' he kept asking, when he appeared at her da's door. 'Why not see me? What have I done?'

'Nothing at all, Kieran. 'Tis just what I said – we have no place in each other's lives. We have no future.'

'We love each other,' he said in a low voice, trying to see over her shoulder if Annie was listening.

But Mae was the only person there, and she would not let him in. 'I was never saying I loved you,' she told him. 'You have been too quick, Kieran. Pushed me too far.'

'Mavourneen, we have all the time in the world! But you cared for me before and you care for me now, only you will not let yourself admit it. Ah, come on now—'

For once, his powers of persuasion did not work, and the nearest he got to being with her again was on that last trip to Cork, when he wore one of his good American suits and looked so handsome, her heart nearly failed her.

But she held firm. How had she done it? Back in Edinburgh, she still didn't know, but was grateful that his farewell kisses on the platform had had to be brief. And that the train had arrived before she need match the melting look in his eyes with one of her own.

'Give me your address,' he said urgently, as he put her case on the rack. 'Quick, now, so that I can write to you.'

'There's no point, Kieran.' She was keeping her gaze averted, not wishing to see the interested faces of her fellow passengers. 'We've been into all of that.'

'Never mind, I can get it from your da.' He kissed her on the cheek and leaped down to the platform, waving his hand and bowing with such style that two elderly ladies sitting next to Mae seemed to be on the point of waving back. 'Ah, you're away! Be in touch, now!'

As the train had gathered speed, bearing her away, Mae sat with her eyes down and her colour high all the way to Dublin.

All that was in the past now, and here she was, back in Wardrobe with people asking about her holiday, saying she looked well, and knowing nothing about the storm she had weathered to reach calm harbour again. Maybe Sandy suspected, though, for she kept eyeing Mae strangely, often seeming about to speak, but saying nothing. Finally, she took the plunge.

'Mae, mind if I ask you – did anything happen on your holiday? You seem – och, I canna say – a wee bit strung up.'

'Strung up, is it?' Mae, busy ironing a pile of period shirts, raised her eyebrows. 'Why, everyone is saying I look very well.'

'You do, you do. Like you've been on holiday, no mistake about that. But – there's something – I canna pin it down.'

Mae set down the iron and sighed. 'I suppose I'd better tell you – I met my cousin's husband again. Kieran Connor.'

Sandy's eyes gleamed. 'That would be ex-husband, eh?'

'Yes, ex-husband. He is back in Traynore. His da is ill and he's helping out at the pub. We met up again.'

'Ah. I think I can guess what happened next.'

'Nothing happened. But he has got the idea into his head that he – cares for me.'

'Like you once cared for him?' Sandy smiled broadly. 'Why, Mae, that's grand! You're both free now, you could marry, it would be right—'

'No, it would not.' Mae picked up the iron and began thumping it down on the shirt on the board. 'It would not be right, Sandy, it would never work out. There's too much against it, so there is, and I was after telling him that. But – I'll not deny – it's been upsetting.'

288

'Oh, Mae, you turned him down?' The brightness in Sandy's eyes faded. 'That's a shame. Mebbe it's no' for me to say, but I think you were too hasty. You should've thought a bit more about being happy, because you've had your share o' sorrow.' She began to thread one of the machines. 'And it's no' always easy, finding happiness again.'

Mae was silent for a time, carefully ironing into the frill of a cuff. 'How have things been for you?' she asked, eventually. 'I mean, with Gareth?'

'Fine.' Sandy hesitated. 'He really loves me, Mae. I've no worries on that score.'

'What have you worries on, then?'

Sandy left her machine and moved to the window, where she stood for some moments.

'He still thinks about what I used to do, and he still thinks about Finlay and Finlay's dad. He never says anything, but I ken fine what's in his mind. I suppose, it's only to be expected, eh? That he'd think about it?'

Mae went to her and put her arm around her.

'Remember what you said just now, Sandy – he really loves you. He's shown that, already.'

'Aye, but I wish he could accept what I told him. We canna do anything, until he does.' Sandy straightened her shoulders. 'I'd better get on, eh? Thank God, you're back, Mae, I was so nervous without you. Every time the door opened and somebody came in, I used to wonder, will I be able to do what they want. Talk about being in a sweat!'

'But then you always could do it, couldn't you?'

'Aye, but I'm glad your holiday wasnae any longer.'

'I'm thinking the same,' said Mae.

Chapter Sixty-Nine

Too hasty. In the days that followed, Sandy's words echoed in Mae's mind. Too hasty she'd been, in turning Kieran down. For she'd had her share of sorrow and should have thought more about being happy.

Should she have thought of that? Mae asked herself, walking to the hostel on her afternoon off. Should she have thought more about her happiness? Accepted that Kieran was, as he said, a free man?

It was true, the euphoria that had consumed her when she first came home was fading fast, and she had begun to remember the passion he had stirred in her when he'd kissed her. Passion such as she'd not felt for years, when it had been hers by right.

Could it be so again? With Kieran?

Dear God, why was she thinking this way? The warm breeze of the late spring day fanned her cheeks as she walked and made her flush – or, so she told herself. In her heart, she knew she was blushing over Kieran – a man she was not likely to see again – seeing as she had insisted that they say goodbye.

Going into Adelaide House, she met Dr Rick hurrying out. He stopped to speak to her, telling her she was looking well, her holiday had suited her.

'And how have things been here, Dr Rick?'

'The same as usual. Hanging on by an eyelash. I've just brought another Scottish laddie into the world – hope he thanks me for it. Nice to see you, Mae.'

Always so cheerful, wasn't he? She said as much when she'd greeted Miss Thorburn and Miss Dow, who gave her a grand welcome and told her, as everyone else had told her, that she was looking well and had obviously enjoyed her holiday.

'Cheerful is the word for Dr Rick,' Miss Dow agreed. 'But then he doesn't like to show his feelings. Virginia's the same, though so sad, poor girl.'

'Mrs Rick's unhappy?' asked Mae.

'Well, she can't have children, you see.'

'Oh,' said Mae, and looked away, as Miss Thorburn shook her head at Miss Dow, who blushed and hastily began to apologise.

'I'm so sorry, Mae, dear, I wouldn't for the world have reminded you, but you know how it is – and all I was going to say is, it's so hard for Dr Rick and poor Virginia, especially with all the babies here that nobody wants.'

'We want them,' Miss Thorburn said shortly. 'Or, at least, we find people who do.'

'Maybe Mrs Rick will adopt?' Mae murmured.

'Maybe. But Mae, it's lovely to see you back. I think your girls are waiting for you.'

'Probably fighting by now,' sniffed Miss Dow.

'I'll go to them,' Mae said at once.

If they were not exactly fighting, some of the young women were certainly looking as if they might come to it soon enough, and were lumbering round the sewing machines, exchanging threatening glances, with one or two even fingering scissors.

'I'm telling you it was me to use that sewing machine!' a tall dark-haired girl was shouting at a strong-chinned fair girl, who was defiantly treadling away, while an audience of half a dozen or so were cheering on two other girls tugging at the same piece of material.

'That's my blue gingham you've got there, Sadie, and you ken that fine!' cried one of the tugging girls, whom Mae recognised as Noreen Wills, a known troublemaker. 'I put ma marker on it last time, so I did, and noo you come along and grab what's no' yours, and if you dinna get out o' ma way, you'll be sorry, eh?'

'You tell her, Noreen!' someone called. 'Sadie's aye takin' what's no' hers. Did I no' lose ma good hairbrush when she slept next tae me, then I sees her doing' her hair before the doctor come, cool as a cucumber, wi' MY brush?'

'I never took your damned hairbrush!' screamed Sadie. 'That was ma own brush, you daft—'

She was searching her mind for the most insulting name, until Miss Thorburn swept in like a tornado, when she fell silent, with the rest of Mae's class.

'Now, what on earth's going on?' cried Miss Thorburn, clapping her hands. 'Are you a class of schoolchildren, scrapping like this? Here's Mae back from her holiday, and I expect she's wishing she'd stayed away!'

'Mae!' The girls at once surrounded her. 'Och, it's grand to see you, then! And looking so well, eh? Did you have a good time? Did you bring us onything!'

'Girls!' wailed Miss Thorburn.

'Sure, I did,' said Mae, smiling. 'I brought some Irish sweeties and some Irish biscuits. They're in the kitchen for later.'

'How aboot a bottle o' Irish whiskey, eh?'

'Can we no' have the sweeties now?'

'And be doing your sewing with sticky fingers?'

Mae, shooing them all away to start work, nodded to Miss Thorburn, who happily left her to it.

Silence fell, punctuated by groans and sighs as the girls, guided by Mae, worked away at cutting out, stitching, and machining, with everyone's turns being worked out fairly and no one being allowed to snatch only the best pieces of material. There was some satisfaction for most of them, in seeing their handiwork gradually take shape, and when they stopped for tea and Mae's biscuits, moods had become as sunny as the light shining through the dusty windows.

'Och, it does you good, eh?' asked the dark-haired girl, stretching and rubbing her back. 'I mean, to see what you've made? Only thing I made before was an apron at school, and you shouldnae seen that! Mae, you'd have had a fit.'

Mae, drinking tea, was laughing, when Miss Dow put her head round the door and called to her.

'Mae, your cousin's here. Just wants a word.'

'My cousin?'

'In the hall, dear. I said you could spare a minute.'

Mae was looking perplexed. Rosaleen, here? Why had she not written? Why had she, in fact, come?

'You girls be finishing your tea,' she murmured. 'I'll be back soon. No arguing while I'm away!'

'Dinna worry, Mae,' they chorused. 'We'll be as good as gold, eh?'

That would be the day, thought Mae, hurrying to the hall, still puzzling over Rosaleen's visit and beginning to worry about it. She would be bound to feel awkward, meeting Kieran's wife, ex-wife though Rosaleen might call herself. Heavens, would she even be able to look her in the eye?

But there was no question of having to look Rosaleen in the eye, for the cousin who was standing in the hall, waiting for her, was Kieran.

Long moments passed, as they stood quite still, gazing – just gazing – into each other's faces. Unlike Mae, Kieran was pale and did not look well. His great charm seemed to have deserted him; his eyes on her face were anxious.

'I had to come,' he said at last. 'I'm sorry.'

''Tis all right.' She took a step towards him, as he stepped towards her. He held out his arms. She went to them. And more long moments passed, as they held each other, not speaking, not kissing, only letting the emotion of the moment flow over them.

'Kieran,' Mae whispered at last. 'We are crazy.'

'No, very sane. Showing sense at last, so we are.'

He made to kiss her, but at last she moved from him.

'Not here, Kieran.'

'Where, then? Mae, where can we go?'

She shook her head, as the reality of their situation came to her.

'Where are you staying?'

He shrugged, and smiled. 'Nowhere. I've just arrived. Got my brother, Frank, over from Liverpool to help my da, booked the sailing, arrived here, was not knowing where to go, so went to the theatre.'

'The Queen's? You went looking for me at the Queen's?'

'You told me where you worked. There was a girl with ginger hair told me you'd be here, and here I am.' His eyes were beginning to dance to the old music, and before she could draw back, he had kissed her swiftly. 'When will you be free, then? How long must I wait?'

'Another half hour.' Mae was fretting a little in case anyone

293

should see them, but they were still alone. 'I must give the girls at least that.'

He looked at his American wristwatch. 'At five, then. I'll go back to the station, pick up my bag, then meet you here.'

'No need to come back here, I'll meet you there. At the station.'

His eyes stopped dancing. 'Guess you don't want anyone to see me? Is that the way of it?'

''Tis not that way at all.' She smiled apologetically. 'Just that the girls will be so interested, I'll never hear the end of it. They see so few people, you understand.'

'So few men, you mean?' He smiled wryly. 'Seems they have not always lived like nuns.'

'They have their troubles, Kieran. But will you wait for me at the station? Say, under the clock?'

With a return to his usual charm, he kissed her hand. 'Mavourneen, I'll wait for you for ever.'

'Hush, now, and away with you,' she said hurriedly, and did not relax until she had seen him out of the front door and into the street.

'Be sure you come!' he cried. 'Promise me!'

'I shall come, Kieran. There is no need to ask me to promise.'

Chapter Seventy

They had a meal in the station buffet, eyeing each other with a mixture of delight and unease. To be together again, when they'd never thought they would be – they couldn't deny that that was thrilling them both to the core. But where was this joy taking them? What was going to happen now?

Ever practical, Mae seized on the immediate problem.

'Where will you stay, Kieran? We must find you somewhere.'

'I was thinking you might help me out there.'

As her colour rose and she looked down at her plate, he leaned forward to touch her hand.

'No need to worry, Mae. I am not asking to stay with you.'

'It would be difficult. Where I live – Harry's people are there, too. And everyone would be wondering – who you were.'

'You could say I am your cousin. Happens to be the truth. You yourself were saying so.'

'I was, but – you will not seem like a cousin to them.'

'So you won't offer me even a cup of tea? I've said I am not asking to stay.'

'A cup of tea, oh, of course I can do that!' Mae's smile was relieved. 'Look, let's go and find a room for you. There is a boarding house where visiting actors sometimes stay – 'tis clean and not expensive. I could take you to see it.'

'And then show me the city. Seems a fine place.' Kieran smiled, as he rose and took up his bag. 'Must be, if you're wanting to live in it.'

The boarding house had a room free, which Kieran, scarcely glancing at, said would be fine. When asked how long he would be

295

staying, his eyes went to Mae, and after a moment's hesitation, he told the landlady his plans were uncertain, he would let her know.

'Depends on you,' he told Mae, outside in the still warm evening air.

'On me?'

'Goes without saying. You are the one I have come to see.'

'But you will not be able to stay long, Kieran. You have your commitments. What about your job with the police?'

'I have compassionate leave, as I was telling you. I needn't turn in my badge yet. And Frank is taking care of things in Traynore. Dying to do it, in fact – he's always had his eye on the pub.' Kieran put Mae's arm in his. 'Now, how about showing me this Princes Street I keep hearing about?'

The city was looking its best on that May evening, with the sun still lingering over the Castle, picking out the new green of the trees and the grass, and the fine silhouette of the skyline. Kieran said he was impressed and smiled on Mae, as though she was to be congratulated. But she was thinking of Harry, who had shown her this part of the city, as she now showed it to another man, and could not respond.

'Hey,' said Kieran, stopping to look into her face. 'You've gone silent on me. Is something wrong?'

'No, no.'

He looked up at the Castle, then back to her, his green eyes bright. 'Are you thinking of him?' he asked softly. 'Of Harry? Was it here you came walking with him?'

'Sometimes.'

'It's only natural, to remember him. I'd not expect anything else.' He ran his hand down her cheek. 'But he's gone, Mae, and you are here. You have a new life to live.'

'I know.'

'Why not let's go back, then? And have that cup of tea you promised me?' When she hesitated, feeling not quite ready to do that, he put his hand under her chin and turned her face to his.

'You are happy, taking me home, mavourneen?'

'Sure, I am,' she answered quickly.

Just as long as they didn't meet Rona.

Chapter Seventy-One

They did not meet Rona. In fact, they were lucky, they saw no one, and all was quiet at Number Eight when Mae unlocked her door and showed Kieran into her flat.

'I'll put the kettle on,' she told him, as he stood looking round at her little domain, admiring the way she had arranged her things, the spring flowers on the table, the light curtains at the window.

'Nice, Mae, it's all very nice. You always did have a gift for homemaking.'

'And how would you know that?'

'Your da's place – weren't you the one kept it so neat, when Rosaleen was never doing a hand's turn?'

'I wouldn't be saying that.'

He had begun to walk about and Mae, waiting for the kettle to boil, showed him her little bathroom, and, after some hesitation, her bedroom.

'When my sister-in-law lived here, she had the two bedrooms, but I made one into a bathroom – something I'd always wanted.'

'Good idea,' he said absently, but she could see that his gaze had gone to the photograph of Harry beside her bed. He made no comment, however, as they went back into the living-room and she told him to sit down.

'I'll make the tea now. Would you like anything to eat?'

'Forget the tea.' He came to her and took her in his arms. 'Who wants tea?'

They began to kiss, quietly at first, then with greater and greater hunger, as though they could not be satisfied, until finally Mae drew away and sank into her chair.

'Oh, Mae,' Kieran sighed, kneeling beside her. 'You see how it is with us? We have to be together. We have to marry, and soon.'

She shook her head. ''Tis too difficult, Kieran. Whichever way we look, 'tis too difficult.'

'Are you thinking of Harry again?' he asked, rising.

'Of Harry and Rosaleen, and everything. All the practical side of it.' She raised her troubled gaze to his. 'Where would we live? Even that, we can't be saying.'

'I'd not ask you to go back to Ireland. It's been bad enough for me, with folk pointing the finger. I couldn't let them treat you the same.'

'There you are, then. 'Tis hopeless.'

'Not at all. You're forgetting – my job is in America. Things would be different there.' He pulled Mae to her feet and held her close. 'And the way things are going, it'd be good for you to leave Europe. There's trouble coming – all the signs are showing it. That Hitler guy and Mussolini – they're preparing for war. In America, we'd be safe.'

Again, she pulled away from him, staring at him in astonishment.

'America, is it? Kieran, how could I be going there? How could I leave my da?'

'Your da? For God's sake, Mae you have to live your own life! People leave Ireland every day of the week! They can't be thinking of their parents. Did I not leave my own? Have you not left your da, anyway?'

'I have not come so far. I can go back, if I am needed. But crossing the Atlantic – that is a different thing, Kieran, as you know to be true.'

He moved to a chair and sat down, rubbing his hand over his eyes. 'Maybe we'd better have that tea now, Mae. Then I'll be going.'

'Wait while I boil up the kettle again,' she said sadly.

The joy they had taken in being together had faded. As they drank the tea, each gazed away from the other, their thoughts turning and tumbling, as they tried to find a way out of their own private maze, but when they set down their cups they were no further forward.

'I'd better be on my way,' Kieran said, taking Mae's hand. 'When can I see you again?'

'You want to?'

'Oh, God, I do! I am not giving up on you, Mae, I promise you. I love you and I want us to be married, whatever the problems.' His eyes on her were fierce. 'Where there's a will, there's a way. It's up to us to find it.'

They kissed again, strongly, as though to seal their intent, then Mae took him to the door and they looked out, as she and Harry had looked out long ago, to see if the coast was clear.

'Nobody,' Kieran was saying with satisfaction, when a child's cry broke the silence of the hall.

'Wee Hamish next door,' Mae whispered. 'Probably cutting more teeth.'

'Poor little devil.' Kieran's eyes were empty again, and Mae, who guessed he had been reminded of Molly, touched his hand in sympathy.

'You never had children,' he whispered, covering her hand with his own. 'I could give you children, Mae.'

But she wouldn't talk of children.

'Goodnight, Kieran. If you want to see me, I have my lunch break at twelve o'clock. Come to the stage door.'

'I'll be there.' Chameleon like, he had changed into his charming self again. 'If the sky falls in, mavourneen.'

Chapter Seventy-Two

'Oh, Mae, did you see him?' cried Sandy in Wardrobe the following morning. 'Kieran Connor? I was the one sent him to the hostel. Did you see him?'

'I did.' Mae took off her hat and sat down at the worktable. 'He found me, all right.'

'So, he came after you.' Sandy's brown eyes on Mae were shining. 'All the way from Ireland. He loves you, Mae, I can tell. You were wrong to turn him down.'

'Nothing's changed.' Mae began to set out her work materials – her scissors, thread, tape-measure – all with precise movements, but slightly trembling hands.

'It has! He's proved he cares for you. And you care for him. You'd be a fool, to shut him out.' Sandy came round the table to put her hand on Mae's arm. 'How often does love come anybody's way, then? I mean, real love?'

Mae knew she was thinking of herself and Gareth, and just as she longed for her own happy ending, wanted one for Mae too.

'The last thing I'm wanting is to shut Kieran out,' she said after a pause. 'But I can't forget that he married my cousin. And in the eyes of some, he is married to her still.'

'Mae, he is legally free. He can marry again. And so can you.'

'We could never live as man and wife in Traynore, Sandy. not where everyone knows us.'

'America, then.' Sandy gave a theatrical sigh. 'Think of it, Mae. America! Why, I'd go tomorrow, if I could!'

'I can't go at all. I have to think of my da.' Mae shook her head. 'Sandy, let's get on. We've work to do.'

'Sorry.' Sandy slipped back to her own seat, and for a while they sewed in silence, though Mae could sense Sandy's mind working overtime, trying to find a solution for her.

'How about Edinburgh?' she finally cried. 'Let Kieran work here! Mae, that's it, eh? I've solved the problem for you.'

Mae, rising to fetch more material, raised her eyebrows. 'Work here, Sandy? And do what?'

'Well, he's a New York cop, isn't he? The polis here could find him something.'

'The way things are, he'd not be likely to find a vacancy. And he's a stranger, anyway. They'd prefer a Scotsman.'

Sandy's face fell and the light faded from her eyes.

'Och, Mae, you've an answer for everything. I'm only trying to help.'

'I'm sorry, I know you are. And I suppose he could always try for a job, anyway.'

'All I'm saying is, that if you want something enough, you find a way to get it. And if you loved Kieran enough, you'd find a way to get him.'

'I do love him.' Mae set down a roll of cloth. ''Tis like the old days, when he cast a spell on me. Took me years to forget him. Now he's back, and the spell is back, too.'

'Can you no' do what he wants, then?'

'I'm afraid I might.'

'Afraid, why? To take the risk? Look, I'm telling you, it'll work out. Sometimes, you have to take risks in this world, eh?'

Mae, studying a paper pattern, was silent for some time.

'Maybe we'll find a way,' she said at last. 'Kieran himself said, "Where there's a will, there's a way."'

'There you are, then!' cried Sandy. 'Och, I'll see you settled yet, Mae!'

And I you, I hope, thought Mae.

'Where can I take you for lunch?' asked Kieran when they met outside the stage door. He had taken her arm and was looking at her with a sort of delighted relief, as though he'd been afraid she might not have appeared.

'Somewhere cheap,' she answered promptly. 'I know a place.'

'Ah, I've money in my pocket. Let's have a treat.'

'Your money will not last for ever, Kieran.'

'True.' He shrugged. 'But let's find this cheap place, then. I'm starving!'

Avoiding the Rowan Tree and anyone in it she might know, Mae took him to a little café in a side street that served a hot meal for a shilling and ninepence, with tea and bread and butter included.

'Feel the better for that,' he told her, when they'd had pies and peas and treacle tart. 'And the better for seeing you, Mae. How long have we got?'

'Not long. I only have an hour.'

'But I can call for you this evening?'

'About six. We can have something to eat at home.'

'Looks like it'll be a long afternoon for me. Where shall I go?'

'The Royal Mile?'

'I'm not interested in royalty.'

'Even old Scottish royalty?'

He grinned. 'Not Edward the Eighth, you mean? Think he's going to marry Mrs Simpson? There's plenty about her in the American papers.'

'He's a king, I suppose he can do as he likes.'

'So can we,' he said with sudden seriousness. 'If we find that way I was talking about. If we want to find it.'

'I do,' she said simply. 'I want to find it.'

'You mean that, Mae?'

She nodded, her eyes as steady as his, and he gave a long sigh.

'Makes me feel good, then.'

'We can both be feeling good.' She rose and picked up her bag. 'Now, I'll have to go back to work.'

'Could I not come with you? Just to see the theatre?' As she hesitated, he took her arm. 'Ah, come on, now, I'm your cousin, eh? That's all you need to tell anybody.'

'You've already seen the theatre, Kieran. When first arrived.'

'Only the stage door. I'd like to see where you work.'

'I suppose I could slide you in, then. For a minute or two.'

His smile was cold. 'Mae, I'm not a guy on the run, or something. All this secrecy – what have we got to hide?'

'I'm sorry, Kieran.' She pressed his hand quickly. 'Sure, I don't want to offend you. I'll be glad to show you where I work.'

302

Immediately, the sun came out for him and his eyes danced because he had won her round.

'Let's go then, mavourneen.'

Mae had thought to find Sandy sewing alone in Wardrobe, but when she opened the door, Kieran following, it was to see Gareth Paget hastily springing from Sandy's side.

'Why, Mae, you're early!' cried Sandy, flushing brightly, as Gareth lowered his eyes.

'Sure, I'm late,' said Mae. 'But I've brought my cousin with me. Gareth, may I introduce Kieran Connor? Kieran, I think you've already met Miss Corrie?'

'I remember Miss Corrie,' said Kieran, giving Sandy his smile. 'Did me a favour.'

'Och, call me Sandy,' she said quickly.

'And Mr Paget is our Director,' Mae went on. 'He runs the theatre.'

Gareth gave a slight bow, but did not, of course, say, 'Call me Gareth'.

'How long are you here for, Mr Connor?' he asked politely.

'A few days, perhaps.'

'And then it's back to Ireland?'

'Probably America. I'm with the New York police.'

'Sounds exciting.'

'Exciting?' Mae's eyes on Kieran were beginning to flash. 'Kieran, I'll see you this evening. I'm afraid I must get on with things now.'

'Hey, was I not to be given a conducted tour?'

'I told you, I am busy.'

As Gareth, exchanging glances with Sandy, quickly removed himself, Kieran took a step towards Mae. But her face was averted.

'This evening, then?' he asked in a low voice.

She simply nodded, and after waiting a moment for her to speak or see him out, he realised she was going to do neither. With a polite goodbye to Sandy, he moved to the door, looked back once, and left.

'So much for finding a way,' snapped Mae, turning her angry gaze on Sandy, when the door had closed on him. 'Seems his way is to go back to America.'

'He only said probably, Mae.'

'And what do you think "probably" means?' Mae gave a scornful laugh and gathered up a folder of sample materials. 'Oh, I'll be saying no more. Just take these up for Brett to see. We've curtains to make for next week's set.'

As Mae swept past her, Sandy thought she had never seen her look so cold. Oh, but what a charmer, eh, that Kieran Connor? He'd be sure to bring the smile back to Mae's pretty face.

Chapter Seventy-Three

'Ah, Mae, you're mad at me,' said Kieran, hurrying to keep up with her as they left the theatre that evening. 'Look, wait, tell me what I've done.'

She gave him a fiery look, and darted across the street, as he followed. 'Sure you are not needing telling!' she cried.

'Something I said, is it?' He dashed his hand to his brow. 'Was it what I told that guy? About going back to the States?'

'And we were to find a way!' Mae said, breathing fast outside Number Eight. 'A way to suit the both of us. So, you say you are going back to America, where I cannot go. 'Tis always the same with you, Kieran. Always the fine talk and never the action!'

'You are not being fair, Mae.' He held her arm as she turned to the front door. 'What did you want me to do, then? Tell him my plans depended on you?'

'You could have said you hadn't decided where you would go. Is that not the truth, Kieran? Or, am I mistaken?'

Standing rigidly on the pavement, they gazed fiercely into each other's eyes, until Kieran gave way.

'If I've upset you, Mae, I'm sorry.' His eyes softened. 'Please, now, let's not quarrel. Our time is precious.'

Her expression, too, began to soften. 'I was upset,' she admitted. 'You might have thought I would be.'

'My trouble, mavourneen – I didn't think.'

'Oh, Kieran—'

She was putting out her hand towards him, would have gone into his arms, but someone spoke her name, and she swung round. It was Rona.

Rona, returning with some messages, her two tall girls, Susie

305

and Jannie, both now in their teens, at her side, their eyes and hers homing in straight to Kieran.

'Rona,' murmured Mae. 'I-I'm glad we've met. I want to introduce you to my cousin, Kieran Connor. My cousin's husband, I should say. Kieran, this is my sister-in-law, Mrs Walker, and Susie and Jannie, my nieces.'

'How very nice to meet you,' said Kieran smoothly.

'Likewise,' murmured Rona. Her eyes moved to Mae, and in their dark-hazel depths, Mae read that she knew. As Kieran himself had said, people always did. 'My cousin's husband,' Mae might say, but Rona knew just who Kieran was, and before her look, Mae's own eyes fell.

Why should she feel guilty? Harry had been dead for years. She had a right to find love again. But with Kieran Connor? Rona would not think so.

'Staying long?' Rona was asking Kieran, as her girls hung on her arms and kept their eyes on him.

'Not long. I'm over in Ireland to see my father. Thought I'd see how Mae was doing.'

'Was Mae no' just over in Ireland, then?'

Rona's voice was sweet and innocent. Kieran's smile in return was easy.

'Sure, she was, but now I am seeing Edinburgh, too. And a fine city it is.'

'Well, nice to meet you, eh?' Rona, loosening herself from her girls, opened the door to Number Eight and began to progress toward the stair. 'Enjoy your visit, Mr Connor. Bye, Mae.'

'Bye Mae!' cried Susie and Jannie, clearly loath to leave this new and exciting fellow who'd arrived on the scene, but in the end obediently following their mother.

'You'd better come in,' Mae told Kieran, opening her own door, but her voice was flat, and for a little while she was not the Mae he knew.

Only when they'd had the meal Mae'd put together quite mechanically, did she gradually begin to thaw. Kieran made her move with him to the sofa, where he took her on his knee and smoothed her hair from her brow and gently kissed her.

'Has she upset you, Mae? Your sister-in-law? She looks a bit of a tartar.'

306

'I'm thinking of how things must seem to her.' Mae fixed him with her large blue eyes. 'She knows about Rosaleen, you see. I told her.'

'And you think she knows about you and me? What of it? You've a right to your own life. She can't expect you to grieve for her brother forever.'

'I have the feeling she will not want me to marry again.' Mae slid from Kieran's knee and sat a little apart from him on the sofa. 'But who says I am to marry you, anyway? If you are set on going back to the States?'

'Ah, Mae—' he ran his hands through his hair. 'What are we to do, then? We can't go back to Ireland.'

She hesitated. 'You could perhaps find a job here.'

He stared. 'Here? In Edinburgh?'

'Why not?'

'I'm a cop, Mae, that's all I know. I might be able to run my da's pub, but there's nothing much else that I can do.'

'There's a police force here.'

He laughed shortly. 'You think I'd get taken on by a Scottish police force? They'll want Scots, not Irish. This isn't New York.'

It was Mae's own point, but she would not accept it. 'You are ruling it out, then? Working here? It would solve all our problems, Kieran.'

He made no reply, and after a moment, she sighed deeply.

'I have found a way for us and you don't want it. There's no more to say.'

'For God's sake, Mae, I've not said I'll not consider it! It's just that – well, I'd never thought of it.' He drew his brows together, looking away. 'I guess I could find out – what the situation is.'

'Would you be willing, to do that?'

'We said we'd find a way.' He shrugged. 'This'd be one.'

'As long as we're together, Kieran? Is that not the main thing?'

'Sure it is.' He drew her back into his arms and began to kiss her, softly at first, then with stronger passion, until only their bodies mattered, and all their talk and considerations melted from their minds.

'Oh, God, Mae, we need each other,' Kieran murmured, releasing her for a moment. 'You need me as much as I need you. Admit it. And you want me, don't you? What the hell does it matter where we live?' Again they held each other, lost in delight, but a

307

certain fear was beginning to build in Mae's mind, a fear of herself and what she might accept.

Oh, God, she prayed, don't let me say I'll go with him to America, don't let me agree.

But already, Kieran was murmuring, 'Mae why not just come with me to the States? It'd be the best place for us. We could start a new life, away from folk here looking down their noses, pointing the finger. Your da's not so old, he's not ill, and you could come back and see him, just like you do from here. I mean, how often do you see him, anyway?'

'Kieran, please—'

'No, Mae, be reasonable. You know in your heart, America's the best place. Safest, too. And I'd never get a job here, not one I'd want. Just say you'll come, and all our worries'll vanish into thin air. Try it, mavourneen. Accept it.'

'There's your own da,' she said faintly. 'Would you leave him?'

'Frank will take care of him. If he gives up the hard work, he'll be OK. Anyway, he knows I've my life to live.' Kieran's eyes on Mae's face were filled with light. 'And so have you.'

They lay quietly in each other's arms, Kieran's hand gently touching Mae's cheek.

'Say it,' he whispered. 'Say you'll come with me.'

The silence in the room was intense, as he held her close to him, closer and closer, so that she began to think she couldn't fight any more. They were one. She must go where he went. If it was America, so be it. Her lips parted – she was ready to speak . . .

Someone was tapping on her door. Tapping gently, not urgently, but with great persistence.

'Oh, God!' cried Kieran. 'It'll be your damned sister-in-law! Don't answer! Don't answer!'

But Mae, rising, was straightening her dress and tidying her hair.

'It might be something serious,' she whispered. 'I might be needed.'

He got to his feet and smoothed back his own hair, his face pale with frustration.

'Answer it, then, if you must. But for God's sake, don't let anybody in.'

As though Mae could not let Rosaleen in! For it was Rosaleen at the door.

Chapter Seventy-Four

She was looking very beautiful. And smart, Mae had to admit, eyeing Rosaleen's navy-blue jacket and long slim skirt, the small hat at an angle on her black hair, the touch of white from the collar at her throat. She carried a pair of white gloves and at her feet was a suitcase. Dear God, a suitcase! How long was she planning to stay? And why had she come?

As though Mae didn't know ... Her eyes went to Kieran, who was staring, transfixed at Rosaleen.

She came towards him, smiling.

'Kieran, would you mind bringing my case in for me? Such a weight, it is. Mae, I'm all confused. I thought you lived next door. Sure, you were there before, is that not right?'

'You went to my old flat?' asked Mae.

'I did, and a fella came to the door with the sweetest little boy.' Rosaleen gave a peal of laughter. 'So, wasn't I thinking he was yours, Mae? And you married again, and me not knowing? But then his da was saying you'd moved. You should have told me.'

'Rosaleen, what the hell are you doing here?' asked Kieran. He brought in her case and banged the door. 'What's the idea, arriving like this, out of the blue?'

'Why, I sent a postcard!' Rosaleen put her arms round Mae's rigid frame and kissed her cheek. ''Tis lost in the post, I expect. I only wanted to see you both.'

'Why?' asked Mae.

'How did you know I was here?' asked Kieran.

'Is nobody going to offer me a cup of tea?' Without being invited, Rosaleen sank into Mae's chair and fanned herself with her gloves. 'Your ma told me, Kieran.'

'Ah,' said Kieran and sat down on the sofa, biting his lip. 'I might have guessed she would.'

Mae, very pale, turned aside.

'I'll make some tea,' she said tonelessly.

'If it's no trouble,' said Rosaleen.

'Of course it's trouble!' cried Kieran, as Mae opened up the stove to make the kettle boil. 'You've come here to make trouble, haven't you, Rosaleen? Soon as you got my mother's letter, you packed your bag and caught the train. Just to make trouble.'

'I only wanted to see you, Kieran. You've never come over to see me in London.'

'We're divorced. Or had you forgotten?'

'We said we'd still be friends.'

'OK, we're friends. But friends shouldn't try to make trouble. Why should Mae go to the bother of putting you up, then?'

'She's my cousin. She put me up before. And I am not trying to make trouble.' Rosaleen's violet eyes were wide. 'You're all I have, you two – apart from Uncle Joseph. It's natural, I'd want to see you.'

'For heaven's sake, let's have this tea!' cried Mae, setting out cups. 'Rosaleen can stay here if she wants to, but there's only the pull-down bed.'

'Wonderful! And that tea looks good, Mae. Is there any sugar, and some of that Scottish shortbread you had before?'

'In the tin,' snapped Mae. 'Help yourself.'

When the awkward moments of drinking tea together had passed, Rosaleen said she'd hang up a few things in Mae's cupboard, if that was all right, and was that a bathroom next door? How lovely! She'd just freshen up, then.

'Wash up, they call it in the States,' she said cheerfully. 'And they call our washing up doing the dishes. 'Twas so funny, wasn't it, Kieran, learning all their different ways?'

'I'm sorry, Mae,' Kieran said in a low voice, when Rosaleen had removed herself. 'This is the last thing I wanted to happen.'

'Not your fault. Though it's a pity you told your mother where you were going.'

'She never needed telling.' Kieran ran his hands through his hair again. 'But don't worry, Mae, I'll just send Rosaleen packing. She can take the first train back to London.'

'I can tell you now, she will not go.'

'What do you think is in her mind, then? Sour grapes. Doesn't want me herself, but doesn't want you to have me either?'

Mae, holding herself as tight as a drum, was managing to show no expression.

'She does want you herself, Kieran. She's changed her mind.'

'Well, I've not changed.' He put his arms around her. 'It's all right, I promise you, I'm not going back to her.'

'Kieran,' called Rosaleen, stepping lightly out of the bathroom. 'Where is it you are staying, then?'

'In a boarding house,' he replied coldly, letting his arms fall from Mae's shoulders.

'Should I be taking a room there, then? To save Mae trouble?'

'No, you stay here. Mae has said, she'll put you up.'

'All right. Fine.' Rosaleen shrugged. 'But what are we going to do tomorrow? Mae, have you the time off?'

'No, I have not. I have to go to work.'

'Rosaleen, you're going back to London tomorrow,' said Kieran. 'That's all you need to worry about.'

Her lip trembled. 'Why, I never thought you could be so unwelcoming. Now that I'm here, I could stay a few days. Mae, you'd not mind?'

'I told you, I have to go to work. I couldn't see you.'

Rosaleen's lovely eyes were fixed on Kieran.

'Will you take me to the station tomorrow, then?'

He hesitated. 'All right. I'll give you a hand with your case. Wasted journey, wasn't it?'

But neither of the women made any reply.

Chapter Seventy-Five

When Kieran left for his boarding house, Mae thought there might be awkwardness between herself and her cousin, but Rosaleen seemed quite at ease. So much so, she almost tore Mae's nerves to shreds, chattering on about this and that, with never a word about what was really on her mind.

So, what did Mae think about the King and Mrs Simpson, then? Would they ever be able to marry? And did Mae like the latest calf-length skirts? Had to be skinny to wear them, of course, but Mae would be all right there. She'd kept wonderfully slim, so she had.

'Not like me!' laughed Rosaleen, though as far as Mae could see there wasn't a spare ounce on her. Typical, of course, thought Mae, of her cousin's habit of talking without meaning.

Yet, as they made up the little pull-down bed in the living-room, there were moments when Mae caught Rosaleen's eyes resting on her with a calculating gaze that belied her artlessness. And Mae knew she was wondering just how far she and Kieran had gone, and of how much there was for Rosaleen herself to do, to win him back.

In the morning, of course, she was still in her bed when Mae was up and about, getting ready for work, yawning and nodding when Mae explained about getting her breakfast, and putting the bed back before she left for the station.

'What time train will you be trying for?' asked Mae.

'Heavens. I've no idea. It's Kieran's idea to make me go home. He must find out the train times.'

'I'll say goodbye, then.'

Rosaleen, throwing back her hair, kissed Mae's cheek.

'Goodbye, dear Mae. I'm sorry you didn't want me to stay.'

'Look, 'tis not that, at all—'

'Ssh, I understand. Take care, then.'

'Will you wish me luck?' asked Mae, after a moment or two.

Again, there was that little considering look from her cousin's eye, but all she said was, 'All the luck in the world.'

The morning in Wardrobe passed like a year. Mae was on pins, waiting for lunchtime, waiting for Kieran. Waiting to see if he was alone.

'Everything all right?' asked Sandy.

'Fine.' Mae, machining the curtains Brett needed for the new set, had decided to keep Rosaleen's visit to herself. After all, she would probably be on her way home by now. Why tell anyone, even Sandy, of something that meant nothing?

'Thought you seemed a bit on edge.'

'You are always thinking that about me.'

Well, if I am, it's because you are, Sandy said to herself sadly.

The hands of the clock moved slowly, oh so slowly, but reached twelve at last, and Mae, leaping up, snatched her hat and jacket and made for the door.

'Is he there?' called Sandy.

But Mae was already on her way out of the theatre, nodding to Sam, hurrying out into the street, looking up and down. One figure, surely, would be coming towards her. One man's figure, running, waving.

There were two figures, walking. One man's, one woman's. Kieran's and Rosaleen's.

I knew it, thought Mae, as her heart plummeted. I knew she'd never take that train. What shall I do? Smile. Be easy. Show nothing.

'Missed the train? she asked, as the two figures reached her.

'I did,' Rosaleen answered with a sunny smile. 'So, we went for a cup of coffee in the buffet to wait for the next one, and then Kieran was saying, well, why not stay a day or two, after all? Such a waste, to go straight home.'

Mae looked at Kieran, whose eyes slid away.

'Seemed a bit foolish, really, when you think about it,' he said in a low voice.

313

'So, you'll be staying on, then, Rosaleen?' she asked Mae.

'I will, but I'm not wanting to put you to any trouble. Kieran's found me a room and we've left my case.'

'At his place?'

'Oh, no.' Rosaleen appeared shocked, though she had herself suggested that same thing. 'A guest house in another street.'

'Not far away,' said Kieran. He was rather pale, and pushing back his hair in the way he had. 'How about something to eat, then? We passed a little place called the Rowan Tree – Rosaleen thought it looked nice. Shall we try that?'

'Why not?' asked Mae. 'The actors like it. Should suit you, too.'

'Why, Mrs Connor, how wonderful to see you again!' cried Roderick, as he and Desmond began hurriedly moving chairs at the actors' table so that they might sit next to Rosaleen, while Lance passed her the menu and Brett gave an indulgent smile. All the young men, it seemed, remembered vividly her first visit.

'And nice to see you, as well, Mae,' said Thea pointedly. 'Haven't seen you in here for a while.'

'And who's this?' asked Sally Anderson, fluttering her eyelashes at Kieran. 'Come and sit next to me – we can squash up, if you like.'

But as Mae made perfunctory introductions, Kieran took her arm and moved with her to a distant table.

'Need more room, I think,' he called to Sally with a smile, at which she pouted a little, but rallied to fix her eyes on Rosaleen and begin dissecting everything she had on.

'I wanted to be with you,' Kieran told Mae, fixing her with an intense gaze.

She said nothing, but studied the menu with unseeing eyes.

'Rosaleen got round me again, Mae. That was the way of it.'

Mae passed him the menu. 'What will you have, then, Kieran? Men usually like the sausages.'

'To hell with sausages. Mae, look at me. Say you understand. She'll be gone in a day or two.'

'I'll have a poached egg on toast,' Mae said to the waitress who had appeared at her elbow. 'And the gentleman will have sausages and mash.'

314

A burst of laughter came from the actors' table, but neither Mae nor Kieran turned their heads.

'I tell you, Mae, Rosaleen will be away in a day or two,' Kieran declared, after an uneasy silence. 'Our marriage is over. It was what she wanted, so she can hardly complain.'

'Rosaleen wanted the divorce?' asked Mae. 'I thought the both of you did.'

'I went along with it.' Kieran was fiddling with his knife and fork. 'And it was easy, you know, to get it.' He raised his eyes to Mae's. 'So that's the situation. Rosaleen will be going home, then we'll be on our own again.'

'Were you asking her why she ever came?'

'She said she'd been thinking of Molly.'

'Molly?' Mae went cold. 'Was it not Molly who came between you? I mean, when you lost her?'

'One poached egg,' said the waitress, putting down plates. 'One sausage and mash. Any tea, or coffee?'

'Later, please,' Mae told her, as Kieran stared down in silence at his sausages.

Back in Wardrobe, Mae left her sewing and moved to stand at the window. She was pretending to be very calm, very hopeful. After all, nothing had been said to make her feel otherwise. But she knew, in her heart, that nothing needed to be said. It was over. What she'd had with Kieran had died, the minute Rosaleen had stepped through Mae's door and back into his life.

He would deny it, of course. Just as he'd spent Mae's lunch hour denying it. But the time would come and soon, when he would say, 'I'm sorry, Mae.'

And she would have to put a good face on it, and say, 'That's all right, Kieran, I understand.'

Why should she? Angry tears gathered in her eyes. Why should she just accept that Rosaleen came first? She was the one who'd left Kieran; who wanted the divorce. Why should he let her just pick him up, when she'd thrown him down? When he'd told Mae he loved her?

Perhaps he didn't love her. Perhaps she'd all along been a substitute Rosaleen. No, no, she wouldn't believe that. No, that would be too hard. It was true he'd taken her for Rosaleen, that first evening in Ireland when they'd met again. But then, she'd taken him for Harry. It had meant nothing. They'd both known the differences, they'd both wanted love. No, she would not accept that he'd never loved her.

As she moved away from the window, dabbing at her eyes, it seemed a small step from that firm stand to letting a glimmer of hope flicker in her heart again. Maybe she would not after all have to hear Kieran say, 'I'm sorry, Mae.'

Chapter Seventy-Six

She did, though – but not until three days had passed. And to begin with, Kieran only said they must talk.

During those three days, they'd spent no time alone. Every morning, Mae had doggedly gone to work, and Kieran had taken Rosaleen sightseeing. Every evening, they'd had a meal together, with Rosaleen talking on as though there were no tension in the air, and Kieran and Mae saying very little. Then Kieran went to his boarding house, Rosaleen to her guesthouse, and Mae went home, wondering when the blow would fall.

'Why d'you no' take a few days off?' asked Sandy, who'd now been told of the situation. 'Dinna leave him and her alone, you're just playing into Rosaleen's hands.'

'If that is all it takes for Kieran to do what she wants, I'm better off without him,' said Mae.

'It's no good thinking like that. You have to fight, it's the only way.'

But Mae had decided – she would let Kieran do the fighting. Sandy was in despair.

With good reason, for on the morning of the fourth day, Kieran came round to Wardrobe, and from the look on his face, it was plain he was not going to do any fighting.

'Mae, can we talk?' he asked, glancing at Sandy, who was ostentatiously busying herself at the other end of the room. His voice was husky, his eyes so full of misery, Mae had to look away.

'Now, Kieran? I'm working.'

'I've made a decision. I have to go back to the States.'

'I see.' Mae hesitated. 'I suppose I could go out for half an hour. Sandy, you'll be here?'

'Aye.' Sandy shot a furious look at Kieran who was already looking away. 'Take your time.'

The morning was fine and warm, but, as they walked slowly away from the theatre, they didn't notice the weather.

'Shall we go to the gardens?' asked Kieran.

'I think we'll just stay here.' Mae sat down on the bench opposite the cathedral. 'I don't want to stay out long. And we have not much to say, have we?'

'Oh, Mae!' He took her hand. 'I feel so bad.'

'About going back to America? Or going back with Rosaleen?'

'She wants us to try again, Mae. That's why she came. She said she'd been thinking about Molly, and how we shouldn't have let ourselves part, because Molly's still with us, you see, and needs the both of us.'

'Rosaleen was not thinking this before?'

'We were so full of grief, we couldn't think straight. Rosaleen said, every time she looked at me, she'd just remember Molly and how happy we'd been, and she couldn't take it, had to get away. I suppose I felt the same.'

Mae quietly removed her hand from his. 'So, where did I fit in, Kieran? All that talk of love – it meant nothing?'

'No! Oh, God, Mae please believe me, I do love you. I truly fell in love with you when I saw you again. I thought we could make each other happy.'

'Until Rosaleen came back?'

'She's Molly's mother,' he said simply. 'We belong together. Oh, Mae, I'm sorry.'

There they were. The words she'd been expecting. Preparing for, except for that silly hope that had kept on flickering. Out now, anyway, and the knife was in her heart instead, but as yet there was no pain. That would come later. For now, there was only numbness, as with a real knife wound, she'd heard. Didn't folk keep going sometimes, not even knowing they'd been hurt? Before they dropped?

'You don't know how bad I feel,' Kieran was saying. 'To know I've hurt you, and you such a grand, sweet person, who's known sorrow already. Rosaleen feels the same—'

'Do not tell me how Rosaleen feels,' said Mae.

'No, well, I'm blaming only myself and that's the truth. I should have looked ahead, worked things out. The only thing is, Mae, I know you never really wanted to go to America with me. And maybe if you had gone, you might have regretted it.'

'Would I?'

'Well, if you'd thought of Rosaleen. Because, deep down, you might have believed – she was still my wife.'

Mae was silent for a time. 'You are probably right,' she said at last. 'But it seems to me, you know, you've worked things out pretty well.' She smiled. 'Made yourself feel better, in fact.'

'No, how can you say that?' He snatched at her hands again. 'I'll never forgive myself, Mae, for what I've done to you. Never!'

'Ah, well maybe, now, you've not done so very much.'

She took a little pleasure in saying that, even though the pain was already beginning in the wound that he had made. But he needn't know.

'I have to go back,' she told him, rising. 'So, I'll say goodbye. Tell Rosaleen I wish her well, but I don't want to see her at the moment.'

'You're saying goodbye – now?'

He had leaped to his feet, his face stricken, she couldn't think why.

'Could I not come round this evening, Mae? Just myself?'

'I have things to do this evening. Better not meet again. Besides, you'll be needing to pack. You'll surely be leaving tomorrow? Going to Ireland, before you go to America?'

He put his hand to his brow. 'I suppose so. But we could have had a meal—'

'Goodbye, Kieran.' She did not put out her hand, or make a move to kiss his cheek. 'And don't bother to walk back with me. I'll go more quickly on my own.'

She guessed he was watching her as she walked away, but she did not, of course, look back. Never again, she decided, would she look back on Kieran Connor.

Chapter Seventy-Seven

As soon as Sandy saw her, she came to her and put her arms around her.

'Oh, Mae!'

'I'm all right,' said Mae, releasing herself. 'Or, I will be.'

'The devil! The rotter!' Sandy's face was scarlet. 'I'd like to kick his teeth in, so I would!'

'I was the foolish one. I knew all along I was taking a risk, getting involved.'

'You believed in him.'

Mae sank into a chair at the table. 'I did. But maybe he believed himself, what he told me.' She rested her head on her hand. 'I nearly went to America with him, you know. And then, 'tis true, I might have regretted it.'

'Did he say you would?'

'He said I might. Might begin thinking again that he was still married to Rosaleen.'

'The snake! He was just trying to make excuses for letting you down.'

'I am better off without him. Everything is easy now. No more problems.' Mae's eyes filled with tears. 'But it hurts, Sandy, I am not denying. All I had of Kieran in my mind is dead.' She shook her head. 'But I will not mourn him, as I mourned Harry.'

'Aye, he's no' worth it. Mae, would you no' like to go home for a bit? You canna work today.'

'I will be better if I work. The best medicine, as they say.'

'Let's work, then.' As she turned aside to pick up her sewing, Mae, looking up, saw that Sandy's colour had faded and that all her energy seemed spent.

'Are you all right yourself?' Mae asked with concern. 'Not feeling faint, or anything?'

'Feeling faint? No.' Sandy smiled grimly. 'And I'm no' in the family way, if that's what you're thinking.'

'I am not!' cried Mae. 'You were just looking – not very well.'

'I'm OK. Had some bad news, that's all.' Sandy heaved a long sigh. 'I didnae tell you, because it's supposed to be a secret, but I suppose he'll be telling us all pretty soon, anyway.'

'Who?'

'Gareth, o' course.' Sandy's eyes were on her work. 'He's leaving, Mae. He's leaving this job. He told me yesterday.'

'Leaving? That can't be true. He's the director. Why would he want to leave?'

'Says the work's no' what he thought. He's too strapped for cash, he canna do what he wants, and seemingly what he wants to do is act.' Sandy shrugged. 'So he told his agent he wanted another job and his agent got him one. You'll never guess where.'

'Where?' whispered Mae.

'Hollywood. Aye, I told you you'd never guess. He's going to make a picture. I think it's from a book. *The Woodlanders*. Have you read it?'

Mae shook her head. She was beginning to feel as sick at heart for Sandy as for herself.

'He's going to play a doctor,' Sandy went on tonelessly. 'And your friend's going to be the heroine.'

'My friend?'

'Lottie Cameron. She's been signed up by the same studio.'

'Lottie is going to Hollywood? I'd no idea. She never told me. Does Brett know?'

'I couldnae say. All I know is that Gareth's leaving me and it's what he wants. He wants to put an ocean between us, eh?'

'No, Sandy, no! He'll come back!'

'He'll no' come back.' Sandy's voice was trembling; she was close to tears. 'He's found a way of getting himself free o' me over there, because he canna do it here. There's no future for us, you see. That's what he thinks.'

'Has he said so?'

'He doesnae have to say so. I always knew it was true, anyway. I always knew he'd never manage to marry me.'

As she began to cry in earnest, it was Mae's turn to put her arm round Sandy.

'You're wrong, Sandy, you're wrong. He'll come back, you'll see. 'Tis only natural he'd want to get on in his career. Any actor'd want to go to Hollywood—'

'Never asked me to go with him,' said Sandy, blowing her nose. 'Och, Mae, you have to face facts. Well, I am.' She smiled faintly. 'What a pair we are, eh? You and me. It's a good job we've got work. Best medicine, as you say.'

She leaped up, and said over her shoulder, 'I forgot to tell you, the chaps are coming in for measuring for the dress suits at two o'clock today.'

'What chaps?'

'Roderick and Lance.' Sandy's tone was contemptuous. 'I'll deal with 'em, Mae, nae bother. And now I'll put the kettle on. We never had our elevenses, eh?'

For the rest of the morning, they worked in silence, not wanting to speak again of what lay closest to their hearts.

Would it always be like this? pondered Mae. Two women, working, putting aside love, because that was safest? Maybe. For now, at least, a time to heal was what they wanted, and this they had. No need to worry about anything else.

And when the young men came in to try on their dress suits, and began playing the fool as they always did, Mae and Sandy responded, in an atmosphere so light-hearted it buoyed up their spirits in spite of themselves.

Anyone would think we had not a care in the world, Mae murmured to herself, and sent up a little prayer that one day it might be true. Or, would that be asking too much?

Chapter Seventy-Eight

Weeks that became months passed slowly by, and life was quiet in Wardrobe. Apart from work, of course. But the country at large was rocked when Edward VIII abdicated in order to marry Mrs Simpson. Their golden king? How could he have done it?

So wounded were the people, there was even talk of Britain becoming a republic. But then the king's brother took the throne, and as he had a sweet-looking wife and two little girls, folk began to think they might after all prefer the monarchy. By the time the Coronation came round in 1937, everyone was happy.

Except Sandy, who said sourly it was all a waste of money. They'd do better to help the unemployed, so they would, and put baths in tenements.

'Ah, now, you don't mean we shouldn't have the Coronation?' asked Danny Weston, an actor who'd replaced Desmond, now in Brighton. 'It's just an excuse for a big party, you know, and we could all do with cheering up.'

He was a cheerful fellow himself. Not handsome – he'd never be destined for matinee idol roles – but he had a friendly, flexible face and steady blue eyes that would always find him work. Already, he was a favourite with the company, and with Sandy, Mae sometimes thought. See how her expression was softening as she looked at him.

'Awful lot o' money being spent, just to cheer folk up, that's all I can say.'

'Well, when it comes to Coronation Night, I say we go out and celebrate anyway. How about it?'

'I might,' said Sandy, finally smiling.

And Mae knew she would.

Some days after the Coronation, when all the parties and parades were over, Mae, returning to Adelaide House for her sewing class, found Miss Thorburn looking out for her. Miss Dow was in the little office, too, and both their faces had a bird-bright expectancy that puzzled her.

'I've had some good news, Mae,' Miss Thorburn told her, when she'd found space for a chair.

'Have some tea, Mae,' said Miss Dow, passing her a cup. 'And would you like a biscuit? They're Garibaldi. I've often wondered why they're called that.'

'Harriet, would you let me tell Mae my news?' asked Miss Thorburn.

'Oh, yes, Anita. I'm sorry. But do take a biscuit, Mae, dear.'

'The thing is, I've been left money.' Miss Thorburn fixed her dark gaze on Mae, as she juggled with her cup of tea and her Garibaldi biscuit and tried not to look too mystified at all the attention being showered on her. 'From my uncle. My last relative, I'm afraid, apart from cousins in Canada.'

'I'm sorry to hear that, Miss Thorburn.'

'Yes, well, it's sad, but I won't pretend I'm not glad about the inheritance. It will mean I can do so much more here, you see. I had been thinking I might have to go cap in hand to the Council, to ask them to take us on, and none of us wanted that—'

'No, indeed!' cried Miss Dow.

'But now, I'll even be able to pay an assistant, which I've never managed to do before.'

Mae turned at once to Miss Dow, who smiled, but shook her head.

'Not me, dear. I've always said I only wanted to come in on a part-time, voluntary basis. That's more my style.'

'And this assistant's job would be full-time?'

'It would,' said Miss Thorburn. 'And with a salary. Oh, heavens, I should come to the point, shouldn't I? Mae, we thought you might be interested.'

'Me?' Mae swallowed a crumb, coughed, and set down her teacup with a clatter. Her eyes widened, going between the two women. 'Me?'

'Well, why not? I've often said you'd be wonderful here. You have the touch. You can reach out to our girls, and they respond to you. I couldn't ask for anyone better, as my right hand.'

'I've no proper nursing experience, or anything.'

'That doesn't matter. I was trained as a nurse myself, but we're not running a hospital here, only a place where the girls can come to have their babies in safety. We've two midwives now, two nursery maids, and a doctor on call, so what we need from you is assistance for me in organising things, keeping the whole place going, making everybody happy. You'd be perfect.'

'And you could always do a little nursing course, to get the basics,' said Miss Dow. 'I did.' She hesitated. 'But, of course, we know you're very happy where you are, and perhaps it's more exciting as a place to work—'

'But not more challenging,' declared Miss Thorburn. 'What do you say, Mae?'

'I don't know. It's – such a surprise.'

'No need to give an answer now. We'd want you to be absolutely sure, in whatever you decide.' Miss Thorburn gave a tight little smile. 'And this place would not be everybody's cup of tea, I'd be the first to agree.'

'I have been happy at the theatre,' Mae said slowly. 'For a long time, it was just what I wanted.'

The older women waited, closely watching her expressive face, as her mind gradually took in the offer that had been made and what it would mean.

'I'm not sure if I can match what you are getting at the Queen's,' Miss Thorburn said at last. 'But I can offer something reasonable.'

'That's all right. I'd not be worrying about the money.' Mae shrugged a little. 'I've only myself to think about.'

'We're all in the same boat,' sighed Miss Dow. 'No children.'

'Mae, would you like to leave this now?' Miss Thorburn asked after a pause. 'And let me know your decision later?'

'No,' answered Mae firmly. 'I know what I want. Thank you for your offer, Miss Thorburn. I'd like to work with you at the hostel. When do I start?'

Had she been too quick to make up her mind? No, she didn't think so. For some time now, since the end of her affair with Kieran, she'd been looking for a new purpose in her life. A new road to travel, where there would be others to help, as well as herself.

It was true, the hostel was not exactly new to her, but her position there would be different. She would be full-time and a professional; able perhaps to make improvements that might change people's lives. Set them on a new road, too, or at least point them in the direction of finding it.

What Sandy would say about being left, of course, was predictable. She would think Mae a fool for giving up the Queen's for Adelaide House, and she wouldn't be the only one to think so. Still, it was Mae's decision that mattered, and if Sandy were promoted to Mae's old job, she might be reconciled to her departure.

Although it was her afternoon off, Mae hurried back to the theatre to break the news to Sandy as soon as possible. Oddly enough, she took it very well. As though she were preoccupied with something else.

'Think I'll get your job?' she asked, testing the iron she was about to use. 'I'd no' bank on it. Point is, could I do it?'

'Of course you could, Sandy! Why, they'll give it to you without an interview.'

'Maybe. But, oh, Lord, Mae, I'm going to miss you. Aren't you the crazy one, eh? Moving to the hostel?'

'I thought you'd say that.'

Sandy suddenly set down the iron and coming to Mae, flung her arms around her.

'But I want to wish you all the luck, eh? I want you to be happy, you ken, like me.'

'Are you happy, Sandy?'

Mae knew that all she'd ever seen of Gareth lately had been his handsome face on the cinema screen, and though he'd written occasionally, she must know the love affair was over. Must, surely, have put it from her mind long ago and be ready for happiness elsewhere.

'I'm happy.' Sandy's brown eyes were glistening with emotion. 'Listen, Danny and me went out again last night, after the play, and you know what, Mae, I told him. I told him everything. Right from the word go, I thought, he'll know everything about me. And, Mae, this is the wonderful bit – he didnae care!'

'Sandy!'

'It's true. He said he didn't go in for judging folk, and he'd never judge me anyway, because what was there to judge? The only one he'd blame would be Finlay's dad for letting me down, and mebbe the way things were that made folk have to struggle so. I couldnae believe it, but he said he meant every word.' Sandy's voice was trembling. 'Mae, I think – mebbe I better no' say what I think—'

'I know what you think, anyway,' Mae said softly. 'You're both in love, is that it?'

'Och, I'm no' putting anything into words.' Sandy blew her nose. 'No' yet. But, Mae, seems like things are looking up for us, eh?'

Maybe, thought Mae. But then you never knew what the future could bring. Some people said there was war around the corner. Best not think of that. Best be grateful for the present.

'Let's get Brett to go out for a bottle of wine,' she cried. 'Let's celebrate!'

'No' yet for me!' cried Sandy. 'Dinna tempt fate, Mae.'

'For me, then, and my new job at Adelaide House.'

So, that was how the company toasted her when the audience had gone home, and kissed her and said they'd miss her. And if anyone thought she was crazy, as Sandy did, they were polite enough not to say so.

Part Five

Chapter Seventy-Nine

A September day in 1945, and early morning in Adelaide House.

Mae had just come down from the small room on the top floor where she had spent the night, and was unlocking her desk in the office – a routine she could have performed blindfold. She had, after all, done the same thing most days since 1940, which was when Miss Thorburn had left to join the RAF Nursing Service.

Now thirty-seven, her black hair still glossy, her complexion still fresh and clear, Mae looked years younger than her age, which often prompted those who knew her to wonder why. For no one could say she'd had an easy or stress-free life. Particularly not in the recent years when she'd run the hostel with only the help of the nursery staff, coping with rationing and wartime restrictions, the blackout, the paperwork, as well as the usual problems of the residents.

'Mae, how'd you look so young?' Jannie Walker, now Mae's assistant, asked her once, and Mae had laughed.

'Luck, I think – if I do. Or else washing my face in rainwater.'

'The only rainwater I ever see is full o' smuts,' Jannie had commented. 'Maybe you've to be Irish for it to work.'

'Ah, now, you Scots girls are lovely.'

And it was true that Jannie, now twenty-two, slim and fair, was very attractive. She had a look of her mother, and also at times, Harry, which could still give Mae a poignant stab. After leaving school, she'd had some nursing experience, and when Miss Thorburn advertised for an assistant for Mae, had been the best candidate.

'Not because she's your niece, Mae,' Miss Thorburn had told her, 'but because I think she will be the most useful to you.

And you'll need someone useful, now that I'm no use to anyone.'

'Don't say that!' Mae had cried, but it was true that poor Anita was only a shadow of her former self. Travelling with her mobile nursing unit in France after D-Day, she had taken a bullet in her lung and though surgery had saved her life, had since developed breathing problems that made it impossible for her to work. She still visited the hostel to pay the bills and give moral support, for which Mae was grateful, as she was grateful to Miss Dow, who came in to help when she could.

On that fine late summer morning, the country was still getting used to being at peace after the long years of battle against Germany and Japan. With VE Day and VJ Day come and gone, and the flag-waving and victory parties over, all folk wanted was to get back to ordinary life, which was not going to happen tomorrow. Demobilisation of the troops was off to a slow start, and if anybody thought rationing was going to end when Hitler was found dead in his bunker, they'd another think coming!

Meanwhile, there was no shortage of customers for the hostel, peacetime being still wartime as far as battered women were concerned, and the numbers of pregnant girls never lessening. Pattie and Linda, replacement nursery staff for two girls who'd moved on, were run off their feet, but then so was everyone at Adelaide House.

'Will the council no' take us over one day?' Jannie sometimes asked, considering all that they did, and Mae wondered, too, if Adelaide House might end up as part of the social services department. But money was tight, and for the time being it seemed that no changes would be made. Miss Thorburn, with the help of various charities, would continue to finance the hostel.

'It's like her baby, eh?' asked Jannie sympathetically.

And mine, thought Mae. The only one I'll ever have.

A familiar smell was beginning to pervade the office, and Mae, sorting through the post, groaned. Oh, Lord, the girls on breakfast duty had burnt the porridge again.

'Jannie!' she called from her door, and Jannie came running down the stairs.

'Yes, Mae?'

'Do I smell porridge burning?'

'Oh, no! That'll be Maisie and Beryl, eh? They're hopeless. But I've been up with Tina Muir. She's feeling bad this morning, but she's no' due. Think we should ring Dr Rick?'

'He's coming in today, anyway, to see Issy Smith, but I'll run up and see Tina. You be trying to sort out the breakfasts. If the porridge is no good, get them to wash out the pan and start again.'

'There'll be complaints in the dining-room if folk have to wait too long. Could we no' give 'em some cornflakes?'

'That might be a good idea. I'll come down as soon as I've seen Tina.'

While Jannie ran down to the kitchen, Mae ran up to the dormitory to see Tina, who turned out to have only a headache, but rather fancied seeing the doctor, 'if he had a minute, eh?'

'He never has much time,' Mae told her. 'How about coming down for breakfast?'

'Breakfast? Och, I can smell that burnt porridge from here. I couldnae eat a thing, Mrs Alpin, and that's the truth.'

'We might be having cornflakes today. That suit?'

'Cornflakes? Aye, mebbe. Will you give me a hond wi' ma dressin' gown, then?'

'I'll just have to look in on Issy next door – can you manage all right?'

'Poor old Issy, eh? She's got varicose veins like ship's ropes, I'm tellin' you. Nae bother, Mrs Alpin, I'll get masel' doon. Just put on a wee bit lipstick. Have to keep lookin' guid, eh?'

Away went Mae, to see 'poor old Issy', who was on bed-rest, to tell her the doctor would be visiting soon. Then it was down the stair to the kitchen, to find Jannie throwing Maisie's cigarette into the sink and Beryl washing out the great black porridge pan and swearing under her breath.

'They're a' banging their spoons in the dining-room,' said Maisie sulkily. 'There'll be trouble if they dinna get something soon.'

'Serve the cornflakes, then,' sighed Mae. 'But how is it you two always let the porridge catch on?'

'It must be the pan,' said Beryl. 'You canna take your eyes off it, eh?'

'Will you folk be quiet?' Jannie called through the kitchen hatch. 'We're doin' our best, eh?'

'What, wi' Maisie and Beryl cookin'?' somebody jeered, and then a young woman with a plaster on her brow came hurrying in to tell Mae she was wanted on the phone.

'Yes?' said Mae, gasping for breath after running back up the stair to her office. 'Adelaide House.'

'Is that Mae?' came a voice she knew. 'Lottie here. Could we meet for lunch?'

Chapter Eighty

They sat on a bench in the Princes Street gardens, eating sandwiches made by Mae, and covertly studying each other to assess any changes, for it was some time since they'd met.

'I'm sorry I have not the time to go out for a proper lunch,' said Mae, deciding that Lottie still had her look of brightness, her own personal starlight, even though that day she was casually dressed in a tweed jacket and slacks and without make-up. 'But 'tis lovely to see you again. How are you, then? How are your parents?'

Lottie's face was serious. 'They're not so well. I'm OK. Starting a new play next week, so I dashed up to see them before that. My father's got terrible arthritis, and Mummy has high blood pressure.'

'I'm sorry to hear that.'

'And of course, she has no maid now. The last one she had was young and joined the ATS, so there's only a daily coming in – not Mrs Ord, she retired – and Mummy gets into such a state. You know what she's like.'

Leopard hasn't changed its spots, thought Mae, relieved that she was not the daily.

'You'll have to calm her down,' she told Lottie, who laughed.

'Who could ever calm my mother down? But tell me about yourself, Mae. You're looking so well, you know. Hard work must suit you, because I know you do work hard.'

'I've done nothing new. Every day's the same, but I'm happy.'

'And how about your father? And your cousins, in America?'

Mae studied her cheese sandwich. She had no wish to discuss Rosaleen and Kieran with Lottie, though the old hurt had long healed, and when Rosaleen sent news of the son she'd called

Joseph after Da, Mae had replied. But in the occasional letters that followed, neither Mae nor Rosaleen ever mentioned Kieran.

'My cousins are fine,' Mae answered at last. 'And my da has married his friend, Annie. I was over for the wedding in nineteen thirty-nine, and when I got back, hadn't the war started!'

'The war.' Lottie threw crumbs from her sandwich towards a visiting sparrow, and shivered. 'Thank God, it's over. If it's over.'

'What do you mean?'

'Well, there were those terrible bombs that were dropped on the Japanese. Everyone says we'll be living in fear of an atomic war for ever more. Quick, let's talk about something else.'

They rose and began to walk towards the east end of Princes Street, passing the old air-raid shelter and all the familiar buildings untouched by the war. Lottie spoke of her time in Hollywood that she'd hated; of how they did everything back to front and how she couldn't wait to get back to the stage. Unlike Gareth Paget, who'd really enjoyed his film work and been very successful. It had been quite a sacrifice for him to come back and join the army when war came.

'But you have to admire him for doing it,' Lottie commented. 'Did he come up to the Queen's at all?'

'He did. Once.'

To see Sandy, was the truth of it, and that was another secret to be kept from Lottie. She need not know that there'd ever been anything between Gareth and Sandy, and anyway it was all forgotten now. Sandy had been able to show Gareth her ring, for by then she and Danny were engaged, and Gareth had said he was very happy for her. They'd parted on good terms, and now Sandy was married, still working at the Queen's, and waiting for Danny's demob.

'A lonely fellow – Gareth,' Lottie commented. 'Never seemed to find the one he wanted. Maybe some gorgeous American girl will find him, when he goes back to the States.'

'You think he'll go back?'

'Sure to, as soon as he's demobbed.'

They crossed Princes Street and turned into Leith Street, coming eventually to Victoria Row, with the Queen's and the cathedral across the road.

'Look, there's Number Eight!' cried Lottie. 'Our old stamping ground!'

'Not so old for me,' Mae retorted. 'I still live there.'

For four nights in every week, she slept at the hostel, while on the remaining three, Jannie took a turn and Mae slept in her flat. Not for anything would she have given up her home.

'How's everyone there?' asked Lottie, putting on an animated show of interest, though she probably hadn't thought of Number Eight for years. 'Mrs Beith? Is she still around?'

'She is, so. Everyone is around, except the young men, of course. They're waiting for demob. Young Kenny Sims is married to Susie, Harry's niece – he's the one who used to tease everybody and throw snowballs. Now he's in the air force. And Norrie Beith was badly wounded in the shoulder, but he was patched up and sent back to Italy.' Mae gave Lottie a sideways glance. 'I suppose you heard about Brett?'

They were standing outside the Queen's, looking at playbills for one of the variety shows that had mostly replaced drama in the war years. Mr Standish had come out of retirement to organise them, but would be handing back to Tony Vincent, when he returned from the navy.

Lottie, not looking at Mae, was colouring deeply.

'I couldn't bear to think about it. His hands – burned.' Her voice was a whisper. 'A ship's fire, wasn't it? I never knew the details.'

'A minesweeper fire. He was lucky to be alive.'

'I did write to him, but I don't know if he ever got the letter. And of course he couldn't write back.'

'He's back at the theatre, Lottie. Came back to his old job after he was invalided out. You could go in and see him, if you liked.'

Lottie was gazing across the road towards her parents' house in Victoria Place.

'I will see him before I leave.' Her clear eyes finally met Mae's gaze. 'Do you see him, Mae?'

'Sometimes, when I look in on Sandy.'

'How is he, then?'

'All right, I suppose. Apart from his hands, but he wears gloves. You needn't look at them.'

'Oh, I shouldn't mind. Of course not.' Lottie took a deep breath. 'I'll go to the theatre tomorrow.'

'Maybe I should be saying that he is a – little changed. Older, you understand.'

'Aren't we all?' Lottie gave a silvery laugh, one she had probably used on stage many times.

'When we first worked at the theatre, though, he was like a boy.'

'Boys grow up, Mae.' Lottie's face was bleak. 'Especially in wartime.'

After an awkward pause, they slowly hugged each other, and Lottie found her charm again.

'So lovely to see you, Mae. I'll be back soon and then we'll fix up for a meal, or something. Perhaps you'd like to see my parents?'

'Please give them my best wishes,' Mae said obliquely. 'Take care, Lottie. Keep in touch.'

Chapter Eighty-One

Dr Rick was coming down the stairs as Mae arrived back at the hostel. He'd been released from the Royal Army Medical Corps only a few weeks before, to take back his practice from his father, a widower and semi-retired doctor, who had held the fort for him, visiting Adelaide House when necessary. A very nice chap, Rick Hurst's father, everyone agreed, but of course it was good to have Rick himself home again.

'Even if he is a shattered man,' Miss Dow had sighed. 'After losing poor Virginia.'

It was now five years since Virginia Hurst had gone south to work as a military nurse and had been killed in the London blitz. Dr Rick was already serving in the Medical Corps; they had seen very little of him, but knew, of course – particularly Mae – how he must be grieving. Time was the healer, as everyone said, and now that he was back, he seemed almost his old self. But then he had never been one for showing his feelings.

'I'm sorry I wasn't here when you came, Dr Rick,' Mae said quickly. 'How did you find Issy Smith, then?'

'I'm afraid I'm a little worried about her. There's the possibility of thrombosis, unless she really rests those legs and wears the elastic stockings.'

'I'll see that she does.'

'Think she hasn't been bothering with the stockings?'

'I couldn't say at all, but 'tis quite likely.' Mae looked away from Dr Rick's concerned gaze. 'I'll read her a little lecture, don't worry.'

'Put the fear of God into her!' He smiled, and moved to the

door. 'And how are you, Mae? Never put on any weight, that's for sure. Don't stay still long enough, do you?'

'I like to keep busy.'

'Another Anita Thorburn.'

'Sure, I'd be flattered to think it.'

They were silent, considering poor Miss Thorburn's inability to keep busy any more.

'I must try to see her sometime,' said Dr Rick.

'She still looks in to pay the bills.'

'Nothing wrong with her brain power.' He touched his hat. 'Well, I must be on my way. Don't forget Issy's little lecture.'

'I'll not do that.'

Back in her office, Mae took some time to settle back to her paperwork. Talking to Dr Rick had unnerved her a little; she didn't know why.

And then there was Lottie and her promise to see Brett. Mae could tell she was finding it hard to face his suffering; relating to other people's problems was always difficult for someone like her, who lived in a world of make-believe. Yet, she would surely want to see him? It was to be hoped, that in his present state, he would want to see her.

Checking over the hostel accounts was always a strain. Every month, costs seemed to rise, however much Mae tried to make economies, and she couldn't help worrying that one day they might not be able to keep going.

But, then, money had always been a problem, hadn't it? Even with Miss Thorburn's inheritance, there'd still never been enough. Yet, they were still afloat. Perhaps always would be.

Just as long as we don't have to go to the Council for help, Mae was thinking, when Jannie came skidding into the office, her face pale with alarm.

'Oh, Mae, guess what – it's Tina Muir! The babby's coming after all, and it's no' due!'

'Oh Lord, and Dr Rick's just gone. Phone Mrs Wilkes, Jannie, and if she's out, try Miss Rowley, while I go up to Tina.'

'What'll I do if I canna get either of 'em?'

'Pray!' cried Mae, and was not altogether joking. Though she and Jannie knew what to do in an emergency, they naturally hoped that the professionals would arrive before one came. Fingers crossed, then, for Tina.

'No need to worry,' Mae told her, when she and Pattie had moved her from the dormitory into the adjoining house for the confinement. 'You'll be fine, though why your baby's coming early is a mystery.'

'And you said I only had a headache!' cried Tina.

'Why, now 'twas you said you had a headache, but let's not argue. I just want to make you comfortable.'

'Comfortable?' Tina gave a groan. 'I like the way you folk talk. Who's comfortable?'

'Mae, it's all right, Miss Rowley's on her way,' said Jannie, flying in, but Tina made a face and said she didn't like Miss Rowley. So cold and thin. Where was Mrs Wilkes, then? Or, better still, Dr Rick?

All these years on, the girls are just the same, thought Mae with a smile, as she remembered Sandy's saying she only wanted the doctor and not Mrs Mennie. But privately she told Jannie that as the baby was premature, they might have to try to get Dr Rick back. They'd see what Miss Rowley thought, and in the meantime, make Tina a cup of tea. Then it would be back to the accounts for Mae.

Maybe she'd rather deliver a baby? No, as soon as she saw Miss Rowley's angular face outside on the step, she was relieved. Even more so, when Dr Rick arrived later in the evening, but then he always had that effect.

But there were going to be problems with the premature baby, he and Miss Rowley both agreed, and Tina would have to go to hospital.

'Och, no,' she wailed. 'I dinna want to be wi' strangers! Can you no' help me, Dr Rick?'

'It's a question of the after-care of the baby,' he told her gently. 'The hospital can help where we can't. But I'll go with you, and you'll be all right, I promise. Mae, can you telephone for an ambulance for us?'

Downstairs, while they waited, Mae gave him a cup of tea, and watched him light a cigarette. At that moment, he appeared anxious, and of course older than when she'd first known him, but it seemed to her that in looks he hadn't changed much. In other ways, though, he seemed different. Someone she no longer knew. Yet, wanted to.

'Always feel I've failed when this happens,' he murmured.

'Maybe we're the ones who've failed.'

'No, you provide the refuge the girls need. Can't be expected to pay for hospital equipment. And to be fair, it doesn't happen often that we have to go elsewhere.'

'Poor Tina, though. Will she be able to come back here?'

'Depends on the baby's progress.' He ground out his cigarette. 'Is there an adoption planned?'

'No, Tina's going to try to keep the baby herself. I can't say how.'

He sighed, staring into space, and she guessed he was thinking of Virginia's longing for the baby that never came.

'Where's that ambulance?' he cried, suddenly glancing at his watch.

Even as he spoke, they heard the knock on the front door and he sprang out of her office and away up the stairs, while Mae admitted the ambulance men.

Thank God, she thought, she could now relax. Until the next emergency.

She was too strung up to sleep well, and when her telephone extension rang in the early morning, answered at once.

'Tina's had her baby,' she heard Dr Rick's voice telling her. 'A girl, not quite four pounds, but they think she'll pull through.'

'Thank God. So, both well?'

'Both well. Thanks, Mae.'

'I did not do much.'

'Oh, yes, you did. You and the Adelaide always do. Sorry to disturb you, but I thought you'd want to know the news.'

'Thank you, Dr Rick.'

'Just Rick will do. Goodnight, Mae. Try to get some more sleep.'

Rick? She'd never called him Rick.

'You're the one needs sleep, Doctor – I mean, Rick. But it's morning, anyway.'

'Is it? I've lost track of time. Good morning, then.'

He laughed and rang off, and Mae looked at her clock. The alarm was just about to sound and she switched it off. Any moment now, Jannie would be arriving. There would be the usual breakfast struggle to supervise, and the usual rounds to make to see how folk were. A nice, typical day after a disturbed night. But as she leaped out of bed, Mae realised she wasn't feeling in the least tired.

Chapter Eighty-Two

Some days later, when Miss Dow came in to help Jannie, Mae was able to take a couple of hours off and visit the Queen's. She would have liked to know if Brett had seen Lottie, but felt she could hardly ask him. Besides, it would have been like checking up on her. Still, she did ask Sandy.

'Have I seen Lottie?' asked Sandy, who was in Wardrobe but refurbishing artificial flowers instead of sewing. Since the start of the war, she'd been expected to turn her hand to anything, as well as doing without an assistant, and spent much of her time preparing scenery for the variety acts. 'Oh, yes, she came in the other day. Looked just the same, eh?'

Sandy herself looked better, now that she was in her thirties, than when she'd been a twenty year old. That, Mae knew, was because she was happy. Even when Danny had been going through the Italian campaign and she was worried sick, she'd still radiated happiness, because she was loved. And now she could look forward to his coming home.

Though Sandy's brothers, Terry and George would be staying on in the army as regulars, Finlay's young uncle and aunt would be demobbed soon. Always made Mae feel her age, to realise that Shona and Johnny were old enough to have been called up. Heavens, even wee Finlay was seventeen now, and at technical college!

'I'm glad Lottie came in,' she said now, helping herself to tea from Sandy's teapot by the kettle. 'She was wanting to see Brett.'

'Aye, she did see him. No' for long, mind. I think she was a wee bit upset.'

'I was hoping she'd cheer him up.'

'The only one he really likes to talk to is you, if you ask me.'

'Ah, now, that's not true. Why would he want to talk to me?'

'Suppose because you're sympathetic. And you've had your troubles. He never likes to talk to folk who've had no troubles.'

'And how many folk without troubles does he know?' Mae asked wryly.

After telling Sandy the latest news of the hostel, which always interested her, they agreed to try to meet on Mae's next evening off, if she could get it, and have something to eat.

'And now I'll leave you to your flowers, Sandy, whatever they're for,' said Mae. 'And see what's happening.'

'They're for decorating the stage for the soprano's act,' Sandy said with a grin. 'Och, you should hear her, Mae. Shatters the light bulbs, nearly, which wouldnae matter if she wasnae flat!'

Hurrying through the passageways to the stage, Mae met Hector Standish, who pecked her cheek and said she was looking marvellous. Though his hair was now snowy white, he had worn well, and she could tell he was enjoying himself, back in the saddle.

'Should never have left us, Mae, but, then, the old place hasn't been itself, has it? I mean – variety acts! Yes, I know, in the old days, we were a variety theatre, but drama's the thing. Could I get the Board to listen to me? No!'

'I'm just on my way to see Brett,' Mae said, stemming the flow. 'How is he, these days?'

'Fine, fine. Never complains. And then, you know, we had Lottie Cameron in a day or two ago. My word, she's a wonder, isn't she? And always grateful to me, for giving her her start.'

Finally breaking free, Mae made her way up to the stage, where she found Brett in conversation with an elderly man who had taken over the lighting after Gerry Ames and Euan MacKail went into the forces. Mae didn't know him and he didn't know her, or that she had been married to a lighting man, and that was the way she preferred it.

'Hello, Brett!' she called, and looking across with a faint smile, he told the lighting man he'd see him later and came to join her.

'Mae, nice to see you. You haven't been in lately.'

''Tis difficult to get the time. How are you, then?'

'You always ask me that. I haven't changed.' He glanced down at his gloved hands, then flushed. 'Sorry. Didn't mean to be sharp.'

Whenever she saw him, it took her a moment or two to recognise him, not only because, as she'd told Lottie, he looked older, but because of his hair. When he was young, it had been long and fine and had fallen over his brow in a great pale brown wave. Now, he wore it as short and brutally cut as when he'd been in the navy, which was perhaps his way of signalling that he was not the same Brett Lester as he had once been.

Well, that was true enough, thought Mae.

'I heard Lottie'd been in to see you,' she said evenly, as he pushed forward a canvas chair for her and took one himself.

'Oh, yes, she looked in.' He glanced at his watch. 'We're doing a lighting rehearsal for a couple of new acts in half an hour. Just a warning.' He smiled. 'You won't want to see 'em.'

'But how did you find Lottie, then?'

'You mean, how did she find me? You sent her, didn't you?'

'Why should you say that? She was keen to come over and see you.'

'All right, she was keen to see me. We had a chat about nothing, then she left. And that was that.'

Mae stood up and began to move away. 'I think you're in one of your moods, Brett. Perhaps I'll see you another day.'

'Ah, no! Look, I'm sorry. Take no notice. It was nice of Lottie to visit me and I'm glad she did.'

He caught up with Mae as she reached the steps leading down from the stage, and they both stood in silence for a moment, gazing out into the silent auditorium. Very soon, this place would be buzzing again with people gathering for rehearsal, but for now there was the feeling that everything was muffled, wrapped in dust, set apart from the vitality of performance.

'Forgive me?' he asked quietly.

'Sure, I do.' And sure, she always would. Poor Brett.

'I was wondering – would you care to go to Queensferry with me some time?'

'Queensferry? You mean Port Edgar?'

She knew he had trained for work on minesweepers at Port Edgar, near the old royal burgh of South Queensferry, and often returned there.

'No, no. I thought we could just look at the bridge, you know. Have a cup of tea.'

'I'd like to, Brett, but I always have this problem of getting time off.'

'That's all right. It was just a thought.'

Seeing his face darken, she said quickly, 'But I'm sure I can arrange something. Maybe one Saturday afternoon?'

The darkness faded; his eyes brightened.

'Will you let me know?'

'I will. And I'll get bus times, shall I?'

'Oh, yes. I won't be driving. Even if I had a car.'

Chapter Eighty-Three

Some two weeks later, Mae and Brett were looking up at the great cantilevers of the Forth Bridge in South Queensferry.

'The eighth wonder of the world, some folk call that,' Brett remarked.

'Sure, 'tis a wonder, anyway,' Mae agreed, glancing from the bridge to Brett's profile.

He had been very quiet on the bus; she had the feeling that this trip he knew so well depressed him. Why make it? Why go back to where he'd trained for the minesweeping? For she was sure he usually liked to walk on to Port Edgar, where he probably sat on a bench and went over and over those days when he'd learned the job that was to end in disaster.

'This place is buzzing,' she went on, looking about her at the crowds. 'So many folk everywhere.'

'It's always busy,' he said indifferently. 'They come from the Rosyth dockyard and HMS *Lochinvar* – that's where I trained. Sometimes have as many as six thousand men there, you know.'

'I have the feeling they're all here, and in the cafés. We'll be lucky to get tea, I'm thinking.'

'We could try for it now, if you like.'

Avoiding the queues waiting for the ferry to Fife, they joined people strolling down the esplanade towards the shops and pubs of the little town. Here they found a café where two sailors were willing to share their table, and an overworked waitress took their order for tea.

'Any scones?' asked Brett, at which the sailors grinned, while at the same time eyeing Mae with interested eyes. As they looked

to be no more than twenty, she guessed they'd consider her somewhat elderly, even if attractive.

'Scones are finished, mate,' said one, in a cockney accent. 'But
they've got toasted teacake.'

'Toasted teacake?' cried Mae. 'Oh, please!'

'Two teas, two toasted teacakes,' said the waitress, hurrying away.

The sailors poured themselves more tea, as Mae and Brett sat in
awkward silence, and the conversation of the rest of the café
rolled around them like waves on the shore. It was a relief when
the waitress came back with their order, and Mae was able to busy
herself 'being mother', while Brett sliced his teacake, not looking
at the sailors. They, however, were looking at his gloved hands.

'Ex-navy?' one asked him.

He looked up, flushing. 'Minesweepers. How did you know?'

'Just a guess. Hurt in action?'

Mae, wondering how Brett would take this intrusion, froze. But
he seemed not to mind.

'Fire on board. In the Atlantic. Nineteen forty-three.'

They sucked in their breath and shook their heads.

'What a thing, eh? Everybody's nightmare.'

'That's right.'

Another silence fell, then the sailors looked at each other and rose.

'Best o' luck, mate. Hope things go OK for you.' They glanced
at Mae, and smiled.

'Good luck to you, too,' said Brett, and as the young men left
them, turned to Mae.

'Nice fellows, weren't they?'

'I was thinking you'd be upset. You don't usually want to talk
about what happened.'

'They're navy men.'

'You mean, they'd understand? I could understand, Brett.'

'May I have some more tea, if there's any in the pot?'

When they came out of the café, a mist from the Forth was changing the fineness of the October afternoon and Mae turned up the
collar of her coat.

'Better get back, Brett. I'm thinking we've had the best of the
weather.'

'I was hoping we could carry on to Port Edgar.'

''Tis not a good idea, for you to keep going there.'

'What do you mean?'

She pulled her hat over her hair, already damp from the mist, and raised her eyes to his.

'I mean, you should let it go – your past in the navy. You have come through, you know. You are still alive. And life can still be good.'

He was taken aback, she could see; had clearly never expected anything so straight to the target from her. It was also clear that he was not going to take it.

'Do you think you have the right to tell me what I should forget, Mae?'

'I have not. Except that I speak as a friend. And I am your friend.'

'I certainly thought you were.'

'Oh, Brett—' She searched his face, now running with moisture and gently touched his cheek. 'I want you not to mind your hands, at all. I want you to be happy again. Is it not what you want, then? To be happy?'

He turned away, shaking his head.

'Let's go back, Mae.'

Sitting next to him in the bus, feeling his resentment like a cold wind blowing against her, she began to wonder if she should have spoken out as she had. Maybe she shouldn't have interfered. Maybe it was true, what he'd implied, that she had no right. A deep sigh shook her frame. Maybe she interfered too much, anyway, in other people's lives.

Suddenly, she felt something touch her arm; it was Brett's covered hand, which he quickly withdrew.

'I'm sorry, Mae,' he said in a low voice. 'You were right to say what you did.'

'Maybe not. You must live your life the way you want. 'Tis not for me to be handing out advice.' She fixed him with serious eyes. 'Believe me, though, I was only thinking of you.'

'I know you were. And it's true, what you say, I'm too wrapped up in the war, in my old days in the navy. Seem to be all I can relate to, you see. And the guys – they're the only ones who know what it's like.'

'Even those young men we just met?'

'Yes, they've escaped the show, because the war's over, but they know what war means, just like the others.'

'Maybe, as time goes by, you'll feel better, Brett. You have your work—'

'Which I can't do as well as I should.'

'That's not true. Everyone says you're managing wonderfully well!'

'Considering my handicap, you mean?'

'You can still do it,' she said doggedly. 'And that's a lot.'

'It is,' he agreed, after a pause. 'You see, Mae, you're good for me. Make me look at things afresh.'

''Tis nice of you to say so,' she said with some relief.

'I was always fond of you, you know. Remember how I used to come into Wardrobe, in the old days?'

'That was to see Sandy.'

'Sandy? No. She's a very attractive girl, but you were the one I came to see. You never knew that?'

How could I know it? Mae thought. Nothing was ever said.

'I never said anything,' he went on, as though reading her thoughts. 'I knew you always thought of me as a boy. A silly young fellow. Maybe I was, at that. But I've changed, haven't I?'

'You have,' she said quietly, and put up her hand to press the bell for their stop.

Fortunately, it was almost dark when they reached the hostel, which meant that no girls looking out of windows would see Mae returning with an escort. She felt a little guilty, depriving them of the excitement, but she knew she'd never hear the last of it, if they saw her with tall, still handsome Brett.

'I've had a lovely day,' she told him, putting out her hand, then taking it back quickly, for of course he did not shake hands. 'Thank you, Brett.'

He stooped and kissed her cheek. 'Will you come out with me again? Not to Queensferry.'

'I will. When I can arrange the time.'

'That reminds me, I'm due at the theatre in ten minutes.' He grinned. 'Thank God I can still run. I'll ring you, Mae.'

'Goodnight, Brett.'

'Had a good time?' asked Jannie, coming into the hall to greet Mae. 'You look a bit wet!'

351

'Mist came down, but guess what, we had toasted teacakes, with butter! Everything all right here?'

'New customer turned up. Woman called Ella Bain. She's waiting in the office.'

'Baby due soon?'

'No babby. She's on the run from her man.'

'Oh dear, they're the difficult ones,' sighed Mae. 'I'd better see her now.'

'She's a bit different from the usual. Comes from Morningside. Husband's got his own insurance firm.'

'Morningside?' Mae raised her eyebrows. 'That is different – for us.'

'Aye. But the set-up's the same. Husband's been knocking her about ever since he got demobbed.' Jannie shook her head. 'You'd expect a fella like that to know better, eh?'

'I've learned never to expect anything,' said Mae.

Chapter Eighty-Four

Brett and Mae went out twice in October, once to the pictures, when they carefully kept their talk to general matters, and once to the King's Theatre, as a change from the Queen's. It was when they were walking home after the show, that Brett suddenly said out of the blue.

'Had my nightmare again last night.'

Mae put her arm in his. 'I never knew you had nightmares, Brett.'

'Most guys who've seen action have nightmares. Mine's always the same.' He quickened his step a little, and she had to quicken hers too. 'About the door.'

'Will you tell me about it?'

He shrugged. 'If you like.'

'Please.'

'OK.' But it took him some time to begin, during which he did not look at Mae, only the street ahead, which she guessed he was not seeing.

'Well, it's locked, this door,' he said at last. 'And I'm trying to open it. I know, if I don't open it, I'll die, but then I can see a light and I know the door's on fire. The whole ship's on fire, because we've been hit.'

Mae said nothing, only hung on to his arm, keeping up with his stride.

'I'm off duty, that's why I'm below, not on deck, but I know everything that's going on, and I know I have to get out of the door. Someone's shouting at me, telling me to get, but I can't get out. I don't know what to do, and I'm trying and trying to open the door—'

353

They had stopped by a street light and Mae could see his face that was no longer his, but a mask of such horror, she unloosed her arm from his and, reaching up to his shoulders, shook him as hard as she could.

'Brett, 'tis all right! 'Tis over! You're here, you're with me!'

Slowly, he came back, his eyes focusing on her, his face becoming his own again.

'That's it,' he muttered. 'That's the dream. I wake up at that point, but in nineteen forty-three, you couldn't wake. I mean, you were there, it was all happening, and you wanted it to be a dream and stop, but it wouldn't.

'I threw my coat over my face and I got the door open, but there were flames and my hands were in them. I think I would have passed out, but there was one of the chaps outside and he dragged me through. We ran up on deck and the whole place was like an inferno. All we could do was go, jump overboard.' Brett shook his head. 'I don't know what happened then. The next thing I remember is coming to, in one of our destroyers. We'd been picked up.'

'Oh, Brett, 'twas a nightmare, all right!' She pressed his arm gently. 'And you must have been so badly burned – not just your hands.'

'Everyone was burned. Some didn't make it, but Colin Melvil, who helped me, survived, thank God. Ended up in the same hospital as me and made a good recovery. So did I, except for my hands. They did what they could – skin grafts, and all that – but there wasn't enough left of 'em to repair.'

'I'm so sorry.'

'I've kept up with Colin, you know. He's in Yorkshire. We meet sometimes.'

'That's good. How is he, then?'

'Pretty well. But he's got a wife and two children – hasn't the time to feel sorry for himself. Like me.'

'No one's said that about you, Brett.'

They began to walk again and Mae could tell he was easier in his mind, even before he said so.

'You know something – you're the first person I've ever really told about the fire, apart from the doctors. And I feel the better for it.'

'You should have talked about it before.'

'Well, I couldn't tell my parents. They're in Sussex – came to see me in hospital a lot, of course – but it'd have only upset them, to hear all the details. And there's been no one else. Until now.'

Mae was silent, not sure of the road she seemed to be travelling with him, yet glad she had in the end been of help to him. When they reached the hostel, she was lifting her face for his usual kiss, still lost in his nightmare world, when a man came hurrying out of the darkness and almost ran into them.

'Hey, what do you think you're doing?' cried Brett. 'You nearly knocked us down!'

Without replying, the man, a shortish figure in a black overcoat, ran up the steps to the hostel and hammered on the front door.

'Excuse me,' called Mae. 'May I help you? My name is Mrs Alpin, I am in charge of Adelaide House.'

He turned and the light above the door shone full on a face that was handsome, yet hard, with dark eyes that stared beneath level brows, and an unforgiving mouth. With a sinking heart, Mae guessed that here was the sort of man she most dreaded to find on her doorstep – a husband come searching for a runaway wife.

'I'm sorry to bother you,' he said now, in a polite Edinburgh accent. 'I've only just found out about this place – that's why I'm so late. But I believe my wife might be staying here, and I'd like to speak to her. Her name is Mrs Bain.'

'I'm afraid it's far too late to let you in now, Mr Bain.'

'I have told you – I want to speak to her.'

'You heard Mrs Alpin – it's too late to visit now,' said Brett. 'You'd better leave, Mr Bain.'

'I have no intention of leaving—' Bain was beginning, when the front door suddenly opened and Jannie appeared on the top step. Before Brett could stop him, he had pushed her out of his way and darted inside.

'Oh, Mae, I thought he was the doctor!' cried Jannie. 'Else, I'd never have opened the door!'

'Never mind, never mind.'

Mae, with Brett at her side, was already in the hall. 'Mr Bain, I am not going to give you any information about your wife,' she said sternly. 'Please leave now.'

The words meant nothing, she could tell, for he had begun to smile, and as she followed his gaze, she gave a groan. Ella Bain, her small face ashen, her eyes full of fear, was beginning to descend the stairs.

'Go back!' cried Mae. 'Ella, go back!'

'Ellie,' said Bain very quietly. 'Ellie, you know this isn't right, now don't you? Why have you come here? You'd no reason. You know I love you.'

She stood very still, halfway down the staircase, making no reply and Mae, running to hold her, could feel her trembling like a plant bending in the wind.

'Now, why don't you just come down those stairs?' Bain asked gently. 'Then we'll go home. Don't worry about the children – we can collect them from your mother tomorrow.' He took another step forward, holding out his hand, as Ella, still with Mae's arm around her, made no move to retreat. 'Come on, darling. Let's go home.'

'Your wife doesn't want to go home with you,' Brett told him roughly. 'Look at her – she's terrified. You'd better just leave, Mr Bain.'

'With Ellie,' he said calmly. 'Or not at all.'

'We're not letting her go with you,' Mae called down to him. 'She has told me many times she does not want to be with you any more.'

'Ellie often says things she doesn't mean.'

Bain was still smiling, he still seemed calm. Then, suddenly, he changed. Like a flash, he was up the stairs and wresting Ella from Mae's arms.

'Come on, we've wasted enough time!' he shouted, his smile gone. 'These people have no power to keep you, Ellie, and you're coming home – with me!'

He was almost at the foot of the stairs, dragging her with him, when Brett moved forward.

'Leave her alone!' he cried. 'Leave her now!'

As Bain paused to stare at him, and then to laugh, Brett ran at him. He first aimed a blow at Bain's shoulder which Bain dodged, still laughing, then frantically began trying to free Ella from Bain's hold. But his hands fell away; he could bring no force to them, and as he stood back, wincing, Bain sent him flying and hurried on.

'Brett!' shrieked Mae, and ran to him where he lay on the last stair, but Bain and Ella were already at the door and Jannie was crying out.

'Mae, he's taking her! He's taking Ella away!'

But standing at the still open front door, medical bag in hand, was Dr Rick.

356

Chapter Eighty-Five

'What's happening?' he asked without raising his voice. 'Mrs Bain, where are you going?'

'Where she should be going,' Bain answered curtly. 'Home, with me, her husband.'

'I don't think so, Mr Bain.'

'If you don't get out of my way, I'll knock you down. I've had enough of this damned conspiracy to come between husband and wife. Get the hell out of it!'

'Certainly not. Please let go of Mrs Bain.'

'I warned you!'

Bain, breathing hard, let go of Ella and struck Dr Rick hard on the side of the face, thinking perhaps he'd done enough to show he meant what he said. But the doctor, shaking his head, threw aside his bag and retaliated with such a blow to Bain's jaw he fell, stunned, to the floor. Astonished, he tried to rise, then fell back again, while Rick watched him.

'Sorry about that, but Mrs Bain isn't going anywhere.' His eyes went to Brett, who was still sitting on the bottom step, holding his head that had been cut. 'Sir, I'll be with you in a moment. Just have to open the door for Mr Bain.'

'I – am – not leaving,' said Bain, struggling up, but his eyes were glazed and he was wavering on his feet. As Rick took him by the arm, voices came from the stairs and Mae, her heart sinking again, saw that the girls, some dressed, some in nightclothes, had appeared on the scene. Even Pattie and Linda were at the back, eyes going everywhere.

'Hey, what's going on?' cried Maisie, wearing a coat over her nightgown. 'Och, is that you, Ellie? Is that your man come after you, then? Dinna worry, hen. We see thae fellas a' the time – we'll no' let him take you!'

'Dinna worry!' the girls echoed. 'He'll no' get past Dr Rick!'

'Please, girls, go back to bed!' cried Mae. 'Pattie – Linda – could you get them out of here?'

'Aye, Mrs Alpin. Come on, now, you lassies. Away to your beds!'

But they were already swarming round the doctor as he propelled Bain through the door, delighted in the drama that was breaking up their routine.

'Want any help, Dr Rick? We'll sort him oot, eh?'

'Just take Ella upstairs,' he told them firmly. ' I can handle this guy.'

'You can't force me to leave,' Bain said thickly, from the doorstep. 'I have a right to see my wife.'

'Not here. You have no right to be on this property, and Mrs Alpin will not hesitate to enforce that. With police help, if necessary.'

'That's tellin' him!' someone shouted.

But Bain was not giving in easily.

'Ellie!' he called, over the heads of the girls to where she was standing, still wide-eyed with fear. 'I'll be back, I promise you. And then we'll go home together, and forget this whole ridiculous business!'

'Out!' cried Rick and closed the door on him.

'Now, I've work to do and you ladies had better get to your beds,' he told his admiring audience. 'Mrs Bain, I'll give you something to make you sleep when I've seen my patient.'

'Sally Teal,' Jannie whispered to Mae. 'She started running a temperature when you were out. Shall I go with the doctor?'

'No, I want you to go home, Jannie. You should have gone hours ago. I can manage here.'

'You look that tired, Mae.'

'We all look tired.'

It was some time later that Mae, Dr Rick and Brett met in Mae's office. Ella had finally drifted into sleep. Dr Rick had done what he could for Sally Teal, but she had flu and must be moved away from the other women tomorrow. Brett, who now had a plaster over his injured brow, said he must be on his way. His face, as Mae noted with apprehension, had taken on its dark look.

'How are you feeling?' asked Rick. 'I'm sorry I don't know your name.'

'I'm fine, thanks.'

'Sure, 'tis my fault, Rick, for not introducing you,' put in Mae. 'This is Brett Lester, a friend of mine from the theatre. Brett, this is Dr Hurst.'

'Like me to have a look at your hands, Mr Lester?'

'My hands are all right.'

'Still, I'd like to check them, if you wouldn't mind. Injured in the war, were they?'

'Burned. But there's nothing you can do. I've had all the treatment.'

'I've a friend at the Royal who is very good in that field. Perhaps if I were to—'

'I told you, they're all right.' Brett leaped to his feet. 'Thanks all the same. You're very kind, I appreciate it. But I'd better get home now. Goodnight, Mae.'

'I'm sorry the evening's had such a terrible ending, Brett—'

'As though it was your fault!'

'Will you be in touch?'

'I – maybe. Goodnight.' Brett glanced at Dr Rick, nodded and began to make his way to the door.

'Are you sure you're all right?' cried Mae, running after him.

'Perfectly.' He looked down at her for a moment, his face working. 'Apart from being useless. Better get back to the doctor there. He's a good man in a crisis.'

When she returned to the office, Rick was sitting with his legs stretched out and smoking a cigarette. A large bruise was forming on his cheekbone.

'Like one of these?' he asked, offering his case. 'Or should I not corrupt you? I'm trying to give 'em up myself.'

Mae, who rarely smoked, took a cigarette and drew on it with some satisfaction.

'I needed something,' she murmured. 'How's your face?'

'Might look quite interesting tomorrow.' He hesitated. 'Have you thought what can be done for Mrs Bain? Could be an idea to get on to Miss Thorburn's lawyer, and fix up an injunction against the husband's coming here.'

'I was thinking maybe it would be better if she went somewhere else, anyway. There's a place in Glasgow might take her – I'll get in touch tomorrow.'

'Not a long-term solution, but would certainly help for now.'

'I can't think of any long-term solution at the moment,' she said with a sigh.

They sat without speaking for a little while, both enjoying peace after storm, then Dr Rick stubbed out his cigarette and said he must away. His grey eyes resting on her face, he seemed to want to say more.

'Mr Lester – he's a special friend, is he?'

'I've known him a long time.'

'That's not really an answer.'

'We go out sometimes. He's been through a lot. I was hoping to help him.' A shadow crossed her face. 'But I'm thinking what happened tonight has undone all I tried to do.'

'I take it, he had a go at Mr Bain?'

'He did, but his hands weren't up to it. Sure, now, he's upset. He will probably not be wanting to see me for a while.'

'He'd be a fool,' Rick said quietly. 'If that were true.'

There was a long, ringing silence between them, then they moved to the door and said goodnight.

That night, Mae lay awake so long, she got up in the end and made some tea. Maybe she was the one who should have had the sleeping pills? But then, some of the thoughts that were keeping her awake were not the sort she wanted to forget in sleep.

Chapter Eighty-Six

On a November morning some days later, Mae was coming out of her door at Number Eight, when Rona called to her from the stair.

'Hey, Mae, wait a minute! Never seem to see you these days, eh? Jannie says you're all run off your feet down at the hostel.'

Now in her forties, Rona was an enlarged version of her former self, but still attractive, with her dark hazel eyes and her fair hair combed up high. Things were comfortable now for her and Jake, with Jake earning good wages back in his old job, and Rona herself working, too. Such ease, after years of anxiety, had sweetened her nature, a fact much appreciated by her neighbours at Number Eight, including Mae.

'Sorry, I'm always in a rush,' she murmured now. 'We must have a cup of tea sometime.'

'That'd be nice. Just wanted to tell you coupla bits o' news. First, Kenny's got his demob date – should be back in a week or two. Susie's acting like it's Christmas – well, it is, nearly.'

'I'm very glad. All the long time of waiting over.'

'Aye, and then it'll be me being a grannie, I expect. Soon as they can get a wee place o' their own. And then the other piece o' news – oh, Mae, you'll laugh, I'm sure.'

'I like to laugh.'

'Well, just lately, Dad's started taking Mrs Beith to the pictures. Would you credit it? Thae two?'

'Why not, though, Rona? 'Tis nice, if they are companions.'

'Thing is, Clara's been that low, worrying over Norrie – you ken how she is – that Dad felt sorry for her and asked her if she'd like to go to the pictures. She said yes, and there you are.' Rona stood back, as though she were a conjuror producing a rabbit. 'Next thing there'll be wedding bells, I'm tellin' you!'

'Why, that would be lovely!' cried Mae. 'My da's been very happy since he married again. Ben and Clara would be happy, too.'

'Aye, well, I'm all for it. Dad could move in wi' Clara, and we could have his place on our own. So, listen out for the news, eh?'

They moved into the street, where they were to part.

'How about you, Mae?' Rona asked, with rare diffidence. 'You've been on your own a long time.'

'I have.'

'I wasnae keen, you ken, for you to marry again. None o' ma business, eh? But I was just thinking o' Harry.'

'No need to talk of that now,' Mae said uncomfortably.

'But I was just going to say – if there was anyone – well, we'd be glad, you ken. Why should you be on your own, then?'

''Tis nice of you to speak, but I'm happy as I am, believe me.'

'But you could p'raps be happier. If someone right came along? Did I no' see you one time wi' that tall fella from the theatre? One that used to go out wi' Miss Cameron?'

'He's just a friend,' Mae replied.

'I've heard that before,' said Rona.

Mae had heard nothing from Brett since the night Victor Bain had tried to take Ella away, and had done nothing herself to contact him. But then she'd been busy, placing Ella in the Glasgow refuge and visiting her mother, who had called in lawyers to see if a divorce could be arranged.

'At least, thae folk have got money,' commented Jannie. 'No' like the rest here.'

'Hasn't helped so far,' sighed Mae. 'But if Ella is safe for the moment, that's something.'

These days, Rick had taken to looking in at her office rather more often than before. Mostly, he would have a word or two about his patients, fixing her with his grey eyes; not staying long. Occasionally, though, he would drop into a chair and relax, maybe even smoke a cigarette, though he kept saying it was the last. Once, he asked after Brett, and Mae told him she hadn't seen him.

'You will be seeing him, though?' he'd pressed.

'Probably. When I go to the Queen's.'

'Just tell him again about that friend of mine at the Royal, who might be able to help. If he's feeling better, he might listen.'

'I'll certainly tell him.'

Rick said no more, and though his eyes were again resting on her face, she couldn't read their expression.

When she did see Brett again, one lunchtime in his office at the theatre, it was clear he was not feeling better and was not prepared to listen.

'It's nice of you to come round,' he told her. 'And good of that doctor to try to get me more help – tell him I appreciate the offer.'

'But you won't take him up on it?'

'Don't need it.'

She waited for a while, watching him slowly and painfully pencilling in details on a stage plan; wondering if he was going to suggest they meet again. At last, he looked up.

'Guess who's back? Tony Vincent. Plus Primmie. Fresh from the navy and the Wrens. He's taken over from Hector Standish and we're going back to drama as soon as the variety programme's finished.'

'That's wonderful.'

'Yes, we're all going to be pretty busy, getting things back to normal.'

'I see. Well, maybe I'll be saying hello to them.'

'Good idea.'

She was turning away, when suddenly she turned back, pushed away his plan, and looked him straight in his shadowed eyes.

'Brett, will you listen to me? You are depressed because your hands let you down, but 'tis only to be expected. You've been injured, you cannot do what you used to do, but there is so much you can do – why not be thinking of that?'

'Anything else?' he asked quietly, as she finished, breathing hard.

'There is not. I've said my say.'

'And I know you mean well, but the thing is I'd just like to be left alone. Whatever I can do, I'm no good to anyone at present. I can't form a relationship, especially with someone like you, because you deserve someone better. Please try to understand.'

She was beginning to retort that he was the one who couldn't or wouldn't understand, when she saw that he was struggling to remove his gloves, and fell silent. For the first time, she saw the shrivelled claws that had once been his hands, and felt the colour rush to her face and the tears to her eyes.

'I just wanted you to see why I think I'm useless.'

'Brett, it doesn't matter, sure, it doesn't.' She gave a sob before she could stop herself. 'You're the person who counts, that's all you have to remember—'

He began to replace his gloves, not listening.

'We'll still see each other, Mae, when you come in. I'll look forward to that.'

'Sure, I'll always be glad to see you.'

He nodded, concentrating on his gloves, and finally, she slipped away.

The Vincents greeted her with what seemed genuine pleasure, both looking so well after their war service, they might have been away on holiday.

'Oh, but how I miss my uniform!' cried Primmie. 'Everyone said the Wrens hat was the most stylish. But, of course, it's lovely to be back.'

'It must be.'

'Seems strange without Thea, though, now she's gone south. And strange without you, Mae. Sandy's wonderful, but Wardrobe's not the same without you.'

'Certainly isn't,' agreed Tony. 'Perhaps you'll come back one day? When you get tired of working with the naughty girls?'

Mae laughed, hoping they wouldn't notice her reddened eye-lids, and said she must go.

'We'll send you some tickets for when we open in December,' said Primmie. 'We're doing J.B. Priestley's *Dangerous Corner* – a sort of mystery with a time twist – you mustn't miss it – I've got a lovely part.'

'That's why you mustn't miss it,' Tony said with a grin, at which she chased him out of the dressing-room, and Mae made her way from the theatre.

She had decided not to look in on Sandy, for Sandy could always spot when she seemed upset. And she was upset. For if Brett Lester believed himself a failure, Mae thought herself another.

Chapter Eighty-Seven

Cheering up the November days was the coming home of more and more service men and women from the war. At Number Eight, Kenny Sims was the first to arrive, followed swiftly by Norrie Beith, with his damaged shoulder. While his mother still fretted over that, though keeping up her cinema outings with Ben Alpin, no one who saw Pauline's face, now that she had her Norrie back, could ever have called her plain.

At the Queen's, Sandy and Danny were reunited and dancing on air, while Lance, Roderick and Gerry were all back at work, with Euan MacKail's return promised for January. And for those at Number Eight who'd been wondering if he'd still have his lodgings at Mrs Beith's, the interesting news was that he had married an ATS girl, so wouldn't want them anyway.

Another interesting piece of news, for Mae, at least, was that the Abercrombys were back visiting Edinburgh. Ronnie and Bernice, as Mae had to remember to call Mrs Ness, had spent the war in Sussex since a dramatic escape from France before the Germans came, but still came north from time to time. Even if Ronnie didn't always turn up, Bernice liked to look in on Mae at the hostel, where she usually bemoaned the loss to the Queen's.

'Still here?' she asked, arriving one afternoon, swathed in thick tweeds, and giving Mae a hug. 'Simply cannot understand why, you being such a lovely seamstress. What possessed you to leave Wardrobe, I'll never know.'

'You wanted a change yourself,' Mae reminded her, taking her into the office.

'And got one!' cried Bernice. 'He's back at the hotel, snoozing. Any tea in that pot, dear?'

Still as plump as ever, she had not changed much, even though her curly hair was now grey and there were a few more lines around her bright eyes.

'How are you, then?' she asked, as Mae gave her tea. 'Still happy being the Good Samaritan?'

'I'm getting paid for what I do, you know.'

'And I suppose it's an ill wind that does nobody any good. I expect Copperknob's doing well in our old job, isn't she? Married, you told me. So should you be.' Bernice stirred sugar into her tea. 'You won't mind me speaking plainly, dear? You're not meant to live alone.'

Same old Mrs Ness, thought Mae, smiling. Blunt as ever.

'I've been alone for many years, Bernice.'

'My point, exactly. Ever see anything of Lottie now? We went to see her in something in London. I have to admit, she was good, damn her eyes!'

Bernice gave a throaty laugh that died as the door opened and Rick appeared.

'Don't worry, I'm not one of the battered wives,' she told him cheerfully, as he apologised for interrupting. 'I used to know Mae at the Queen's long ago.'

'Mrs Abercromby was my boss in Wardrobe,' Mae explained. 'Bernice, this is Dr Hurst.'

Polite murmurings were exchanged, but Rick soon excused himself, saying he'd see Mae later and giving her a long last look from the door, which Bernice didn't fail to observe.

'Why, Mae, you've got an admirer!' she exclaimed. 'And isn't he nice?'

'Sure, I don't know what you're talking about!' cried Mae, colouring to her brow. 'Dr Hurst is not my admirer.'

'Is he married, dear?'

'He lost his wife in the London blitz.'

'That's very sad, but it was some years ago. Folk have to move on, you know.'

'Not everyone wants to do that.'

'It's the way of the world, Mae. For most, anyway.' Bernice's face softened. 'Oh, look, I'm sorry if I've embarrassed you. That's me, with the big foot in the big mouth again, eh? Let's forget I said anything, and you come and have a meal with us at the hotel. Don't tell me you can't get away.'

'I'll get my diary now,' said Mae, relieved that the subject was changed and her colour was fading.

She was too busy, after Bernice had gone, to think too much about what she'd said. Anyway, it was nonsense. Rick, her admirer? It was only when she was in her bed at home, being one of her nights away from the hostel, that she found herself remembering those grey eyes of his, and of how, when she looked up, she'd so often find them studying her.

Was it true, what folk said, that a woman always knew when a man was interested in her? Bernice had seemed to know, even when a man was interested in someone else, but Mae would never dare to let herself think that Rick was her admirer.

In the old days, he'd always been someone seen from afar, someone all the girls were half in love with, while later, he'd been a devoted husband to Virginia when Mae herself had been a devoted wife to Harry. Now, they were both older, and perhaps a little worn by circumstances and sorrow. It would be too much, wouldn't it, to expect . . .

Here, Mae moved her thoughts away from any further speculation. She didn't know what she expected, or what Rick might be expecting, if anything.

Better just try to get some sleep. But as the world began to slip away, the dark-blue eyes of Brett Lester came unexpectedly to her mind, and at their pain, she stirred and buried her face in her pillow. Her sleep when it came was troubled.

Chapter Eighty-Eight

Mae was half disappointed, half relieved, not to see Rick for the next few days. That was the way of it, sometimes; time could pass before a case needed his attention. On the other hand, he did seem to have been calling quite a lot recently.

The first post-war Christmas was on the horizon, and an atmosphere of determined enjoyment was making itself felt in the city. The killing was over, the lads and lassies were coming home. Everybody was going to have a good time, come what may, and that included the girls at Adelaide House.

'When are we gettin' oor tree?' they kept asking. 'And can we no' have some proper decorations? Why've we got to make paper chains?'

'Cost less,' Mae told them. 'Money's tight, I'm afraid.'

'Ah, come on, they'd no' cost much.'

'I suppose we might run to something new if there's anything to buy, and I'll get some holly, anyway.'

But one dark December morning, after Miss Thorburn had arrived by taxi and discussed the accounts, even buying new decorations looked by no means certain.

Sitting in Mae's office, sipping hot water and lemon, Miss Thorburn's breathing was so laboured and her appearance so frail, it almost hurt to be with her. But Mae wanted to be with her, just to appreciate again that spirit of hers that still drove her, in her fight to help others.

'The problem is, Mae, we're not breaking even,' she said now, speaking slowly and painfully. 'My accountant saw me recently – and my bank manager. Seems my investments are not doing well – I no longer have enough – to fund the hostel without help.'

'But we've always had help,' Mae said quickly. 'I mean, from the charities.'

'True, but it's been reduced.' Miss Thorburn paused, as a fit of coughing racked her. 'Excuse me, Mae – I'll just take a drink—'

'Let me help you—'

'No, no, I can manage.' She sipped her water and set down her glass. 'Point is – what we have from the charities – has never – been the same – since the war. Other needs – I suppose.'

'How bad are things?' asked Mae, after a silence.

The older woman gave a long rattling sigh. 'Bad enough. Well – you must know – from your own accounts.'

''Tis true, I've been worried. I've tried to economise, but got nowhere.'

'I know, I know. Don't blame yourself, Mae. This – has nothing – to do with you.'

'I mean, the girls do all the cooking and the cleaning and most of the laundry. I buy food in bulk, I find the cheapest markets—'

'There's no more you could do, my dear.' Miss Thorburn's dark eyes were sorrowful. 'Seems – we're coming to the end of the road. Sad – but, there it is. I'd hoped – I wouldn't live to see it.'

'Ah, don't be saying that!' Mae's own eyes were bright. 'We'll find a way out. We'll keep on. Maybe I'll try to rustle up some more supporters—'

'No. We'll just have to – bite on the bullet. Go to the Council. Ask if they'll take us on, as one of their hostels. Of course, their concern is more for the homeless, but I know they are interested in what we do.'

''Tis our only choice, you think?'

'Our only choice. I'm sorry, Mae.'

'I am thinking of you.'

Miss Thorburn shrugged her narrow shoulders. 'I've had my good years. Now, I'll have to let go.'

'You would like me to speak to somebody at the Council?'

'No, no, I will do that myself. It's my responsibility. The last thing I can do – for Adelaide House.'

After a long silence, Miss Thorburn asked Mae to telephone for a taxi, then, leaning on her stick made her slow progress to the front door.

'I will – of course – let you know – what happens,' she whispered. 'Don't worry – I'm sure you will be kept on – Jannie, too.'

'Oh, we'll be all right,' said Mae, her fingers firmly crossed. 'No need to worry.'

The taxi arrived and Miss Thorburn, having been helped into it, gave a last smile at Mae and a wave to one of the girls looking out of the window, before being driven away. For some moments, Mae stood in the cold, watching the taxi working its way through the traffic, until Jannie appeared on the front step and called to her.

'Hey, Mae, come on in, you'll catch your death!'

But the only cold Mae felt was inside.

It was later that day when she was at her desk again, that Rick appeared at her door. She raised her eyes in surprise.

'Why, Rick, we weren't expecting you.'

'No, this is just a social call.'

He pulled up a chair facing her.

'You're looking depressed. Are you worrying about going to the Council?'

'I am. Miss Thorburn gave me the news today.' Mae rolled a pencil between her fingers. 'Always makes me sad to see her, anyway.'

'I know. She's not improving.' Rick took out his cigarette case, then put it back. 'But this Council idea – it's been on the cards for some time, hasn't it?'

'We were hoping it would never happen.'

'Might not be a bad thing, though. A good deal needs to be done here, you know, to bring it into line with modern practice.'

Mae's eyes flashed. 'I would not be saying that.'

'Ah, now, don't misunderstand me. It's a wonderful place – you're all doing a terrific job.' He briefly touched her hand. 'You know I think that. You know how I admire Miss Thorburn and all she's done, and you and everyone. It's just that a bit of extra money could make such a difference.'

'Well, we shall see, if we get it. The Council might not want us, anyway.'

'It'll be a damned shame, if Adelaide House has to close. I mean, just think of someone like poor Mrs Bain for instance, and how she was able to come here for help. Haven't seen the husband again, I hope?'

'Thank the good Lord, we have not. Ellie is going to try for divorce, but then there'll be the problem with the custody of the children. We're just hoping for the best.' Mae put her pencil aside. 'Rick, you said this was a social call. Is there anything I can do for you?'

'Come to the theatre with me,' he said without hesitation, as though he were confident, but his eyes on her were anxious.

'The theatre?' Mae's heart was jumping.

'Maybe it'd be too much of a busman's night out for you. I mean, you might be sick of it.'

'I like it. Are you meaning the Queen's?'

'Yes, they're doing *Dangerous Corner*. One of Priestley's "time" plays, I was told – if that means anything to you.'

Mae gave a smile, and took an envelope from her desk. 'You'll never believe this, Rick. They've just sent me two complimentary tickets for the opening night. Would you like to have them?'

'If we can go together.'

'Sure, we'll go together.'

But Rick was studying the tickets. 'You know what this means, though? You'll be taking me to the theatre, instead of the other way round.'

'Why not? I'd like to take you, Rick.'

He laughed uncertainly, running his fingers through his curly hair. 'I'm not used to be taken anywhere, I'll have to admit, but thank you very much, Mae.'

'Thank the Queen's. Now, I'll have to work out if I can arrange to be free for that date.'

'I'm OK. I've got a new practice partner now – Arthur Frazer – he'll take surgery for me.' Rick touched Mae's hand again. 'And if I have to bribe Jannie to stand in for you, Mae, just let me know.'

They stood up, exchanging last long looks again, then as Jannie came flying in, Rick smiled and left.

'Didnae ken Dr Rick was due,' said Jannie, rubbing her cold hands together. 'Who's ill, then?'

'Nobody,' answered Mae. 'Everyone's very well, as far as I know.'

Chapter Eighty-Nine

It was a long time since Mae had been 'out front' at the Queen's, and sitting with Rick in the stalls, waiting for the Priestley play to begin, she felt as nervous as though she were on stage. In fact, her nerves had been getting the better of her ever since he'd asked her out, even though she herself had provided the tickets. Full of confidence then, the nearer the evening came, the less confident she'd become.

Even what to wear had been a problem. Like most women, Mae hadn't had anything new for years, material for dressmaking and ready-made clothes being equally scarce. 'Make do and mend' was the rule of the day, but she had the feeling now that all her clothes were tired-looking and dreary and that nothing would do.

Having tried on everything she owned, she'd settled on a familiar blue two-piece and white blouse for the theatre outing. The white blouse had a lace collar, and she'd hoped Rick might not remember how many times he'd seen it. Men never noticed clothes anyway, did they?

Sure, wasn't it the first thing he'd said, then, when she took off her coat? 'Nice to see you're wearing your pretty lace blouse, Mae – I've always liked that one.'

Oh, fancy his remembering what she wore! Was that a good or a bad sign?

Settled now in her seat, she was studying the programme Rick had bought, sometimes glancing at him, to see if she could guess what he was thinking, but he was looking round with interest at the theatre she knew so well. Was he really so interested? Wasn't he as nervous as she was herself? Two lonely people. Should they be out together at all, then?

'I suppose you know a lot of these names?' he asked, when she passed him the programme.

'As a matter of fact, most of the people I used to know are gone. But there's Primmie Day – Vincent, as she is now – she's married to the Director, Antony Vincent – and two fellows – Lance Jenkins and Danny Weston. And one name you'll know yourself, Rick. See, "Wardrobe – Sandy Corrie". She still calls herself Corrie, but of course she's Sandy Weston now.'

'One of your successes,' Rick said with a smile.

'She was her own success,' Mae answered seriously. 'I helped a bit, but she worked things out for herself. I know 'tis the best way.'

'For your other friend, too.'

'Who?'

'Brett. Brett Lester. He needs help, but it would be best if it came from within. I'm not talking about his hands, you understand.'

'I know.' Mae was looking away. 'But 'tis not easy for him.'

'Oh, that's true and I've every sympathy.' Rick cleared his throat. 'Hope I'm not talking out of turn, Mae. I know you have a special interest in him.'

She looked down at the programme, longing for the lights to dim and the curtains to part.

'How is he, then?' asked Rick. 'Have you seen him lately?'

'Only once, here.'

'I wouldn't want, you know, to intrude. I mean, if there was anything – Mae, I think you know what I'm trying to say.'

'I do, and it's all right.'

'That's a relief.'

The lights were beginning to dim; the curtains were parting.

Mae felt her own relief that they'd stopped talking about Brett.

In the interval, they had coffee in the bar and were discussing the play, which was intriguing, when Sandy came into the bar, clearly thrilled at finding them together.

'Mae – Dr Rick! I saw you from the stage before curtain up – couldnae be sure at first it was you.'

'It's us, all right,' said Rick with a return of his cheerfulness. 'Taking an evening off.'

'And why not? You deserve it.'

'They sent me complimentary tickets,' Mae said quickly. 'Had to use them.'

'Aye, of course.' After a pause during which her bright gaze went from Mae to Rick, Sandy said she'd better get back. 'In case anybody needs a quick repair, or something. You ken how it is, Mae.'

'I do.'

'Well, nice seeing you both, then. Keep in touch.'

'Looks well,' Rick murmured, as Sandy, with some reluctance, left them.

'Very well. So happy, you see. She and Danny have their own flat now, with Finlay – they're not in the Cowgate. In fact, I think her mother's moved as well.'

'On to better things?'

'Maybe, but they say the Cowgate will be improved some time. Money will be spent.'

'That'll be the day. Is that the bell?'

Leaving the theatre after the play, Mae said they should have gone backstage, to say how much they'd enjoyed it.

'Do you want to do that?' asked Rick, buttoning his overcoat against the December cold.

'Maybe not.' In fact, Mae knew it could only be an ordeal, to meet more interested stares when she introduced Rick. And then there was Brett . . . Perhaps Rick himself had remembered Brett.

'I'd rather just take you for supper, Mae. You'll let me do that? After all, you provided the tickets.'

'Well – thank you, then. We needn't go backstage. I did thank Primmie for the tickets, after all.'

Chapter Ninety

They went to a little restaurant in the High Street, which provided as good a meal as possible in post-war circumstances.

'Can't expect much wherever we go,' said Rick, but Mae thought the main dish on offer – a ham fricassee – was delicious. And then they were allowed a glass of wine! She couldn't remember when she'd last had any wine.

'At least, one glass won't give me a hangover for morning surgery,' Rick said.

Over the coffee, he offered Mae his cigarette case, but she shook her head.

'Don't feel the need tonight?' he asked lightly.

'I've had a lovely evening.'

'Me too.' He looked down at his case, then put it away, and gave a grin that made him look again like the Dr Rick she used to know. 'Thanks for taking me out, Mae.'

'Sure, was a pleasure,' she answered, laughing.

Out in the clear December night, he said he'd see her home, apologising again for not having his car, which he could only use for work, petrol of course being strictly rationed.

'As though I'd expect to be driven anywhere!' exclaimed Mae.

'Shall we take the tram, then?'

''Tis not raining – let's walk.'

Arm in arm, they stepped out well, but Mae, sensing that Rick had lost his ease of manner, had begun to brace herself for serious talk. Of Brett, perhaps? In fact, it was of his wife that Rick wanted to speak. I should have been prepared, thought Mae.

'You and I have something in common,' he murmured, as they

made their way down the Mound. 'We've both had to learn to live without the people we loved. Did you think at first you'd never manage it, Mae?'

'I did, but someone gave me good advice. Just to take it one day at a time.'

'But then the days stretch ahead into years, and you think you'll never feel any different. When I first lost Virginia, I couldn't imagine ever getting used to being without her. Nothing mattered, except work.'

'I understand.'

'My work was terrible, though. Truly terrible. it made no sense, what I saw. Any more than Virginia's death made any sense.' Rick glanced down at Mae and shook his head. 'I was a man in the dark. Like a miner, picking my way through God knows what.'

'The world was fighting evil, Rick. That was the darkness.'

'And we won, you're going to say, and I suppose we did. At a price.'

They were crossing Princes Street, glittering with lights never seen since 1939, and Mae felt their hearts should be lifting, but Rick's maybe was not yet ready. 'Most guys who've seen action have nightmares,' Brett had said. It seemed that Rick, who'd had to clear up after action, had his nightmares too.

'Life can still be good,' she told him, using the same words she'd used to Brett, and he pressed her arm in his.

'That's true, Mae. What I'm aiming to say to you, is that I've begun to realise it again. Very slowly, I'm climbing out of the pit.' He smiled a little. 'Out of the darkness.'

'Out of the darkness,' she echoed, and they walked on to Victoria Row.

'Here's Number Eight, where I live,' she told him, as they stood at the front door. 'I'm thinking you know these tenements, Rick?'

'I've visited one or two patients here. Very solid buildings.' He looked up at the high windows. 'You've been happy here, Mae?'

'I have.' She hesitated, wondering what she should do. Ask him in? Would he expect that? Did she want to? She did.

'Would you like to come in for a moment, Rick?'

'Better not. We both have early starts tomorrow, haven't we?' He touched her face with gentle fingers. 'I'll just say goodnight.'

'Goodnight then, Rick.'

'Shall we go out together again? If I get the tickets?'

'Sure, you're teasing me over those tickets!'

'But you'll see me again? Not just at the hostel, I mean?'

'I'll see you again.'

He left her, setting off on his way home to his father's house in Murrayfield. She knew he'd let the flat he'd shared with Virginia; probably would never live in it again. As she looked for her key in the passageway of Number Eight, Mae's thoughts dwelt on the young wife who had died. How much did she still count in Rick's life? Perhaps, a great deal.

'Hello, Mae,' called a voice, as she was still staring down at her key and she turned to see Mrs Beith and Ben coming in, their faces cheerful and rosy with the cold.

'Been out, dear?' asked Clara. 'We thought we saw that doctor, didn't we, Ben? The one who works at your place, Mae. Hope nobody's ill, eh?'

'Och, he was walking,' said Ben. 'He'd have had his car, if he'd been called oot.'

'I was just over at the theatre,' said Mae, opening her door. 'Have you seen the play?'

'No, dear, we've been to see *Meet me in Saint Louis*, with Judy Garland. Oh, what a lovely picture!' Clara's gaze on Mae was limpid. 'You get the doctor to take you, Mae, that's my advice.'

'Goodnight, Mrs Beith,' called Mae, letting herself into her flat. 'Goodnight, Ben.'

'Goodnight, Mae!' they cried, exchanging glances.

Chapter Ninety-One

Rick was in the forefront of Mae's mind. Even though it was Christmas, and she'd presents to find for her da and Annie and folk in Edinburgh. Even though she'd the party to organise for Adelaide House. Even though any day now she might hear from Miss Thorburn that her world was turning upside down. And even though she'd no certain idea of where she featured in the mind of Rick himself.

He was attracted to her, of course. She knew that, and marvelled that no one else seemed to notice how often he would look in on her, and spend time with her that he couldn't spare. But, then, to those at the hostel, Dr Rick was just Dr Rick – even if no longer a shattered man, not one to be interested in anyone in particular. And Mae was Mae, exactly the same. Never would the girls think of putting them together.

But what raged in Mae's mind like toothache, was whether or not Rick would think of putting the two of them together. Calling in on her and looking at her was one thing; wanting more than that was another. But, oh Lord, how much more did she want herself?

Sometimes, she thought it might be the case that she wasn't really interested in another relationship. Not if there were to be any chance of heartbreak. And there might be. She and Rick had not been out together again.

It would be best, she decided, just to get on with all the things she had to do, and try to keep Rick at the back of her mind, rather than the front.

She sent off her presents to Ireland with a letter promising to come over when she could, and found just the right things for Sandy and her family, for Rona and the girls, for Ben and Clara, who were expected to make an exciting announcement any time. She bought bulbs in bowls for Anita Thorburn and Harriet Dow, and scent for Lottie, who'd said she'd be coming up, which only left – she drooped at the thought – Brett and Rick.

Need she buy anything for Brett? Wouldn't he be embarrassed? And Rick – he'd never expect anything, but in the old days, he and Virginia had always brought in chocolates for the hostel – beautiful boxes, that of course you couldn't find now. Shouldn't she get him something? Some little thing, in case they went out again before Christmas?

How foolish she was, to be worrying about things that didn't matter. Only, of course, they did matter – to her.

The hostel party was arranged for the week before Christmas. Mae and Jannie set up the tree, and decorated it with Miss Thorburn's old lights, and though the girls did make paper chains for the dining room, Mae splashed out on holly and some Chinese lanterns and garlands she found in a shop in the High Street.

'In for a penny, in for a pound,' she told Jannie. 'Who knows if we'll even be here next year? Let's make this a good party.'

'Always think it's a funny party wi' no men,' commented Jannie.

'Well, nobody wants to invite the men they know, so who else would come?'

'Poor old Dr Rick?'

'I'll see if he's willing.'

He was willing, arriving with a Christmas cake he'd managed to buy from Logie's, and even agreeing to play the piano for carol singing.

'I don't know what we'd do without you,' Mae told him. 'Miss Thorburn isn't up to coming, your dad's away, you said, and Miss Dow's got the flu.'

'Have to do my bit, I suppose.' His gaze as usual was lingering on her face. 'You're not going to Ireland for Christmas, then?'

'Sure, you know I can't leave the hostel. Always get the battered wives in at Christmas, I don't know why.'

'Too much festive spirit,' he said dryly. 'I'm going down to the Borders on Christmas Eve to join Dad at my aunt's. Arthur's agreed to be on call, if I do the same for him at New Year.'

'I see.' She was feeling strangely desolate that Rick would be away for Christmas. Not that she could have seen him, anyway.

'I expect we'll meet before then, though.' He glanced at the women milling around the dining-room. 'Want me to man the gramophone?'

'Well, there aren't many of the girls who can be dancing.'

'They've probably got their eye on the buffet. So've I. looks very good.'

'Should be.' Mae laughed shortly. 'We nearly drew blood, getting it ready. Oh, let's start, shall we? Everybody's starving.'

After the buffet table had been cleared, and the lemonade drunk, board games were played for a while, until tempers frayed, threats were made, and so many faces went dangerously red, Mae called a halt and said Dr Rick would play for carols.

Ah, that was better! Everybody calmed down and gathered round the elderly, donated piano, as Rick went through his repertoire of 'Good King Wenceslas', 'Once in Royal David's City', and so on, adding his baritone to the women's thin voices, and evidently enjoying himself.

All went well, until 'Silent Night', the final carol, had been played, and Rick was rising to his feet, bowing to the applause, when Gloria Hunter, a heavy-faced young woman, with scarlet cheeks and raven hair, suddenly produced a sprig of mistletoe.

'Merry Christmas, Dr Rick!' she cried, and waving the sprig over his head as far as she could reach, gave him a smacking kiss on the mouth.

'Ooh, Gloria!' the girls cried, while the midwives, Miss Rowley and Mrs Wilkes, looked shocked and Mae's eyes flashed, as she took the mistletoe from Gloria's fingers.

'Were we not saying we wouldn't go in for this?' she asked coolly.

'Och, it's Christmas, Mrs Alpin! Where's the harm?'

'No harm,' said Rick agreeably. 'Merry Christmas, Gloria, but I can't kiss everyone, you know.'

'Just me, was ma plan,' she said, winking at her friends.

'Kiss Mrs Alpin!' someone cried, and others joined in. 'Kiss Mae, Dr Rick! She'll do for all of us!'

'Sure, now you're being silly,' said Mae, flushing, but she still had the sprig of mistletoe in her hand and Rick took it from her.

'Merry Christmas, Mae,' he said quietly, and holding the sprig aloft, bent his head and kissed her.

Only a mistletoe kiss, of course, but very sweet, very gentle, with something about it that made the watchers fall silent, as though knowing this was not the time to laugh. When it was over and Rick had stepped away, Mae, who had gone rather pale, began to busy herself packing up the board games.

'Ladies, it's late,' she called. 'Let's clear away.'

The party was over.

Rick was at the front door, Mae with him, her face averted. He had asked if he could help; she had said he was not needed.

'Thank you for coming,' she said now, her manner stiff. 'And for the cake and everything.'

'I didn't embarrass you just then, did I?' he asked awkwardly.

''Twas difficult for me, I'll not deny.'

'The girls didn't laugh.'

''Tis true, they didn't.'

'Perhaps they could tell I wanted to kiss you.'

'In front of all the hostel?'

'Oh, God, I'm sorry. It was just something that happened. Something I wanted to happen. But not like that.'

She turned her face towards his. 'Goodnight, Rick. I'd better go. I'm needed in the kitchen.'

'Wait.' He grasped her wrist. 'I'm sorry, things seem to be sliding away from us. I do want to see you again – you know that—'

'Do I?'

He dropped her wrist and put his hand to his brow, trying to give one of his old cheerful grins; it didn't quite work.

'Bear with me, Mae. I'm not sure what I'm up to. But, could we meet after I get back?'

She looked away without replying, and after a moment or two, he sighed.

'I don't blame you, Mae, for not wanting to see me. Why should you wait for me to call the tune? But if we could just meet and talk, it would mean a lot to me.' He looked around the hall. 'Can't talk here, can we?'

'Hardly.'

'So, can we meet?'

Her expression softening a little, she turned her eyes on his and he drew her into his arms.

'Wasn't such a crime, was it?' he whispered. 'Stealing a kiss under the mistletoe?'

''Twas the first one, Rick.'

'And shouldn't have been public? I know. Well, this one's private. Just for you and me.'

Their second kiss, in the empty hall, where the noises off told of a houseful of women still busy elsewhere, some singing, some arguing, all quite unaware of what they were missing. For this kiss was very different from the one under the mistletoe. This kiss, so strong and passionate, was a lover's kiss, and those who were kissing knew it.

'Rick, someone might have seen,' Mae gasped, when they finally parted.

'No, there was just the two of us.' He was smiling; breathless. 'I checked.'

Reluctantly, he opened the door and looked back.

'Goodnight, Mae. I'll see you before I leave.'

'You mean, if you're called out?'

'Even if I'm not called out.'

'Goodnight, Rick,' she said softly.

Chapter Ninety-Two

The twenty-third of December brought Lottie round to the hostel with her Christmas present for Mae. She had only arrived from London by sleeper that morning; declared she'd hardly had a wink of sleep, but was determined to drag Mae off to the Queen's for a lunchtime drink with Tony Vincent and the company.

'Not that it's really a company yet – he's still putting it together – so they don't want to go north this year. There'll be no pantomime, but they're going to do *The Snow Queen* themselves. Primmie's the Snow Queen, of course.'

'I haven't got time to go for drinks,' protested Mae. 'Christmas is a terrible time for me, so it is.'

'Och, you can slip out at dinner time,' said Jannie. 'You're letting me have all the holiday off – you go, Mae, it'll do you good.'

'Though you're looking pretty good, anyway,' commented Lottie, eyeing Mae's bright eyes and scarcely concealed air of happiness. 'Like the cat that's swallowed the cream, no less. Has something happened?'

''Tis Christmas, I suppose.'

'Why, you just said Christmas was terrible for you.' Lottie laughed. 'But come on, get your coat. Jannie says it's OK, so let's go.'

'So, how did you get away from your play?' asked Mae, when they were on their way to the Queen's. 'Is the theatre closing for the holiday?'

'Only for Christmas Day – my understudy's taking over. I said I had to see my parents, which is true. They're not well at all. Wish you'd look in on them some time.'

'I'm sorry they are no better.' Mae glanced sideways at Lottie, and wondered if she should tell her about Rick. But what could she say? It was too soon to say anything, too soon to risk words. Too soon to share her wonderful warm feeling inside; her sensation of floating everywhere; of having moved on to a different plane from normal life.

'I'm glad to be getting the chance to see Brett,' she told Lottie, in an attempt to divert her interest. 'I've a little present for him. just a tie, nothing special.'

Lottie stared. 'You're taking Brett a present?'

'Why not? He's an old friend.'

'Oh, of course. Well, I've got him something, too. Cufflinks, which I'm sure he'll never use, but what can you do? Men always have everything, which is so mysterious, isn't it?'

They heard the noise of the drinks party in Tony's office before they reached it. Like wolves baying at the moon, as Lottie described it. 'Just shows you should never stand outside a cocktail party, Mae.'

'I'm not one for making a practice of it,' she answered with a laugh. 'Tea and buns is what we go in for at Adelaide House. If we can get the buns.'

Still, it was very pleasant to see all the familiar faces gathered together – Tony, Primmie, Sandy, Danny, Lance – and new people, who didn't know Mae but were glad to meet her and welcome her in. Of course, they all recognised Lottie, from her photographs. But where was Brett?

'Oh, don't say he hasn't come!' cried Lottie.

But he was there, propped in the corner, in conversation with one of the new young actresses.

'Doing my old role, I bet,' Lottie whispered. 'Assistant Stage Manager. She's got that harrassed look.'

Brett, though, was looking rather better, Mae thought. Not quite so thin in the face, not quite so lost in his own personal nightmare. But she could be wrong.

She and Lottie pressed through the crowd to join him, at which his companion, seeing Lottie so close, gave a sigh and melted away. Brett raised his eyebrows.

'You frightened her off, Lottie. Such is fame.'

'How are you, Brett?' asked Lottie warmly. 'You're looking well.'

384

'Not half so well as you, or Mae.' His eyes slid to Mae. 'Not half so well,' he repeated. 'How's your doctor friend, Mae? Been knocking out any more troublemakers?'

'What doctor friend?' asked Lottie. 'What troublemakers?'

'Sure, Brett's just teasing,' said Mae, her already high colour deepening. 'Merry Christmas, Brett. This is just a little something for your stocking.'

He straightened up, looking contrite. 'Oh, God, and I never got you anything! Thanks, Mae. Can I open it now?'

'Christmas morning,' ordered Lottie. 'With mine.'

'Not you, too? I don't know what to say. Except it's nice of you both, to think of me. I appreciate it.'

'We think of you all the time,' said Lottie. 'And it's the thought that counts.'

'Well, then, I'll say you have my thoughts, too.'

He leaned forward and kissed each of them on the cheek. 'Merry Christmas to you both. How long are you here for, Lottie?'

'A few days. How about coming round to Victoria Place some time?'

'Very kind of you, but I'm going down to Sussex. I won't be back until after Boxing Day.'

'There'd still be time to meet,' she pressed. 'You know my home number.'

'Sure. Well – better circulate, eh?'

'I must talk to Sandy,' said Mae, aware, as she turned away that Lottie hadn't moved from Brett's side. Conscience pricking her? But they had been close once; she knew she owed him her interest.

'Have you no' brought Dr Rick?' asked Sandy, who had been matchmaking for Mae and Rick ever since she'd seen them together at the theatre. But for once she didn't press for news, being preoccupied with news of her own.

'Would you credit it?' she cried. 'Finlay's going to have to join up next year! Here's all these guys coming home, and then they go and call up a whole lot more. I never thought a Labour government would be so daft.'

'To be fair, they need the men,' said Danny. 'There'll be occupation troops needed for a hell of a long time. They're even bringing in National Service some time in the future.'

'And Finlay won't be in danger,' Mae put in soothingly. 'That's the difference.'

'He'll be away from home,' Sandy answered moodily.

'Still got me,' said Danny, putting his arm round her waist.

'Och, get on!' cried Sandy delightedly.

She and Mae exchanged their presents and with a promise to meet over the holiday, parted, so that Mae could make hasty good-byes to Tony and Primmie and return to the hostel.

'I'll be in touch!' cried Lottie, hurrying across the room towards her.

'Don't forget,' said Mae.

Chapter Ninety-Three

Back at the hostel, sorting through a few late cards, Mae could have burst into song, she felt so happy. But then she opened a letter from Anita Thorburn, and felt the axe fall. The Council had considered the matter and was now willing to take over Adelaide House, though its function might be extended to take in a more general mix of those in need.

> Sorry, to tell you at this time, Mae, (Anita had written in her still firm hand) but sometimes it's better to grasp the nettle as soon as possible. I'll see you after Christmas, when we can discuss all the implications, but I am confident that our work will continue, and that's the important thing. I send my best wishes to you and everyone at Adelaide House, and my prayers that 1946 may bring good luck to us all. Yours most sincerely, Anita Thorburn.

How long she sat considering the letter, Mae never knew, but she was roused from her thoughts by a hand touching her shoulder. It was Rick's.

'I didn't hear the door,' she said, as though it mattered how he'd got in.

'One of the girls opened it.' His eyes were on her letter. 'Bad news, Mae?'

She passed it to him. 'Better see for yourself.'

Soon, he had lowered it, to look at her with compassionate eyes. 'Mae, I'm so sorry. I know you didn't want this.'

'You said it might be for the best.'

'Now I'm only thinking that I don't want you upset.'

387

'I'm all right. 'Tis just the uncertainty that's worrying. Not knowing what's going to happen.'

She stood up, trying to smile. 'Feel better, seeing you, though. But I didn't call you out.'

'I said I'd look in anyway.' He took a package from his overcoat pocket. 'I wanted to give you this. It's just a scarf.'

'Rick, I have one for you.'

'A scarf?'

'I couldn't think what to get.'

'Snap.'

They laughed together as they opened their presents. Hers from him was exquisite – a blue silk scarf he said would match her eyes. His was Irish tweed, bought in the Edinburgh High Street, but made in Donegal.

'Mae, thank you. I'll put it on this minute.'

'Ah, no, on Christmas Day. That's the rule.'

'What a stickler you are for rules, then.'

He drew her towards him. 'We should make our own rules, I think.'

Time passed as they kissed and held each other, until Mae released herself, searching his face with a thoughtful gaze.

'You're remembering we were going to talk?' he asked, his own face serious.

'Can't talk here, we said.'

'When we meet, then. I'm back on the twenty-ninth. But I want to say, Mae, don't worry too much about the future. I think it'll be all right.'

'For Jannie, as well?'

'I wasn't thinking of Jannie. Just us.'

'Oh,' said Mae.

They walked slowly to the door, Mae looking round to see if anyone was watching.

'Did you get any new customers?' Rick asked, as he carefully stowed away his present in his pocket. 'You thought you might.'

'Sure, we did. Two poor women who managed to get in the way of their husbands' celebrations. Black eyes, no ration books – 'tis Christmas, of course.'

'Oh, no. Want me to see 'em?'

'They're all right for the moment. Need more than a doctor.'

For a time, they did not speak.

'Let me kiss you goodbye,' Rick said at last. 'There's no one to see. I think I can hear 'em all, singing carols again.'

They were caught in their embrace, lost to the world, when their world intervened and they were startled to hear a burst of clapping and hoarse cheers.

'Oh, my God!' cried Rick, as Mae sprang from his arms, and they both stood staring up at rows of smiling faces looking down at them from the stairs.

'Well done, Dr Rick!' cried the girls. 'Och, Mrs Alpin, we couldnae be more pleased! Two lovely people, eh? Is it no' grand? When's the weddin', then?'

''Tis just a Christmas greeting,' Mae murmured, colouring scarlet.

'And you ticked me off aboot the mistletoe!' shouted Gloria, grinning with delight. 'Shame on you, eh?'

'I'm away,' said Rick hurriedly. 'Sorry, Mae, sorry. See you when I come back.'

'Everyone down to the kitchen,' called Mae. 'Then we'll have our mince pies.'

'Are they no' for Christmas Eve?' someone asked politely.

'Christmas Eve as well,' said Mae recklessly. 'Why not?'

She put her hands to her burning cheeks and chased her charges down the back stairs.

389

Chapter Ninety-Four

On the evening of 29 December, the performance of *The Snow Queen* at the Queen's theatre finished at half-past ten. The audience moved quickly into the winter's night, but the members of the cast and the theatre staff remained for a while, changing clothes, removing make-up, tidying up, doing all the tasks that had to be done before closing for the night. The safety curtain was down.

Meanwhile, in the restaurant of the North British Hotel, at the east end of Princes Street, Rick and Mae were having dinner and enjoying their surroundings. Except that Mae was a little over-awed.

'I've never been here before,' she whispered to Rick. 'Sure, it's very grand.'

Of course, she was worrying about her clothes again, even though she had on her beautiful Christmas scarf. Same old blue suit, though. Whatever else happened in 1946, she was going to have to make herself something different to wear.

Her eye was caught suddenly by an elderly couple at a corner table, and her colour rose.

'Rick, don't look now, but those people over there are Lottie's parents. Oh, dear Lord, I hope they don't see me!'

'Parents of the great Charlotte? Now, why shouldn't you want them to see you?'

'Don't you remember?' Her colour was still high. 'I used to be their maid.'

'Ah, Mae, what of it?' He covered her hand quickly. 'You're not their maid now, and even if you were, what does it matter?'

'Some think these things matter. Mrs Cameron would.'

'They don't matter to you and me. Come on, drink your wine.'

But as she sipped her wine, Mae was thinking how much older and more worn Lottie's parents were looking, and her heart smote her. Lottie had wanted her to see them and she never had, but she would call at the New Year, that was a promise. They'd been nice, after all, at Lottie's farewell party long ago, and it was good to be friendly. All the same, when the Camerons left without noticing her, she breathed a sigh of relief.

'Mae,' said Rick, when their coffee had been served. 'We said we'd talk.'

'Here?' Mae's eyes went round the restaurant. 'There are too many people, Rick.'

'They're not near us.'

'The waiters are watching.'

'Can't hear us, though. And there are things I'd like to say.'

She stirred her coffee with a trembling hand. 'Sure, I'm listening, then.'

'It's just—' He drank his own coffee as though he needed it. 'Just that I want to apologise.'

'Oh.' Mae's face was blank; she had been expecting something else.

'I feel I let you down, you see.'

'Let me down? When?'

'After we went out together. We were so happy – well, I was—'

'So was I.'

'I asked if you wanted to see me again, and you said yes.' He ran a hand through his hair. 'And then what? I didn't ask you. What the devil did you think of me, Mae?'

'I cannot say,' she answered truthfully. 'I couldn't be sure what was in your mind.'

'You must have known how I felt about you?'

'I couldn't be sure,' she said again. 'I wondered if I had been mistaken.'

'No.' He leaned across to press her hand. 'You weren't mistaken. I fell in love with you as soon as I saw you again.'

She stared at him, her lips parted. Then? Her hand still trembling, she stirred her coffee again and drank it, though it was cold.

'I didn't even realise I was ready to find new love,' Rick went on, watching her. 'But when I came back after the war, there you were. The Mae I'd known for years, just as beautiful, but somehow different. Been through the mill. Maybe I was different, too.'

'My war was not as hard as yours, Rick.'

'I'm talking about grief.'

They were silent for a time, then Rick said, 'All I wanted was to be with you, and when we went out together that first time, I thought it was wonderful, we were both ready for a new relationship. Then – the guilt came.'

'For Virginia?' asked Mae.

'I knew she'd have wanted me to be happy – she was that sort of person – but I couldn't get it out my head, that I shouldn't be. She was dead and would never be happy again, and here was I, wanting happiness with someone else. I felt so bad, Mae. Can you understand?'

'A lot of people feel like that,' she said gently. 'When they are ready to live again.'

'Did you?'

''Twas not quite the same for me. For years after I lost Harry, I never wanted anyone but him.'

'I see. There was never anyone else, then?'

Mae looked down. She had been waiting for this moment, this question, and was glad in a way that it had come. Be brave, she told herself. Answer him. He has to know. She raised her eyes.

'For a while, Rick, there was. Someone in Ireland.'

His gaze wavered. 'Always thought there would have been somebody. Maybe Brett.'

'Brett?' She smiled. 'No.'

'Tell me about this other fellow, then.'

'I used to know him before, when we were young. By the time I met him again, I'd been alone for many years. I suppose I was ready – to move on.'

'What happened?'

'Nothing. He wasn't right for me, I wasn't right for him.'

'He's not important to you?'

'He is not. I think now, he never was.'

'Something else to get over, though?'

'And is over,' she said in a low voice.

For a long time, neither spoke, then Rick said quietly. 'Let's forget about him, then. Because what matters is us. I've learned that, Mae. I'll not forget Virginia, but I've said goodbye to her. My love for her is of the past.'

'Like mine, for Harry.'

'And ours is of the present. That's the way things have to be.'

They touched hands again over the table, then Rick glanced around at the emptying restaurant. 'Mae, how many proposals do you think are made here, in the North British? Because I'm making one now. Will you marry me?'

Her face gave him her answer, but she still whispered across the table, 'I will,' while the waiters looked on and wished they would go.

Finally, they did go, out into the night and the lighted streets.

'Jannie's sleeping at the hostel?' asked Rick, tucking his new scarf into his coat collar. 'You're in your own flat tonight?'

'I am. Want to come in for a while?'

'You bet. This wind cuts like a knife.' He laughed. 'As if that were the only reason.'

Suddenly, he halted at the pavement edge.

'Mae, do you smell burning?'

'Burning?' She stood for a moment, with her face to the wind. 'I do. 'Tis quite strong.'

As she spoke, a fire engine roared past, and they noticed that an unusual number of people seemed to be hurrying towards Leith Street.

'Always frightens me to see a fire engine,' murmured Mae. 'I think, is it my place that's on fire?'

'Now, what are the odds for that?' asked Rick. He took her arm. 'It probably is a tenement somewhere, but there's no need to think it's yours.'

'I see another fire engine!' cried Mae. 'It's somewhere big, Rick, it must be. Look at the people running!'

They ran too, joining the others already on their way, making for Victoria Row, and filled now with dread. Somewhere big? What might that be?

It was the Queen's.

Chapter Ninety-Five

For a moment, they couldn't move, as their eyes took in the horror of the scene before them. The flames at every window of the theatre's façade; the smoke rising to the sky, fanned by the winter wind. The crowds of people already standing, watching; the fire-engines skewed across the street; the firemen on turntable ladders, sending fountains of water splashing against the theatre's stone.

Every resident from Victoria Row seemed to be out on the pavement outside the tenements, some with blankets round their shoulders, some holding small children. Other children were running in and out of the crowd, being screamed at by their parents, one being Hamish Beith before he was caught by Norrie and Pauline.

Standing with Ben, Rona and Jake, was Mrs Beith herself, wearing an outdoor coat and a scarf over the curlers in her hair, who called Mae's name.

'Mae! Mae! Och, is it no' terrible?'

'They say we might all have to be evacuated!' cried Rona. 'Susie's out wi' Kenny – wish they'd come home. Thank God, Jannie's over at your place, Mae.'

'See the priests from the cathedral lookin' up at the roof?' asked Jake, animated for once. 'Everybody's hopin' the flames'll no' spread. Did before, I heard.'

'Are the theatre folk safe?' cried Mae, jerked into action. 'I must find them. I must find Sandy!'

'Wait!' shouted Rick as she darted in and out of the people watching, searching every face. 'Wait for me, Mae!'

It was all right. They found the actors huddled together, as close as they could get to the theatre entrance. Tony Vincent, his face ghastly white in the light of the flames, had his arm round Primmie, who was sobbing, while the rest were standing in silence, stunned by what they were seeing. Hector Standish was murmuring to several older, well-dressed men – the rarely seen theatre board members, Mae realised – and beyond them she saw Sandy and Danny holding hands and shaking, and burst into tears with relief.

'Oh, Mae!' Sandy kept saying over and over again, as they hugged each other. 'Oh, Mae!'

'What happened? What happened?'

'Well, I'd been on duty, and Danny and me were getting ready to go, when the night watchman came running doon and said there was a fire in the gallery. We couldnae believe it, I mean, things must have been fine when the audience was leaving. But Jim kept saying, "get out, get out", and we didnae waste time, I can tell you. Och, it was a nightmare, Mae, a nightmare!'

'A nightmare,' chimed Danny, mopping his brow with a blackened handkerchief. 'It spread like wildfire – probably from an electrical fault, one of the chaps told us. They say the gallery'll have gone, and the circle, and the auditorium. Only the dressing rooms'll be OK behind the safety curtain.'

'Wardrobe's full o' smoke – what'll happen to ma costumes?' asked Sandy. 'Och, what of it? I'll no' have a job, anyway.'

'Is there anything I can do?' asked Rick.

'Thank God, they say no one's hurt, but they've got an ambulance standing by. They want us to move along, but we're no' leaving.'

'Mae!' cried another voice, and Lottie, a wraith in a black shawl, came hurrying through the crowds to throw her arms around Mae. 'Oh, God, I've looked everywhere – I can't find Brett.'

'He must be here somewhere,' said Sandy. 'He was in his wee office next to Wardrobe and I banged on the door and told him to hurry.'

'You knocked on his door?' whispered Mae, the colour draining from her face. 'You told him to get out?'

'Aye, I did. What's wrong?'

'It's his nightmare. He dreams it every night. There's a fire, same as in the ship in the war, and someone is knocking on his door, and he can't open the door, he can't get out.'

'He can open the door!' cried Sandy. 'It's no' locked. Why should it be locked?'

'Sandy, he's still there, he's still in his office. 'I'm going to him!'

'Mae, are you mad?' cried Rick, following her as she sped away towards the stage door. 'Mae, come back!'

But Lottie was already ahead of her, running like a deer, and before anyone could stop her, was into the building.

'Oh, the stupid idiot!' cried a fireman. 'What's she think she's doing?'

'She thinks there's someone still in there,' gasped Rick, holding Mae tightly to him. 'I'll go in myself, if you'll hold this lady here.'

'You stay where you are,' said the fireman, and shouted to others. 'We've got breathing masks.'

''Tis all right, Rick.' Mae was freeing herself from his grasp. 'I'll leave it to them. But, oh, God, what'll happen to Lottie? What'll happen to Brett?'

He took off his coat and wrapped it round her, trying to keep her from shivering, trying to soothe her.

'How could you risk yourself like that?' he whispered, as she grew calmer.

''Twas Lottie who took the risk.'

An eternity seemed to pass, before a fireman emerged, carrying Lottie, followed by a second man supporting Brett. A cheer went up from the watchers, as attendants from the waiting ambulance ran forward with blankets, and the firemen handed their charges into their care.

'Rick, try to go with them to the hospital,' urged Mae. 'You're a doctor, they'll let you. Then I'll follow.'

'It wasnae ma fault,' Sandy was wailing. 'I didnae ken he had nightmares.'

'Sure, it's not your fault, then,' said Mae. 'You were only trying to help. They're safe now, anyway.'

'Hope so,' said Rick, on his way to the ambulance. 'Which hospital, driver? I'm a doctor, I want to go with you.'

'The Royal. Step aboard, doctor. Do what you can, they've escaped the flames, but it'll be the smoke that's got 'em.'

Chapter Ninety-Six

It was some hours later that Rick and Mae returned from the Royal to Number Eight. Both Lottie and Brett were indeed suffering from smoke inhalation, but would survive. Lottie's parents had sat with Mae in the waiting-room, while Rick had been in conference with the doctors, and when he brought the good news, Mrs Cameron and Mae wept together, and Mr Cameron patted their shoulders and groaned a little.

Afterwards, the Camerons had been allowed to see Lottie for a minute or two, while Rick and Mae had been allowed to see Brett. He couldn't speak, he was clearly in pain, yet there was a sort of peace about him as he lay back against his pillows, and in the reddened eyes that rested on Mae, a tenderness. He's going to get better, she thought, her heart rising within her, and not just from the smoke inhalation.

'Lottie's all right,' she whispered. 'Have they told you? There's no need to worry.'

He nodded, his gaze on her intense.

'She tried to save you, Brett. Sure, she did save you, didn't she? 'Twas all she wanted.'

At that, he slowly closed his eyes, as though he must cherish the thought alone, and Mae quietly rose.

'I'll see you again soon,' she murmured, and looked across to Rick.

'Let's go back.'

The residents of Victoria Row had not after all been evacuated, and the cathedral had not been harmed, but the sight of the still smouldering theatre, surrounded by firemen and onlookers even so late into the night, was too much for Mae.

'I just want to go indoors, Rick. Blot it out.'

'You're exhausted, Mae. You'll feel better in the morning.'

'Maybe.' She looked at him with weary, dark-rimmed eyes. 'Are you coming in?'

'I'm coming in.'

She had been looking forward to showing him her flat, but now was not the time and they only stood, clasped together, in her living-room.

'I feel like a rag doll,' she said weakly. 'But I'm thanking God, everyone's all right. I was so terrified at first, for Lottie and Brett.'

'You do care for him,' Rick said after a pause.

She ran her hand softly down his face. 'As a friend, is all. 'Tis Lottie who cares for him.'

'Certainly seems so. To do what she did.'

'Sure, they'd drifted apart – she let her work come first – but I'm thinking she knew what she felt tonight. And she was always the only one for him.'

'I told you, I used to think you might be the one for him.'

'I never was. You know that now?'

'I know it. I love you. Tell me that you love me.'

'I love you, Rick.'

They sighed, buoyed by their words, their commitment, all thought of Brett and Lottie put aside as they looked into their future. They'd been given another chance for happiness; they would take it.

After some time they moved to the door, where Mae said it was her turn to be feeling guilty.

'Because of what's outside, Rick. The fire. Can you believe, I'd forgotten it?'

'Me, too.'

They held each other again.

'Will you come to Ireland with me?' she whispered. 'Meet my da?'

'I will. I want to meet him. It's good you already know my father.'

'So like you,' she said fondly.

Swaying with weariness, they stayed, wrapped in their bliss, until finally they opened the outer door. And saw again the ruin of the Queen's.

'There it is, then,' said Rick bleakly.

'Think it will ever be rebuilt?'

'I don't see why not. They'll be busy rebuilding the rest of the world pretty soon. On the other hand, there'll be money needed and it might not be forthcoming. We'll have to wait and see.'

'I cannot imagine the city without the Queen's.'

'There are always changes. Cities change, like people. Like us.'

They exchanged a last kiss, while the lights of the fire across the street flickered down and the crowds began at last to turn away.

'I'll see you in the morning,' whispered Rick. 'Try to get some sleep.'

But they both knew they would not sleep. Dream, perhaps, even though awake. Until they met again.

PostScript

Three special weddings amongst many took place in 1946.

Clara married Ben at the local kirk, Lottie married Brett at an Edinburgh register office, and Mae married Rick at St Mary's Cathedral.

All Victoria Row came to Clara's and Ben's wedding. All the scattered actors from the Queen's came to Lottie's and Brett's. And everyone – Joseph and Annie from Ireland, neighbours, actors, patients, girls from the hostel, Miss Thorburn, Miss Dow, as well as Sandy, Danny, and the Abercrombys, came to Mae's and Rick's. Even the newsagent, who'd taken over his mother's shop after her retirement, stood with the onlookers and cheered.

These were wonderful days of celebration, even if no one could bear to look at the twisted black skeleton of the theatre next to Mae's cathedral. Surely, one day, it would be rebuilt?

It never was, and finally, in 1956 the site was bought by the cathedral for an extension. Very soon people forgot that there had ever been a theatre opposite Victoria Row, though Katie, the young daughter of Mae and Rick, knew all about it, because her mother told her.

Adelaide House survived, but as a council-run hostel, and though Mae still worked there as a volunteer, it never seemed quite the same to her. Sure, it was a shame, as she once said to Rick, that there should still be a need for such a place. Perhaps one day, there wouldn't be?

'Pie in the sky, I'm afraid,' said Rick, who some time before had handed over his role at the hostel to a young woman doctor.

But Mae, ever hopeful, didn't agree.

The Road to the Sands

Anne Douglas

The war has brought devastating changes to the people of Portobello, a seaside district of Edinburgh. But as VE day nears, Tess Gillespie and her mother are feeling hopeful. Tess is looking forward to being able to walk on her beloved beaches for the first time since war was declared. More importantly, her father and sister will soon be back home and they can all be a family once again.

However, the war has changed Don Gillespie and no longer content to settle back in to his former life. The future will bring both betrayal and heartbreak for all the Gillespie women. And it will take all their courage and resolution to rebuild their lives and find new happiness.

Yesterday's Dreams

Jessica Blair

Local Whitby girl, Colette Shipley has become fascinated by the mysteries of the new art of photography and begins to create a record of her scenic home town with its tall ships and twin lighthouses, street urchins and weathered old fishermen. One day she encounters Arthur Newton who shares her passion for the town's unique atmosphere. Colette and Arthur begin a friendship that develops further. However, unbeknown to Collette, Arthur is also married with a young child.

Arthur has tried to be content with his steady job at the railways and his marriage to his childhood sweetheart Rose. However even before meeting Colette, Arthur had been living a secret life, one which he has not shared with his family, friends or even Rose: he has a real talent for painting. His talent has blossomed under the tutelage of a sympathetic gallery owner, Ebenezer Hirst, and the patronage of Laurence Steel, an established painter in the Pre-Raphaelite school. Arthur is now faced with a difficult decision: remain comfortably in his railway job or risk the security of his wife and child by becoming a full-time artist. A decision not made any easier by his growing attraction for Colette, who is supportive of his artistic endeavours in a way that his practical wife never has . . .

Simply Unforgettable

Mary Balogh

They meet in a ferocious snowstorm. She is a young teacher with a secret past. He is the cool, black-caped stranger who unexpectedly comes to her rescue. Between these two unlikely strangers, desire is instantaneous ... and utterly impossible to resist. Stranded together in a country inn, Lucius Marshall – the Viscount Sinclair – and Frances Allard share a night of glorious, unforgettable passion. But Frances knows her place – and it is far from the privileged world of the sensual aristocrat. Due to begin her teaching position at Miss Martin's School in Bath, Frances must try to forget that one extraordinary night – and the man who touched her with such exquisite tenderness and abandon.

But Frances cannot hide forever. And when fate once again throws them together, Lucius refuses to take no for an answer. If Frances will not be his wife, he will make her his mistress. So begins an odyssey fraught with intrigue – one that defies propriety and shocks the strait-laced ton. For Lucius's passionate, single-minded pursuit is about to force Frances to give up all her secrets – except one – to win the heart of the man she already loves.

Angels Fall

Nora Roberts

The sole survivor of a brutal crime, Reece Gilmore has been on the run, desperately fighting the nightmares and panic attacks that haunt her. She doesn't intend to stay in the sleepy town of Angels Fall one second longer than she needs to, despite its friendly – if curious – inhabitants, and the irresistible attraction of local writer Brody. However, on a hike into the mountains she witnesses a couple having a vicious argument that culminates in murder. By the time Reece finds Brody and brings him to the scene, both killer and victim are gone.

Faced with a lack of evidence, the authorities in Angels Fall find it hard to believe Reece's story. After all, she's a newcomer in town and yet has already gained a reputation for being jumpy – maybe even a little fragile. But when a series of menacing occurrences makes it clear that someone wants her out of the way, Reece must put her trust in Brody – the one person who does believe her – to find the murderer before it's too late . . .

Cover the Butter

Carrie Kabak

The year is 1965, and Kate Cadogan has just got her first bra ...
and corset. It's a watershed moment, even if she hates the way the
girdle chafes the tops of her thighs, and even though what she
really wanted was a polka-dot shift dress with a cool Peter Pan
collar. Undaunted, Kate jumps headfirst into the thrills and
heartaches of her teenage years, albeit under the watchful eye of
her mother, Biddy, a woman so repressed and controlling she
gives new meaning to the word 'matriarch'.

From her first crush, on local bad boy Barry Finch, through to
her scandalous period of 'living in sin' during her years at teacher
training college, right up to her passionless marriage to Rodney,
Kate seems to have a talent for picking the wrong men. Ultimately
seeking Biddy's approval in everything she does, Kate finds the
parameters of her life shrinking before her eyes, and feels powerless to stop it. Fortunately, her lifelong friends, Moira and Ingrid,
are on hand, giving her more support than a foundation garment
ever could, helping her to realise that she can create a life for herself, and that starting over has no age limit.